IN T

Gray Alys ~~~~~~~~~~~~~~~~~~~~~~ fire. Boyce had begun to change.

She watched his body twist as bone and muscle changed within, watched his pale white hair grow longer and longer, watched his lazy smile turn into a wide red grin that split his face, watched the wine cup fall as his hands melted and writhed and became paws. Then he threw back his head and howled, and he ripped at his clothing until it lay in tatters, and he was Boyce no longer. Across the fire from Gray Alys the wolf stood, half again the size of an ordinary wolf, with a savage red slash of a mouth and glowing scarlet eyes. Gray Alys stared into those eyes as she rose and shook the dust from her feathered cloak.

The wolf howled once again, a long wild sound that melted into the wind. And then he leapt, straight across the embers of the fire he had built.

Gray Alys threw her arms out, her cloak bunched in her hands, and changed. Her change was faster than his had been, over almost as soon as it begun. She beat her vast silvery wings, each pinion tipped with black, and the dust swirled as she rose up into the moonlight, up to safety high above the white wolf's bound, up and up until the ruins shrunk to insignificance far beneath her. Her cruel curving beak opened and closed and opened again, though no sound came forth. Her wings beat and beat again, and she began to descend, shrieking down through the night air, plunging toward her prey....

PORTRAITS OF HIS CHILDREN

GEORGE R.R. MARTIN

BAEN BOOKS

PORTRAITS OF HIS CHILDREN

Copyright © 1987 by George R. R. Martin

A Baen Book

Baen Publishing Enterprises
P.O. Box 1403
Riverdale, N.Y. 10471

ISBN: 0-671-72124-0

Cover art by Paul Chadwick

First Baen printing, June 1992

Distributed by
SIMON & SCHUSTER
1230 Avenue of the Americas
New York, N.Y. 10020

Printed in the United States of America

To Denise
who brought the magic back
and helped me through the dark.

Hi.

TABLE OF CONTENTS

PORTRAITS OF HIS CHILDREN

A SKETCH OF THEIR FATHER
by
Roger Zelazny

George R. R. Martin and I go back for well over a decade. I first got to know him when we taught a science fiction section together at the Indiana University Writers' Conference. That was where I became aware of the clearness of his vision into storytelling processes, through what I felt to be perfect analyses and critiques of everything that came across the desk. I also noted just how helpful he was to the would-be writers in attendance. It was his idea to set up extra, informal evening sessions, where we could depart from the class format and discuss anything concerning the area in which the participants were interested. He really cared about those people, and he wanted to arm them with every weapon he could for the big combat zone of professional writing. I respected him for that, and since I already respected him for things he had written I wound up the week on that attractive campus full of good feelings toward George and I resolved to follow his career.

Now, I'd learned of his history in chess, both in running tournaments and in playing the game himself (he's rated Expert), I'd learned of his academic background in Journalism and I'd even learned what the two Rs stand for, during our association that week. Later, I heard that he had accepted a job teaching Journalism in Iowa. (He moved there from Chicago—he has a couple of degrees from Northwestern—and he originally hails from New Jersey.) I did not at that time know of his interest in Mississippi riverboats, a thing anyone can now see by reading his fine novel, *Fevre Dream.* Nor did I learn anything which would have caused me to anticipate his powerful *Armageddon Rag,* which leads me to conclude that science fiction writers themselves have, through exposure, become immune to the extrapolative process even in the hands of others of their kind.

I skip over reunions at various conventions and professional functions to a later period when George quit teaching to write full-time, departed the windswept plains of Iowa and became my neighbor here in the mountain-girt fastnesses of Santa Fe, New Mexico. I have already told the story elsewhere of how he jokingly suggested I write the story—which I jokingly decided to do—that became "Unicorn Variation," one of my better-known pieces. We have eaten and drunk together on many occasions, and he gives good parties—a thing that's never been one of my own strong points—and I'll let this be my thank you note for a lot of fine times, even the one where I set off his fire alarm when I stepped out into the hallway to light my pipe.

I have since known him as an exceptional editor, in his management of the complex mosaic-novel Wild Card series—which, upon reflection, I realize that only a chess expert could coordinate. I have also seen his sensitivity to another writer's work in his adaptation of my story "The Last Defender of Camelot" as a *Twilight Zone* episode. Not only did he do a better job of scripting it than I could have myself, but he phoned me regularly to explain the necessity for changes (no horses on the sound stage, though we could have night there; horses out-of-doors, but not at night—too tricky to film) and to report on problems as they developed (good armor is not always that easy to come by, Stonehenge wasn't built in a day and Hollow Knights upset Special Effects people) and problems in the course of filming (why Lancelot's cane became a scarf) and disasters (the stunt man whose nose was cut off during the sword-fighting scene). I listened in awe to the problems with which he wrestled in attempting to preserve the integrity of my story, I knew gratitude for his attempts through six rewrites to save lines he could tell were favorites of mine and I was totally pleased with the result when it finally glowed into being and moved.

Now I have before me the MS of this collection, and I've just finished reading through it. I'm glad that it's so good—though I don't think George capable of writing a really bad story—and I see that it contains tales from all over his career, including "The Lonely Songs of Laren Dorr"—one of the few stories by someone else which I wish I'd written. Reading through this many this way, I was impressed by his range. There are a number of good writers who are Johnny One-Notes, who tell a certain sort of story very well or use a particular type of character very skillfully, but never seem to go beyond that. This is not the case with George. His themes are as varied as his characters, and there is a temporal progession to his subtlety and complexity; that is, he continues to grow and develop, which is the life-principle for an artist.

There is a certain wistfulness to "With Morning Comes Mistfall," a high poignancy to pieces such as "The Glass

Flower," "Portraits of His Children," and "The Lonely Songs of Laren Dorr," madness and violence in "The Second Kind of Loneliness" and "Under Seige," and there is also humor, in "The Last Super Bowl" and "Closing Time." There is dignity and perhaps even nobility in "Unsound Variations," irony in "In the Lost Lands" and a kind of bitter-sweet fairy tale quality to "The Ice Dragon." All in all, it's an impressive array of tellings. Anyone picking up this book will get a full return on the investment.

A story is, among other things, a judgment of reality. The better ones merge thought and feeling to achieve an experience of such judgments. A concern for values in the face of individual extinction and universal entropy, for example, is one of the high themes in both philosopy and literature. To deal with such a matter at all, as opposed to dispensing simple entertainments, is to reach toward the upper limits of fiction. There seem to be as many different ways of presenting the Values v. Death theme as there are writers willing to work at that uncomfortable level. The willingness to try may be what separates the artist from the hack. Look at the final conversation between Kleronomas and Cyrain of Ash in "The Glass Flower." There is a deadly, icy balancing of philosophical positions in this exchange. Here, George found the perfect vehicle for merging his thoughts and feelings on the matter. Reading stuff such as this is an uncommon experience. Behind those few pages are years of living sensitive to the forces that create and destroy, and coming up with a series of judgments. Of course, it helps to have a poet's way with words and a dramatist's ear for dialogue. But I was talking about ideas, pure judgments of reality, and their translation into fiction. George does not draw away from the greater judgments, and so achieves a background feeling of honesty in his work which separates it from the run-of-the-mill.

I pause, since this is an introduction and not a dissertation, and also because I fear that too much of such talk could make him sound heavy and stuffy, which he is not, rather than graceful and engaging, which he is.

I could change the subject now and tell you that George is a gentle soul, fond of cats, hats, good food and drink, music and the company of friends, that he lives in a pleasant house full of books and awards, and that he seems to be one of those people who has no enemies. I could say that, having known him as teacher, writer, editor, critic, inspirer and adapter, I am continually impressed by his sensitivity in all areas concerning writing. I could also disregard my earlier conclusion about extrapolation and perform a series of progressively brightening predictions on the course of his career.

However, I feel obliged to point out that since I am prejudiced in his favor because he's a friend of mine I have subtracted lots of good things I could say about him to sort of balance things out.

WITH MORNING COMES MISTFALL

I was early to breakfast that morning, the first day after landing. But Sanders was already out on the dining balcony when I got there. He was standing alone by the edge, looking out over the mountains and the mists.

I walked up behind him and muttered hello. He didn't bother to reply. "It's beautiful, isn't it?" he said, without turning.

And it was.

Only a few feet below balcony level the mists rolled, sending ghostly breakers to crash against the stones of Sanders' castle. A thick white blanket extended from horizon to horizon, cloaking everything. We could see the summit of the Red Ghost, off to the north; a barbed dagger of scarlet rock jabbing into the sky. But that was all. The other mountains were still below mist level.

But we were above the mists. Sanders had built his hotel atop the tallest mountain in the chain. We were floating alone in a swirling white ocean, on a flying castle amid a sea of clouds.

Castle Cloud, in fact. That was what Sanders had named the place. It was easy to see why.

"Is it always like this?" I asked Sanders, after drinking it all in for awhile.

"Every mistfall," he replied, turning towards me with a wistful smile. He was a fat man, with a jovial red face. Not the sort who should smile wistfully. But he did.

He gestured towards the east, where Wraithworld's sun rising above the mists made a crimson and orange spectacle out of the dawn sky.

"The sun," he said. "As it rises, the heat drives the mists back into the valleys, forces them to surrender the mountains they've conquered during the night. The mists sink, and one by one the peaks come into view. By noon the whole range is visible for miles and miles. There's nothing like it on Earth, or anywhere else."

He smiled again, and led me over to one of the tables scattered around the balcony. "And then, at sunset, it's all reversed. You must watch mistrise tonight," he said.

We sat down, and a sleek robowaiter came rolling out to serve us as the chairs registered our presence. Sanders ignored it. "It's war, you know," he continued. "Eternal war between the sun and the mists. And the mists have the better of it. They have the valleys, and the plains, and the seacoasts. The sun has only a few mountaintops. And them only by day."

He turned to the robowaiter and ordered coffee for both of us, to keep us occupied until the others arrived. It would be fresh-brewed, of course. Sanders didn't tolerate instants or synthetics on his planet.

"You like it here," I said, while we waited for the coffee.

Sanders laughed. "What's not to like? Castle Cloud has everything. Good food, entertainment, gambling, and all the other comforts of home. Plus this planet. I've got the best of both worlds, don't I?"

"I suppose so. But most people don't think in those terms. Nobody comes to Wraithworld for the gambling, or the food."

Sanders nodded. "But we do get some hunters. Out after rockcats and plains devils. And once in a while someone will come to look at the ruins."

"Maybe," I said. "But those are your exceptions. Not your rule. Most of your guests are here for one reason."

"Sure," he admitted, grinning. "The wraiths."

"The wraiths," I echoed. "You've got beauty here, and hunting and fishing and mountaineering. But none of that brings the tourists here. It's the wraiths they come for."

The coffee arrived then, two big steaming mugs accompanied by a pitcher of thick cream. It was very strong, and very hot, and very good. After weeks of spaceship synthetic, it was an awakening.

Sanders sipped at his coffee with care, his eyes studying me over the mug. He set it down thoughtfully. "And it's the wraiths you've come for, too," he said.

I shrugged. "Of course. My readers aren't interested in scenery, no matter how spectacular. Dubowski and his men are here to find wraiths, and I'm here to cover the search."

Sanders was about to answer, but he never got the chance. A sharp, precise voice cut in suddenly. "If there are any wraiths to find," the voice said.

We turned to face the balcony entrance. Dr. Charles Dubowski, head of the Wraithworld Research Team, was standing in the doorway, squinting at the light. He had managed to shake the gaggle of research assistants who usually trailed him everywhere.

Dubowski paused for a second, then walked over to our table, pulled out a chair, and sat down. The robowaiter came rolling out again.

Sanders eyed the thin scientist with unconcealed distaste. "What makes you think the wraiths aren't there, Doctor?" he asked.

Dubowski shrugged, and smiled lightly. "I just don't feel there's enough evidence," he said. "But don't worry. I never let my feelings interfere with my work. I want the truth as much as anyone. So I'll run an impartial expedition. If your wraiths *are* out there, I'll find them."

"Or they'll find you," Sanders said. He looked grave. "And that might not be too pleasant."

Dubowski laughed. "Oh, come now, Sanders. Just because you live in a castle doesn't mean you have to be so melodramatic."

"Don't laugh, Doctor. The wraiths have killed people before, you know."

"No proof of that," said Dubowski. "No proof at all. Just as there's no proof of the wraiths themselves. But that's why we're here. To find proof. Or disproof. But come, I'm famished." He turned to our robowaiter, who had been standing by and humming impatiently.

Dubowski and I ordered rockcat steaks, with a basket of hot, freshly baked biscuits. Sanders took advantage of the Earth supplies our ship had brought in last night, and got a massive slab of ham with a half-dozen eggs.

Rockcat has a flavor that Earth meat hasn't had in centuries. I loved it, although Dubowski left much of his steak uneaten. He was too busy talking to eat.

"You shouldn't dismiss the wraiths so lightly," Sanders said after the robowaiter had stalked off with our orders. "There is evidence. Plenty of it. Twenty-two deaths since this planet was discovered. And eyewitness accounts of wraiths by the dozens."

"True," Dubowski said. "But I wouldn't call that real evidence. Deaths? Yes. Most are simple disappearances, however. Probably people who fell off a mountain, or got eaten by a rockcat, or something. It's impossible to find the bodies in the mists.

"More people vanish every day on Earth, and nothing is thought of it. But here, everytime someone disappears, people claim the wraiths got him. No, I'm sorry. It's not enough."

"Bodies have been found, Doctor," Sanders said quietly. "Slain horribly. And not by falls or rockcats, either."

It was my turn to cut in. "Only four bodies have been recovered that I know of," I said. "And I've backgrounded myself pretty thoroughly on the wraiths."

Sanders frowned. "All right," he admitted. "But what about those four cases? Pretty convincing evidence, if you ask me."

The food showed up about then, but Sanders continued as we ate. "The first sighting, for example. That's never been explained satisfactorily. The Gregor Expedition."

I nodded. Dave Gregor had captained the ship that had discovered Wraithworld, nearly 75 years earlier. He had probed through the mists with his sensors, and set his ship down on the seacoast plains. Then he sent teams out to explore.

There were two men in each team, both well armed. But in one case, only a single man came back, and he was in hysteria. He and his partner had gotten separated in the mists, and suddenly he heard a blood-curdling scream. When he found his friend, he was quite dead. And something was standing over the body.

The survivor described the killer as man-like, eight feet tall, and somehow insubstantial. He claimed that when he fired at it, the blaster bolt went right through it. Then the creature had wavered, and vanished in the mists.

Gregor sent other teams out to search for the thing. They recovered the body, but that was all. Without special instruments, it was difficult to find the same place twice in the mists. Let alone something like the creature that had been described.

So the story was never confirmed. But nonetheless, it caused a sensation when Gregor returned to Earth. Another ship was sent to conduct a more thorough search. It found nothing. But one of its search teams disappeared without a trace.

And the legend of the mist wraiths was born, and began to grow. Other ships came to Wraithworld, and a trickle of colonists came and went, and Paul Sanders landed one day and erected the Castle Cloud so the public might safely visit the mysterious planet of the wraiths.

And there were other deaths, and other disappearances, and many people claimed to catch brief glimpses of wraiths prowling through the mists. And then someone found the ruins. Just tumbled stone blocks, now. But once, structures of some sort. The homes of the wraiths, people said.

There was evidence, I thought. And some of it was hard to deny. But Dubowski was shaking his head vigorously.

"The Gregor affair proves nothing," he said. "You know as well as I this planet has never been explored thoroughly. Especially the plains area, where Gregor's ship put down. It was probably some sort of animal that killed that man. A rare animal of some sort native to that area."

"What about the testimony of his partner?" Sanders asked.

"Hysteria, pure and simple."

"The other sightings? There have been an awful lot of them. And the witnesses weren't always hysterical."

"Proves nothing," Dubowski said, shaking his head. "Back on Earth, plenty of people still claim to have seen ghosts and flying saucers. And here, with those damned mists, mistakes and hallucinations are naturally even easier."

He jabbed at Sanders with the knife he was using to butter a biscuit. "It's these mists that foul up everything. The wraith myth would have died long ago without the mists. Up to now, no one has had the equipment or the money to conduct a really thorough investigation. But we do. And we will. We'll get the truth once and for all."

Sanders grimaced. "If you don't get yourself killed first. The wraiths may not like being investigated."

"I don't understand you, Sanders," Dubowski said. "If you're so afraid of the wraiths and so convinced that they're down there prowling about, why have you lived here so long?"

"Castle Cloud was built with safeguards," Sanders said. "The brochure we send prospective guests describes them. No one is in any danger here. For one thing, the wraiths won't come out of the mists. And we're in sunlight most of the day. But it's a different story down in the valleys."

"That's superstitious nonsense. If I had to guess, I'd say these mist wraiths of yours were nothing but transplanted Earth ghosts. Phantoms of someone's imagination. But I won't guess—I'll wait until the results are in. Then we'll see. If they are real, they won't be able to hide from us."

Sanders looked over at me. "What about you? Do you agree with him?"

"I'm a journalist," I said carefully. "I'm just here to cover what happens. The wraiths are famous, and my readers are interested. So I've got no opinions. Or none that I'd care to broadcast, anyway."

Sanders lapsed into a disgruntled silence, and attacked his ham and eggs with a renewed vigor. Dubowski took over for him, and steered the conversation over to the details of the investigation he was planning. The rest of the meal was a montage of eager talk about wraith traps, and search plans, and roboprobes, and sensors. I listened carefully and took mental notes for a column on the subject.

Sanders listened carefully, too. But you could tell from his face that he was far from pleased by what he heard.

Nothing much else happened that day. Dubowski spent his time at the spacefield, built on a small plateau below the castle, and supervised the unloading of his equipment. I wrote a column on his plans for the expedition, and beamed it back to Earth. Sanders tended to his other guests, and did whatever else a hotel manager does, I guess.

I went out to the balcony again at sunset, to watch the mists rise.

It was war, like Sanders had said. At mistfall, I had seen the sun victorious in the first of the daily battles. But now the conflict was renewed. The mists began to creep back to the heights as the temperature fell. Wispy gray-white tendrils stole up silently from the valleys, and curled around the jagged mountain peaks like ghostly fingers. Then the fingers began to grow thicker and stronger, and after awhile they pulled the mists up after them.

One by one the stark, wind-carved summits were swallowed up for another night. The Red Ghost, the giant to the north, was the last mountain to vanish in the lapping white ocean. And then the mists began to pour in over the balcony ledge, and close around Castle Cloud itself.

I went back inside. Sanders was standing there, just inside the doors. He had been watching me.

"You were right," I said. "It was beautiful."

He nodded. "You know, I don't think Dubowski has bothered to look yet," he said.

"Busy, I guess."

Sanders sighed. "Too damn busy. C'mon. I'll buy you a drink."

The hotel bar was quiet and dark, with the kind of mood that promotes good talk and serious drinking. The more I saw of Sanders' castle, the more I liked the man. Our tastes were in remarkable accord.

We found a table in the darkest and most secluded part of the room, and ordered drinks from a stock that included liquors from a dozen worlds. And we talked.

"You don't seem very happy to have Dubowski here," I said after the drinks came. "Why not? He's filling up your hotel."

Sanders looked up from his drink, and smiled. "True. It is the slow season. But I don't like what he's trying to do."

"So you try to scare him away?"

Sanders' smile vanished. "Was I that transparent?"

I nodded.

He sighed. "Didn't think it would work," he said. He sipped thoughtfully at his drink. "But I had to try something."

"Why?"

"Because. Because he's going to destroy this world, if I let him. By the time he and his kind get through, there won't be a mystery left in the universe."

"He's just trying to find some answers. Do the wraiths exist? What about the ruins? Who built them? Didn't you ever want to know those things, Sanders?"

He drained his drink, looked around, and caught the waiter's eye to order another. No robowaiters in here. Only human help. Sanders was particular about atmosphere.

"Of course," he said when he had his drink. "Everyone's wondered about those questions. That's why people come here to Wraithworld, to the Castle Cloud. Each guy who touches down here is secretly hoping he'll have an adventure with the wraiths, and find out all the answers personally.

"So he doesn't. So he slaps on a blaster and wanders around the mist forests for a few days, or a few weeks, and finds nothing. So what? He can come back and search again. The dream is still there, and the romance, and the mystery.

"And who knows? Maybe one trip he glimpses a wraith drifting through the mists. Or something he thinks is a wraith. And then he'll go home happy, 'cause he's been part of a legend. He's touched a little bit of creation that hasn't had all the awe and the wonder ripped from it yet by Dubowski's sort."

He fell silent, and stared morosely into his drink. Finally, after a long pause, he continued. "Dubowski! Bah! He makes me boil. He comes here with his ship full of lackeys and his million credit grant and all his gadgets, to hunt for wraiths. Oh, he'll get them all right. That's what frightens me. Either he'll prove they don't exist, or he'll find them, and they'll turn out to be some kind of submen or animal or something."

He emptied his glass again, savagely. "And that will ruin it. Ruin it, you hear! He'll answer all the questions with his gadgets, and there'll be nothing left for anyone else. It isn't fair."

I sat there and sipped quietly at my drink and said nothing. Sanders ordered another. A foul thought was running around in my head. Finally I had to say it aloud.

"If Dubowski answers all the questions," I said, "then there will be no reason to come here anymore. And you'll be put out of business. Are you sure that's not why you're so worried?"

Sanders glared at me, and I thought he was going to hit me for a second. But he didn't. "I thought you were different. You looked at mistfall, and understood. I thought you did, anyway. But I guess I was wrong." He jerked his head toward the door. "Get out of here," he said.

I rose. "Alright," I said. "I'm sorry, Sanders. But it's my job to ask nasty questions like that."

He ignored me, and I left the table. When I reached

the door, I turned and looked back across the room. Sanders was staring into his drink again, and talking loudly to himself.

"Answers," he said. He made it sound obscene. "Answers. Always they have to have answers. But the questions are so much finer. Why can't they leave them alone?"

I left him alone then. Alone with his drinks.

The next few weeks were hectic ones, for the expedition and for me. Dubowski went about things thoroughly, you had to give him that. He had planned his assault on Wraithworld with meticulous precision.

Mapping came first. Thanks to the mists, what maps there were of Wraithworld were very crude by modern standards. So Dubowski sent out a whole fleet of robo-probes, to skim above the mists and steal their secrets with sophisticated sensory devices. From the information that came pouring in, a detailed topography of the region was pieced together.

That done, Dubowski and his assistants then used the maps to carefully plot every recorded wraith sighting since the Gregor Expedition. Considerable data on the sightings had been compiled and analyzed long before we left Earth, of course. Heavy use of the matchless collection on wraiths in the Castle Cloud library filled in the gaps that remained. As expected, sightings were most common in the valleys around the hotel, the only permanent human habitation on the planet.

When the plotting was completed, Dubowski set out his wraith traps, scattering most of them in the areas where wraiths had been reported most frequently. He also put a few in distant, outlying regions, however, including the seacoast plain where Gregor's ship had made the initial contact.

The traps weren't really traps, of course. They were squat duralloy pillars, packed with most every type of sensing and recording equipment known to earth science. To the traps, the mists were all but nonexistent. If some unfortunate wraith wandered into survey range, there would be no way it could avoid detection.

Meanwhile, the mapping roboprobes were pulled in to be overhauled and reprogrammed, and then sent out again. With the topography known in detail, the probes could be sent through the mists on low-level patrols without fear of banging into a concealed mountain. The sensing equipment carried by the probes was not the equal of that in the wraith traps, of course. But the probes had a much greater range, and could cover thousands of square miles each day.

Finally, when the wraith traps were deployed and the roboprobes were in the air, Dubowski and his men took to the mist forests themselves. Each carried a heavy backpack of sensors and detection devices. The human search teams had more mobility than the wraith traps, and more sophisticated equipment than the probes. They covered a different area each day, in painstaking detail.

I went along on a few of those trips, with a backpack of my own. It made for some interesting copy, even though we never found anything. And while on search, I fell in love with the mist forests.

The tourist literature likes to call them "the ghastly mist forests of haunted Wraithworld." But they're not ghastly. Not really. There's a strange sort of beauty there, for those who can appreciate it.

The trees are thin and very tall, with white bark and pale gray leaves. But the forests are not without color. There's a parasite, a hanging moss of some sort, that's very common, and it drips from the overhanging branches in cascades of dark green and scarlet. And there are rocks, and vines, and low bushes choked with misshapen purplish fruits.

But there's no sun, of course. The mists hide everything. They swirl and slide around you as you walk, caressing you with unseen hands, clutching at your feet.

Once in a while, the mists play games with you. Most of the time you walk through a thick fog, unable to see more than a few feet in any direction, your own shoes lost in the mist carpet below. Sometimes, though, the fog closes in suddenly. And then you can't see at all. I blundered into more than one tree when that happened.

At other times, though, the mists—for no apparent reason—will roll back suddenly, and leave you standing alone in a clear pocket within a cloud. That's when you can see the forest in all its grotesque beauty. It's a brief, breathtaking glimpse of never-never land. Moments like that are few and short-lived. But they stay with you.

They stay with you.

In those early weeks, I didn't have much time for walking in the forests, except when I joined a search team to get the feel of it. Mostly I was busy writing. I did a series on the history of the planet, highlighted by the stories of the most famous sightings. I did feature profiles on some of the more colorful members of the expedition. I did a piece on Sanders, and the problems he encountered and overcame in building Castle Cloud. I did science pieces on the little known about the planet's ecology. I did mood pieces about the forests and the mountains. I did speculative thought pieces about the ruins. I wrote about rockcat hunting, and mountain climbing, and the huge and dangerous swamp lizards native to some offshore islands.

And, of course, I wrote about Dubowski and his search. On that I wrote reams.

Finally, however, the search began to settle down into dull routine, and I began to exhaust the myriad other topics Wraithworld offered. My output began to decline. I started to have time on my hands.

That's when I really began to enjoy Wraithworld. I began to take daily walks through the forests, ranging

wider each day. I visited the ruins, and flew half a conti-
nent away to see the swamp lizards first hand instead of
by holo. I befriended a group of hunters passing through,
and shot myself a rockcat. I accompanied some other
hunters to the western seacoast, and nearly got myself
killed by a plains devil.

And I began to talk to Sanders again.

Through all of this, Sanders had pretty well ignored
me and Dubowski and everyone else connected with the
wraith research. He spoke to us grudgingly if at all,
greeted us curtly, and spent all his free time with his
other guests.

At first, after the way he had talked in the bar that
night, I worried about what he might do. I had visions
of him murdering someone out in the mists, and trying
to make it look like a wraith killing. Or maybe just sabo-
taging the wraith traps. But I was sure he would try
something to scare off Dubowski or otherwise undermine
the expedition.

Comes of watching too much holovision, I guess. Sanders did nothing of the sort. He merely sulked, glared
at us in the castle corridors, and gave us less than full
cooperation at all times.

After a while, though, he began to warm up again. Not
towards Dubowski and his men. Just towards me.

I guess that was because of my walks in the forests.
Dubowski never went out into the mists unless he had
to. And then he went out reluctantly, and came back
quickly. His men followed their chief's example. I was
the only joker in the deck. But then, I wasn't really part
of the same deck.

Sanders noticed, of course. He didn't miss much of
what went on in his castle. And he began to speak to me
again. Civilly. One day, finally, he even invited me for
drinks again.

It was about two months into the expedition. Winter
was coming to Wraithworld and Castle Cloud, and the

air was getting cold and crisp. Dubowski and I were out on the dining balcony, lingering over coffee after another superb meal. Sanders sat at a nearby table, talking to some tourists.

I forget what Dubowski and I were discussing. Whatever it was, Dubowski interrupted me with a shiver at one point. "It's getting cold out here," he complained. "Why don't we move inside?" Dubowski never liked the dining balcony very much.

I sort of frowned. "It's not that bad," I said. "Besides, it's nearly sunset. One of the best parts of the day."

Dubowski shivered again, and stood up. "Suit yourself," he said. "But I'm going in. I don't feel like catching a cold just so you can watch another mistfall."

He started to walk off. But he hadn't taken three steps before Sanders was up out of his seat, howling like a wounded rockcat.

"Mistfall," he bellowed. *"Mistfall!"* He launched into a long, incoherent string of obscenities. I had never seen Sanders so angry, not even when he threw me out of the bar that first night. He stood there, literally trembling with rage, his face flushed, his fat fists clenching and unclenching at his sides.

I got up in a hurry, and got between them. Dubowski turned to me, looking baffled and scared. "Wha—" he started.

"Get inside," I interrupted. "Get up to your room. Get to the lounge. Get somewhere. Get anywhere. But get out of here before he kills you."

"But—but—what's wrong? What happened? I don't—"

"Mistfall is in the morning," I told him. "At night, at sunset, it's mistrise. Now *go.*"

"That's *all*? Why should that get him so—so—"

"GO!"

Dubowski shook his head, as if to say he still didn't understand what was going on. But he went.

I turned to Sanders. "Calm down," I said. "Calm down."

He stopped trembling, but his eyes threw blaster bolts at Dubowski's back. "Mistfall," he muttered. "Two months that bastard has been here, and he doesn't know the difference between mistfall and mistrise."

"He's never bothered to watch either one," I said. "Things like that don't interest him. That's his loss, though. No reason for you to get upset about it."

He looked at me, frowning. Finally he nodded. "Yeah," he said. "Maybe you're right." He sighed. "But *mistfall*! Hell." There was a short silence, then, "I need a drink. Join me?"

I nodded.

We wound up in the same dark corner as the first night, at what must have been Sanders' favorite table. He put away three drinks before I had finished my first. Big drinks. Everything in Castle Cloud was big.

There were no arguments this time. We talked about mistfall, and the forests, and the ruins. We talked about the wraiths, and Sanders lovingly told me the stories of the great sightings. I knew them all already, of course. But not the way Sanders told them.

At one point, I mentioned that I'd been born in Bradbury when my parents were spending a short vacation on Mars. Sanders' eyes lit up at that, and he spent the next hour or so regaling me with Earthman jokes. I'd heard them all before, too. But I was getting more than a little drunk, and somehow they all seemed hilarious.

After that night, I spent more time with Sanders than with anyone else in the hotel. I thought I knew Wraithworld pretty well by that time. But that was an empty conceit, and Sanders proved it. He showed me hidden spots in the forests that have haunted me ever since. He took me to island swamps, where the trees are of a very different sort and sway horridly without a wind. We flew to the far north, to another mountain range where the peaks are higher and sheathed in ice, and to a southern plateau where the mists pour eternally over the edge in a ghostly imitation of a waterfall.

I continued to write about Dubowski and his wraith hunt, of course. But there was little new to write about, so most of my time was spent with Sanders. I didn't worry too much about my output. My Wraithworld series had gotten excellent play on Earth and most of the colony worlds, so I thought I had it made.

Not so.

I'd been on Wraithworld just a little over three months when my syndicate beamed me. A few systems away, a civil war had broken out on a planet called New Refuge. They wanted me to cover it. No news was coming out of Wraithworld anyway, they said, since Dubowski's expedition still had over a year to run.

Much as I liked Wraithworld, I jumped at the chance. My stories had been getting a little stale, and I was running out of ideas, and the New Refuge thing sounded like it could be very big.

So I said goodbye to Sanders and Dubowski and Castle Cloud, and took a last walk through the mist forests, and booked passage on the next ship through.

The New Refuge civil war was a firecracker. I spent less than a month on the planet, but it was a dreary month. The place had been colonized by religious fanatics, but the original cult had schismed, and both sides accused the other of heresy. It was all very dingy. The planet itself had all the charm of a Martian suburb.

I moved on as quickly as I could, hopping from planet to planet, from story to story. In six months, I had worked myself back to Earth. Elections were coming up, so I got slapped onto a political beat. That was fine by me. It was a lively campaign, and there was a ton of good stories to be mined.

But throughout it all, I kept myself up on the little news that came out of Wraithworld. And finally, as I'd expected, Dubowski announced a press conference. As the syndicate's resident wraith, I got myself assigned to cover, and headed out on the fastest starship I could find.

I got there a week before the conference, ahead of everyone else. I had beamed Sanders before taking ship, and he met me at the spaceport. We adjourned to the dining balcony, and had our drinks served out there.

"Well?" I asked him, after we had traded amenities. "You know what Dubowski's going to announce?"

Sanders looked very glum. "I can guess," he said. "He called in all his damn gadgets a month ago, and he's been cross-checking findings on a computer. We've had a couple of wraith sightings since you left. Dubowski moved in hours after each sighting, and went over the areas with a fine-tooth comb. Nothing. That's what he's going to announce, I think. Nothing."

I nodded. "Is that so bad, though? Gregor found nothing."

"Not the same," Sanders said. "Gregor didn't look the way Dubowski has. People will believe him, whatever he says."

I wasn't so sure of that, and was about to say so, when Dubowski arrived. Someone must have told him I was there. He came striding out on the balcony, smiling, spied me, and came over to sit down.

Sanders glared at him, and studied his drink. Dubowski trained all of his attention on me. He seemed very pleased with himself. He asked what I'd been doing since I left, and I told him, and he said that was nice.

Finally I got to ask him about his results. "No comment," he said. "That's what I've called the press conference for."

"C'mon," I said. "I covered you for months when

everybody else was ignoring the expedition. You can give me some kind of beat. What have you got?"

He hesitated. "Well, okay," he said doubtfully. "But don't release it yet. You can beam it out a few hours ahead of the conference. That should be enough time for a beat."

I nodded agreement. "What do you have?"

"The wraiths," he said. "I have the wraiths, bagged neatly. They don't exist. I've got enough evidence to prove it beyond a shadow of a doubt." He smiled broadly.

"Just because you didn't find anything?" I started. "Maybe they were avoiding you. If they're sentient, they might be smart enough. Or maybe they're beyond the ability of your sensors to detect."

"Come now," Dubowski said. "You don't believe that. Our wraith traps had every kind of sensor we could come up with. If the wraiths existed, they would have registered on something. But they didn't. We had the traps planted in the areas where three of Sanders' so-called sightings took place. Nothing. Absolutely nothing. Conclusive proof that those people were seeing things. Sightings, indeed."

"What about the deaths, the vanishings?" I asked. "What about the Gregor Expedition and the other classic cases?"

His smile spread. "Couldn't disprove all the deaths, of course. But our probes and our searches turned up four skeletons." He ticked them off on his fingers. "Two were killed by a rockslide, and one had rockcat claw marks on the bones."

"The fourth?"

"Murder," he said. "The body was buried in a shallow grave, clearly by human hands. A flood of some sort had exposed it. It was down in the records as a disappearance. I'm sure all the other bodies could be found, if we searched long enough. And we'd find that all died perfectly normal deaths."

Sanders raised his eyes from his drink. They were bitter eyes. "Gregor," he said stubbornly. "Gregor and the other classics."

Dubowski's smile became a smirk. "Ah, yes. We searched that area quite thoroughly. My theory was right. We found a tribe of apes nearby. Big brutes. Like giant baboons, with dirty white fur. Not a very successful species, either. We found only one small tribe, and they were dying out. But clearly, that was what Gregor's man sighted. And exaggerated all out of proportion."

There was silence. Then Sanders spoke, but his voice was beaten. "Just one question," he said softly. "Why?"

That brought Dubowski up short, and his smile faded. "You never have understood, have you, Sanders?" he said. "It was for truth. To free this planet from ignorance and superstition."

"Free Wraithworld?" Sanders said. "Was it enslaved?"

"Yes," Dubowski answered. "Enslaved by foolish myth. By fear. Now this planet will be free, and open. We can find out the truth behind those ruins now, without murky legends about half-human wraiths to fog the facts. We can open this planet for colonization. People won't be afraid to come here, and live, and farm. We've conquered the fear."

"A colony world? Here?" Sanders looked amused. "Are you going to bring big fans to blow away the mists, or what? Colonists have come before. And left. The soil's all wrong. You can't farm here, with all these mountains. At least not on a commercial scale. There's no way you can make a profit growing things on Wraithworld.

"Besides, there are hundreds of colony worlds crying for people. Did you need another so badly? Must Wraithworld become yet another Earth?"

He shook his head sadly, drained his drink, and continued. "You're the one who doesn't understand, Doctor. Don't kid yourself. You haven't freed Wraithworld.

You've destroyed it. You've stolen its wraiths, and left an empty planet."

Dubowski shook his head. "I think you're wrong. They'll find plenty of good, profitable ways to exploit this planet. But even if you were correct, well, it's just too bad. Knowledge is what man is all about. People like you have tried to hold back progress since the beginning of time. But they failed, and you failed. Man needs to know."

"Maybe," Sanders said. "But is that the *only* thing man needs? I don't think so. I think he also needs mystery, and poetry, and romance. I think he needs a few unanswered questions, to make him brood and wonder."

Dubowski stood up abruptly, and frowned. "This conversation is as pointless as your philosophy, Sanders. There's no room in my universe for unanswered questions."

"Then you live in a very drab universe, Doctor."

"And you, Sanders, live in the stink of your own ignorance. Find some new superstitions if you must. But don't try to foist them off on me with your tales and legends. I've got no time for wraiths." He looked at me. "I'll see you at the press conference," he said. Then he turned and walked briskly from the balcony.

Sanders watched him depart in silence, then swiveled in his chair to look out over the mountains. "The mists are rising," he said.

Sanders was wrong about the colony too, as it turned out. They did establish one, although it wasn't much to boast of. Some vineyards, some factories, and a few thousand people; all belonging to a couple of big companies.

Commercial farming did turn out to be unprofitable, you see. With one exception—a native grape, a fat gray thing the size of a lemon. So Wraithworld has only one export, a smoky white wine with a mellow, lingering flavor.

They call it mistwine, of course. I've grown fond of it

over the years. The taste reminds me of mistfall somehow, and makes me dream. But that's probably me, not
the wine. Most people don't care for it much.

Still, in a very minor way, it's a profitable item. So
Wraithworld is still a regular stop on the spacelanes. For
freighters, at least.

The tourists are long gone, though. Sanders was right
about that. Scenery they can get closer to home, and
cheaper. The wraiths were why they came.

Sanders is long gone, too. He was too stubborn and too
impractical to buy in on the mistwine operations when he
had the chance. So he stayed behind his ramparts at
Castle Cloud until the last. I don't know what happened
to him afterwards, when the hotel finally went out of
business.

The castle itself is still there. I saw it a few years ago,
when I stopped for a day en route to a story on New
Refuge. It's already crumbling, though. Too expensive to
maintain. In a few years, you won't be able to tell it from
those other, older ruins.

Otherwise the planet hasn't changed much. The mists
still rise at sunset, and fall at dawn. The Red Ghost is
still stark and beautiful in the early morning light. The
forests are still there, and the rockcats still prowl.

Only the wraiths are missing.

Only the wraiths.

THE SECOND KIND
OF LONELINESS

june 18

My relief left Earth today.

It will be at least three months before he gets here, of course. But he's on his way.

Today he lifted off from the Cape, just as I did, four long years ago. Out at Komarov Station he'll switch to a moon boat, then switch again in orbit around Luna, at Deepspace Station. There his voyage will really begin. Up to then he's still been in his own backyard.

Not until the *Charon* casts loose from Deepspace Station and sets out into the night will he feel it, *really* feel it, as I felt it four years ago. Not until Earth and Luna vanish behind him will it hit. He's known from the first that there's no turning back, of course. But there's a

difference between knowing it and feeling it. Now he'll
feel it.

There will be an orbital stopover around Mars, to send
supplies down to Burroughs City. And more stops in the
belt. But then the *Charon* will begin to gather speed. It
will be going very fast when it reaches Jupiter. And much
faster after it whips by, using the gravity of the giant
planet like a slingshot to boost its acceleration.

After that there are no stops for the *Charon*. No stops
at all until it reaches me, out here at the Cerberus Star
Ring, six million miles beyond Pluto.

My relief will have a long time to brood. As I did.

I'm still brooding now, today, four years later. But
then, there's not much else to do out here. Ringships are
infrequent, and you get pretty weary of films and tapes
and books after a time. So you brood. You think about
your past, and dream about your future. And you try to
keep the loneliness and the boredom from driving you
out of your skull.

It's been a long four years. But it's almost over now.
And it will be nice to get back. I want to walk on grass
again, and see clouds, and eat an ice cream sundae.

Still, for all that, I don't regret coming. These four
years alone in the darkness have done me good, I think.
It's not as if I had left much. My days on Earth seem
remote to me now, but I can still remember them if I
try. The memories aren't all that pleasant. I was pretty
screwed up back then.

I needed time to think, and that's one thing you get
out here. The man who goes back on the *Charon* won't
be the same one who came out here four years ago. I'll
build a whole new life back on Earth. I know I will.

june 20

Ship today.

I didn't know it was coming, of course. I never do.
The ringships are irregular, and the kind of energies I'm

playing with out here turn radio signals into crackling chaos. By the time the ship finally punched through the static, the station's scanners had already picked it up and notified me.

It was clearly a ringship. Much bigger than the old system rustbuckets like the *Charon*, and heavily armored to withstand the stresses of the nullspace vortex. It came straight on, with no attempt to decelerate.

While I was heading down to the control room to strap in, a thought hit me. This might be the last. Probably not, of course. There's still three months to go, and that's time enough for a dozen ships. But you can never tell. The ringships are irregular, like I said.

Somehow the thought disturbed me. The ships have been part of my life for four years now. An important part. And the one today might have been the last. If so, I want it all down here. I want to remember it. With good reason, I think. When the ships come, that makes everything else worthwhile.

The control room is in the heart of my quarters. It's the center of everything, where the nerves and the tendons and the muscles of the station are gathered. But it's not very impressive. The room is very small, and once the door slides shut the walls and floor and ceiling are all a featureless white.

There's only one thing in the room: a horseshoe-shaped console that surrounds a single padded chair.

I sat down in that chair today for what might be the last time. I strapped myself in, and put on the earphones, and lowered the helmet. I reached for the controls and touched them and turned them on.

And the room vanished.

It's all done with holographs, of course. I *know* that. But that doesn't make a bit of difference when I'm sitting in that chair. Then, as far as I'm concerned, I'm not inside anymore. I'm out *there*, in the void. The control console is still there, and the chair. But the rest has gone.

Instead, the aching darkness is everywhere, above me, below me, all around me. The distant sun is only one star among many, and all the stars are terribly far away.

That's the way it always is. That's the way it was today. When I threw that switch I was alone in the universe with the cold stars and the ring. The Cerberus Star Ring.

I saw the ring as if from outside, looking down on it. It's a vast structure, really. But from out here, it's nothing. It's swallowed by the immensity of it all, a slim silver thread lost in the blackness.

But I know better. The ring is huge. My living quarters take up but a single degree in the circle it forms, a circle whose diameter is more than a hundred miles. The rest is circuitry and scanners and power banks. And the engines, the waiting nullspace engines.

The ring turned silent beneath me, its far side stretching away into nothingness. I touched a switch on my console. Below me, the nullspace engines woke.

In the center of the ring, a new star was born.

It was a tiny dot amid the dark at first. Green today, bright green. But not always, and not for long. Nullspace has many colors.

I could see the far side of the ring then, if I'd wanted to. It was glowing with a light of its own. Alive and awake, the nullspace engines were pouring unimaginable amounts of energy inward, to rip wide a hole in space itself.

The hole had been there long before Cerberus, long before man. Men found it, quite by accident, when they reached Pluto. They built the ring around it. Later they found two other holes, and built other star rings.

The holes were small, too small. But they could be enlarged. Temporarily, at the expense of vast amounts of power, they could be ripped open. Raw energy could be pumped through that tiny, unseen hole in the universe until the placid surface of nullspace roiled and lashed back, and the nullspace vortex formed.

And now it happened.

The star in the center of the ring grew and flattened. It was a pulsing disc, not a globe. But it was still the brightest thing in the heavens. And it swelled visibly. From the spinning green disc, flame-like orange spears lanced out, and fell back, and smoky bluish tendrils uncoiled. Specks of red danced and flashed among the green, grew and blended. The colors all began to run together.

The flat, spinning, multi-colored star doubled in size, doubled again, again. A few minutes before it had not been. Now it filled the ring, lapped against the silver walls, seared them with its awful energy. It began to spin faster and faster, a whirlpool in space, a maelstrom of flame and light.

The vortex. The nullspace vortex. The howling storm that is not a storm and does not howl, for there is no sound in space.

To it came the ringship. A moving star at first, it took on visible form and shape almost faster than my human eyes could follow. It became a dark silver bullet in the blackness, a bullet fired at the vortex.

The aim was good. The ship hit very close to the center of the ring. The swirling colors closed over it.

I hit my controls. Even more suddenly than it had come, the vortex was gone. The ship was gone too, of course. Once more there was only me, and the ring, and the stars.

Then I touched another switch, and I was back in the blank white control room, unstrapping. Unstrapping for what might be the last time, ever.

Somehow I hope not. I never thought I'd miss anything about this place. But I will. I'll miss the ringships. I'll miss moments like today.

I hope I get a few more chances at it before I give it up forever. I want to feel the nullspace engines wake again under my hands, and watch the vortex boil and churn while I float alone between the stars. Once more, at least. Before I go.

june 23

That ringship has set me to thinking. Even more than usual.

It's funny that with all the ships I've seen pass through the vortex, I've never even given a thought to riding one. There's a whole new world on the other side of nullspace; Second Chance, a rich green planet of a star so far away that astronomers are still unsure whether it shares the same galaxy with us. That's the funny thing about the holes—you can't be sure where they lead until you go through.

When I was a kid, I read a lot about star travel. Most people didn't think it was possible. But those that did always mentioned Alpha Centauri as the first system we'd explore and colonize. Closest, and all that. Funny how wrong they were. Instead, our colonies orbit suns we can't even see. And I don't think we'll *ever* get to Alpha Centauri—

Somehow I never thought of the colonies in personal terms. Still can't. Earth is where I failed before. That's got to be where I succeed now. The colonies would be just another escape.

Like Cerberus?

june 26

Ship today. So the other wasn't the last, after all. But what about this one?

june 29

Why does a man volunteer for a job like this? Why does a man run to a silver ring six million miles beyond Pluto, to guard a hole in space? Why throw away four years of life alone in the darkness?

Why?

I used to ask myself that, in the early days. I couldn't answer it then. Now I think I can. I bitterly regretted the impulse that drove me out here, then. Now I think I understand it.

And it wasn't really an impulse. I ran to Cerberus. Ran. Ran to escape from loneliness.

That doesn't make sense?

Yet it does. I know about loneliness. It's been the theme of my life. I've been alone for as long as I can remember.

But there are two kinds of loneliness.

Most people don't realize the difference. I do. I've sampled both kinds.

They talk and write about the loneliness of the men who man the star rings. The lighthouses of space, and all that. And they're right.

There are times, out here at Cerberus, when I think I'm the only man in the universe. Earth was just a fever dream. The people I remember were just creations of my own mind.

There are times, out here, when I want someone to talk to so badly that I scream, and start pounding on the walls. There are times when the boredom crawls under my skin and all but drives me mad.

But there are *other* times, too. When the ringships come. When I go outside to make repairs. Or when I just sit in the control chair, imaging myself out into the darkness to watch the stars.

Lonely? Yes. But a solemn, brooding, tragic loneliness that a man hates with a passion—and yet loves so much he craves for more.

And then there is the second kind of loneliness.

You don't need the Cerberus Star Ring for that kind. You can find it anywhere on Earth. I know. I did. I found it everywhere I went, in everything I did.

It's the loneliness of people trapped within themselves. The loneliness of people who have said the wrong thing so often that they don't have the courage to say anything anymore. The loneliness, not of distance, but of fear.

The loneliness of people who sit alone in furnished rooms in crowded cities, because they've got nowhere to go and no one to talk to. The loneliness of guys who go to bars to meet someone, only to discover they don't know how to strike up a conversation, and wouldn't have the courage to do so if they did.

There's no grandeur to that kind of loneliness. No purpose and no poetry. It's loneliness without meaning. It's sad and squalid and pathetic, and it stinks of self-pity.

Oh yes, it hurts at times to be alone among the stars.

But it hurts a lot more to be alone at a party. A lot more.

june 30
Reading yesterday's entry. Talk about self-pity—

july 1
Reading *yesterday's* entry. My flippant mask. After four years, I still fight back whenever I try to be honest with myself. That's not good. If things are going to be any different this time, I have to understand myself.

So why do I have to ridicule myself when I admit that I'm lonely and vulnerable? Why do I have to struggle to admit that I was scared of life? No one's ever going to read this thing. I'm talking to myself, about myself.

So why are there so many things I can't bring myself to say?

july 4
No ringship today. Too bad. Earth ain't never *had* no fireworks that could match the nullspace vortex, and I felt like celebrating.

But why do I keep Earth calendar out here, where the years are centuries and the seasons a dim memory? July is just like December. So what's the use?

july 10

I dreamed of Karen last night. And now I can't get her out of my skull.

I thought I buried her long ago. It was all a fantasy anyway. Oh, she liked me well enough. Loved me, maybe. But no more than a half-dozen other guys. I wasn't really *special* to her, and she never realized just how special she was to me.

Nor how much I wanted to be special to her—how much I needed to be special to someone, somewhere.

So I elected her. But it was all a fantasy. And I knew it was, in my more rational moments. I had no right to be so hurt. I had no special claim on her.

But I thought I did, in my daydreams. And I *was* hurt. It was my fault, though, not hers. Karen would never hurt anyone willingly. She just never realized how fragile I was.

Even out here, in the early years, I kept dreaming. I dreamed of how she'd change her mind. How she'd be waiting for me. Etc.

But that was more wish fulfillment. It was before I came to terms with myself out here. I know now that she won't be waiting. She doesn't need me, and never did. I was just a friend.

So I don't much like dreaming about her. That's bad. Whatever I do, I must *not* look up Karen when I get back. I have to start all over again. I have to find someone who *does* need me. And I won't find her if I try to slip back into my old life.

july 18

A month since my relief left Earth. The *Charon* should be in the belt by now. Two months to go.

july 23

Nightmares. God help me.

I'm dreaming of Earth again. And Karen. I can't stop. Every night it's the same.

It's funny, calling Karen a nightmare. Up to now she's always been a dream. A beautiful dream, with her long, soft hair, and her laugh, and that funny way she had of grinning. But those dreams were always wish fulfillments. In the dreams Karen needed me and wanted me and loved me.

The nightmares have the bite of truth to them. They're all the same. It's always a replay of me and Karen, together on that last night.

It was a good night, as nights went for me. We ate at one of my favorite restaurants, and went to a show. We talked together easily, about many things. We laughed together, too.

Only later, back at her place, I reverted to form. When I tried to tell her how much she meant to me. I remember how awkward and stupid I felt, how I struggled to get things out, how I stumbled over my own words. So much came out wrong.

I remember how she looked at me then. Strangely. How she tried to disillusion me. Gently. She was always gentle. And I looked into her eyes and listened to her voice. But I didn't find love, or need. Just—just pity, I guess.

Pity for an inarticulate jerk who'd been letting life pass him by without touching it. Not because he didn't want to. But because he was afraid to, and didn't know how. She'd found that jerk, and loved him, in her way—she loved everybody. She'd tried to help, to give him some of her self-confidence, some of the courage and bounce that she faced life with. And, to an extent, she had.

Not enough, though. The jerk liked to make fantasies about the day he wouldn't be lonely anymore. And when Karen tried to help him, he thought she was his fantasy come to life. Or deluded himself into thinking that. The jerk suspected the truth all along, of course, but he lied to himself about it.

And when the day came that he couldn't lie any longer,

he was still vulnerable enough to be hurt. He wasn't the type to grow scar tissue easily. He didn't have the courage to try again with someone else. So he ran.

I hope the nightmares stop. I can't take them, night after night. I can't take reliving that hour in Karen's apartment.

I've had four years out here. I've looked at myself hard. I've changed what I didn't like, or tried to. I've tried to cultivate that scar-tissue, to gather the confidence I need to face the new rejections I'm going to meet before I find acceptance. But I know myself damn well now, and I know it's only been a partial success. There will always be things that will hurt, things that I'll never be able to face the way I'd like to.

Memories of that last hour with Karen are among those things. *God,* I hope the nightmares end.

july 26

More nightmares. Please, Karen. I loved you. Leave me alone. Please.

july 29

There was a ringship yesterday, thank God. I needed one. It helped take my mind off Earth, off Karen. And there was no nightmare last night, for the first time in a week. Instead I dreamed of the nullspace vortex. The raging silent storm.

august 1

The nightmares have returned. Not always Karen, now. Older memories too. Infinitely less meaningful, but still painful. All the stupid things I've said, all the girls I never met, all the things I never did.

Bad. Bad. I have to keep reminding myself. I'm not like that anymore. There's a new me, a me I built out here, six million miles beyond Pluto. Made of steel and

stars and nullspace, hard and confident and self-assured.
And not afraid of life.

The past is behind me. But it still hurts.

august 2

Ship today. The nightmares continue. Damn.

august 3

No nightmare last night. Second time for that, that
I've rested easy after opening the hole for a ringship
during the day. (Day? Night? Nonsense out here—but I
still write as if they had meaning. Four years haven't
even touched the Earth in me.) Maybe the vortex is
scaring Karen away. But I never wanted to scare Karen
away before. Besides, I shouldn't need crutches.

august 13

Another ship came through a few nights ago. No
dream afterwards. A pattern!

I'm fighting the memories. I'm thinking of other things
about Earth. The good times. There were a lot of them,
really, and there will be lots more when I get back. I'm
going to make sure of that.

These nightmares are stupid. I won't permit them to
continue. There was so much else I shared with Karen,
so much I'd like to recall. Why can't I?

august 18

The *Charon* is about a month away. I wonder who my
relief will be. I wonder what drove *him* out here?

Earth dreams continue. No. Call them Karen dreams.
Am I even afraid to write her name now?

august 20

Ship today. After it was through I stayed out and
looked at stars. For several hours, it seems. Didn't seem
as long at the time.

It's beautiful out here. Lonely, yes. But such a loneliness! You're alone with the universe, the stars spread out at your feet and scattered around your head.

Each one is a sun. Yet they still look cold to me. I find myself shivering, lost in the vastness of it all, wondering how it got there and what it means.

My relief, whoever it is, I hope he can appreciate this, as it should be appreciated. There are so many who can't, or won't. Men who walk at night, and never look up at the sky. I hope my relief isn't like that.

august 24

When I get back to Earth, I *will* look up Karen. I must. How can I pretend that things are going to be different this time if I can't even work up the courage to do that? And they *are* going to be different. So I *must* face Karen, and prove that I've changed. Really changed.

august 25

The nonsense of yesterday. *How* could I face Karen? What would I *say* to her? I'd only start deluding myself again, and wind up getting burned all over again. No. I must *not* see Karen. Hell, I can even take the dreams.

august 30

I've been going down to the control room and flipping myself out regularly of late. No ringships. But I find that going outside makes the memories of Earth dim.

More and more I know I'll miss Cerberus. A year from now, I'll be back on Earth, looking up at the night sky, and remembering how the ring shone silver in the starlight. I know I will.

And the vortex. I'll remember the vortex, and the ways the colors swirled and mixed. Different every time.

Too bad I was never a holo buff. You could make a fortune back on Earth with a tape of the way the vortex looks when it spins. The ballet of the void. I'm surprised no one's ever thought of it.

Maybe I'll suggest it to my relief. Something to do to fill the hours, if he's interested. I hope he is. Earth would be richer if someone brought back a record.

I'd do it myself, but the equipment isn't right, and I don't have the time to modify it.

september 4

I've gone outside every day for the last week, I find. No nightmares. Just dreams of the darkness, laced with the colors of nullspace.

september 9

Continue to go outside, and drink it all in. Soon, soon now, all this will be lost to me. Forever. I feel as though I must take advantage of every second. I must memorize the way things are out here at Cerberus, so I can keep the awe and the wonder and the beauty fresh inside me when I return to Earth.

september 10

There hasn't been a ship in a long time. Is it over, then? Have I seen my last?

september 12

No ship today. But I went outside and woke the engines and let the vortex roar.

Why do I always write about the vortex roaring and howling? There is no sound in space. I hear nothing. But I watch it. And it does roar. It does.

The sounds of silence. But not the way the poets meant.

september 13

I've watched the vortex again today, though there was no ship.

I've never done that before. Now I've done it twice.
It's forbidden. The costs in terms of power are enormous,
and Cerberus lives on power. So why?

It's almost as though I don't want to give up the vortex.
But I have to. Soon.

september 14

Idiot, idiot, idiot. What have I been doing? The
Charon is less than a week away, and I've been gawking
at the stars as if I'd never seen them before. I haven't
even started to pack, and I've got to clean up my records
for my relief, and get the station in order.

Idiot! Why am I wasting time writing in this damn *book*!

september 15

Packing almost done. I've uncovered some weird
things, too. Things I tried to hide in the early years. Like
my novel. I wrote it in the first six months, and thought
it was great. I could hardly wait to get back to Earth,
and sell it, and become an Author. Ah, yes. Read it over
a year later. It stinks.

Also, I found a picture of Karen.

september 16

Today I took a bottle of Scotch and a glass down to
the control room, set them down on the console, and
strapped myself in. Drank a toast to the blackness and
the stars and the vortex. I'll miss them.

september 17

A day, by my calculations. A day. Then I'm on my way
home, to a fresh start and a new life. If I have the courage to live it.

september 18

Nearly midnight. No sign of the *Charon*. What's
wrong?

Nothing, probably. These schedules are never precise. Sometimes as much as a week off. So why do I worry? Hell, I was late getting here myself. I wonder what the poor guy I replaced was thinking then?

september 20

The *Charon* didn't come yesterday, either. After I got tired of waiting, I took that bottle of Scotch and went back to the control room. And out. To drink another toast to the stars. And the vortex. I woke the vortex and let it flame, and toasted it.

A lot of toasts. I finished the bottle. And today I've got such a hangover I think I'll never make it back to Earth.

It was a stupid thing to do. The crew of the *Charon* might have seen the vortex colors. If they report me, I'll get docked a small fortune from the pile of money that's waiting back on Earth.

september 21

Where is the *Charon*? Did something happen to it? Is it coming?

september 22

I went outside again.

God, so beautiful, so lonely, so vast. Haunting, that's the word I want. The beauty out there is haunting. Sometimes I think I'm a fool to go back. I'm giving up all of eternity for a pizza and a lay and a kind word.

NO! What the hell am I writing! No. I'm going back, of course I am. I need Earth, I miss Earth, I want Earth. And this time it *will* be different.

I'll find another Karen, and this time I won't blow it.

september 23

I'm sick. God, but I'm sick. The things I've been thinking. I thought I had changed, but now I don't know. I find myself actually thinking about staying, about signing on for another term. I don't want to. No. But I think I'm still afraid of life, of Earth, of everything.

Hurry, *Charon*. Hurry, before I change my mind.

september 24

Karen or the vortex? Earth or eternity?

Dammit, how can I *think* that! Karen! Earth! I have to have courage, I have to risk pain, I have to taste life.

I am *not* a rock. Or an island. Or a star.

september 25

No sign of the *Charon*. A full week late. That happens sometimes. But not very often. It will arrive soon. I know it.

september 30

Nothing. Each day I watch, and wait. I listen to my scanners, and go outside to look, and pace back and forth through the ring. But nothing. It's never been this late. What's wrong?

october 3

Ship today. Not the *Charon*. I thought it was at first, when the scanners picked it up. I yelled loud enough to wake the vortex. But then I looked, and my heart sank. It was too big, and it was coming straight on without decelerating.

I went outside and let it through. And stayed out for a long time afterward.

october 4

I want to go home. Where are they? I don't understand. I don't understand.

They can't just leave me here. They can't. They won't.

october 5

Ship today. Ringship again. I used to look forward to them. Now I hate them, because they're not the *Charon*. But I let it through.

october 7

I unpacked. It's silly for me to live out of suitcases when I don't know if the *Charon* is coming, or when.

I still look for it, though. I wait. It's coming, I know. Just delayed somewhere. An emergency in the belt maybe. There are lots of explanations.

Meanwhile, I'm doing odd jobs around the ring. I never did get it in proper shape for my relief. Too busy star watching at the time, to do what I should have been doing.

january 8 (or thereabouts)

Darkness and despair.

I know why the *Charon* hasn't arrived. It isn't due. The calendar was all screwed up. It's January, not October. And I've been living on the wrong time for months. Even celebrated the Fourth of July on the wrong day.

I discovered it yesterday when I was doing those chores around the ring. I wanted to make sure everything was running right. For my relief.

Only there won't be any relief.

The *Charon* arrived three months ago. I—I destroyed it.

Sick. It was sick. I was sick, mad. As soon as it was done, it hit me. What I'd done. Oh, God. I screamed for hours.

And then I set back the wall calendar. And forgot. Maybe deliberately. Maybe I couldn't bear to remember. I don't know. All I know is that I forgot.

But now I remember. Now I remember it all.

The scanners had warned me of the *Charon*'s approach. I was outside, waiting. Watching. Trying to get enough of the stars and the darkness to last me forever.

Through that darkness, *Charon* came. It seemed so slow compared to the ringships. And so small. It was my salvation, my relief, but it looked fragile, and silly, and somehow ugly. Squalid. It reminded me of Earth.

It moved towards docking, dropping into the ring from above, groping towards the locks in the habitable section of Cerberus. So very slow. I watched it come. Suddenly I wondered what I'd say to the crewmen, and my relief. I wondered what they'd think of me. Somewhere in my gut, a fist clenched.

And suddenly I couldn't stand it. Suddenly I was afraid of it. Suddenly I hated it.

So I woke the vortex.

A red flare, branching into yellow tongues, growing quickly, shooting off bluegreen bolts. One passed near the *Charon*. And the ship shuddered.

I tell myself, now, that I didn't realize what I was doing. Yet I knew the *Charon* was unarmored. I knew it couldn't take vortex energies. I knew.

The *Charon* was so slow, the vortex so fast. In two heartbeats the maelstrom was brushing against the ship. In three it had swallowed it.

It was gone so fast. I don't know if the ship melted, or burst asunder, or crumpled. But I know it couldn't have survived. There's no blood on my star ring, though. The debris is somewhere on the other side of nullspace. If there is any debris.

The ring and the darkness looked the same as ever.

That made it so easy to forget. And I must have wanted to forget very much.

And now? What do I do *now*? Will Earth find out? Will there ever be relief? I want to go home.

Karen, I—

june 18

My relief left Earth today.

At least I think he did. Somehow the wall calendar was broken, so I'm not precisely sure of the date. But I've got it back into working order.

Anyway, it can't have been off for more than a few hours, or I would have noticed. So my relief *is* on the way. It will take him three months to get here, of course.

But at least he's coming.

THE LAST SUPER BOWL

The last Super Bowl was played in January, 2016, on a muddy field in Hoboken, New Jersey.

It was attended by 832 aging fans, 12 sportswriters, a Boy Scout troop, and the commissioner of the National Football League. The commissioner brought the Boy Scouts. He was also a scoutmaster.

The Packers were the favorites, and that was as it should be. It was somehow right, and appropriate, and just that the Packers should be in the final game.

They were still the Green Bay Packers, after all, the same now, at the end, as in the dim beginnings so many years ago. The teams of the great cities had come and gone, but the Packers stayed on, eternal and unchanging.

They had a perfect record going into the champion-

ship, and a defense the likes of which football had never
seen. Or at least so the sportswriters wrote. But claims
like that had to be taken with several grains of salt.
Sportswriters were a dying breed, and they exaggerated
a lot to stave off extinction.

The underdogs in the last, lonely showdown were the
Hoboken Jets. Formerly the Jersey City Jets. Formerly
the Newark Jets. Formerly the New York Jets. The
sportswriters, in their fading wisdom, had decreed that
the Jets would lose by two touchdowns.

Not that Hoboken had a bad team. They were pretty
good, actually. They'd won their conference going away.
But then, it was a weak conference, and the Jet defense
was a little sloppy. They didn't have a great offense
either.

What they did have was Keith Lancer. Lancer, so said
the sportswriters, was the greatest quarterback ever to
throw a football. Better than Namath, Unitas, Graham,
Baugh, any of them. A golden arm; great range, fantastic
accuracy. He was a scrambler too. And a brilliant field
general.

But he was only one man, and he had never faced a
team like the Packers. The Packer front four were creatures out of a nightmare. Their rush had been known
to drive brilliant quarterbacks into blithering, terrified
idiocy.

The sportswriters claimed the Packer defense would
grind Lancer into little bits and scatter him all over the
field. But that was just what the sportswriters claimed.
And nobody listened to sportswriters anymore.

It was a classic confrontation. Offense against defense.
One brilliant man against a smoothly oiled machine. A
lone hero against a hoard of monsters.

The last page of football history. But a great page, a
great moment, a great game.

And it was played before 832 fans, 12 sportswriters, a

Boy Scout troop, and the commissioner of the National Football League.

It had begun, long ago, when someone decided to settle an old argument.

Arguments are the stuff of which sports are made. They go on and on, forever, and no one has ever stopped to figure out how many bars they keep in business. The arguments were all different, but all the same. Who's the greatest heavyweight champion of all time? Who should play center field on the all-time All Star team? Name the best football team ever.

Ask a man those questions and listen to his answers. Then you'll know when he was growing up, and where he once lived, and what kind of a man he was.

Eternal questions, never-ending arguments, the raucous music of the locker room and the tavern. Not questions that could be answered. Nor questions that should be answered. There are some things man was not meant to know.

But one day someone tried to answer them. He used a computer.

Computers were still in diapers back then. But still they were treated with deference. They didn't make mistakes. When a computer said something, the man in the street generally listened. And believed.

So they decided to ask a computer to pick the greatest heavyweight champion of all time.

But they didn't merely ask a question. They had more imagination than that. They arranged a tournament, a great tournament between all the heavyweight champions of history, each fighting in his prime. They fed each man's style into the machine, and told it about his strengths and weaknesses and habits and quirks.

And the machine digested all the glass chins and snappy left jabs and dazzling footwork, and set to work producing simulated fights. One by one the heavyweight

champions eliminated each other in computerized bouts
that were jazzed up and dramatized and broadcast over
the radio.

Rocky Marciano won the thing.

It began to rain shortly after the two teams had come
onto the field. Not a heavy rain, at first. Just a thin, cold,
soggy-wet drizzle that came down and down and wouldn't
stop.

Green Bay won the toss and elected to receive. Hoboken decided to defend the south goal.

The kickoff was shallow and wobbly, probably because
of the rain and the muddy condition of the field. Mike
Strawn, the Packers' speed merchant, fielded the kick
and ran it back fifteen yards before being pulled down
at the thirty.

The Packer offense took the field. They were a coldly
determined bunch that afternoon. They had something
to prove. They were tired of hearing, over and over again,
about how defense made the Packers great. And Dave
Sandretti, the Packers' scrappy young quarterback, was
especially tired of hearing about Keith Lancer.

Sandretti went to the air immediately, hitting on a
short, flat pass to the sideline for a quick first down. On
the next play he handed off, and Mule Mitchell smashed
through the center of the Jet line for a four yard gain.
Then Strawn went around end for another first down.

The Packers drove.

Their offense was nothing fancy. The Packer coach
believed in basic football. But it was effective. Alternating
skillfully between his short passes and his potent running
game, Sandretti moved the Packers across the fifty and
into enemy territory before the drive finally bogged down
near the thirty-five.

The field goal attempt was wide. The Jets took over
on their own twenty.

*   *   *

Inevitably, other tournaments followed in the wake of the first one. They settled the argument about the greatest middleweight champion of all time, and the best college football team, and the finest baseball squad ever assembled.

And each simulated fight and computerized game seemed to draw larger radio audiences than the one before it. People liked the idea. They didn't always agree with the computer's verdict, but that was okay. It gave them something new to argue about.

It wasn't long before the sponsors of the computerized tournaments realized they had a gold mine on their hands. And, once they did realize it, it took them no time at all to abandon their original purposes. Settling the old arguments, after all, was dangerous. It might lead to loss of interest in forthcoming computerized bouts.

So they announced that the computer's verdicts were far from final. Different tournament pairings might give different results, they claimed. And so it was when they ran the heavyweight elimination over again.

The lords of sport looked on tolerantly. Computerized sports were an interesting sideshow, they thought, but hardly anything to worry about. After all, a phony football game broadcast over the radio could never match the violent color and excitement of the real thing on television.

They even went so far as to feature computer simulations in their pregame shows, to add a little spice to the presentation. The computer predictions were almost always wrong, and the computer games were drab compared to the spectacle that invariably followed.

The lords of sport were absolutely certain that computer simulations would never be anything more than minor sideshows. Absolutely certain.

At first, Lancer set out to establish his running game. He abandoned that idea two plays later, after the

Packer defense had twice snagged Jet runners short of the line of scrimmage. On third and fifteen, Lancer took to the air for the first time. The pass was complete for a first down.

On first and ten, he went for a long bomb. It fell incomplete when his receiver slipped on the muddy field. But the Jets got a first down anyway. The Packer rush put a bit too much pressure on Lancer, and got assessed fifteen yards for roughing the passer. Lancer had been hit solidly by two defensemen after getting the pass away.

He got up covered with mud, a little shaken, and very mad. When Lancer was mad, the Jets were mad. The team began to move.

If the Packer offense was the soul of simplicity, the Jet offense was a study in devious complexity. Lancer used a whole array of different formations, kept his backfield in constant motion with shift after shift, and had a mind-boggling number of plays to choose from.

The Packers knew all that, of course. They had studied game films. But watching films was not quite the same thing as facing an angry Keith Lancer.

Lancer let the Packers have both barrels now. He started to razzle-dazzle with a vengeance. The Packer rush dumped him a few more times. But in between the Jets were registering long gains.

It took Lancer nine plays to put Hoboken into the end zone. The Jets went ahead, 7-0.

The sportswriters started muttering.

The problem with the early computer simulations was their lack of depth. Computer games were presented either as flat, colorless predictions, or as overdramatized radio shows. Which was all right. But not to be compared to actually watching a real game.

Then someone got a bright idea. They made a movie.

Rocky Marciano had been retired for years, but he was still around. Muhammed Ali was still one of the premier heavyweights of the era. So they paired them in a computer fight, got Marciano back into reasonable shape, and had the two men act out the computer's prediction of what would have happened if they had met when each was in his prime. Marciano won by a knockout.

The film got wide publicity, and was shown in theatres from coast to coast. It outdrew the crowds that real bouts got in the same theatres when they appeared via closed-circuit television.

The newspapers seemed confused over how to cover it. Some sent movie critics. But many sent sportswriters. And while most of those sportswriters treated it as a joke, a minor and inconsequential diversion, others wrote up the fight quite seriously.

The handwriting was on the wall. But the lords of sport didn't read it. After all, the circumstances that allowed a film like this to be made were pretty unique, they reasoned. The computer people could hardly dig up John L. Sullivan or the Four Horsemen or Babe Ruth for future films. And the public would never accept actors.

So there was nothing to worry about. Nothing at all.

Through the mud and the steadily building rain, the Packers came driving back. They relied mostly on their running game, on Mule Mitchell's tanklike rushes and Mike Strawn's darting zigzags and quick end runs. But Sandretti's passing played a role, too. He didn't have Lancer's arm, by any means. But he was good, and he was accurate, and when the chips were down he seldom missed.

Back upfield they moved, back into Jet territory. The first quarter ended with them on the Jet thirty.

The drive continued in the second period, but once again the Packers seemed to run out of gas when they got within the shadow of the goalposts. They had to settle for a field goal.

*   *   *

More movies followed the success of the first. But the lords of sport had been correct. The idea had built-in limitations. A lavish production that used actors to pit Jack Dempsey against Joe Louis underlined that point. It was a total bust. The fans wanted the real thing. Or close to it, anyway.

But some films could be made, and they were made, and they made money. It became a respectable movie subgenre. One studio, Versus Productions, specialized in film versions of computer sports, and made modest profits.

But real sports continued to do better than ever. The public had more and more leisure, and a voracious hunger for vicarious violence. The lords of sport feasted on huge television contracts, and grew fat and rich. And blind.

They hardly even noticed when some of the old computer films began to turn up on late shows here and there.

They should have.

Lancer got the Jets driving again. But this time their momentum ebbed quickly. The Packer defense wasn't about to get pushed around all day. They were quick to adapt, and now they were beginning to get used to Lancer's bag of tricks.

The Hoboken drive sputtered to a halt on the Green Bay forty, when Lancer was dumped twice in a row by the Packer rush. The field goal attempt was a valiant but misguided effort to buck the wind and the rain. It fell absurdly short.

The Packers took over. At once they began to move. Sandretti clicked on a series of passes, and Mitchell punched through the Hoboken line again and again.

When the Packers crossed the fifty, the Jets decided to surprise Sandretti with a blitz. They did surprise him. Once.

The next time they tried it, Sandretti slipped a screen pass to Strawn in the flat. He shook off one tackler, sidestepped two more, and outran everybody else on the field.

That made it 10–7 Packers. The sportswriters began to breathe a little easier.

It was such a simple idea.

The name of the man who first thought of it is lost. But there is a legend. The legend says it was an electronics engineer employed by one of the networks, and that the idea came to him when he was watching a television rerun of a computer fight movie.

It wasn't a very good movie, and his attention began to wander, says the legend. He began to think about why filmed computer simulations had never really made it big. The problem, he decided, was actors.

Computer simulations had more veracity and realism than fictional fight movies. But they lost it when they used actors. The public wouldn't buy actors. But, without actors, the possible number of productions was severely limited.

What was needed was another way to make the simulations.

He looked at the television wall, the legend says. And the idea came.

He wasn't watching a picture. Not really. He knew that. He was watching a pattern of multicolored dots. A complex pattern that deluded the human eye into thinking it was a picture. But it wasn't. There was nothing there but a bunch of electronic impulses.

If you get those impulses to join together and form an image of some actor playing Joe Louis, then there was no damn reason in the world that you couldn't get them to join together to form an image of Joe Louis himself.

It was easier if there was a pattern to be broken down and reassembled, of course. But that didn't mean it was impossible to build patterns out of whole cloth. And it wouldn't matter if those patterns had ever really existed anywhere but on the television screen. The images could be made just as real.

Yes. It could work. If you had an instrument fast enough to assemble such complex patterns, and change them smoothly enough to simulate motion and action. If you had a computer, a big one. Yes.

The next day, the legend says, the nameless electronics engineer went to speak to the president of his network.

On the second play after the kickoff, the Packers blitzed. Their normal rush was fierce enough. Their blitz was devastating. The Hoboken line shattered under the impact, and the Packers stormed through, hungry for quarterback blood.

Lancer, back to pass, searched desperately for a receiver. He found none. He danced out of the way of the first Packer to reach him, tucked the ball under his arm, and tried to scramble. He got about five yards back towards the line of scrimmage before the Green Bay meatgrinder closed in around him.

Afterwards, he couldn't get up. They carried him off the field limping.

There was a stunned silence, then a slowly building cheer as Lancer was carried to the sidelines.

Or as much of a cheer as could be produced by 832 fans, 12 sportswriters, a Boy Scout troop, and the commissioner of the National Football League.

Sports were very big business, and all three networks fought tooth-and-nail in the bloody bidding wars for the right to telecast the major events. And of all the wars, the football wars were the most gory.

One network won the NFL that year. Another won the NCAA. The third, according to tradition, was in for a bad time. It was going to get badly bludgeoned in the ratings until those contracts ran out.

But that year, the third network refused to lie down meekly and accept its fate. It broke with tradition. It scheduled something new. A show called *Unplayed Football Classics*.

The show featured televised computer simulations of great games between the top football teams, both pro and college, in the history of the game. It did not use actors. A gigantic network computer, specially designed and built for the purpose, produced the simulations from scratch.

The show was a bombshell. A glorious, shouting, screaming, disgustingly successful smash hit.

With Lancer out, the Jets went nowhere. They bogged down in the mud and were forced to punt.

Sandretti, sensing that the Hoboken team was badly shaken by the loss of its star quarterback, pressed his advantage ruthlessly. He went for the bomb on the first play from scrimmage.

Strawn, sent out wide on the play, snagged the long throw neatly and took it all the way in for another Packer touchdown. The extra point made it 17–7.

All of a sudden, it seemed to be raining a little harder on the Hoboken side of the field. A few of the 832 fans, those of the least faith, began to drift from the stadium.

Unplayed Football Classics was followed by *Matchup*, a boxing show that telecast the imaginary bouts most requested by the viewers. Other spinoffs followed in good time when *Matchup* too made it big.

After the third year of smash ratings, *Unplayed Football Classics* was sent into the front lines. Its time slot was moved so it conflicted, directly, with the NFL Game-of-the-Week.

The resulting holocaust was a ratings draw. But even

that was enough to wake the lords of sport from their slumber and set them to yelping. For the very first time, computer simulations had demonstrated that they could compete successfully with the real product.

The lords of sport fought back, at first, with an advertising campaign. They set out to convince the public that the computer games were cheap imitations that no *real* sports fan would accept for a moment as a substitute for the real thing.

They failed. The fans were too far removed from the stadium to grasp the point. They were a generation of sports fans that had never seen a football game, except over television. And, over television, the computer games were just as dramatic and unpredictable and exciting as anything the NFL could offer.

So, the games weren't real. So what. They *looked* real. It wasn't like they used actors, or anything.

The lords of sport reeled from their failure, grasped for another weapon. The lawsuits began.

You can't call your simulated team the Green Bay Packers, the lawyers for the lords told the computer people. That name is our property. You can't use it. Or the names of all those players. You'll have to make up your own.

They went to court to prove their point.

They lost.

After all, the judges ruled, they weren't using real games. Besides, they asked the lords of sport, why didn't you object to all those people who did the same thing on radio? No, it's too late. You've set your precedents already.

Meanwhile, the third network was building a bigger computer. It was called Sportsmaster.

Hoboken held onto the ball for the rest of the second quarter, but only to run out the clock. There wasn't enough time left to do anything before the half anyway.

The halftime show was a dreary affair. The NFL had long passed the point when it could stage big productions. But, given its budget, it still tried. There were a few high school bands on hand, and a holoshow that was an utter disaster thanks to the rain.

It didn't matter. Nobody was watching anyway. The fans had all gone for hot dogs, and the sportswriters were down in the locker room trying to find out how Keith Lancer was.

The Boy Scouts, meanwhile, went to the Packer locker room, to get autographs. On orders from the scoutmaster, who was also commissioner of the National Football League.

Sportsmaster was the largest civilian computer ever built, and there were some that said it was even bigger than the Pentagon computer that controlled the nation's defenses. Its master memory banks contained all the data on sports and sports figures that anyone anywhere had ever bothered to put down on paper or film or tape. It was designed to prepare detailed, full-color, whole-cloth simulations, for both standard television wallscreens and the new holovision sets.

Its method of operation was an innovation, too. Instead of isolated games, Sportsmaster featured league competition, complete with seasons and schedules. But in the Sportsmaster Baseball League, every team was a pennant winner. In the Sportsmaster Boxing Tournament, every fighter was a champion. In the Sportsmaster Football League, every competitor had at least a divisional crown to its credit.

Sportsmaster games would not be presented as mere television shows. They would be presented as events, as news, it was decreed. The network sponsoring Sportsmaster immediately begin to give the same build-up to future computer simulations as to real sports events. The newspapers, at first, refused to go along. Most insisted on covering Sportsmaster broadcasts in the entertainment section instead of the sports pages.

For awhile they insisted, that is. Then, one by one, they began to come around. The fans, it seems, wanted sports coverage of Sportsmaster presentations.

And the lords of sport suddenly faced war.

Hoboken took the kickoff at the opening of the second half. But Keith Lancer still sat on the sidelines, and without him the Jets seemed vaguely unsure of what they were supposed to do with the ball. They made one first down, then stalled and were forced to punt.

The Packer offense came back onto the field, and they radiated a cold confidence. With methodical precision, Sandretti led his team down the field. He was taking no chances now, so he kept the ball out of the air and relied on his running backs. Again and again Mitchell slammed into the line, and Strawn danced through it, to pick up a yard or two or four. Slowly but inexorably the Packer steamroller ground ahead.

The drive was set back by a few penalties, and slowed here and there when the Jet defense toughened momentarily. But it was never stopped. It was late in the third quarter before Mitchell finally plunged over tackle into the end zone for another Packer touchdown.

Then came the extra point, and it was 24–7 Packers, and a lot of the fans seemed to be leaving.

For a decade the war raged, fierce and bloody. At first, Sportsmaster was the underdog, fighting for acceptance, fighting to be taken seriously. The NFL and the NHL and the NBA won all the early battles.

And then the gap began to close. The viewers and the fans got used to Sportsmaster, and the distinction began to blur. After all, the games all looked the same over television. Except that the Sportsmaster Leagues seemed to have better teams, and their games seemed to be a little more exciting.

That was deliberate. The Sportsmaster people had programmed in a drama factor. They were careful about it, however. They knew that nothing can kill a sport faster than obvious staging of games for effect. The predictable, standard scripts of wrestling and roller derby were strictly avoided. Sportsmaster games remained always as unpredictable as the real thing.

Only, they were slightly more exciting, on the average. There were dull games in the Sportsmaster Leagues, of course. But never quite as many as in the real leagues.

The turning point in the war was the Battle of the Super Bowl in January, 1994.

In the NFL Super Bowl, the New York Giants were facing the Denver Broncos. The Broncos were one of the most exciting teams in decades; blinding speed, a colorful quarterback, and the highest-scoring offense in football history. The Giants were the mediocre champions of a weak division, who had gotten lucky in the playoffs.

In the Sportsmaster Super Bowl, the 1993 Denver Broncos were facing the Green Bay Packers of the Vince Lombardi era.

In the NFL Super Bowl, the Broncos beat the Giants 34–9 in an utterly undistinguished game. The outcome of the contest was never in doubt for a second.

In the Sportsmaster Super Bowl, the Broncos beat the Packers 21–17, on a long bomb thrown with seconds remaining on the clock.

The two Super Bowls got almost identical ratings. But those who watched the NFL game found that they had missed a classic to watch a dud. It was the last time that would happen, they vowed.

Sportsmaster began to pull ahead.

* * *

It was the moment of truth for Hoboken.

The Jets took the Packer kickoff, and started upfield with determination. Yard by yard they fought their way through the mud and the rain, back into the game. And the Packer defense made them pay for every inch with blood.

The Jets drove to the fifty, then past it. They moved into Packer territory. When the quarter ended, they were on the Packer thirty-three yard line.

Two plays into the fourth quarter, the second-string quarterback fumbled on a handoff. The Packers recovered.

Sandretti took over, and the Packers moved the ball back towards midfield. They picked up one first down. But then, suddenly, the Jet defense got tough.

They stopped the Packers on the forty-five. Green Bay was forced to punt. The punt, against the wind, was a bad one. The Jets called for a fair catch and took the ball on their own thirty.

First and ten. The Jets tried an end sweep. No gain.

Second and ten. A reverse. A three-yard loss.

Third and thirteen. The Jets called time out.

And Keith Lancer came back in.

He wasn't limping now. But he still looked unsteady, wobbly on his feet. This was it for the Jets, the fans told themselves. This was the do-or-die play. A pass, of course. It had to be a pass.

The Packers were thinking the same thing. When the ball was snapped and Lancer faded back, their front four came roaring in like demons out of hell.

Lancer lateralled to one of his halfbacks on the sideline. The rushers changed direction in mid-stride, and streaked past him.

Lancer, suddenly ignored, ran slowly upfield and caught the pass for a first down. He was tackled with a vengeance. But all that got the Packers was a fifteen-yard penalty.

Lancer stayed in, and started passing. In seven plays, he put Hoboken on the scoreboard again to cut the Packer margin to 24–14.

The long twilight of spectator sports had begun.

Sportsmaster II was unveiled in 1995, a computer bigger and more sophisticated than the original. Sportsmaster, Inc., was sliced from the network that had founded it by government decree, since the combined empire was growing too large.

By the late 1990s, television and confrontations between Sportsmaster shows and real sports events were confrontations in name only. Sportsmaster ran away with the ratings with monotonous regularity.

In 1996, the network that had been broadcasting NFL games refused to pick up the contract unless the price was slashed almost in half. The league was forced to agree.

In 1998, the NBA television contract was worth only a fourth of what it had gone for five years earlier.

In 1999, no one bid for the right to telecast NHL hockey.

Still, the sports promoters hung on. They still had some television audiences. And the games themselves were still packed.

But the Sportsmaster men were ruthless. They analyzed the reasons why real sports still attracted people. And came up with some innovations.

People who still went to games did so because they preferred to view sports outdoors, or as part of a crowd, they decided. Fine. So they built Sportsmaster Theatres, where fans could eat hog dogs and watch the games as part of a crowd. And they erected giant Sportsmaster Stadium, where the simulations were staged outdoors as full-color, three-dimensional holoshows.

In 2003, the Super Bowl was not a sellout. The World

Series had already failed to sell out for several years running. The live crowds started to shrink.

And didn't stop.

Despite the Jet touchdown, the Packers were still comfortably out in front. The game was theirs, if they could only run out the clock.

Sandretti kept his team on the ground, handing off to Mitchell and Strawn, chalking up one first down after another the hard way by churning through the mud. The Jets began to use their time-outs. The minutes flew by.

The Packers finally were held just past the mid-field stripe. But Sandretti had wreaked his damage. There was time left for maybe one Jet drive, but hardly for two.

But Hoboken did not give up. Their time-outs were gone and the clock was against them. But Lancer was in the game again. And that made anything possible.

The Packers went into a prevent defense to guard against the bomb. They were willing to give up the short gain, the first down. That was alright. Lancer could drive for a touchdown if he wanted to, so long as it wasn't a quick score.

The Jet quarterback tried one bomb, but it fizzled, incomplete, in the rain. Packer defenders were all over the Hoboken deep men. The Jets had no recourse but to drive for the score, eat up the clock, and pray for a break.

They drove. Lancer, no longer wobbly, hit on one short pass after another. Hoboken moved upfield. Hoboken scored. The extra point was dead on target. The score stood at 24–21.

But there was less than a minute left to play.

In 2005, they introduced Sportsmaster III, and the Home Matchmaker. It was a fatal blow.

Sportsmaster III was ten times the size of Sportsmaster II, and had more than a hundred times the capacity. It was built underground in Kansas, and was larger than most cities. Regional extensions were scattered over the nation.

The Home Matchmakers were expensive devices that linked up directly with the Sportsmaster extensions, and, through them, with Sportsmaster III. They were programming devices. They allowed each Sportsmaster subscriber to select his own games for home viewing.

Sportsmaster III could accommodate any request, could set up any match, could arrange any conditions. If a subscriber wanted to see the 1962 Los Angeles Rams play the 1980 Notre Dame junior varsity in the Astrodome, Sportsmaster III would digest that request, search its awesome memory banks, and beam up simulation to the subscriber's holovision.

The variations were infinite. The subscriber could punch in weather, injuries, and location. The subscriber could select his own team of All Stars, and pit them against someone else's team, or against a real team of any era. With Sportsmaster III and the Home Matchmaker, the sports fan could sit at home and watch any sort of contest he could dream up.

At first, the Home Matchmakers were very costly. Only the very rich could afford them. Others were forced to pool their resources, form Sportsmaster clubs, and vote on the games they wanted to see.

But soon the price began to come down.

And when it got low enough, spectator sports died.

Boxing went first. It had always been the weak sister. The champions continued to defend their crowns, but there were fewer and fewer challengers, since the game was far from lucrative. The intervals between fights grew steadily longer. And after a while, there were no more fights.

The other sports followed. People continued to play tennis and golf, but they were no longer willing to pay to watch others play. Not when they could watch much better matches, of their own selection, on Sportsmaster hookups. Tournament after tournament was cancelled. Until there were no more left to cancel.

The NHL and the NBA both disbanded in 2010. They had been suffering billion-dollar losses for several years before they closed up shop.

Baseball, hoary with age, held on four years longer. It moved its teams to progressively smaller cities, where the novelty always brought out crowds for awhile. It slashed costs desperately. It sold stadiums, cut salaries to the bone, skimped on field and equipment maintenance. It went before Congress, and argued that the national past-time should be preserved with a subsidy.

And, in 2014, it folded.

Football was the last to go. Since the 1970s, it had been the biggest, and the richest, and the most arrogant sport of all. It had fought the most bitterly in the days of ads and lawsuits, and it had carried the brunt of the battle throughout the long television war.

And now it refused to die. It used every trick the baseball leagues had tried, and then some. It cut teams, added teams, moved teams, changed the rules, began sideshows. But nothing worked. No one came. No one was interested.

And so it was that the last Super Bowl was played in January, 2016, on a muddy field in Hoboken, New Jersey.

It was going to be an on-sides kick. The Jets knew that. The Packers knew that. Every fan in the stadium knew that. They were all waiting.

But, even as they lined up for the kickoff, the rains came.

They came in earnest, a torrent, a sudden downpour. The sky darkened, and the wind howled, and the water came rushing down and down and down. It was a blinding rain, lashing at the mud, sending the remaining fans scrambling for shelter.

In that rain came the kickoff.

It was an on-sides kick, of course. Neither team could see the ball very well. Both converged on it. A Packer reached it first. He threw himself on top of it.

And the mud-covered ball squirted out from under him. Squirted towards Hoboken.

The Jets had the break they needed. It was first and ten near the fifty, and it was their ball. But the clock was ticking, and the rain was a shrieking wall of water that refused to let up.

Lancer and the Jet offense came running back onto the field, and lined up quickly. They didn't bother with a huddle. They had their plays down already.

The Packer defensemen walked out slowly, dragging their heels through the mud, dawdling, eating up the clock. Finally they got lined up, and the ball was snapped.

It was impossible to pass in that rain. Impossible. You couldn't throw through that much water. You couldn't run through mud like that, and puddles that looked like oceans. You couldn't even see the ball in that kind of rain.

It was impossible to pass in that rain. But the Jets had to pass. Their time was running out.

So Lancer passed. Somehow, somehow, he passed.

His first throw was a bullet to the sidelines, good for twenty yards. The receiver didn't see the ball coming. But he caught it anyway, because Lancer laid it right into his hands. Then he stepped out of bounds, and stopped the clock.

There were eighteen seconds left to play.

Lancer passed again. Somehow, through that blinding rain, in that sea of mud, somehow, he passed again. It was complete.

It was complete to the other sideline, to the five. The receiver clutched at the ball, and bobbled it for a second, then grasped it tightly, and took a step towards the goal line.

And the Packer defender roared into him like a mack truck and knocked him out of bounds. The clock stopped again. With about six seconds left.

It was the last touchdown drive. The very, very last. And now was its climax.

They lined up at the three, with seconds left. Both teams looked the same by now; spattered, soaking, hulking figures in uniforms that had all turned an identical mud-brown.

It was the last confrontation. The Packer defense, in its ultimate test: a wall, an iron-hard, determined, teeth-clenched, mud-brown human wall. Lancer, the last great quarterback: wet and muddy and injured and angry and brilliant.

And the rain, the pounding rain around them both.

The ball was snapped.

Lancer took it. The Jet line surged forward, smashing at the Packers, fighting to clear a hole, clearing one. Lancer moved to it, through it, towards the goal line, the goal line only feet away.

And something rose up from the ground and hit him. Hard and low.

It was the last touchdown drive, the last ever. And it was brilliant and it was poetic and they should have scored. They should have scored.

But they didn't.

And the gun sounded, and the game was over, and the Packers had won. The players began to drift away to the locker room.

And Keith Lancer, who drove for the final touchdown, and didn't make it, picked himself up from the mud, and sighed, and helped up the man who had tackled him.

They shook hands in the rain, and Lancer smiled to hide the tears. And so, strangely, did the Packer. They walked together from the field.

Neither one bothered to look up, at the stands.

The empty stands.

THE LONELY SONGS OF LAREN DORR

There is a girl who goes between the worlds.

She is grey-eyed and pale of skin, or so the story goes, and her hair is a coal-black waterfall with half-seen hints of red. She wears about her brow a circlet of burnished metal, a dark crown that holds her hair in place and sometimes puts shadows in her eyes. Her name is Sharra; she knows the gates.

The beginning of her story is lost to us, with the memory of the world from which she sprang. The end? The end is not yet, and when it comes we shall not know it.

We have only the middle, or rather a piece of that middle, the smallest part of the legend, a mere fragment of the quest. A small tale within the greater, of one world

71

where Sharra paused, and of the lonely singer Laren
Dorr and how they briefly touched.

One moment there was only the valley, caught in twilight. The setting sun hung fat and violet on the ridge
above, and its rays slanted down silently into a dense
forest whose trees had shiny black trunks and colorless
ghostly leaves. The only sounds were the cries of the
mourning-birds coming out for the night, and the swift
rush of water in the rocky stream that cut the woods.

Then, through a gate unseen, Sharra came tired and
bloodied to the world of Laren Dorr. She wore a plain
white dress, now stained and sweaty, and a heavy fur
cloak that had been half-ripped from her back. And her
left arm, bare and slender, still bled from three long
wounds. She appeared by the side of the stream, shaking,
and she threw a quick, wary glance about her before she
knelt to dress her wounds. The water, for all its swiftness,
was a dark and murky green. No way to tell if it was
safe, but Sharra was weak and thirsty. She drank, washed
her arm as best she could in the strange and doubtful
water, and bound her injuries with bandages ripped from
her clothes. Then, as the purple sun dipped lower behind
the ridge, she crawled away from the water to a sheltered
spot among the trees, and fell into exhausted sleep.

She woke to arms around her, strong arms that lifted
her easily to carry her somewhere, and she woke struggling. But the arms just tightened, and held her still.
"Easy," a mellow voice said, and she saw a face dimly
through gathering mist, a man's face, long and somehow
gentle. "You are weak," he said, "and night is coming.
We must be inside before darkness."

Sharra did not struggle, not then, though she knew she
should. She had been struggling a long time, and she was
tired. But she looked at him, confused. "Why?" she asked.
Then, not waiting for an answer, "Who are you? Where
are we going?"

"To safety," he said.

"Your home?" she asked, drowsy.

"No," he said, so soft she could scarcely hear his voice. "No, not home, not ever home. But it will do." She heard splashing then, as if he were carrying her across the stream, and ahead of them on the ridge she glimpsed a gaunt, twisted silhouette, a triple-towered castle etched black against the sun. Odd, she thought, that wasn't there before.

She slept.

When she woke, he was there, watching her. She lay under a pile of soft, warm blankets in a curtained, canopied bed. But the curtains had been drawn back, and her host sat across the room in a great chair draped by shadows. Candlelight flickered in his eyes, and his hands locked together neatly beneath his chin. "Are you feeling better?" he asked, without moving.

She sat up, and noticed she was nude. Swift as suspicion, quicker than thought, her hand went to her head. But the dark crown was still there, in place, untouched, its metal cool against her brow. Relaxing, she leaned back against the pillows and pulled the blankets up to cover herself. "Much better," she said, and as she said it she realized for the first time that her wounds were gone.

The man smiled at her, a sad wistful sort of smile. He had a strong face, with charcoal-colored hair that curled in lazy ringlets and fell down into dark eyes somehow wider than they should be. Even seated, he was tall. And slender. He wore a suit and cape of some soft grey leather, and over that he wore melancholy like a cloak. "Claw marks," he said speculatively, while he smiled. "Claw marks down your arm, and your clothes almost ripped from your back. Someone doesn't like you."

"Something," Sharra said. "A guardian, a guardian at the gate." She sighed. "There is always a guardian at the gate. The Seven don't like us to move from world to world. Me they like least of all."

His hands unfolded from beneath his chin, and rested on the carved wooden arms of his chair. He nodded, but the wistful smile stayed. "So, then," he said. "You know the Seven, and you know the gates." His eyes strayed to her forehead. "The crown, of course. I should have guessed."

Sharra grinned at him. "You did guess. More than that, you knew. Who are you? What world is this?"

"My world," he said evenly. "I've named it a thousand times, but none of the names ever seem quite right. There was one once, a name I liked, a name that fit. But I've forgotten it. It was a long time ago. *My* name is Laren Dorr, or that was my name, once, when I had use for such a thing. Here and now it seemed somewhat silly. But at least I haven't forgotten *it*."

"Your world," Sharra said. "Are you a king, then? A god?"

"Yes," Laren Dorr replied, with an easy laugh. "And more. I'm whatever I choose to be. There is no one around to dispute me."

"What did you do to my wounds?" she asked.

"I healed them." He gave an apologetic shrug. "It's my world. I have certain powers. Not the powers I'd like to have, perhaps, but powers nonetheless."

"Oh." She did not look convinced.

Laren waved an impatient hand. "You think it's impossible. Your crown, of course. Well, that's only half right. I could not harm you with my ah, powers, not while you wear that. But I can help you." He smiled again, and his eyes grew soft and dreamy. "But it doesn't matter. Even if I could I would never harm you, Sharra. Believe that. It has been a long time."

Sharra looked startled. "You know my name. How?"

He stood up, smiling, and came across the room to sit beside her on the bed. And he took her hand before replying, wrapping it softly in his and stroking her with his thumb. "Yes, I know your name. You are Sharra, who moves between the worlds. Centuries ago, when the hills had a different shape and the violet sun burned scarlet at the very beginning of its cycle, they came to me and told me you would come. I hate them, all Seven, and I will always hate them, but that night I welcomed the vision they gave me. They told me only your name, and that you would come here, to my world. And one thing more. But that was enough. It was a promise, a promise of an ending or a start, of a change. And any change is welcome on this world. I've been alone here through a thousand suncycles, Sharra, and each cycle lasts for centuries. There are few events to mark the death of time."

Sharra was frowning. She shook her long black hair, and in the dim light of the candles the soft red highlights glowed. "Are they that far ahead of me, then?" she said. "Do they know what will happen?" Her voice was troubled. She looked up at him. "This other thing they told you?"

He squeezed her hand, very gently. "They told me I would love you," Laren said. His voice still sounded sad. "But that was no great prophecy. I could have told them so much. There was a time long ago—I think the sun was yellow then—when I realized that I would love *any* voice that was not an echo of my own."

Sharra woke at dawn, when shafts of bright purple light spilled into her room through a high arched window that had not been there the night before. Clothing had been laid out for her; a loose yellow robe, a jeweled dress of bright crimson, a suit of forest green. She chose the suit, dressed quickly. As she left, she paused to look out the window.

She was in a tower, looking out over crumbling stone battlements and a dusty triangular courtyard. Two other towers, twisted matchstick things with pointed conical spires, rose from the other corners of the triangle. There was a strong wind that whipped the rows of grey pennants set along the walls, but no other motion to be seen.

And, beyond the castle walls, no sign of the valley, none at all. The castle with its courtyard and its crooked towers was set atop a mountain, and far and away in all directions taller mountains loomed, presenting a panorama of black stone cliffs and jagged rocky walls and shining clean ice steeples that gleamed with a violet sheen. The window was sealed and closed, but the wind *looked* cold.

Her door was open. Sharra moved quickly down a twisting stone staircase, out across the courtyard into the main building, a low wooden structure built against the wall. She passed through countless rooms, some cold and empty save for dust, others richly furnished, before she found Laren Dorr eating breakfast.

There was an empty seat at his side; the table was heavily laden with food and drink. Sharra sat down, and took a hot biscuit, smiling despite herself. Laren smiled back.

"I'm leaving today," she said, in between bites. "I'm sorry, Laren. I must find the gate."

The air of hopeless melancholy had not left him. It never did. "So you said last night," he replied, sighing. "It seems I have waited a long time for nothing."

There was meat, several types of biscuits, fruit, cheese, milk. Sharra filled a plate, face a little downcast, avoiding Laren's eyes. "I'm sorry," she repeated.

"Stay a while," he said. "Only a short time. You can afford it, I would think. Let me show you what I can of my world. Let me sing to you." His eyes, wide and dark and very tired, asked the question.

She hesitated. "Well . . . it takes time to find the gate. Stay with me for a while, then. But Laren, eventually I must go. I have made promises. You understand?"

He smiled, gave a helpless shrug. "Yes. But look. I

know where the gate is. I can show you, save you a search. Stay with me, oh, a month. A month as you measure time. Then I'll take you to the gate." He studied her. "You've been hunting a long, long time, Sharra. Perhaps you need a rest."

Slowly, thoughtfully, she ate a piece of fruit, watching him all the time. "Perhaps I do," she said at last, weighing things. "And there will be a guardian, of course. You could help me then. A month . . . that's not so long. I've been on other worlds far longer than a month." She nodded, and a smile spread slowly across her face. "Yes," she said, still nodding. "That would be all right."

He touched her hand lightly. After breakfast, he showed her the world they had given him.

They stood side by side on a small balcony atop the highest of the three towers, Sharra in dark green and Laren tall and soft in grey. They stood without moving, and Laren moved the world around them. He set the castle flying over restless churning seas, where long black serpent-heads peered up out of the water to watch them pass. He moved them to a vast echoing cavern under the earth, all aglow with a soft green light, where dripping stalactites brushed down against the towers and herds of blind white goats moaned outside the battlements. He clapped his hands and smiled, and steam-thick jungle rose around them; trees that climbed each other in rubber ladders to the sky, giant flowers of a dozen different colors, fanged monkeys that chittered from the walls. He clapped again, and the walls were swept clean, and suddenly the courtyard dirt was sand and they were on an endless beach by the shore of a bleak grey ocean, and above them the slow wheeling of a great blue bird with tissue-paper wings was the only movement to be seen. He showed her this, and more, and more, and in the end as dusk seemed to threaten in one place after another, he took the castle back to the ridge above the valley. And Sharra looked down on the forest of black-barked trees where he had found her, and heard the mourning-birds whimper and weep among transparent leaves.

"It is not a bad world," she said, turning to him on the balcony.

"No," Laren replied. His hands rested on the cold stone railing, his eyes on the valley below. "Not entirely. I explored it once, on foot, with a sword and a walking stick. There was a joy there, a real excitement. A new mystery behind every hill." He chuckled. "But that, too, was long ago. Now I know what lies behind every hill. Another empty horizon."

He looked at her, and gave his characteristic shrug. "There are worse hells, I suppose. But this is mine."

"Come with me, then," she said. "Find the gate with me, and leave. There are other worlds. Maybe they are less strange and less beautiful, but you will not be alone."

He shrugged again. "You make it sound so easy," he said in a careless voice. "I have found the gate, Sharra. I have tried it a thousand times. The guardian does not stop me. I step through, briefly glimpse some other world, and suddenly I'm back in the courtyard. No. I cannot leave."

She took his hand in hers. "How sad. To be alone so long. I think you must be very strong, Laren. I would go mad in only a handful of years."

He laughed, and there was a bitterness in the way he did it. "Oh, Sharra. I have gone mad a thousand times, also. They cure me, love. They always cure me." Another shrug, and he put his arm around her. The wind was cold and rising. "Come," he said. "We must be inside before full dark."

They went up in the tower to her bedroom, and they sat together on her bed and Laren brought them food; meat burned black on the outside and red within, hot bread, wine. They ate and they talked.

"Why are you here?" she asked him, in between

mouthfuls, washing her words down with wine. "How did you offend them? Who were you, before?"

"I hardly remember, except in dreams," he told her. "And the dreams—it has been so long, I can't even recall which ones are truth and which are visions born of my madness." He sighed. "Sometimes I dream I was a king, a great king in a world other than this, and my crime was that I made my people happy. In happiness they turned against the Seven, and the temples fell idle. And I woke one day, within my room, within my castle, and found my servants gone. And when I went outside, my people and my world were also gone, and even the woman who slept beside me.

"But there are other dreams. Often I remember vaguely that I was a god. Well, an almost-god. I had powers, and teachings, and they were not the teachings of the Seven. They were afraid of me, each of them, for I was a match for any of them. But I could not meet all Seven together, and that was what they forced me to do. And then they left me only a small bit of my power, and sent me here. It was cruel irony. As a god, I'd taught that people should turn to each other, that they could keep away the darkness by love and laughter and talk. So all these things the Seven took from me.

"And even that is not the worst. For there are other times when I think that I have always been here, that I was born here some endless age ago. And the memories are all false ones, sent to make me hurt the more."

Sharra watched him as he spoke. His eyes were not on her, but far away, full of fog and dreams and half-dead rememberings. And he spoke very slowly, in a voice that was also like fog, that drifted and curled and hid things, and you knew that there were mysteries there and things brooding just out of sight and far-off lights that you would never reach.

Laren stopped, and his eyes woke up again. "Ah, Sharra," he said. "Be careful how you go. Even your

crown will not help you should they move on you directly.
And the pale child Bakkalon will tear at you, and Naa-
Slas feed upon your pain, and Saagael on your soul."

She shivered, and cut another piece of meat. But it
was cold and tough when she bit into it, and suddenly
she noticed that the candles had burned very low. How
long had she listened to him speak?

"Wait," he said then, and he rose and went outside,
out the door near where the window had been. There
was nothing there now but rough grey stone; the windows all changed to solid rock with the last fading of the
sun. Laren returned in a few moments, with a softly
shining instrument of dark black wood slung around his
neck on a leather cord. Sharra had never quite seen its
like. It had sixteen strings, each a different color, and all
up and down its length brightly glowing bars of light
were inlaid amid the polished wood. When Laren sat,
the bottom of the device rested on the floor and the top
came to just above his shoulder. He stroked it lightly,
speculatively; the lights glowed, and suddenly the room
was full of swift-fading music.

"My companion," he said, smiling. He touched it
again, and the music rose and died, lost notes without
a tune. And he brushed the lightbars and the very air
shimmered and changed color.

He began to sing.

> *I am the Lord of loneliness,*
> *Empty my domain . . .*

. . . the first words ran, sung low and sweet in Laren's
mellow far-off fog voice. The rest of the song—Sharra
clutched at it, heard each word and tried to remember,
but lost them all. They brushed her, touched her, then
melted away, back into the fog, here and gone again so
swift that she could not remember quite what they had
been. With the words, the music; wistful and melancholy

and full of secrets, pulling at her, crying, whispering promises of a thousand tales untold. All around the room the candles flamed up brighter, and globes of light grew and danced and flowed together until the air was full of color.

Words, music, light; Laren Dorr put them all together and wove for her a vision.

She saw him then as he saw himself in his dreams; a king, strong and tall and still proud, with hair as black as hers and eyes that snapped. He was dressed all in shimmering white, pants that clung tight and a shirt that ballooned at the sleeves, and a great cloak that moved and curled in the wind like a sheet of solid snow. Around his brow he wore a crown of flashing silver, and a slim, straight sword flashed just as bright at his side. This Laren, this younger Laren, this dream vision, moved without melancholy, moved in a world of sweet ivory minarets and languid blue canals. And the world moved around him, friends and lovers and one special woman who Laren drew with words and lights of fire, and there was an infinity of easy days and laughter. Then, sudden, abrupt; darkness. He was here.

The music moaned; the lights dimmed; the words grew sad and lost. Sharra saw Laren wake, in a familiar castle now deserted. She saw him search from room to room, and walk outside to face a world he'd never seen. She watched him leave the castle, walk off towards the mists of a far horizon in the hope that those mists were smoke. And on and on he walked, and new horizons fell beneath his feet each day, and the great fat sun waxed red and orange and yellow, but still his world was empty. All the places he had shown her he walked to; all those and more; and finally, lost as ever, wanting home, the castle came to him.

By then his white had faded to dim grey. But still the song went on. Days went, and years, and centuries, and Laren grew tired and mad but never old. The sun shone green and violet and a savage hard blue-white, but with each cycle there was less color in his world. So Laren sang, of endless empty days and nights when music and memory were his only sanity, and his songs made Sharra feel it.

And when the vision faded and the music died and his soft voice melted away for the last time and Laren paused and smiled and looked at her, Sharra found herself trembling.

"Thank you," he said softly, with a shrug. And he took his instrument and left her for the night.

The next day dawned cold and overcast, but Laren took her out into the forests, hunting. Their quarry was a lean white thing, half cat, half gazelle, with too much speed for them to chase easily and too many teeth for them to kill. Sharra did not mind. The hunt was better than the kill. There was a singular, striking joy in that run through the darkling forest, holding a bow she never used and wearing a quiver of black wood arrows cut from the same dour trees that surrounded them. Both of them were bundled up tightly in grey fur, and Laren smiled out at her from under a wolf's-head hood. And the leaves beneath their boots, as clear and fragile as glass, cracked and splintered as they ran.

Afterwards, unblooded but exhausted, they returned to the castle and Laren set out a great feast in the main dining room. They smiled at each other from opposite ends of a table fifty feet long, and Sharra watched the clouds roll by the window behind Laren's head, and later watched the window turn to stone.

"Why does it do that?" she asked. "And why don't you ever go outside at night?"

He shrugged. "Ah. I have reasons. The nights are, well, not good here." He sipped hot spice wine from a great jeweled cup. "The world you came from, where you started—tell me, Sharra, did you have stars?"

She nodded. "Yes. It's been so long, though. But I still remember. The nights were very dark and black, and the stars were little pinpoints of light, hard and cold and far away. You could see patterns sometimes. The men of my world, when they were young, gave names to each of those patterns, and told grand tales about them."

Laren nodded. "I would like your world, I think," he said. "Mine was like that, a little. But our stars were a thousand colors, and they moved, like ghostly lanterns in the night. Sometimes they drew veils around them to hide their light, and then our nights would be all shimmer and gossamer. Often I would go sailing at startime, myself and she whom I loved. Just so we could see the stars together. It was a good time to sing." His voice was growing sad again.

Darkness had crept into the room, darkness and silence, and the food was cold and Sharra could scarce see his face fifty long feet away. So she rose and went to him, and sat lightly on the great table near to his chair. And Laren nodded and smiled, and at once there was a whoosh, and all along the walls torches flared to sudden life in the long dining hall. He offered her more wine, and her fingers lingered on his as she took the glass.

"It was like that for us, too," Sharra said. "If the wind was warm enough, and other men were far away, then we liked to lie together in the open. Kaydar and I." She hesitated, looked at him.

His eyes were searching. "Kaydar?"

"You would have liked him, Laren. And he would have liked you, I think. He was tall and he had red hair and there was a fire in his eyes. Kaydar had powers, as did I, but his were greater. And he had such a will. They took him one night, did not kill him, only took him from me and from our world. I have been hunting for him ever since. I know the gates, I wear the dark crown, and they will not stop me easily."

Laren drank his wine and watched the torchlight on

the metal of his goblet. "There are an infinity of worlds, Sharra."

"I have as much time as I require. I do not age, Laren, no more than you do. I will find him."

"Did you love him so much?"

Sharra fought a fond, flickering smile, and lost. "Yes," she said, and now it was her voice that seemed a little lost. "Yes, so much. He made me happy, Laren. We were only together for a short time, but he *did* make me happy. The Seven cannot touch that. It was a joy just to watch him, to feel his arms around me and see the way he smiled."

"Ah," he said, and he did smile, but there was something very beaten in the way he did it. The silence grew very thick.

Finally Sharra turned to him. "But we have wandered a long way from where we started. You still have not told me why your windows seal themselves at night."

"You have come a long way, Sharra. You move between the worlds. Have you seen worlds without stars?"

"Yes. Many, Laren. I have seen a universe where the sun is glowing ember with but a single world, and the skies are vast and vacant by night. I have seen the land of frowning jesters, where there is no sky and the hissing suns burn below the ocean. I have walked the moors of Carradyne, and watched dark sorcerers set fire to a rainbow to light that sunless land."

"This world has no stars," Laren said.

"Does that frighten you so much, that you stay inside?"

"No. But it has something else instead." He looked at her. "Would you see?"

She nodded.

As abruptly as they had lit, the torches all snuffed out. The room swam with blackness. And Sharra shifted on the table to look over Laren's shoulder. Laren did not move. But behind him, the stones of the window fell away like dust and light poured in from outside.

The sky was very dark, but she could see clearly, for against the darkness a shape was moving. Light poured from it, and the dirt in the courtyard and the stones of the battlements and the grey pennants were all bright beneath its glow. Puzzling, Sharra looked up.

Something looked back. It was taller than the mountains and it filled up half the sky, and though it gave off light enough to see the castle by, Sharra knew that it was dark beyond darkness. It had a man-shape, roughly, and it wore a long cape and a cowl, and below that was blackness even fouler than the rest. The only sounds were Laren's soft breathing and the beating of her heart and the distant weeping of a mourning-bird, but in her head Sharra could hear demonic laughter.

The shape in the sky looked down at her, in her, and she felt the cold dark in her soul. Frozen, she could not move her eyes. But the shape did move. It turned, and raised a hand, and then there was something else up there with it, a tiny man-shape with eyes of fire that writhed and screamed and called to her.

Sharra shrieked, and turned away. When she glanced back, there was no window. Only a wall of safe, sure stone, and a row of torches burning, and Laren holding her within strong arms. "It was only a vision," he told her. He pressed her tight against him, and stroked her hair. "I used to test myself at night," he said, more to himself than to her. "But there was no need. They take turns up there, watching me, each of the Seven. I have seen them too often, burning with black light against the clean dark of the sky, and holding those I loved. Now I don't look. I stay inside and sing and my windows are made of night-stone."

"I feel . . . fouled," she said, still trembling a little.

"Come," he said. "There is water upstairs, you can clean away the cold. And then I'll sing for you." He took her hand, and led her up into the tower.

Sharra took a hot bath while Laren set up his instrument and tuned it in the bedroom. He was ready when she returned, wrapped head to foot in a huge fluffy brown towel. She sat on the bed, drying her hair and waiting.

And Laren gave her visions.

He sang his other dream this time, the one where he was a god and the enemy of the Seven. The music was a savage pounding thing, shot through with lightning and tremors of fear, and the lights melted together to form a scarlet battlefield where a blinding-white Laren fought shadows and the shapes of nightmare. There were seven of them, and they formed a ring around him and darted in and out, stabbing him with lances of absolute black, and Laren answered them with fire and storm. But in the end they overwhelmed him, the light faded, and then the song grew soft and sad again and the vision blurred as lonely dreaming centuries flashed by.

Hardly had the last notes fallen from the air and the final shimmers died then Laren started once again. A new song this time, and one he did not know so well. His fingers, slim and graceful, hesitated and retraced themselves more than once, and his voice was shaky too, for he was making up some of the words as he went along. Sharra knew why. For this time he sang of her, a ballad of her quest. Of burning love and endless searching, of worlds beyond worlds, of dark crowns and waiting guardians that fought with claws and tricks and lies. He took every word that she had spoken, and used each, and transformed each. In the bedroom, glittering panoramas formed where hot white suns burned beneath eternal oceans and hissed in clouds of steam, and men ancient beyond time lit rainbows to keep away the dark. And he sang Kaydar, and he sang him true somehow, he caught and drew the fire that had been Sharra's love and made her believe anew.

But the song ended with a question, the halting finale lingering in the air, echoing, echoing. Both of them waited for the rest, and both knew there was no more. Not yet.

Sharra was crying. "My turn, Laren," she said. Then: "Thank you. For giving Kaydar back to me."

"It was only a song," he said, shrugging. "It's been a long time since I had a new song to sing."

Once again he left her, touching her cheek lightly at the door as she stood there with the blanket wrapped around her. Then Sharra locked the door behind him and went from candle to candle, turning light to darkness with a breath. And she threw the towel over a chair and crawled under the blankets and lay a long long time before drifting off to sleep.

It was still dark when she woke, not knowing why. She opened her eyes and lay quietly and looked around the room, and nothing was there, nothing was changed. Or was there?

And then she saw him, sitting in the chair across the room with his hands locked under his chin, just as he had sat that first time. His eyes steady and unmoving, very wide and dark in a room full of night. He sat very still. "Laren?" she called, softly, still not quite sure the dark form was him.

"Yes," he said. He did not move. "I watched you last night, too, while you slept. I have been alone here for longer than you can ever imagine, and very soon now I will be alone again. Even in sleep, your presence is a wonder."

"Oh, Laren," she said. There was a silence, a pause, a weighing and an unspoken conversation. Then she threw back the blanket, and Laren came to her.

Both of them had seen centuries come and go. A month, a moment; much the same.

They slept together every night, and every night Laren sang his songs while Sharra listened. They talked throughout dark hours, and during the day they swam nude in crystalline waters that caught the purple glory of the sky. They made love on beaches of fine white sand, and they spoke a lot of love.

But nothing changed. And finally the time drew near. On the eve of the night before the day that was end, at twilight, they walked together through the shadowed forest where he'd found her.

Laren had learned to laugh during his month with Sharra, but now he was silent again. He walked slowly, clutched her hand hard in his, and his mood was more grey than the soft silk shirt he wore. Finally, by the side of the valley stream, he sat and pulled her down by his side. They took off their boots and let the water cool their feet. It was a warm evening, with a lonely restless wind and already you could hear the first of the mourning-birds.

"You must go," he said, still holding her hand but never looking at her. It was a statement, not a question.

"Yes," she said, and the melancholy had touched her too, and there were leaden echoes in her voice.

"My words have all left me, Sharra," Laren said. "If I could sing for you a vision now I would. A vision of a world once empty, made full by us and our children. I could offer that. My world has beauty and wonder and mystery enough, if only there were eyes to see it. And if the nights are evil, well, men have faced dark nights before, on other worlds in other times. I would love you, Sharra, as much as I am able. I would try to make you happy."

"Laren . . . ," she started. But he quieted her with a glance.

"No. I could say that, but I will not. I have no right. Kaydar makes you happy. Only a selfish fool would ask you to give up that happiness to share my misery. Kaydar is all fire and laughter, while I am smoke and song and sadness. I have been alone too long, Sharra. The grey is part of my soul now, and I would not have you darkened. But still . . ."

She took his hand in both of hers, lifted it, and kissed it quickly. Then, releasing him, she lay her head on his unmoving shoulder. "Try to come with me, Laren," she said. "Hold my hand when we pass through the gate, and perhaps the dark crown will protect you."

"I will try anything you ask. But don't ask me to believe that it will work." He sighed. "You have countless worlds ahead of you, Sharra, and I cannot see your ending. But it is not here. That I know. And maybe that is best. I don't know anymore, if I ever did. I remember love vaguely, I think I can recall what it was like, and I remember that it never lasts. Here, with both of us unchanging and immortal, how could we help but to grow bored? Would we hate each other then? I'd not want that." He looked at her then, and smiled an aching melancholy smile. "I think that you had known Kaydar for only a short time, to be so in love with him. Perhaps I'm being devious after all. For in finding Kaydar, you may lose him. The fire will go out some day, my love, and the magic will die. And then you may remember Laren Dorr."

Sharra began to weep, softly. Laren gathered her to him, and kissed her, and whispered a gentle "No." She kissed back, and they held each other wordless.

When at last the purple gloom had darkened to near-black, they put back on their boots and stood. Laren hugged her and smiled.

"I *must* go," Sharra said. "I *must*. But leaving is hard, Laren, you must believe that."

"I do," he said. "I love you *because* you will go, I think. Because you cannot forget Kaydar, and you will not forget the promises you made. You are Sharra, who goes between the worlds, and I think the Seven must fear you far more than any god I might have been. If you were not you, I would not think as much of you."

"Oh. Once you said you would love any voice, that was not any echo of your own."

Laren shrugged. "As I have often said, love, *that* was a very long time ago."

They were back inside the castle before darkness, for a final meal, a final night, a final song. They got no sleep that night, and Laren sang to her again just before dawn. It was not a very good song, though; it was an aimless, rambling thing about a wandering minstrel on some nondescript world. Very little of interest ever happened to the minstrel; Sharra couldn't quite get the point of the song, and Laren sang it listlessly. It seemed an odd farewell, but both of them were troubled.

He left her with the sunrise, promising to change clothes and meet her in the courtyard. And sure enough, he was waiting when she got there, smiling at her calm and confident. He wore a suite of pure white; pants that clung, a shirt that puffed up at the sleeves, and a great heavy cape that snapped and billowed in the rising wind. But the purple sun stained him with its shadow rays.

Sharra walked out to him and took his hand. She wore tough leather, and there was a knife in her belt, for dealing with the guardian. Her hair, jet black with light-born glints of red and purple, blew as freely as his cape, but the dark crown was in place. "Goodbye, Laren," she said. "I wish I had given you more."

"You have given me enough. In all the centuries that come, in all the sun-cycles that lie ahead, I will remember. I shall measure time by you, Sharra. When the sun rises one day and its color is blue fire, I will look at it and say, 'yes, this is the first blue sun after Sharra came to me.'"

She nodded. "And I have a new promise. I will find Kaydar, some day. And if I free him, we will come back to you, both of us together, and we will pit my crown and Kaydar's fires against all the darkness of the Seven."

Laren shrugged. "Good. If I'm not here, be sure to leave a message," he said. And then he grinned.

"Now, the gate. You said you would show me the gate."

Laren turned and gestured at the shortest tower, a sooty stone structure Sharra had never been inside. There was a wide wooden door in its base. Laren produced a key.

"Here?" she said, looking puzzled. "In the castle?"

"Here," Laren said. They walked across the courtyard, to the door. Laren inserted the heavy metal key and began to fumble with the lock. While he worked, Sharra took one last look around, and felt the sadness heavy on her soul. The other towers looked bleak and dead, the courtyard was forlorn, and beyond the high icy mountains was only an empty horizon. There was no sound but Laren working at the lock, and no motion but the steady wind that kicked up the courtyard dust and flapped the seven grey pennants that hung along each wall. Sharra shivered with sudden loneliness.

Laren opened the door. No room inside; only a wall of moving fog, a fog without color or sound or light. "Your gate, my lady," the singer said.

Sharra watched it, as she had watched it so many times before. What world was next? she wondered. She never knew. But maybe in the next one, she would find Kaydar.

She felt Laren's hand on her shoulder. "You hesitate," he said, his voice soft.

Sharra's hand went to her knife. "The guardian," she said suddenly: "There is always a guardian." Her eyes darted quickly round the courtyard.

Laren sighed. "Yes. Always. There are some who try to claw you to pieces, and some who try to get you lost, and some who try to trick you into taking the wrong gate. There are some who hold you with weapons, some with chains, some with lies. And there is one, at least, who tried to stop you with love. Yet he was true for all that, and he never sang you false."

And with a hopeless, loving shrug, Laren shoved her through the gate.

Did she find him, in the end, her lover with the eyes of fire? Or is she searching still? What guardian did she face next?

When she walks at night, a stranger in a lonely land, does the sky have stars?

I don't know. He doesn't. Maybe even the Seven do not know. They are powerful, yes, but all power is not theirs, and the number of worlds is greater than even they can count.

There is a girl who goes between the worlds, but her path is lost in legend by now. Maybe she is dead, and maybe not. Knowledge moves slowly from world to world, and not all of it is true.

But this we know; in an empty castle below a purple sun, a lonely minstrel waits, and sings of her.

THE ICE DRAGON

Adara liked the winter best of all, for when the world grew cold the ice dragon came.

She was never quite sure whether it was the cold that brought the ice dragon or the ice dragon that brought the cold. That was the sort of question that often troubled her brother Geoff, who was two years older than her and insatiably curious, but Adara did not care about such things. So long as the cold and the snow and the ice dragon all arrived on schedule, she was happy.

She always knew when they were due because of her birthday. Adara was a winter child, born during the worst freeze that anyone could remember, even Old Laura, who lived on the next farm and remembered things that had happened before anyone else was born. People still talked about that freeze. Adara often heard them.

They talked about other things as well. They said it was the chill of that terrible freeze that had killed her mother, stealing in during her long night of labor past the great fire that Adara's father had built, and creeping under the layers of blankets that covered the birthing bed. And they said that the cold had entered Adara in the womb, that her skin had been pale blue and icy to the touch when she came forth, and that she had never warmed in all the years since. The winter had touched her, left its mark upon her, and made her its own.

It was true that Adara was always a child apart. She was a very serious little girl who seldom cared to play with the others. She was beautiful, people said, but in a strange, distant sort of way, with her pale skin and blond hair and wide clear blue eyes. She smiled, but not often. No one had ever seen her cry. Once when she was five she had stepped upon a nail imbedded in a board that lay concealed beneath a snowbank, and it had gone clear through her foot, but Adara had not wept or screamed even then. She had pulled her foot loose and walked back to the house, leaving a trail of blood in the snow, and when she had gotten there she had said only, "Father, I hurt myself." The sulks and tempers and tears of ordinary childhood were not for her.

Even her family knew that Adara was different. Her father was a huge, gruff bear of a man who had little use for people in general, but a smile always broke across his face when Geoff pestered him with questions, and he was full of hugs and laughter for Teri, Adara's older sister, who was golden and freckled, and flirted shamelessly with all the local boys. Every so often he would hug Adara as well, especially when he was drunk, which was frequent during the long winters. But there would be no smiles then. He would only wrap his arms around her, and pull her small body tight against him with all his massive strength, sob deep in his chest, and fat wet tears would run down his ruddy cheeks. He never hugged her at all during the summers. During the summers he was too busy.

Everyone was busy during the summers except for Adara. Geoff would work with his father in the fields and ask endless questions about this and that, learning everything a farmer had to know. When he was not working he would run with his friends to the river, and have adventures. Teri ran the house and did the cooking, and worked a bit at the inn by the crossroads during the busy season. The innkeeper's daughter was her friend, and his youngest son was more than a friend, and she would always come back giggly and full of gossip and news from travellers and soldiers and king's messengers. For Teri and Geoff the summers were the best time, and both of them were too busy for Adara.

Their father was the busiest of all. A thousand things needed to be done each day, and he did them, and found a thousand more. He worked from dawn to dusk. His muscles grew hard and lean in summer, and he stank from sweat each night when he came in from the fields, but he always came in smiling. After supper he would sit with Geoff and tell him stories and answer his questions, or teach Teri things she did not know about cooking, or stroll down to the inn. He was a summer man, truly.

He never drank in summer, except for a cup of wine now and again to celebrate his brother's visits.

That was another reason why Teri and Geoff loved the summers, when the world was green and hot and bursting with life. It was only in summer that Uncle Hal, their father's younger brother, came to call. Hal was a dragonrider in service to the king, a tall slender man with a face like a noble. Dragons cannot stand the cold, so when winter fell Hal and his wing would fly south. But each summer he returned, brilliant in the king's green-and-gold uniform, en route to the battlegrounds to the north and west of them. The war had been going on for all of Adara's life.

Whenever Hal came north, he would bring presents; toys from the king's city, crystal and gold jewelry, candies, and always a bottle of some expensive wine that he and his brother could share. He would grin at Teri and make her blush with his compliments, and entertain Geoff with tales of war and castles and dragons. As for Adara, he often tried to coax a smile out of her, with gifts and jests and hugs. He seldom succeeded.

For all his good nature, Adara did not like Hal; when Hal was there, it meant that winter was far away.

Besides, there had been a night when she was only four, and they thought her long asleep, that she overheard them talking over wine. "A solemn little thing," Hal said. "You ought to be kinder to her, John. You cannot blame *her* for what happened."

"Can't I?" her father replied, his voice thick with wine. "No, I suppose not. But it is hard. She looks like Beth, but she has none of Beth's warmth. The winter is in her, you know. Whenever I touch her I feel the chill, and I remember that it was for her that Beth had to die."

"You are cold to her. You do not love her as you do the others."

Adara remembered the way her father laughed then. "Love her? Ah, Hal. I loved her best of all, my little winter child. But she has never loved back. There is nothing in her for me, or you, any of us. She is such a cold little girl." And then he began to weep, even though it was summer and Hal was with him. In her bed, Adara listened and wished that Hal would fly away. She did not quite understand all that she had heard, not then, but she remembered it, and the understanding came later.

She did not cry; not at four, when she heard, or six, when she finally understood. Hal left a few days later, and Geoff and Teri waved to him excitedly when his wing passed overhead, thirty great dragons in proud formation against the summer sky. Adara watched with her small hands by her sides.

There were other visits in other summers, but Hal never made her smile, no matter what he brought her.

Adara's smiles were a secret store, and she spent of them only in winter. She could hardly wait for her birthday to come, and with it the cold. For in winter she was a special child.

She had known it since she was very little, playing with the others in the snow. The cold had never bothered her the way it did Geoff and Teri and their friends. Often Adara stayed outside alone for hours after the others had fled in search of warmth, or run off to Old Laura's to eat the hot vegetable soup she liked to make for the children. Adara would find a secret place in the far corner of the fields, a different place each winter, and there she would build a tall white castle, patting the snow in place with small bare hands, shaping it into towers and battlements like those Hal often talked about on the king's castle in the city. She would snap icicles off from the lower branches of trees, and use them for spires and spikes and guardposts, ranging them all about her castle. And often in the dead of winter would come a brief thaw and a sudden freeze, and overnight her snow castle would turn to ice, as hard and strong as she imagined real castles to be. All through the winters she would build on her castle, and no one ever knew. But always the spring would come, and a thaw not followed by a freeze; then all the ramparts and walls would melt away, and Adara would begin to count the days until her birthday came again.

Her winter castles were seldom empty. At the first frost each year, the ice lizards would come wriggling out of their burrows, and the fields would be overrun with the tiny blue creatures, darting this way and that, hardly seeming to touch the snow as they skimmed across it. All the children played with the ice lizards. But the others were clumsy and cruel, and they would snap the fragile little animals in two, breaking them between their fingers as they might break an icicle hanging from a roof. Even Geoff, who was too kind ever to do something like that, sometimes grew curious, and held the lizards too long in his efforts to examine them, and the heat of his hands would make them melt and burn and finally die.

Adara's hands were cool and gentle, and she could hold the lizards as long as she liked without harming them, which always made Geoff pout and ask angry questions. Sometimes she would lie in the cold, damp snow and let the lizards crawl all over her, delighting in the light touch of their feet as they skittered across her face. Sometimes she would wear ice lizards hidden in her hair as she went about her chores, though she took care never to take them inside where the heat of the fires would kill them. Always she would gather up scraps after the family ate, and bring them to the secret place where her castle was a-building, and there she would scatter them. So the castles she erected were full of kings and courtiers every winter; small furry creatures that snuck out from the woods, winter birds with pale white plumage, and hundreds and hundreds of squirming, struggling ice lizards, cold and quick and fat. Adara liked the ice lizards better than any of the pets the family had kept over the years.

But it was the ice dragon that she loved.

She did not know when she had first seen it. It seemed to her that it had always been a part of her life, a vision glimpsed during the deep of winter, sweeping across the frigid sky on wings serene and blue. Ice dragons were rare, even in those days, and whenever it was seen the children would all point and wonder, while the old folks muttered and shook their heads. It was a sign of a long and bitter winter when ice dragons were abroad in the land. An ice dragon had been seen flying across the face of the moon on the night Adara had been born, people said, and each winter since it had been seen again, and those winters had been very bad indeed, the spring coming later each year. So the people would set fires and pray and hope to keep the ice dragon away, and Adara would fill with fear.

But it never worked. Every year the ice dragon returned. Adara knew it came for her.

The ice dragon was large, half again the size of the scaled green war dragons that Hal and his fellows flew. Adara had heard legends of wild dragons larger than mountains, but she had never seen any. Hal's dragon was big enough, to be sure, five times the size of a horse, but it was small compared to the ice dragon, and ugly besides.

The ice dragon was a crystalline white, that shade of white that is so hard and cold that it is almost blue. It was covered with hoarfrost, so when it moved its skin broke and crackled as the crust on the snow crackles beneath a man's boots, and flakes of rime fell off.

Its eyes were clear and deep and icy.

Its wings were vast and batlike, colored all a faint translucent blue. Adara could see the clouds through them, and oftentimes the moon and stars, when the beast wheeled in frozen circles through the skies.

Its teeth were icicles, a triple row of them, jagged spears of unequal length, white against its deep blue maw.

When the ice dragon beat its wings, the cold winds blew and the snow swirled and scurried and the world seemed to shrink and shiver. Sometimes when a door flew open in the cold of winter, driven by a sudden gust of wind, the householder would run to bolt it and say, "An ice dragon flies nearby."

And when the ice dragon opened its great mouth, and exhaled, it was not fire that came streaming out, the burning sulfurous stink of lesser dragons.

The ice dragon breathed *cold.*

Ice formed when it breathed. Warmth fled. Fires guttered and went out, shriven by the chill. Trees froze through to their slow secret souls, and their limbs turned brittle and cracked from their own weight. Animals turned blue and whimpered and died, their eyes bulging and their skin covered over with frost.

The ice dragon breathed death into the world; death and quiet and *cold*. But Adara was not afraid. She was a winter child, and the ice dragon was her secret.

She had seen it in the sky a thousand times. When she was four, she saw it on the ground.

She was out building on her snow castle, and it came and landed close to her, in the emptiness of the snow-covered fields. All the ice lizards ran away. Adara simply stood. The ice dragon looked at her for ten long heartbeats, before it took to the air again. The wind shrieked around her and through her as it beat its wings to rise, but Adara felt strangely exulted.

Later that winter it returned, and Adara touched it. Its skin was very cold. She took off her glove nonetheless. It would not be right otherwise. She was half afraid it would burn and melt at her touch, but it did not. It was much more sensitive to heat than even the ice lizards, Adara knew somehow. But she was special, the winter child, cool. She stroked it, and finally gave its wing a kiss that hurt her lips. That was the winter of her fourth birthday, the year she touched the ice dragon.

The winter of her fifth birthday was the year she rode upon it for the first time.

It found her again, working on a different castle at a different place in the fields, alone as ever. She watched it come, and ran to it when it landed, and pressed herself against it. That had been the summer when she had heard her father talking to Hal.

They stood together for long minutes until finally Adara, remembering Hal, reached out and tugged at the dragon's wing with a small hand. And the dragon beat its great wings once, and then extended them flat against the snow, and Adara scrambled up to wrap her arms about its cold white neck.

Together, for the first time, they flew.

She had no harness or whip, as the king's dragonriders use. At times the beating of the wings threatened to shake her loose from where she clung, and the coldness of the dragon's flesh crept through her clothing and bit and numbed her child's flesh. But Adara was not afraid.

They flew over her father's farm, and she saw Geoff looking very small below, startled and afraid, and knew he could not see her. It made her laugh an icy, tinkling laugh, a laugh as bright and crisp as the winter air.

They flew over the crossroads inn, where crowds of people came out to watch them pass.

They flew above the forest, all white and green and silent.

They flew high into the sky, so high that Adara could not even see the ground below, and she thought she glimpsed another ice dragon, way off in the distance, but it was not half so grand as *hers*.

They flew for most of the day, and finally the dragon swept around in a great circle, and spiraled down, gliding on its stiff and glittering wings. It let her off in the field where it had found her, just after dusk.

Her father found her there, and wept to see her, and hugged her savagely. Adara did not understand that, nor why he beat her after he had gotten her back to the house. But when she and Geoff had been put to sleep, she heard him slide out of his own bed and come padding over to hers. "You missed it all," he said. "There was an ice dragon, and it scared everybody. Father was afraid it had eaten you."

Adara smiled to herself in the darkness, but said nothing.

She flew on the ice dragon four more times that winter, and every winter after that. Each year she flew further and more often than the year before, and the ice dragon was seen more frequently in the skies above their farm.

Each winter was longer and colder than the one before.

Each year the thaw came later.

And sometimes there were patches of land, where the ice dragon had lain to rest, that never seemed to thaw properly at all.

There was much talk in the village during her sixth year, and a message was sent to the king. No answer ever came.

"A bad business, ice dragons," Hal said that summer when he visited the farm. "They're not like real dragons, you know. You can't break them or train them. We have tales of those that tried, found frozen with their whip and harness in hand. I've heard about people that have lost hands or fingers just by touching one of them. Frostbite. Yes, a bad business."

"Then why doesn't the king do something?" her father demanded. "We sent a message. Unless we can kill the beast or drive it away, in a year or two we won't have any planting season at all."

Hal smiled grimly. "The king has other concerns. The war is going badly, you know. They advance every summer, and they have twice as many dragonriders as we do. I tell you, John, it's hell up there. Some year I'm not going to come back. The king can hardly spare men to go chasing an ice dragon." He laughed. "Besides, I don't think anybody's ever killed one of the things. Maybe we should just let the enemy take this whole province. Then it'd be *his* ice dragon."

But it wouldn't be, Adara thought as she listened. No matter what king ruled the land, it would always be *her* ice dragon.

Hal departed and summer waxed and waned. Adara counted the days until her birthday. Hal passed through again before the first chill, taking his ugly dragon south for the winter. His wing seemed smaller when it came flying over the forest that fall, though, and his visit was briefer than usual, and ended with a loud quarrel between him and her father.

"They won't move during the winter," Hal said. "The winter terrain is too treacherous, and they won't risk an advance without dragonriders to cover them from above. But come spring, we aren't going to be able to hold them. The king may not even try. Sell the farm now, while you can still get a good price. You can buy another piece of land in the south."

"*This* is my land," her father said. "I was born here. You too, though you seem to have forgotten it. Our parents are buried here. And Beth too. I want to lie beside her when I go."

"You'll go a lot sooner than you'd like if you don't listen to me," Hal said angrily. "Don't be stupid, John. I know what the land means to you, but it isn't worth your life." He went on and on, but her father would not be moved. They ended the evening swearing at each other, and Hal left in the dead of night, slamming the door behind him as he went.

Adara, listening, had made a decision. It did not matter what her father did or did not do. She would stay. If she moved, the ice dragon would not know where to find her when winter came, and if she went too far south it would never be able to come to her at all.

It did come to her, though, just after her seventh birthday. That winter was the coldest one of all. She flew so often and so far that she scarcely had time to work on her ice castle.

Hal came again in the spring. There were only a dozen dragons in his wing, and he brought no presents that year. He and her father argued once again. Hal raged and pleaded and threatened, but her father was stone. Finally Hal left, off to the battlefields.

That was the year the king's line broke, up north near

some town with a long name that Adara could not pronounce.

Teri heard about it first. She returned from the inn one night flushed and excited. "A messenger came through, on his way to the king," she told them. "The enemy won some big battle, and he's to ask for reinforcements. He said our army is retreating."

Their father frowned, and worry lines creased his brow. "Did he say anything of the king's dragonriders?" Arguments or no, Hal was family.

"I asked," Teri said. "He said the dragonriders are the rear guard. They're supposed to raid and burn, delay the enemy while our army pulls back safely. Oh, I hope Uncle Hal is safe!"

"Hal will show them," Geoff said. "Him and Brimstone will burn 'em all up."

Their father smiled. "Hal could always take care of himself. At any rate, there is nothing we can do. Teri, if any more messengers come through, ask them how it goes."

She nodded, her concern not quite covering her excitement. It was all quite thrilling.

In the weeks that followed, the thrill wore off, as the people of the area began to comprehend the magnitude of the disaster. The king's highway grew busier and busier, and all the traffic flowed from north to south, and all the travellers wore green-and-gold. At first the soldiers marched in disciplined columns, led by officers wearing golden helmets, but even then they were less than stirring. The columns marched wearily, and the uniforms were filthy and torn, and the swords and pikes and axes the soldiers carried were nicked and oftimes stained. Some men had lost their weapons; they limped along blindly, empty-handed. And the trains of wounded that followed the columns were often longer than the columns themselves. Adara stood in the grass by the side of the road and watched them pass. She saw a man with no eyes supporting a man with only one leg, as the two of them walked together. She saw men with no legs, or no arms, or both. She saw a man with his head split open by an axe, and many men covered with caked blood and filth, men who moaned low in their throats as they walked. She *smelled* men with bodies that were horribly greenish and puffed-up. One of them died and was left abandoned by the side of the road. Adara told her father and he and some of the men from the village came out and buried him.

Most of all, Adara saw the burned men. There were dozens of them in every column that passed, men whose skin was black and seared and falling off, who had lost an arm or a leg or half of a face to the hot breath of a dragon. Teri told them what the officers said, when they stopped at the inn to drink or rest; the enemy had many, many dragons.

For almost a month the columns flowed past, more every day. Even Old Laura admitted that she had never seen so much traffic on the road. From time to time a lone messenger on horseback rode against the tide, galloping towards the north, but always alone. After a time everyone knew there would be no reinforcements.

An officer in one of the last columns advised the people of the area to pack up whatever they could carry, and move south. "They are coming," he warned. A few listened to him, and indeed for a week the road was full of refugees from towns further north. Some of them told frightful stories. When they left, more of the local people went with them.

But most stayed. They were people like her father, and the land was in their blood.

The last organized force to come down the road was a ragged troop of cavalry, men as gaunt as skeletons riding horses with skin pulled tight around their ribs. They thundered past in the night, their mounts heaving and foaming, and the only one to pause was a pale young officer, who reigned his mount up briefly and shouted, "Go, go. They are burning everything!" Then he was off after his men.

The few soldiers who came after were alone or in small groups. They did not always use the road, and they did not pay for the things they took. One swordsman killed a farmer on the other side of town, raped his wife, stole his money, and ran. His rags were green-and-gold.

Then no one came at all. The road was deserted.

The innkeeper claimed he could smell ashes when the wind blew from the north. He packed up his family and went south. Teri was distraught. Geoff was wide-eyed and anxious and only a bit frightened. He asked a thousand questions about the enemy, and practiced at being a warrior. Their father went about his labors, busy as ever. War or no war, he had crops in the field. He smiled less than usual, however, and he began to drink, and Adara often saw him glancing up at the sky while he worked.

Adara wandered the fields alone, played by herself in the damp summer heat, and tried to think of where she would hide if her father tried to take them away.

Last of all, the king's dragonriders came, and with them Hal.

There were only four of them. Adara saw the first one, and went and told her father, and he put his hand on her shoulder and together they watched it pass, a solitary green dragon with a vaguely tattered look. It did not pause for them.

Two days later, three dragons flying together came into view, and one of them detached itself from the others and circled down to their farm while the other two headed south.

Uncle Hal was thin and grim and sallow-looking. His dragon looked sick. Its eyes ran, and one of its wings had been partially burned, so it flew in an awkward, heavy manner, with much difficulty. "Now will you go?" Hal said to his brother, in front of all the children.

"No. Nothing has changed."

Hal swore. "They will be here within three days," he said. "Their dragonriders may be here even sooner."

"Father, I'm scared," Teri said.

He looked at her, saw her fear, hesitated, and finally turned back to his brother. "I am staying. But if you would, I would have you take the children."

Now it was Hal's turn to pause. He thought for a moment, and finally shook his head. "I can't, John. I would, willingly, joyfully, if it were possible. But it isn't. Brimstone is wounded. He can barely carry me. If I took on any extra weight, we might never make it."

Teri began to weep.

"I'm sorry, love," Hal said to her. "Truly I am." His fists clenched helplessly.

"Teri is almost full-grown," their father said. "If her weight is too much, then take one of the others."

Brother looked at brother, with despair in their eyes. Hal trembled. "Adara," he said finally. "She's small and light." He forced a laugh. "She hardly weighs anything at all. I'll take Adara. The rest of you take horses, or a wagon, or go on foot. But go, damn, you, go."

"We will see," their father said non-committally. "You take Adara, and keep her safe for us."

"Yes," Hal agreed. He turned and smiled at her. "Come, child. Uncle Hal is going to take you for a ride on Brimstone."

Adara looked at him very seriously. "No," she said. She turned and slipped through the door and began to run.

They came after her, of course, Hal and her father and even Geoff. But her father wasted time standing in the door, shouting at her to come back, and when he began to run he was ponderous and clumsy, while Adara was indeed small and light and fleet of foot. Hal and

Geoff stayed with her longer, but Hal was weak, and
Geoff soon winded himself, though he sprinted hard at
her heels for a few moments. By the time Adara reached
the nearest wheat field, the three of them were well
behind her. She quickly lost herself amid the grain, and
they searched for hours in vain while she made her way
carefully towards the woods.

When dusk fell, they brought out lanterns and torches
and continued their search. From time to time she heard
her father swearing, or Hal calling out her name. She
stayed high in the branches of the oak she had climbed,
and smiled down at their lights as they combed back and
forth through the fields. Finally she drifted off to sleep,
dreaming about the coming of winter and wondering how
she would live until her birthday. It was still a long time
away.

Dawn woke her; dawn and a noise in the sky.

Adara yawned and blinked, and heard it again. She
shinnied to the uppermost limb of the tree, as high as it
would bear her, and pushed aside the leaves.

There were dragons in the sky.

She had never seen beasts quite like these. Their scales
were dark and sooty, not green like the dragon Hal rode.
One was a rust color and one was the shade of dried
blood and one was black as coal. All of them had eyes
like glowing embers, and steam rose from their nostrils,
and their tails flicked back and forth as their dark, leathery wings beat the air. The rust-colored one opened its
mouth and roared, and the forest shook to its challenge,
and even the branch that held Adara trembled just a
little. The black one made a noise too, and when it
opened its maw a spear of flame lanced out, all orange
and blue, and touched the trees below. Leaves withered
and blackened, and smoke began to rise from where the
dragon's breath had fallen. The one the color of blood
flew close overhead, its wings creaking and straining, its
mouth half-open. Between its yellowed teeth Adara saw

soot and cinders, and the wind stirred by its passage was fire and sandpaper, raw and chafing against her skin. She cringed.

On the backs of the dragons rode men with whip and lance, in uniforms of black-and-orange, their faces hidden behind dark helmets. The one on the rust dragon gestured with his lance, pointing at the farm buildings across the fields. Adara looked.

Hal came up to meet them.

His green dragon was as large as their own, but somehow it seemed small to Adara as she watched it climb upwards from the farm. With its wings fully extended, it was plain to see how badly injured it was; the right wing tip was charred, and it leaned heavily to one side as it flew. On its back, Hal looked like one of the tiny toy soldiers he had brought them as a present years before.

The enemy dragonriders split up and came at him from three sides. Hal saw what they were doing. He tried to turn, to throw himself at the black dragon head-on, and flee the other two. His whip flailed angrily, desperately. His green dragon opened its mouth, and roared a weak challenge, but its flame was pale and short and did not reach the oncoming enemy.

The others held their fire. Then, on a signal, their dragons all breathed as one. Hal was wreathed in flames.

His dragon made a high wailing noise, and Adara saw that it was burning, *he* was burning, they were all burning, beast and master both. They fell heavily to the ground, and lay smoking amidst her father's wheat.

The air was full of ashes.

Adara craned her head around in the other direction, and saw a column of smoke rising from beyond the forest and the river. That was the farm where Old Laura lived with her grandchildren and *their* children.

When she looked back, the three dark dragons were circling lower and lower above her own farm. One by one they landed. She watched the first of the riders dismount and saunter towards their door.

She was frightened and confused and only seven, after all. And the heavy air of summer was a weight upon her, and it filled her with a helplessness and thickened all her fears. So Adara did the only thing she knew, without thinking, a thing that came naturally to her. She climbed down from her tree and ran. She ran across the fields and through the woods, away from the farm and her family and the dragons, away from all of it. She ran until her legs throbbed with pain, down in the direction of the river. She ran to the coldest place she knew, to the deep caves underneath the river bluffs, to chill shelter and darkness and safety.

And there in the cold she hid. Adara was a winter child, and cold did not bother her. But still, as she hid, she trembled.

Day turned into night. Adara did not leave her cave.

She tried to sleep, but her dreams were full of burning dragons.

She made herself very small as she lay in the darkness, and tried to count how many days remained until her birthday. The caves were nicely cool; Adara could almost imagine that it was not summer after all, that it was winter, or near to winter. Soon her ice dragon would come for her, and she would ride on its back to the land of always-winter, where great ice castles and cathedrals of snow stood eternally in endless fields of white, and the stillness and silence were all.

It almost felt like winter as she lay there. The cave grew colder and colder, it seemed. It made her feel safe. She napped briefly. When she woke, it was colder still. A white coating of frost covered the cave walls, and she was sitting on a bed of ice. Adara jumped to her feet and looked up towards the mouth of the cave, filled with a wan dawn light. A cold wind caressed her. But it was coming from outside, from the world of summer, not from the depths of the cave at all.

She gave a small shout of joy, and climbed and scrambled up the ice-covered rocks.

Outside, the ice dragon was waiting for her.

It had breathed upon the water, and now the river was frozen, or at least a part of it was, although one could see that the ice was fast melting as the summer sun rose. It had breathed upon the green grass that grew along the banks, grass as high as Adara, and now the tall blades were white and brittle, and when the ice dragon moved its wings the grass cracked in half and tumbled, sheared as clean as if it had been cut down with a scythe.

The dragon's icy eyes met Adara's, and she ran to it and up its wing, and threw her arms about it. She knew she had to hurry. The ice dragon looked smaller than she had ever seen it, and she understood what the heat of summer was doing to it.

"Hurry, dragon," she whispered. "Take me away, take me to the land of always-winter. We'll never come back here, never. I'll build you the best castle of all, and take care of you, and ride you every day. Just take me away, dragon, take me home with you."

The ice dragon heard and understood. Its wide translucent wings unfolded and beat the air, and bitter arctic winds howled through the fields of summer. They rose. Away from the cave. Away from the river. Above the forest. Up and up. The ice dragon swung around to the north. Adara caught a glimpse of her father's farm, but it was very small and growing smaller. They turned their back to it, and soared.

Then a sound came to Adara's ears. An impossible sound, a sound that was too small and too far away for her to ever have heard it, especially above the beating of the ice dragon's wings. But she heard it nonetheless. She heard her father scream.

Hot tears ran down her cheeks, and where they fell

upon the ice dragon's back they burned small pockmarks in the frost. Suddenly the cold beneath her hands was biting, and when she pulled one hand away Adara saw the mark that it had made upon the dragon's neck. She was scared, but still she clung. "Turn back," she whispered. "Oh, *please*, dragon. Take me back."

She could not see the ice dragon's eyes, but she knew what they would look like. Its mouth opened and a blue-white plume issued, a long cold streamer that hung in the air. It made no noise; ice dragons are silent. But in her mind Adara heard the wild keening of its grief.

"Please," she whispered once again. "Help me." Her voice was thin and small.

The ice dragon turned.

The three dark dragons were outside of the barn when Adara returned, feasting on the burned and blackened carcasses of her father's stock. One of the dragonriders was standing near them, leaning on his lance and prodding his dragon from time to time.

He looked up when the cold gust of wind came shrieking across the fields, and shouted something, and sprinted for the black dragon. The beast tore a last hunk of meat from her father's horse, swallowed, and rose reluctantly into the air. The rider flailed his whip.

Adara saw the door of the farmhouse burst open. The other two riders rushed out, and ran for their dragons. One of them was struggling into his pants as he ran. He was barechested.

The black dragon roared, and its fire came blazing up at them. Adara felt the searing of heat, and a shudder went through the ice dragon as the flames played along its belly. Then it craned its long neck around, and fixed its baleful empty eyes upon the enemy, and opened its frost-rimmed jaws. Out from among its icy teeth its breath came streaming, and that breath was pale and cold.

It touched the left wing of the coal-black dragon

beneath them, and the dark beast gave a shrill cry of pain, and when it beat its wings again, the frost-covered wing broke in two. Dragon and dragonrider began to fall.

The ice dragon breathed again.

They were frozen and dead before they hit the ground.

The rust-colored dragon was flying at them, and the dragon the color of blood with its barechested rider. Adara's ears were filled with their angry roaring, and she could feel their hot breath around her, and see the air shimmering with heat, and smell the stink of sulfur.

Two long swords of fire crossed in midair, but neither touched the ice dragon, though it shriveled in the heat, and water flew from it like rain whenever it beat its wings.

The blood-colored dragon flew too close, and the breath of the ice dragon blasted the rider. His bare chest turned blue before Adara's eyes, and moisture condensed on him in an instant, covering him with frost. He screamed, and died, and fell from his mount, though his harness had remained behind, frozen to the neck of his dragon. The ice dragon closed on it, wings screaming the secret song of winter, and a blast of flame met a blast of cold. The ice dragon shuddered once again, and twisted away, dripping. The other dragon died.

But the last dragonrider was behind them now, the enemy in full armor on the dragon whose scales were the brown of rust. Adara screamed, and even as she did the fire enveloped the ice dragon's wing. It was gone in less than an instant, but the wing was gone with it, melted, destroyed.

The ice dragon's remaining wing beat wildly to slow its plunge, but it came to earth with an awful crash. Its legs shattered beneath it, and its wing snapped in two places, and the impact of the landing threw Adara from its back. She tumbled to the soft earth of the field, and rolled, and struggled up, bruised but whole.

The ice dragon seemed very small now, and very broken.

Its long neck sank wearily to the ground, and its head rested amid the wheat.

The enemy dragonrider came swooping in, roaring with triumph. The dragon's eyes burned. The man flourished his lance and shouted.

The ice dragon painfully raised its head once more, and made the only sound that Adara ever heard it make: a terrible thin cry full of melancholy, like the sound the north wind makes when it moves around the towers and battlements of the white castle that stands empty in the land of always-winter.

When the cry had faded, the ice dragon sent cold into the world one final time: a long smoking blue-white stream of cold that was full of snow and stillness and the end of all living things. The dragonrider flew right into it, still brandishing whip and lance. Adara watched him crash.

Then she was running, away from the fields, back to the house and her family within, running as fast as she could, running and panting and crying all the while like a seven year old.

Her father had been nailed to the bedroom wall. They had wanted him to watch while they took their turns with Teri. Adara did not know what to do, but she untied Teri, whose tears had dried by then, and they freed Geoff, and then they got their father down. Teri nursed him and cleaned out his wounds. When his eyes opened and he saw Adara, he smiled. She hugged him very hard, and cried for him.

By night he said he was fit enough to travel. They crept away under cover of darkness, and took the king's road south.

Her family asked no questions then, in those hours of darkness and fear. But later, when they were safe in the south, there were questions endlessly. Adara gave them the best answers she could. But none of them ever believed her, except for Geoff, and he grew out of it when he got older. She was only seven, after all, and she did not understand that ice dragons are never seen in summer, and cannot be tamed nor ridden.

Besides, when they left the house that night, there was no ice dragon to be seen. Only the huge dark corpses of three war dragons, and the smaller bodies of three dragonriders in black-and-orange. And a pond that had never been there before, a small quiet pool where the water was very cold. They had walked around it carefully, headed towards the road.

Their father worked for another farmer for three years in the south. His hands were never as strong as they had been, before the nails had been pounded through them, but he made up for that with the strength of his back and his arms, and his determination. He saved whatever he could, and he seemed happy. "Hal is gone, and my land," he would tell Adara, "and I am sad for that. But it is all right. I have my daughter back." For the winter was gone from her now, and she smiled and laughed and even wept like other little girls.

Three years after they had fled, the king's army routed the enemy in a great battle, and the king's dragons burned the foreign capitol. In the peace that followed, the northern provinces changed hands once more. Teri had recaptured her spirit and married a young trader, and she remained in the south. Geoff and Adara returned with their father to the farm.

When the first frost came, all the ice lizards came out, just as they had always done. Adara watched them with a smile on her face, remembering the way it had been. But she did not try to touch them. They were cold and fragile little things, and the warmth of her hands would hurt them.

IN THE LOST LANDS

You can buy anything you might desire from Gray Alys.
But it is better not to.

* * *

The Lady Melange did not come herself to Gray Alys.
She was said to be a clever and a cautious young woman,
as well as exceedingly fair, and she had heard the stories.
Those who dealt with Gray Alys did so at their own peril,
it was said. Gray Alys did not refuse any of those who
came to her, and she always got them what they wanted.
Yet somehow, when all was done, those who dealt with
Gray Alys were never happy with the things that she
brought them, the things that they had wanted. The Lady
Melange knew all this, ruling as she did from the high
keep built into the side of the mountain. Perhaps that
was why she did not come herself.

Instead, it was Jerais who came calling on Gray Alys that day; Blue Jerais the lady's champion, foremost of the paladins who secured her high keep and led her armies into battle, captain of her colorguard. Jerais wore an underlining of pale blue silk beneath the deep azure plate of his enameled armor. The sigil on his shield was a malestrom, done in a hundred subtle hues of blue, and a sapphire large as an eagle's eye was set in the hilt of his sword. When he entered Gray Alys' presence and removed his helmet, his eyes were a perfect match for the jewel in his sword, though his hair was a startling and inappropriate red.

Gray Alys received him in the small, ancient stone house she kept in the dim heart of the town beneath the mountain. She waited for him in a windowless room full of dust and the smell of mold, seated in an old high-backed chair that seemed to dwarf her small, thin body. In her lap was a gray rat the size of a small dog. She stroked it languidly as Jerais entered and took off his helmet and let his bright blue eyes adjust to the dimness.

"Yes?" Gray Alys said at last.

"You are the one they call Gray Alys," Jerais said.

"I am."

"I am Jerais. I come at the behest of the Lady Melange."

"The wise and beautiful Lady Melange," said Gray Alys. The rat's fur was soft as velvet beneath her long, pale fingers. "Why does the Lady send her champion to one as poor and plain as I?"

"Even in the keep, we hear tales of you," said Jerais.

"Yes."

"It is said, for a price, you will sell things strange and wonderful."

"Does the Lady Melange wish to buy?"

"It is said also that you have powers, Gray Alys. It is said that you are not always as you sit before me now, a slender woman of indeterminate age, clad all in gray. It is said that you become young and old as you wish. It is said that sometimes you are a man, or an old woman, or a child. It is said that you know the secrets of shapeshifting, that you go abroad as a great cat, a bear, a bird, and that you change your skin at will, not as a slave to the moon like the werefolk of the lost lands."

"All of these things are said," Gray Alys acknowledged.

Jerais removed a small leather bag from his belt and stepped closer to where Gray Alys sat. He loosened the drawstring that held the bag shut, and spilled out the contents on the table by her side. Gems. A dozen of them, in as many colors. Gray Alys lifted one and held it to her eye, watching the candle flame through it. When she placed it back among the others, she nodded at Jerais and said, "What would the Lady buy of me?"

"Your secret," Jerais said, smiling. "The Lady Melange wishes to shapeshift."

"She is said to be young and beautiful," Gray Alys replied. "Even here beyond the keep, we hear many tales of her. She has no mate but many lovers. All of her colorguard are said to love her, among them yourself. Why should she wish to change?"

"You misunderstand. The Lady Melange does not seek youth or beauty. No change could make her fairer than she is. She wants from you the power to become a beast. A wolf."

"Why?" asked Gray Alys.

"That is none of your concern. Will you sell her this gift?"

"I refuse no one," said Gray Alys. "Leave the gems here. Return in one month, and I shall give you what the Lady Melange desires."

Jerais nodded. His face looked thoughtful. "You refuse no one?"

"No one."

He grinned crookedly, reached into his belt, and extended his hand to her. Within the soft blue crushed velvet of his gloved palm rested another jewel, a sapphire even larger than the one set in the hilt of his sword. "Accept this as payment, if you will. I wish to buy for myself."

Gray Alys took the sapphire from his palm, held it up between thumb and forefinger against the candle flame, nodded, and dropped it among the other jewels. "What would you have, Jerais?"

His grin spread wider. "I would have you fail," he said. "I do not want the Lady Melange to have this power she seeks."

Gray Alys regarded him evenly, her steady gray eyes fixed on his own cold blue ones. "You wear the wrong color, Jerais," she said at last. "Blue is the color of loyalty, yet you betray your mistress and the mission she entrusted to you."

"I am loyal," Jerais protested. "I know what is good for her, better than she knows herself. Melange is young and foolish. She thinks it can be kept secret, when she finds this power she seeks. She is wrong. And when the people know, they will destroy her. She cannot rule these folk by day, and tear out their throats by night."

Gray Alys considered that for a time in silence, stroking the great rat that lay across her lap. "You lie, Jerais," she said when she spoke again. "The reasons you give are not your true reasons."

Jerais frowned. His gloved hand, almost casually, came to rest on the hilt of his sword. His thumb stroked the great sapphire set there. "I will not argue with you," he said gruffly. "If you will not sell to me, give me back my gem and be damned with you!"

"I refuse no one," Gray Alys replied.

Jerais scowled in confusion. "I shall have what I ask?"

"You shall have what you want."

"Excellent," said Jerais, grinning again. "In a month, then!"

"A month," agreed Gray Alys.

* * *

And so Gray Alys sent the word out, in ways that only
Gray Alys knew. The message passed from mouth to
mouth through the shadows and alleys and the secret
sewers of the town, and even to the tall houses of scarlet
wood and colored glass where dwelled the noble and the
rich. Soft gray rats with tiny human hands whispered it
to sleeping children, and the children shared it with each
other, and chanted a strange new chant when they
skipped rope. The word drifted to all the army outposts
to the east, and rode west with the great caravans into
the heart of the old empire of which the town beneath
the mountain was only the smallest part. Huge leathery
birds with the cunning faces of monkeys flew the word
south, over the forests and the rivers, to a dozen different
kingdoms, where men and women as pale and terrible
as Gray Alys herself heard it in the solitude of their
towers. Even north, past the mountains, even into the
lost lands, the word traveled.

It did not take long. In less than two weeks, he came
to her. "I can lead you to what you seek," he told her.
"I can find you a werewolf."

He was a young man, slender and beardless. He
dressed in the worn leathers of the rangers who lived
and hunted in the windswept desolation beyond the
mountains. His skin had the deep tan of a man who
spent all his life outdoors, though his hair was as white
as mountain snow and fell about his shoulders, tangled
and unkempt. He wore no armor and carried a long knife
instead of a sword, and he moved with a wary grace.
Beneath the pale strands of hair that fell across his face,
his eyes were dark and sleepy. Though his smile was
open and amiable, there was a curious indolence to him
as well, and a dreamy, sensuous set to his lips when he
thought no one was watching. He named himself Boyce.

Gray Alys watched him and listened to his words and
finally said, "Where?"

"A week's journey north," Boyce replied. "In the lost lands."

"Do you dwell in the lost lands, Boyce?" Gray Alys asked of him.

"No. They are no fit place for dwelling. I have a home here in town. But I go beyond the mountains often, Gray Alys. I am a hunter. I know the lost lands well, and I know the things that live there. You seek a man who walks like a wolf. I can take you to him. But we must leave at once, if we are to arrive before the moon is full."

Gray Alys rose. "My wagon is loaded, my horses are fed and shod. Let us depart then."

Boyce brushed the fine white hair from his eyes, and smiled lazily.

The mountain pass was high and steep and rocky, and in places barely wide enough for Gray Alys' wagon to pass. The wagon was a cumbersome thing, long and heavy and entirely enclosed, once brightly painted but now faded so by time and weather that its wooden walls were all a dreary gray. It rode on six clattering iron wheels, and the two horses that pulled it were of necessity monsters half again the size of normal beasts. Even so, they kept a slow pace through the mountains. Boyce, who had no horse, walked ahead or alongside, and sometimes rode up next to Gray Alys. The wagon groaned and creaked. It took them three days to ascend to the highest point on the mountain road, where they looked through a cleft in the mountains out onto the wide barren plains of the lost lands. It took them three more days to descend.

"Now we will make better time," Boyce promised Gray Alys when they reached the lost lands themselves. "Here the land is flat and empty, and the going will be easy. A day now, perhaps two, and you shall have what you seek."

"Yes," said Gray Alys.

They filled the water barrels full before they left the

mountains, and Boyce went hunting in the foothills and returned with three black rabbits and the carcass of a small deer, curiously deformed, and when Gray Alys asked him how he had brought them down with only a knife as a weapon, Boyce smiled and produced a sling and sent several small stones whistling through the air. Gray Alys nodded. They made a small fire and cooked two of the rabbits, and salted the rest of the meat. The next morning, at dawn, they set off into the lost lands.

Here they moved quickly indeed. The lost lands were a cold and empty place, and the earth was packed as hard and firm as the roads that wound through the empire beyond the mountains. The wagon rolled along briskly, creaking and clattering, shaking a bit from side to side as it went. In the lost lands there were no thickets to cut through, no rivers to cross. Desolation lay before them on all sides, seemingly endless. From time to time they saw a grove of trees, gnarled and twisted all together, limbs heavy with swollen fruit with skin the color of indigo, shining. From time to time they clattered through a shallow, rocky stream, none deeper than ankle level. From time to time vast patches of white fungus blanketed the desolate gray earth. Yet all these things were rare. Mostly there was only the emptiness, the shuddering dead plains all around them, and the winds. The winds were terrible in the lost lands. They blew constantly, and they were cold and bitter, and sometimes they smelled of ash, and sometimes they seemed to howl and shriek like some poor doomed soul.

At last they had come far enough so Gray Alys could see the end of the lost lands: another line of mountains far, far north of them, a vague bluish-white line across the gray horizon. They could travel for weeks and not reach those distant peaks, Gray Alys knew, yet the lost lands were so flat and so empty that even now they could make them out, dimly.

At dusk Gray Alys and Boyce made their camp, just

beyond a grove of the curious tortured trees they had glimpsed on their journey north. The trees gave them a partial respite from the fury of the wind, but even so they could hear it, keening and pulling at them, twisting their fire into wild suggestive shapes.

"These lands are lost indeed," Gray Alys said as they ate.

"They have their own beauty," Boyce replied. He impaled a chunk of meat on the end of his long knife, and turned it above the fire. "Tonight, if the clouds pass, you will see the lights rippling above the northern mountains, all purple and gray and maroon, twisting like curtains caught in this endless wind."

"I have seen those lights before," said Gray Alys.

"I have seen them many times," Boyce said. He bit off a piece of meat, pulling at it with his teeth, and a thin line of grease ran down from the corner of his mouth. He smiled.

"You come to the lost lands often," Gray Alys said.

Boyce shrugged. "I hunt."

"Does anything live here?" asked Gray Alys. "Live amidst all this desolation?"

"Oh yes," Boyce replied. "You must have eyes to find it, you must know the lost lands, but it is there. Strange twisted beasts never seen beyond the mountains, things out of legends and nightmares, enchanted things and accursed things, things whose flesh is impossibly rare and impossibly delicious. Humans, too, or things that are almost human. Werefolk and changelings and gray shapes that walk only by twilight, shuffling things half-living and half-dead." His smile was gentle and taunting. "But you are Gray Alys, and all this you must know. It is said you came out of the lost lands yourself once, long ago."

"It is said," Gray Alys answered.

"We are alike, you and I," Boyce replied. "I love the town, the people, song and laughter and gossip. I savor the comforts of my house, good food and good wine. I relish the players who come each fall to the high keep and perform for the Lady Melange. I like fine clothes and jewels and soft, pretty women. Yet part of me is only at home here, in the lost lands, listening to the wind, watching the shadows warily each dusk, dreaming things the townfolk never dare." Full dark had fallen by then. Boyce lifted his knife and pointed north, to where dim lights had begun to glow faintly against the mountains. "See there, Gray Alys. See how the lights shimmer and shift. You can see shapes in them if you watch long enough. Men and women and things that are neither, moving against the darkness. Their voices are carried by the wind. Watch and listen. There are great dramas in those lights, plays grander and stranger than any ever performed on the Lady's stage. Do you hear? Do you see?"

Gray Alys sat on the hard-packed earth with her legs crossed and her gray eyes unreadable, watching in silence. Finally she spoke. "Yes," she said, and that was all.

Boyce sheathed his long knife and came around the campfire—it had died now to a handful of dim reddish embers—to sit beside her. "I knew you would see," he said. "We are alike, you and I. We wear the flesh of the city, but in our blood the cold wind of the lost lands is blowing always. I could see it in your eyes, Gray Alys."

She said nothing; she sat and watched the lights, feeling the warm presence of Boyce beside her. After a time he put an arm about her shoulders, and Gray Alys did not protest. Later, much later, when the fire had gone entirely dark and the night had grown cold, Boyce reached out and cupped her chin within his hand and turned her face to his. He kissed her, once, gently, full upon her thin lips.

And Gray Alys woke, as if from a dream, and pushed him back upon the ground and undressed him with sure, deft hands and took him then and there. Boyce let her do it all. He lay upon the chill hard ground with his hands clasped behind his head, his eyes dreamy and his lips curled up in a lazy, complacent smile, while Gray Alys rode him, slowly at first, then faster and faster, building to a shuddering climax. When she came her body went stiff and she threw her head back; her mouth opened, as if to cry out, but no sound came forth. There was only the wind, cold and wild, and the cry it made was not a cry of pleasure.

The next day dawned chill and overcast. The sky was full of thin, twisted gray clouds that raced before them faster than clouds ought to race. What light filtered through seemed wan and colorless. Boyce walked beside the wagon while Gray Alys drove it forward at a leisurely pace. "We are close now," Boyce told her. "Very close."

"Yes."

Boyce smiled up at her. His smile had changed since they had become lovers. It was fond and mysterious, and more than a bit indulgent. It was a smile that presumed. "Tonight," he told her.

"The moon will be full tonight," Gray Alys said.

Boyce smiled and pushed the hair from his eyes and said nothing.

Well before dusk, they drew up amidst the ruins of some nameless town long forgotten even by those who dwelled in the lost lands. Little remained to disturb the sweeping emptiness, only a huddle of broken masonry, forlorn and pitiful. The vague outlines of town walls could still be discerned, and one or two chimneys remained standing jagged and half-shattered, gnawing at the horizon like rotten black teeth. No shelter was to be found here, no life. When Gray Alys had fed her horses, she wandered through the ruins, but found little. No pottery, no rusted blades, no books. Not even bones. Nothing at all to hint of the people who had once lived here, if people they had been.

The lost lands had sucked the life out of this place, and blown away even the ghosts, so not a trace of memory remained. The shrunken sun was low on the horizon, obscured by scuttling clouds, and the scene spoke to her with the wind's voice, cried out in loneliness and despair. Gray Alys stood for a long time, alone, watching the sun sink while her thin tattered cloak billowed behind her and the cold wind bit through into her soul. Finally she turned away and went back to the wagon.

Boyce had built a fire, and he sat in front of it, mulling some wine in a copper pot, adding spices from time to time. He smiled his new smile for Gray Alys when she looked at him. "The wind is cold," he said. "I thought a hot drink would make our meal more pleasant."

Gray Alys glanced away towards the setting sun, then back at Boyce. "This is not the time or the place for pleasure, Boyce. Dusk is all but upon us, and soon the full moon shall rise."

"Yes," said Boyce. He ladled some of the hot wine into his cup, and tried a swallow. "No need to rush off hunting, though," he said, smiling lazily. "The wolf will come to us. Our scent will carry far in this wind, in this emptiness, and the smell of fresh meat will bring him running."

Gray Alys said nothing. She turned away from him and climbed the three wooden steps that led up to the interior of her wagon. Inside she lit a brazier carefully, and watched the light shift and flicker against the weathered gray wallboards and the pile of furs on which she slept. When the light had grown steady, Gray Alys slid back a wall panel, and stared at the long row of tattered garments that hung on pegs within the narrow closet. Cloaks and capes and billowing loose shirts, strangely cut gowns and suits that clung like a second skin from head to toe, leather and fur and feathers. She hesitated briefly, then reached in and chose a great cloak made of a thousand long silver feathers, each one tipped delicately with black. Removing her simple cloth cloak, Gray Alys fastened the flowing feathered garment at her neck. When she turned it billowed all about her, and the dead air inside the wagon stirred and briefly seemed alive before the feathers settled and stilled once again. Then Gray Alys bent and opened a huge oaken chest, bound in iron and leather. From within she drew out a small box. Ten rings rested against worn gray felt, each set with a long, curving silver claw instead of a stone. Gray Alys donned them methodically, one ring to each finger, and when she rose and clenched her fists, the claws shone dimly and menacingly in the light from the brazier.

Outside, it was twilight. Boyce had not prepared any food, Gray Alys noted as she took her seat across the fire from where the pale-haired ranger sat quaffing his hot wine.

"A beautiful cloak," Boyce observed amiably.

"Yes," said Gray Alys.

"No cloak will help you when *he* comes, though."

Gray Alys raised her hand, made a fist. The silver claws caught the firelight. Gleamed.

"Ah," said Boyce. "Silver.

"Silver," agreed Gray Alys, lowering her hand.

"Still," Boyce said. "Others have come against him, armed with silver. Silver swords, silver knives, arrows tipped with silver. They are dust now, all those silvered warriors. He gorged himself on their flesh."

Gray Alys shrugged.

Boyce stared at her speculatively for a time, then smiled and went back to his wine. Gray Alys drew her cloak more tightly about herself to keep out the cold wind. After a while, staring off into the far distance, she saw lights moving against the northern mountains. She remembered the stories that she had seen there, the tales that Boyce had conjured for her from that play of colored shadows. They were grim and terrible stories. In the lost lands, there was no other kind.

At last another light caught her eye. A spreading dimness in the east, wan and ominous. Moonrise.

Gray Alys stared calmly across the dying campfire. Boyce had begun to change.

She watched his body twist as bone and muscle changed within, watched his pale white hair grow longer and longer, watched his lazy smile turn into a wide red grin that split his face, saw the canines lengthen and the tongue come lolling out, watched the wine cup fall as his hands melted and writhed and became paws. He started to say something once, but no words came out, only a low, coarse snarl of laughter, half-human and half-animal. Then he threw back his head and howled, and he ripped at his clothing until it lay in tatters all about him and he was Boyce no longer. Across the fire from Gray Alys the wolf stood, a great shaggy white beast, half again the size of an ordinary wolf, with a savage red slash of a mouth and glowing scarlet eyes. Gray Alys stared into those eyes as she rose and shook the dust from her feathered cloak. They were knowing eyes, cunning, wise. Inside those eyes she saw a smile, a smile that presumed.

A smile that presumed too much.

The wolf howled once again, a long wild sound that melted into the wind. And then he leapt, straight across the embers of the fire he had built.

Gray Alys threw her arms out, her cloak bunched in her hands, and changed.

Her change was faster than his had been, over almost as soon as it begun, but for Gray Alys it lasted an eternity. First there was the strange choking, clinging feeling as the cloak adhered to her skin, then dizziness and a curious liquid weakness as her muscles began to run and flow and reshape themselves. And finally exhilaration, as the power rushed into her and came coursing through

her veins, a wine fiercer and hotter and wilder than the
poor stuff Boyce had mulled above their fire.

She beat her vast silvery wings, each pinion tipped
with black, and the dust stirred and swirled as she rose
up into the moonlight, up to safety high above the white
wolf's bound, up and up until the ruins shrunk to insignificance far beneath her. The wind took hold of her,
caressed her with trembling icy hands, and she yielded
herself to it and soared. Her great wings filled with the
dread melody of the lost lands, carrying her higher and
higher. Her cruel curving beak opened and closed and
opened again, though no sound came forth. She wheeled
across the sky, drunken with flight. Her eyes, sharper
than any human eyes could be, saw far into the distance,
spied out the secrets of every shadow, glimpsed all the
dying and half-dead things that stirred and shambled
across the barren face of the lost lands. The curtains of
light to the north danced before her, a thousand times
brighter and more gorgeous than they had been before,
when she had only the dim eyes of the little thing called
Gray Alys to perceive them with. She wanted to fly to
them, to soar north and north and north, to cavort among
those lights, shredding them into glowing strips with her
talons.

She lifted her talons as if in challenge. Long and wick-
edly curved they were, and razor sharp, and the moonlight flashed along their length, pale upon the silver. And
she remembered then, and she wheeled about in a great
circle, reluctantly, and turned away from the beckoning
lights of the northlands. Her wings beat and beat again,
and she began to descend, shrieking down through the
night air, plunging toward her prey.

She saw him far beneath her, a pale white shape hur-
tling away from the wagon, away from the fire, seeking
safety in the shadows and the dark places. But there was
no safety in the lost lands. He was strong and untiring,
and his long powerful legs carried him forward in a

steady swift lope that ate up the miles as if they were nothing. Already he had come a long way from their camp. But fast as he was, she was faster. He was only a wolf, after all, and she was the wind itself.

She descended in a dead silence, cutting through the wind like a knife, silver talons outstretched. But he must have spied her shadow streaking towards him, etched clear by the moonlight, for as she closed he spurted forward wildly, driven by fear. It was useless. He was running full out when she passed above him, raking him with her talons. They cut through fur and twisted flesh like ten bright silver swords, and he broke stride and staggered and went down.

She beat her wings and circled overhead for another pass, and as she did the wolf regained his feet and stared up at her terrible silhouette dark against the moon, his eyes brighter now than ever, turned feverish by fear. He threw back his head and howled a broken bloody howl that cried for mercy.

She had no mercy in her. Down she came, and down, talons drenched with blood, her beak open to rend and tear. The wolf waited for her, and leapt up to meet her dive, snarling, snapping. But he was no match for her. She slashed at him in passing, evading him easily, opening five more long gashes that quickly welled with blood.

The next time she came around he was too weak to run, too weak to rise against her. But he watched her turn and descend, and his huge shaggy body trembled just before she struck.

Finally his eyes opened, blurred and weak. He groaned and moved feebly. It was daylight, and he was back in the camp, lying beside the fire. Gray Alys came to him when she heard him stir, knelt, and lifted his head. She held a cup of wine to his lips until he had drunk his fill. When Boyce lay back again, she could see the wonder in his eyes, the surprise that he still lived. "You knew," he said hoarsely. "You knew . . . what I was."

"Yes," said Gray Alys. She was herself once more; a slender, small, somehow ageless woman with wide gray eyes, clad in faded cloth. The feathered cloak was hung away, the silver claws no longer adorned her fingers.

Boyce tried to sit up, winced at the pain, and settled back on to the blanket she had laid beneath him. "I thought . . . thought I was dead," he said.

"You were close to dead," Gray Alys replied.

"Silver," he said bitterly. "Silver cuts and burns so."

"Yes."

"But you saved me," he said, confused.

"I changed back to myself, and brought you back, and tended you."

Boyce smiled, though it was only a pale ghost of his old smile. "You change at will," he said wonderingly. "Ah, there is a gift I would kill for, Gray Alys!"

She said nothing.

"It was too open here," he said. "I should have taken you elsewhere. If there had been cover . . . buildings, a forest, anything . . . then you should not have had such an easy time with me."

"I have other skins," Gray Alys replied. "A bear, a cat. It would not have mattered."

"Ah," said Boyce. He closed his eyes. When he opened them again, he forced a twisted smile. "You were beautiful, Gray Alys. I watched you fly for a long time before I realized what it meant, and began to run. It was hard to tear my eyes from you. I knew you were the doom of me, but still I could not look away. So beautiful. All smoke and silver, with fire in your eyes. The last time, as I watched you swoop towards me, I was almost glad. Better to perish at the hands of she who is so terrible and fine, I thought, than by some dirty little swordsman with his sharpened silver stick."

"I am sorry," said Gray Alys.

"No," Boyce said quickly. "It is better that you saved me. I will mend quickly, you will see. Even silver wounds bleed but briefly. Then we will be together."

"You are still weak," Gray Alys told him. "Sleep."

"Yes," said Boyce. He smiled at her, and closed his eyes.

Hours had passed when Boyce finally woke again. He was much stronger, his wounds all but mended. But when he tried to rise, he could not. He was bound in place, spreadeagled, hands and feet tied securely to stakes driven into the hard gray earth.

Gray Alys watched him make the discovery, heard him cry out in alarm. She came to him, held up his head, and gave him more wine.

When she moved back, his head twisted around wildly, staring at his bonds, and then at her. "What have you done?" he cried.

Gray Alys said nothing.

"Why?" he asked. "I do not understand, Gray Alys. *Why?* You saved me, tended me, and now I am bound."

"You would not like my answer, Boyce."

"The moon!" he said wildly. "You are afraid of what might happen tonight, when I change again." He smiled, pleased to have figured it out. "You are being foolish. I would not harm you, not now, after what has passed between us, after what I know. We belong together, Gray Alys. We are alike, you and I. We have watched the lights together, and I have seen you fly! We must have trust between us! Let me loose."

Gray Alys frowned and sighed and gave no other answer.

Boyce stared at her uncomprehending. "Why?" he asked again. "Untie me, Alys, let me prove the truth of my words. You need not fear me."

"I do not fear you, Boyce," she said sadly.

"Good," he said eagerly. "Then free me, and change

with me. Become a great cat tonight, and run beside me, hunt with me. I can lead you to prey you never dreamed of. There is so much we can share. You have felt how it is to change, you know the truth of it, you have tasted the power, the freedom, seen the lights from a beast's eyes, smelled fresh blood, gloried in a kill. You know . . . the freedom . . . the intoxication of it . . . all the . . . you know . . ."

"I know," Gray Alys acknowledged.

"Then free me! We are meant for one another, you and I. We will live together, love together, hunt together."

Gray Alys shook her head.

"I do not understand," Boyce said. He strained upward wildly at his bonds, and swore, then sunk back again. "Am I hideous? Do you find me evil, unattractive?"

"No."

"Then what?" he said bitterly. "Other women have loved me, have found me handsome. Rich, beautiful ladies, the finest in the land. All of them have wanted me, even when they knew."

"But you have never returned that love, Boyce," she said.

"No," he admitted. "I have loved them after a fashion. I have never betrayed their trust, if that is what you think. I find my prey here, in the lost lands, not from among those who care for me." Boyce felt the weight of Gray Alys' eyes, and continued. "How could I love them more than I did?" he said passionately. "They could know only half of me, only the half that lived in town and loved wine and song and perfumed sheets. The rest of me lived out here, in the lost lands, and knew things that they could never know, poor soft things. I told them so, those who pressed me hard. To join with me wholly they must run and hunt beside me. Like you. Let me go, Gray Alys. Soar for me, watch me run. Hunt with me."

Gray Alys rose and sighed. "I am sorry, Boyce. I would spare you if I could, but what must happen must happen.

Had you died last night, it would have been useless. Dead things have no power. Night and day, black and white, they are weak. All strength derives from the realm between, from twilight, from shadow, from the terrible place between life and death. From the gray, Boyce, from the gray."

He wrenched at his bonds again, savagely, and began to weep and curse and gnash his teeth. Gray Alys turned away from him and sought out the solitude of her wagon. There she remained for hours, sitting alone in the darkness and listening to Boyce swear and cry out to her with threats and pleadings and professions of love. Gray Alys stayed inside until well after moonrise. She did not want to watch him change, watch his humanity pass from him for the last time.

At last his cries had become howls, bestial and abandoned and full of pain. That was when Gray Alys finally reemerged. The full moon cast a wan pale light over the scene. Bound to the hard ground, the great white wolf writhed and howled and struggled and stared at her out of hungry scarlet eyes.

Gray Alys walked toward him calmly. In her hand was the long silver skinning knife, its blade engraved with fine and graceful runes.

When he finally stopped struggling, the work went more quickly, but still it was a long and bloody night. She killed him the instant she was done, before the dawn came and changed him and gave him back a human voice to cry his agony. Then Gray Alys hung up the pelt and brought out tools and dug a deep, deep grave in the packed cold earth. She piled stones and broken pieces of masonry on top of it, to protect him from the things that roamed the lost lands, the ghouls and the carrion crows and the other creatures that did not flinch at dead flesh. It took her most of the day to bury him, for the ground was very hard indeed, and even as she worked she knew it was a futile labor.

And when at last the work was done, and dusk had almost come again, she went once more into her wagon, and returned wearing the great cloak of a thousand silver feathers, tipped with black. Then she changed, and flew, and flew, a fierce and tireless flight, bathed in strange lights and wedded to the dark. All night she flew beneath a full and mocking moon, and just before dawn she cried out once, a shrill scream of despair and anguish that rang and keened on the sharp edge of the wind and changed its sound forever.

Perhaps Jerais was afraid of what she might give him, for he did not return to Gray Alys alone. He brought two other knights with him, a huge man all in white whose shield showed a skull carved out of ice, and another in crimson whose sigil was a burning man. They stood at the door, helmeted and silent, while Jerais approached Gray Alys warily. "Well?" he demanded.

Across her lap was a wolfskin, the pelt of some huge massive beast, all white as mountain snow. Gray Alys rose and offered the skin to Blue Jerais, draping it across his outstretched arm. "Tell the Lady Melange to cut herself, and drip her own blood onto the skin. Do this at moonrise when the moon is full, and then the power will be hers. She need only wear the skin as a cloak, and will the change thereafter. Day or night, full moon or no moon, it makes no matter."

Jerais looked at the heavy white pelt and smiled a hard smile. "A wolfskin, eh? I had not expected that. I thought perhaps a potion, a spell."

"No," said Gray Alys. "The skin of a werewolf."

"A werewolf?" Jerais' mouth twisted curiously, and there was a sparkle in his deep sapphire eyes. "Well, Gray Alys, you have done what the Lady Melange asked, but you have failed me. I did not pay you for success. Return my gem."

"No," said Gray Alys. "I have earned it, Jerais."

"I do not have what I asked for."

"You have what you wanted, and that is what I promised." Her gray eyes met his own without fear. "You thought my failure would help you get what you truly wanted, and that my success would doom you. You were wrong."

Jerais looked amused. "And what do I truly desire?"

"The Lady Melange," said Gray Alys. "You have been one lover among many, but you wanted more. You wanted all. You knew you stood second in her affections. I have changed that. Return to her now, and bring her the thing that she has bought."

That day there was bitter lamentation in the high keep on the mountain, when Blue Jerais knelt before the Lady Melange and offered her a white wolfskin. But when the screaming and the wailing and the mourning was done, she took the great pale cloak and bled upon it and learned the ways of change. It is not the union she desired, but it is a union nonetheless. So every night she prowls the battlements and the mountainside, and the townfolk say her howling is wild with grief.

And Blue Jerais, who wed her a month after Gray Alys returned from the lost lands, sits beside a madwoman in the great hall by day, and locks his doors by night in terror of his wife's hot red eyes, and does not hunt anymore, or laugh, or lust.

* * *

You can buy anything you might desire from Gray Alys. But it is better not to.

UNSOUND VARIATIONS

After they swung off the Interstate, the road became a narrow two-lane that wound a tortuous path through the mountains in a series of switchbacks, each steeper than the last. Peaks rose all around them, pine-covered and crowned by snow and ice, while swift cold waterfalls flashed by, barely seen, on either side. The sky was a bright and brilliant blue. It was exhilarating scenery, but it did nothing to lighten Peter's mood. He concentrated blindly on the road, losing himself in the mindless reflexes of driving.

As the mountains grew higher, the radio reception grew poorer, stations fading in and out with every twist in the road, until at last they could get nothing at all. Kathy went from one end of the band to the other, searching, and then back again. Finally she snapped off the radio in disgust. "I guess you'll just have to talk to me," she said.

Peter didn't need to look at her to hear the sharpness in her tone, the bitter edge of sarcasm that had long ago replaced fondness in her voice. She was looking for an argument, he knew. She was angry about the radio, and she resented him dragging her on this trip, and most of all she resented being married to him. At times, when he was feeling very sorry for himself, he did not even blame her. He had not turned out to be much of a bargain as a husband; a failed writer, failed journalist, failing businessman, depressed and depressing. He was still a lively sparring partner, however. Perhaps that was why she tried to provoke fights so often. After all the blood had been let, one or both of them would start crying, and then they would usually make love, and life would be pleasant for an hour or two. It was about all they had left.

Not today, though. Peter lacked the energy, and his mind was on other things. "What do you want to talk about?" he asked her. He kept his tone amicable and his eyes on the road.

"Tell me about these clowns we're going to visit," she said.

"I did. They were my teammates on the chess team, back when I was at Northwestern."

"Since when is chess a team sport anyway?" Kathy said. "What'd you do, vote on each move?"

"No. In chess, a team match is really a bunch of individual matches. Usually four or five boards, at least in college play. There's no consultation or anything. The team that wins the most individual games wins the match point. The way it works—"

"I get it," she said sharply. "I may not be a chessplayer, but I'm not stupid. So you and these other three were the Northwestern team?"

"Yes and no," Peter said. The Toyota was straining; it wasn't used to grades this steep, and it hadn't been adjusted for altitude before they took off from Chicago. He drove carefully. They were up high enough now to come across icy patches, and snow drifting across the road.

"Yes and no," Kathy said sarcastically. "What does that mean?"

"Northwestern had a big chess club back then. We played in a lot of tournaments—local, state, national. Sometimes we fielded more than one team, so the line-up was a bit different every tournament. It depended on who could play and who couldn't, who had a midterm, who'd played in the last match—lots of things. We four were Northwestern's B team in the North American Intercollegiate Team Championships, ten years ago this week. Northwestern hosted that tournament, and I ran it, as well as playing."

"What do you mean *B team*?"

Peter cleared his throat and eased the Toyota around a sharp curve, gravel rattling against the underside of the car as one wheel brushed the shoulder. "A school wasn't limited to just one team," he said. "If you had the money and a lot of people who wanted to play, you could enter several. Your best four players would make up your A team, the real contender. The second four would be the B team, and so on." He paused briefly, and continued with a faint note of pride in his voice. "The nationals at Northwestern were the biggest ever held, up to that time, although of course that record has since been broken. We set a second record, though, that still stands. Since the tournament was on our home grounds, we had lots of players on hand. We entered six teams. No other school has ever had more than four in the nationals, before or after." The record still brought a smile to his face. Maybe it wasn't much of a record, but it was the only one he had, and it was *his*. Some people lived and died without ever setting a record of any kind, he reflected silently. Maybe he ought to tell Kathy to put his on his tombstone: HERE LIES PETER K. NORTEN. HE FIELDED SIX TEAMS. He chuckled.

"What's so funny?"

"Nothing."

She didn't pursue it. "So you ran this tournament, you say?"

"I was the club president and the chairman of the local committee. I didn't direct, but I put together the bid that brought the nationals to Evanston, made all the preliminary arrangements. And I organized all six of our teams, decided who would play on each one, appointed the team captains. But during the tournament itself I was only the captain of the B team."

She laughed. "So you were a big deal on the second-string. It figures. The story of our life."

Peter bit back a sharp reply, and said nothing. The Toyota swerved around another hairpin, and a vast Colorado mountain panorama opened up in front of them. It left him strangely unmoved.

After a while Kathy said, "When did you stop playing chess?"

"I sort of gave it up after college. Not a conscious decision, really. I just kind of drifted out of it. I haven't played a game of tournament chess in almost nine years. I'm probably pretty rusty by now. But back then I was fairly good."

"How good is fairly good?"

"I was rated as a Class A player, like everyone else on our B team."

"What does that mean?"

"It means my USCF rating was substantially higher than that of the vast majority of tournament chess players in the country," he said. "And the tournament players are generally much better than the unrated wood-pushers you encounter in bars and coffee houses. The ratings went all the way down to Class E. Above Class A you had Experts, and Masters, and Senior Masters at the top, but there weren't many of them."

"Three classes above you?"

"Yes."

"So you might say, at your very best, you were a fourth-class chess player."

At that Peter did look over at her. She was leaning back in her seat, a faint smirk on her face. "Bitch," he said. He was suddenly angry.

"Keep your eyes on the road!" Kathy snapped.

He wrenched the car around the next turn hard as he could, and pressed down on the gas. She hated it when he drove fast. "I don't know why the hell I try to talk to you," he said.

"My husband, the big deal," she said. She laughed. "A fourth-class chess player playing on the junior varsity team. And a fifth-rate driver, too."

"Shut up," Peter said furiously. "You don't know what the hell you're talking about. Maybe we were only the B team, but we were good. We finished better than anyone had any right to expect, only a half-point behind Northwestern A. And we almost scored one of the biggest upsets in history."

"Do tell."

Peter hesitated, already regretting his words. The memory was important to him, almost as important as his silly little record. *He* knew what it meant, how close they had come. But she'd never understand, it would only be another failure for her to laugh at. He should never have mentioned it.

"Well?" she prodded. "What about this great upset, dear? Tell me."

It was too late, Peter realized. She'd never let him drop it now. She'd needle him and needle him until he told her. He sighed and said, "It was ten years ago this week. The nationals were always held between Christmas and New Year's, when everyone was on break. An eight-round team tournament, two rounds a day. All of our teams did moderately well. Our A team finished seventh overall."

"You were on the B team, sweetie."

Peter grimaced. "Yes. And we were doing best of all, up to a point. Scored a couple nice upsets late in the tournament. It put us in a strange position. Going into the last round, the University of Chicago was in first place, alone, with a 6–1 match record. They'd beaten our A team, among their other victims, and they were defending national champions. Behind them were three other schools at 5½–1½. Berkeley, the University of Massachusetts, and—I don't know, someone else, it doesn't matter. What mattered was that all three of those teams had already played U of C. Then you had a whole bunch of teams at 5–2, including both Northwestern A and B. One of the 5–2 teams had to be paired up against Chicago in the final round. By some freak, it turned out to be us. Everyone thought that cinched the tournament for them.

"It was really a mismatch. They were the defending champions, and they had an awesome team. Three Masters and an Expert, if I recall. They outrated us by hundreds of points on every board. It should have been easy. It wasn't.

"It was never easy between U. of C. and Northwestern. All through my college years, we were the two big midwestern chess powers, and we were arch-rivals. The Chicago captain, Hal Winslow, became a good friend of mine, but I gave him a lot of headaches. Chicago *always* had a stronger team than we did, but we gave them fits nonetheless. We met in the Chicago Intercollegiate League, in state tournaments, in regional tournaments, and several times in the nationals. Chicago won most of those, but not all. We took the city championship away from them once, and racked up a couple other big upsets too. And that year, in the nationals, we came *this* close"—he held up two fingers, barely apart—"to the biggest upset of all." He put his hand and back on the wheel, and scowled.

"Go on," she said. "I'm breathless to know what comes next."

Peter ignored the sarcasm. "An hour into the match, we had half the tournament gathered around our tables, watching. Everyone could see that Chicago was in trouble. We clearly had superior positions on two boards, and we were even on the other two.

"It got better. I was playing Hal Winslow on third board. We had a dull, even position, and we agreed to a draw. And on fourth board, E.C. gradually got outplayed and finally resigned in a dead lost position."

"E.C.?"

"Edward Colin Stuart. We all called him E.C. Quite a character. You'll meet him up at Bunnish's place."

"He lost?"

"Yes."

"This doesn't sound like such a thrilling upset to me," she said dryly. "Though maybe by your standards, it's a triumph."

"E.C. lost," Peter said, "but by that time, Delmario had clearly busted his man on board two. The guy dragged it out, but finally we got the point, which tied the score at 1½–1½, with one game in progress. And we were winning that one. It was incredible. Bruce Bunnish was our first board. A real turkey, but a half-decent player. He was another A player, but he had a trick memory. Photographic. Knew every opening backwards and forwards. He was playing Chicago's big man." Peter smiled wryly. "In more ways than one. A Master name of Robinson Vesselere. Damn strong chessplayer, but he must have weighed four hundred pounds. He'd sit there absolutely immobile as you played him, his hands folded on top of his stomach, little eyes squinting at the board. And he'd crush you. He should have crushed Bunnish easily. Hell, he was rated four hundred points higher.

But that wasn't what had gone down. With that trick memory of his, Bunnish had somehow outplayed Vesselere in an obscure variation of the Sicilian. He was swarming all over him. An incredible attack. The position was as complicated as anything I'd ever seen, very sharp and tactical. Vesselere was counterattacking on the queenside, and he had some pressure, but nothing like the threats Bunnish had on the kingside. It was a won game. We were all sure of that."

"So you almost won the championship?"

"No," Peter said. "No, it wasn't that. If we'd won the match, we would have tied Chicago and a few other teams at 6–2, but the championship would have gone to someone else, some team with 6½ match points. Berkeley maybe, or Mass. It was just the upset itself we wanted. It would have been *incredible*. They were the best college chess team in the country. We weren't even the best at our school. If we had beaten them, it would have caused a sensation. And we came so close."

"What happened?"

"Bunnish blew it," Peter said sourly. "There was a critical position. Bunnish had a sac. A sacrifice, you know? A double piece sac. Very sharp, but it would have busted up Vesselere's kingside and driven his king out into the open. But Bunnish was too timid for that. Instead he kept looking at Vesselere's queenside attack, and finally he made some feeble defensive move. Vesselere shifted another piece to the queenside, and Bunnish defended again. Instead of following up his advantage, he made a whole series of cautious little adjustments to the position, and before long his attack had dissipated. After that, of course, Vesselere overwhelmed him." Even now, after ten years, Peter felt the disappointment building inside him as he spoke. "We lost the match 2½–1½, and Chicago won another national championship. Afterwards, even Vesselere admitted that he was busted if Brucie had played knight takes pawn at the critical point. *Damn.*"

"You lost. That's what this amounts to. You lost."

"We came close."

"Close only counts in horseshoes and grenades," Kathy said. "You lost. Even then you were a loser, dear. I wish I'd known."

"*Bunnish* lost, damn it," Peter said. "It was just like him. He had a Class A rating, and that trick memory, but as a team player he was worthless. You don't know how many matches he blew for us. When the pressure was on, we could always count on Bunnish to fold. But that time was the worst, that game against Vesselere. I could have killed him. He was an arrogant asshole, too."

Kathy laughed. "Isn't this arrogant asshole the one we are now speeding to visit?"

"It's been ten years. Maybe he's changed. Even if he hasn't, well, he's a multimillionaire asshole now. Electronics. Besides, I want to see E.C. and Steve again, and Bunnish said they'd be there."

"Delightful," said Kathy. "Well, rush on, then. I wouldn't want to miss this. It might be my only opportunity to spend four days with an asshole millionaire and three losers."

Peter said nothing, but he pressed down on the accelerator, and the Toyota plunged down the mountain road, faster and faster, rattling as it picked up speed. Down and down, he thought, down and down. Just like my goddamned life.

Four miles up Bunnish's private road, they finally came within sight of the house. Peter, who still dreamed of buying his own house after a decade of living in cheap apartments, took one look and knew he was gazing at a three million dollar piece of property. There were three levels, all blending into the mountainside so well you hardly noticed them, built of natural wood and native stone and tinted glass. A huge solar greenhouse was the most conspicuous feature. Beneath the house, a four-car garage was sunk right into the mountain itself.

Peter pulled into the last empty spot, between a brand new silver Cadillac Seville that was obviously Bunnish's, and an ancient rusted VW Beetle that was obviously not. As he pulled the key from the ignition, the garage doors shut automatically behind them, blocking out daylight and the gorgeous mountain vistas. The door closed with a resounding metallic clang.

"Someone knows we're here," Kathy observed.

"Get the suitcases," Peter snapped.

To the rear of the garage they found the elevator, and Peter jabbed the topmost of the two buttons. When the elevator doors opened again, it was on a huge living room. Peter stepped out and stared at a wilderness of potted plants beneath a vaulting skylight, at thick brown carpets, fine wood panelling, bookcases packed with leather-bound volumes, a large fireplace, and Edward Colin Stuart, who rose from a leather-clad armchair across the room when the elevator arrived.

"E.C.," Peter said, setting down his suitcase. He smiled.

"Hello, Peter," E.C. said, coming toward them quickly. They shook hands.

"You haven't changed a goddamned bit in ten years," Peter said. It was true. E.C. was still slender and compact, with a bushy head of sandy blond hair and a magnificent handlebar mustache. He was wearing jeans and a tapered purple shirt, with a black vest, and he seemed just as he had a decade ago: brisk, trim, efficient. "Not a damn bit," Peter repeated.

"More's the pity," E.C. said. "One is supposed to change, I believe." His blue eyes were as unreadable as ever. He turned to Kathy, and said, "I'm E.C. Stuart."

"Oh, pardon," Peter said. "This is my wife, Kathy."

"Delighted," she said, taking his hand and smiling at him.

"Where's Steve?" Peter asked. "I saw his VW down in the garage. Gave me a start. How long has he been driving that thing now? Fifteen years?"

"Not quite," E.C. said. "He's around somewhere, probably having a drink." His mouth shifted subtly when he said it, telling Peter a good deal more than his words did.

"And Bunnish?"

"Brucie has not yet made his appearance. I think he was waiting for you to arrive. You probably want to settle in to your rooms."

"How do we find them, if our host is missing?" Kathy asked dryly.

"Ah," said E.C., "you haven't been acquainted with the wonders of Bunnishland yet. Look." He pointed to the fireplace.

Peter would have sworn that there had been a painting above the mantle when they had entered, some sort of surreal landscape. Now there was a large rectangular screen, with words on it, vivid red against black. WELCOME, PETER. WELCOME, KATHY. YOUR SUITE IS ON THE SECOND LEVEL, FIRST DOOR. PLEASE MAKE YOURSELF COMFORTABLE.

Peter turned. "How . . . ?"

"No doubt triggered by the elevator," E.C. said. "I was greeted the same way. Brucie is an electronics genius, remember. The house is full of gadgets and toys. I've explored a bit." He shrugged. "Why don't you two unpack and then wander back? I won't go anywhere."

They found their rooms easily enough. The huge, tiled bath featured an outside patio with a hot tub, and the suite had its own sitting room and fireplace. Above it was an abstract painting, but when Kathy closed the room door it faded away and was replaced by another message: I HOPE YOU FIND THIS SATISFACTORY.

"Cute guy, this host of ours," Kathy said, sitting on the edge of the bed. "Those TV screens or whatever they are better not be two-way. I don't intend to put on any show for any electronic voyeur."

Peter frowned. "Wouldn't be surprised if the house *was* bugged. Bunnish was always a strange sort."

"How strange?"

"He was hard to like," Peter said. "Boastful, always bragging about how good he was as a chessplayer, how smart he was, that sort of thing. No one really believed him. His grades were good, I guess, but the rest of the time he seemed close to dense. E.C. has a wicked way with hoaxes and practical jokes, and Bunnish was his favorite victim. I don't know how many laughs we had at his expense. Bunnish was kind of a goon in person, too. Pudgy, round-faced with big cheeks like some kind of chipmunk, wore his hair in a crew cut. He was in ROTC. I've never seen anyone who looked more ridiculous in a uniform. He never dated."

"Gay?"

"No, not hardly. Asexual is closer to it." Peter looked around the room and shook his head. "I can't imagine how Bunnish made it this big. Him of all people." He sighed, opened his suitcase, and started to unpack. "I might have believed it of Delmario," he continued. "Steve and Bunnish were both in Tech, but Steve always seemed much brighter. We all thought he was a real whiz-kid. Bunnish just seemed like an arrogant mediocrity."

"Fooled you," Kathy said. She smiled sweetly. "Of course, he's not the only one to fool you, is he? Though perhaps he was the first."

"Enough," Peter said, hanging the last of his shirts in the closet. "Come on, let's get back downstairs. I want to talk to E.C."

They had no sooner stepped out of their suite when a voice hailed them. "*Pete?*"

Peter turned, and the big man standing in the doorway

down the hall smiled a blurry smile at him. "Don't you recognize me, Peter?"

"Steve?" Peter said wonderingly.

"Sure, hey, who'd you think?" He stepped out of his own room, a bit unsteadily, and closed the door behind him. "This must be the wife, eh? Am I right?"

"Yes," Peter said. "Kathy, this is Steve Delmario. Steve, Kathy." Delmario came over and pumped her hand enthusiastically, after clapping Peter roundly on the back. Peter found himself staring. If E.C. had scarcely changed at all in the past ten years, Steve had made up for it. Peter would never have recognized his old teammate on the street.

The old Steve Delmario had lived for chess and electronics. He was a fierce competitor, and he loved to tinker things together, but he was frustratingly uninterested in anything outside his narrow passions. He had been a tall, gaunt youth with incredibly intense eyes held captive behind coke-bottle lenses in heavy black frames. His black hair had always been either ruffled and unkempt or—when he treated himself to one of his do-it-yourself haircuts—grotesquely butchered. He was equally careless about his clothing, most of which was Salvation Army chic minus the chic: baggy brown pants with cuffs, ten-year-old shirts with frayed collars, a zippered and shapeless grey sweater he wore everywhere. Once E.C. had observed that Steve Delmario looked like the last man left alive on earth after a nuclear holocaust, and for almost a semester thereafter the whole club had called Delmario, "the last man on earth." He took it with good humor. For all his quirks, Delmario had been well-liked.

The years had been cruel to him, however. The coke-bottle glasses in the black frames were the same, and the clothes were equally haphazard—shabby brown cords, a short-sleeved white shirt with three felt-tip pens in the pocket, a faded sweater-vest with every button buttoned, scuffed hush puppies—but the rest had all changed.

Steve had gained about fifty pounds, and he had a bloated, puffy look about him. He was almost entirely bald, nothing left of the wild black hair but a few sickly strands around his ears. And his eyes had lost their fever-ish intensity, and were filled instead with a fuzziness that Peter found terribly disturbing. Most shocking of all was the smell of alcohol on his breath. E.C. had hinted at it, but Peter still found it difficult to accept. In college, Steve Delmario had never touched anything but an infre-quent beer.

"It is good to see you again," Peter said, though he was no longer quite sure that was true. "Shall we go on downstairs? E.C. is waiting."

Delmario nodded. "Sure, sure, let's do it." He clapped Peter on the back again. "Have you seen Bunnish yet? Damn, this is some place he's got, isn't it? You seen those message screens? Clever, real clever. Never would have figured Bunnish to go as far as this, not our old Funny Bunny, eh?" He chuckled. "I've looked at some of his patents over the years, you know. Real ingenious. Real fine work. And from *Bunnish*. I guess you just never know, do you?"

The living room was awash with classical music when they descended the spiral stair. Peter didn't recognize the composition; his own tastes had always run to rock. But classical music had been one of E.C.'s passions, and he was sitting in an armchair now, eyes closed, listening.

"Drinks," Delmario was saying. "I'll fix us all some drinks. You folks must be thirsty. Bunny's got a wet bar right behind the stair here. What do you want?"

"What are the choices?" Kathy asked.

"Hell, he's got anything you could think of," said Delmario.

"A Beefeater martini, then," she said. "Very dry."

Delmario nodded. "Pete?"

"Oh," said Peter. He shrugged. "A beer, I guess."

Delmario went behind the stair to fix up their drinks,

and Kathy arched her eyebrows at him. "Such refined tastes," she said. "A *beer*!"

Peter ignored her and went over to sit beside E.C. Stuart. "How the hell did you find the stereo?" he asked. "I don't see it anywhere." The music seemed to be coming right out of the walls.

E.C. opened his eyes, gave a quirkish little smile, and brushed one end of his mustache with a finger. "The message screen blabbed the secret to me," he said. "The controls are built into the wall back over there," nodding, "and the whole system is concealed. It's voice activated, too. Computerized. I *told* it what album I wanted to hear."

"Impressive," Peter admitted. He scratched his head. "Didn't Steve put together a voice-activated stereo back in college?"

"Your beer," Delmario said. He was standing over them, holding out a cold bottle of Heineken. Peter took it, and Delmario—with a drink in hand—seated himself on the ornate tiled coffee table. "I had a system," he said. "Real crude, though. Remember, you guys used to kid me about it."

"You bought a good cartridge, as I recall," E.C. said, "but you had it held by a tone-arm you made out of a bent coathanger."

"It worked," Delmario protested. "It was voice-activated too, like you said, but real primitive. Just on and off, that's all, and you had to speak real loud. I figured I could improve on it after I got out of school, but I never did." He shrugged. "Nothing like this. This is real sophisticated."

"I've noticed," E.C. said. He craned up his head slightly and said, in a very loud clear voice, "I've had enough music now, thank you." The silence that followed was briefly startling. Peter couldn't think of a thing to say.

Finally E.C. turned to him and said, all seriously, "How did Bunnish get you here, Peter?"

Peter was puzzled. "Get me here? He just invited us. What do you mean?"

"He paid Steve's way, you know," E.C. said. "As for me, I turned down this invitation. Brucie was never one of my favorite people, you know that. He pulled strings to change my mind. I'm with an ad agency in New York. He dangled a big account in front of them, and I was told to come here or lose my job. Interesting, eh?"

Kathy had been sitting on the sofa, sipping her martini and looking bored. "It sounds as though this reunion is important to him," she observed.

E.C. stood up. "Come here," he said. "I want to show you something. The rest of them rose obediently, and followed him across the room. In a shadowy corner surrounded by bookcases, a chessboard had been set up, with a game in progress. The board was made of squares of light and dark wood, painstakingly inlaid into a gorgeous Victorian table. The pieces were ivory and onyx. "Take a look at that," E.C. said.

"That's a beautiful set," Peter said, admiringly. He reached down to lift the Black queen for a closer inspection, and grunted in surprise. The piece wouldn't move.

"Tug away," E.C. said. "It won't do you any good. I've tried. The pieces are glued into position. Every one of them."

Steve Delmario moved around the board, his eyes blinking behind his thick glasses. He set his drink on the table and sank into the chair behind the White pieces. "The position," he said, his voice a bit blurry with drink. "I know it."

E.C. Stuart smiled thinly and brushed his mustache. "Peter," he said, nodding toward the chessboard. "Take a good look."

Peter stared, and all of a sudden it came clear to him, the position on the board became as familiar as his own

features in a mirror. "The game," he said. "From the
nationals. This is the critical position from Bunnish's
game with Vesselere."

E.C. nodded. "I thought so. I wasn't sure."

"Oh, *I'm* sure," Delmario said loudly. "How the hell
could I *not* be sure? This is right where Bunny blew it,
remember? He played king to knight one, instead of the
sac. Cost us the match. Me, I was sitting right next to
him, playing the best damned game of chess I ever
played. Beat a Master, and what good did it do? Not a
damn bit of good, thanks to Bunnish." He looked at the
board and glowered. "Knight takes pawn, that's all he's
got to play, busts Vesselere wide open. Check, check,
check, check, got to be a mate there somewhere."

"You were never able to find it, though, Delmario,"
Bruce Bunnish said from behind them.

None of them had heard him enter. Peter started like
a burglar surprised while copping the family silver.

Their host stood in the doorway a few yards distant.
Bunnish had changed, too. He had lost weight since college, and his body looked hard and fit now, though he
still had the big round cheeks that Peter remembered.
His crew cut had grown out into a healthy head of brown
hair, carefully styled and blow-dried. He wore large,
tinted glasses and expensive clothes. But he was still Bunnish. His voice was loud and grating, just as Peter
remembered it.

Bunnish strolled over to the chessboard almost casually. "You analyzed that position for weeks afterward,
Delmario," he said. "You never found the mate."

Delmario stood up. "I found a dozen mates," he said.

"Yes," Bunnish said, "but none of them were forced.
Vesselere was a Master. He wouldn't have played into
any of your so-called mating lines."

Delmario frowned and took a drink. He was going to
say something else—Peter could see him fumbling for
the words—but E.C. stood up and took away his chance.

"Bruce," he said, holding out his hand. "Good to see you again. How long has it been?"

Bunnish turned and smiled superciliously. "Is that another of your jokes, E.C.? You know how long it has been, and I know how long it has been, so why do you ask? Norten knows, and Delmario knows. Maybe you're asking for Mrs. Norten." He looked at Kathy. "Do you know how long it has been?"

She laughed. "I've heard."

"Ah," said Bunnish. He swung back to face E.C. "Then we all know, so it must be another of your jokes, and I'm not going to answer. Do you remember how you used to phone me at three in the morning, and ask me what time it was? Then I'd tell you, and you'd ask me what I was doing calling you at that hour?"

E.C. frowned and lowered his hand.

"Well," said Bunnish, into the awkward silence that followed, "no sense standing here around this stupid chessboard. Why don't we all go sit down by the fireplace, and talk." He gestured. "Please."

But when they were seated, the silence fell again. Peter took a swallow of beer and realized that he was more than just ill-at-ease. A palpable tension hung in the air. "Nice place you've got here, Bruce," he said, hoping to lighten the atmosphere.

Bunnish looked around smugly. "I know," he said. "I've done awfully well, you know. Awfully well. You wouldn't believe how much money I have. I hardly know what to do with it all." He smiled broadly and fatuously. "And how about you, my friends? Here I am boasting once again, when I ought to be listening to all of you recount your own triumphs." Bunnish looked at Peter. "You first, Norten. You're the captain, after all. How have you done?"

"All right," Peter said, uncomfortably. "I've done fine. I own a bookstore."

"A *bookstore*! How wonderful! I recall that you always

wanted to be in publishing, though I rather thought you'd be writing books instead of selling them. Whatever happened to those novels you were going to write, Peter? Your literary career?"

Peter's mouth was very dry. "I ... things change, Bruce. I haven't had much time for writing." It sounded so feeble, Peter thought. All at once, he was desperately wishing he was elsewhere.

"No time for writing," echoed Bunnish. "A pity, Norten. You had such promise."

"He's still promising," Kathy put in sharply. "You ought to hear him promise. He's been promising as long as I've known him. He never writes, but he does promise."

Bunnish laughed. "Your wife is very witty," he said to Peter. "She's almost as funny as E.C. was, back in college. You must enjoy being married to her a great deal. I recall how fond you were of E.C.'s little jokes." He looked at E.C. "Are you still a funny man, Stuart?"

E.C. looked annoyed. "I'm hysterical," he said, in a flat voice.

"Good," said Bunnish. He turned to Kathy and said, "I don't know if Peter has told you all the stories about old E.C., but he really played some amazing pranks. Hilarious man, that's our E.C. Stuart. Once, when our chess team had won the city championship, he had a girlfriend of his call up Peter and pretend to be an AP reporter. She interviewed him for an hour before he caught on."

Kathy laughed. "Peter is sometimes a bit slow," she said.

"Oh, that was nothing. Normally I was the one E.C. liked to play tricks on. I didn't go out much, you know. Deathly afraid of girls. But E.C. had a hundred girlfriends, all of them gorgeous. One time he took pity on me and offered to fix me up on a blind date. I accepted eagerly, and when the girl arrived on the corner where we were supposed to meet, she was wearing dark glasses and carrying a cane. Tapping. You know."

Steve Delmario guffawed, tried to stifle his laughter, and nearly choked on his drink. "Sorry," he wheezed, "sorry."

Bunnish waved casually. "Oh, go ahead, laugh. It *was* funny. The girl wasn't really blind, you know, she was a drama student who was rehearsing a part in a play. But it took me all night to find that out. I was such a fool. And that was only one joke. There were hundreds of others."

E.C. looked somber. "That was a long time ago. We were kids. It's all behind us now, Bruce."

"Bruce?" Bunnish sounded surprised. "Why, Stuart, that's the first time you've ever called me *Bruce*. You *have* changed. You were the one who started calling me Brucie. God, how I hated that name! Brucie, Brucie, Brucie, I *loathed* it. How many times did I ask you to call me Bruce? How many times? Why, I don't recall. I do recall, though, that after three years you finally came up to me at one meeting and said that you'd thought it over, and now you agreed that I was right, that Brucie was not an appropriate name for a Class A chessplayer, a twenty-year old, an officer in ROTC. Your exact words. I remember the whole speech, E.C. It took me so by surprise that I didn't know what to say, so I said, '*Good, it's about time!*' And then you grinned, and said that Brucie was out, that you'd never call me Brucie again. From now on, you said, you'd call me *Bunny*."

Kathy laughed, and Delmario choked down an explosive outburst, but Peter only felt cold all over. Bunnish's smile was genial enough, but his tone was pure iced venom as he recounted the incident. E.C. did not look amused either. Peter took a swallow of his beer, casting about for some ploy to get the conversation onto a different track. "Do any of you still play?" he heard himself blurt out.

They all looked at him. Delmario seemed almost befuddled. "Play?" he said. He blinked down at his empty glass.

"Help yourself to a refill," Bunnish told him. "You know where it is." He smiled at Peter as Delmario moved off to the bar. "You mean chess, of course."

"Chess," Peter said. "You remember chess. Odd little pastime played with black and white pieces and lots of two-faced clocks." He looked around. "Don't tell me we've *all* given it up?"

E.C. shrugged. "I'm too busy. I haven't played a rated game since college."

Delmario had returned, ice cubes clinking softly in a tumbler full of bourbon. "I played a little after college," he said, "but not for the last five years." He sat down heavily, and stared into the cold fireplace. "Those were my bad years. Wife left me, I lost a couple jobs. Bunny here was way ahead of me. Every goddamn idea I came up with, he had a patent on it already. Got so I was useless. That was when I started to drink." He smiled, and took a sip. "Yeah," he said. "Just then. And I stopped playing chess. It all comes out, you know, it all comes out over the board. I was losing, losing lots. To all these *fish*, God, I tell you, I couldn't take it. Rating went down to Class B." Delmario took another drink, and looked at Peter. "You need something to play good chess, you know what I'm saying? A kind of . . . hell, I don't know . . . a kind of arrogance. Self-confidence. It's all wrapped up with ego, that kind of stuff, and I didn't have it any more, whatever it was. I used to have it, but I lost it all. I had bad luck, and I looked around one day and it was gone, and my chess was gone with it. So I quit." He lifted the tumbler to his lips, hesitated, and drained it all. Then he smiled for them. "Quit," he repeated. "Gave it up. Chucked it away. Bailed out." He chuckled, and stood up, and went off to the bar again.

"I play," Bunnish said forcefully. "I'm a Master now."

Delmario stopped in midstride, and fixed Bunnish with such a look of total loathing that it could have killed. Peter saw that Steve's hand was shaking.

"I'm very happy for you, Bruce," E.C. Stuart said. "Please do enjoy your Mastership, and your money, and Bunnishland." He stood and straightened his vest, frowning. "Meanwhile, I'm going to be going."

"Going?" said Bunnish. "Really, E.C., so soon? Must you?"

"Bunnish," E.C. said, "you can spend the next four days playing your little ego games with Steve and Peter, if you like, but I'm afraid I am not amused. You always were a pimple-brain, and I have better things to do with my life than to sit here and watch you squeeze out ten-year-old pus. Am I making myself clear?"

"Oh, perfectly," Bunnish said.

"Good," said E.C. He looked at the others. "Kathy, it was nice meeting you. I'm sorry it wasn't under better circumstances. Peter, Steve, if either of you comes to New York in the near future, I hope you'll look me up. I'm in the book."

"E.C., don't you . . ." Peter began, but he knew it was useless. Even in the old days, E.C. Stuart was headstrong. You could never talk him into or out of anything.

"Goodbye," he said, interrupting Peter. He went briskly to the elevator, and they watched the wood-panelled doors close on him.

"He'll be back," Bunnish said after the elevator had gone.

"I don't think so," Peter replied.

Bunnish got up, smiling broadly. Deep dimples appeared in his large, round cheeks. "Oh, but he will, Norten. You see, it's my turn to play the little jokes now, and E.C. will soon find that out."

"What?" Delmario said.

"Don't you fret about it, you'll understand soon enough," Bunnish said. "Meanwhile, please do excuse me. I have to see about dinner. You all must be ravenous. I'm making dinner myself, you know. I sent my servants away, so we could have a nice private reunion." He looked at his watch, a heavy gold Swiss. "Let's all meet in the dining room in, say, an hour. Everything should be ready by then. We can talk some more. About life. About chess." He smiled, and left.

Kathy was smiling too. "Well," she said to Peter after Bunnish had left the room, "this is all vastly more entertaining than I would have imagined. I feel as if I just walked into a Harold Pinter play."

"Who's that?" Delmario asked, resuming his seat.

Peter ignored him. "I don't like any of this," he said. "What the hell did Bunnish mean about playing a joke on us?"

He didn't have to wait long for an answer. While Kathy went to fix herself another martini, they heard the elevator again, and turned expectantly toward the doors. E.C. stepped out frowning. "Where is he?" he said in a hard voice.

"He went to cook dinner," Peter said. "What is it? He said something about a joke. . . ."

"Those garage doors won't open," E.C. said. "I can't get my car out. There's no place to go without it. We must be fifty miles from the nearest civilization."

"I'll go down and ram out with my VW," Delmario said helpfully. "Like in the movies."

"Don't be absurd," E.C. said. "That door is stainless steel. There's no way you're going to batter it down." He scowled and brushed back one end of his mustache. "Battering down Brucie, however, is a much more viable proposition. Where the hell is the kitchen?"

Peter sighed. "I wouldn't if I were you, E.C.," he said. "From the way he's been acting, he'd just love a chance to clap you in jail. If you touch him, it's assault, you know that."

"Phone the police," Kathy suggested.

Peter looked around. "Now that you mention it, I don't see a phone anywhere in this room. Do you?" Silence. "There was no phone in our suite, either, that I recall."

"Hey!" Delmario said. "That's right, Pete, you're right."

E.C. sat down. "He appears to have us checkmated," he said.

"The exact word," said Peter. "Bunnish is playing some kind of game with us. He said so himself. A joke."

"Ha ha," said E.C. "What do you suggest we do, then? Laugh?"

Peter shrugged. "Eat dinner, talk, have our reunion, find out what the hell Bunnish wants with us."

"Win the game, guys, that's what we do," Delmario said.

E.C. stared at him. "What the hell does that mean?"

Delmario sipped his bourbon and grinned. "Peter said Bunny was playing some kind of game with us, right? OK, fine. Let's play. Let's beat him at this goddamned game, whatever the hell it is." He chuckled. "Hell, guys, this is the Funny Bunny we're playing. Maybe he is a Master, I don't give a good goddamn, he'll still find a way to blow it in the end. You know how it was. Bunnish *always* lost the big games. He'll lose this one, too."

"I wonder," said Peter. "I wonder."

Peter brought another bottle of Heineken back to the suite with him, and sat in a deck chair on the patio drinking it while Kathy tried out the hot tub.

"This is nice," she said from the tub. "Relaxing. Sensuous, even. Why don't you come on in?"

"No, thanks," Peter said.

"We ought to get one of these."

"Right. We could put it in our living room. The people in the apartment downstairs would love it." He took a swallow of beer and shook his head.

"What are you thinking about?" Kathy asked.

Peter smiled grimly. "Chess, believe it or not."

"Oh? Do tell."

"Life is a lot like chess," he said.

She laughed. "Really? I'd never noticed, somehow."

Peter refused to let her needling get to him. "All a matter of choices. Every move you face choices, and every choice leads to different variations. It branches and then branches again, and sometimes the variation you pick isn't as good as it looked, isn't sound at all. But you don't know that until your game is over."

"I hope you'll repeat this when I'm out of the tub," Kathy said. "I want to write it all down for posterity."

"I remember, back in college, how many possibilities life seemed to hold. Variations. I knew, of course, that I'd only live one of my fantasy lives, but for a few years there, I had them all, all the branches, all the variations. One day I could dream of being a novelist, one day I would be a journalist covering Washington, the next— oh, I don't know, a politician, a teacher, whatever. My dream lives. Full of dream wealth and dream women. All the things I was going to do, all the places I was going to live. They were mutually exclusive, of course, but since I didn't have any of them, in a sense I had them all. Like when you sit down at a chessboard to begin a game, and you don't know what the opening will be. Maybe it will be a Sicilian, or a French, or a Ruy Lopez. They all co-exist, all the variations, until you start making the moves. You always dream of winning, no matter what line you choose, but the variations are still . . . different." He drank some more beer. "Once the game begins, the possibilities narrow and narrow and narrow, the other variations fade, and you're left with what you've got—a position half of your own making, and half chance, as embodied by that stranger across the board. Maybe you've got a good game, or maybe you're in trouble, but in any case there's just that one position to work from. The might-have-beens are gone."

Kathy climbed out of the hot tub and began towelling herself off. Steam rose from the water, and moved gently around her. Peter found himself looking at her almost with tenderness, something he had not felt in a long time. Then she spoke, and ruined it. "You missed your calling," she said, rubbing briskly with the towel. "You should have taken up poster-writing. You have a knack for poster profundity. You know, like, '*I am not in this world to live up to your expect—*'"

"Enough," Peter said. "How much blood do you have to draw, damn it?"

Kathy stopped and looked at him. She frowned. "You're really down, aren't you?" she said.

Peter stared off at the mountains, and did not bother to reply.

The concern left her voice as quickly as it had come. "Another depression, huh? Drink another beer, why don't you? Feel sorry for yourself some more. By midnight you'll have worked yourself up to a good crying jag. Go on."

"I keep thinking of that match," Peter said.

"Match?"

"In the nationals," he said. "Against Chicago. It's weird, but I keep having this funny feeling, like . . . like it was right there that it all started to go bad. We had a chance to do something big, something special. But it slipped away from us, and nothing has been right since. A losing variation, Kathy. We picked a losing variation, and we've been losing ever since. All of us."

Kathy sat down on the edge of the tub. "All of you?"

Peter nodded. "Look at us. I failed as a novelist, failed as a journalist, and now I've got a failing bookstore. Not to mention a bitch wife. Steve is a drunk who couldn't even get together enough money to pay his way out here. E.C. is an aging account executive with an indifferent track record, going nowhere. Losers. You said it, in the car."

She smiled. "Ah, but what about our host? Bunnish lost bigger than any of you, and he seems to have won everything since."

"Hmmmm," said Peter. He sipped thoughtfully at his beer. "I wonder. Oh, he's rich enough, I'll give you that. But he's got a chessboard in his living room with the pieces glued into position, so he can stare every day at the place he went wrong in a game played ten years ago. That doesn't sound like a winner to me."

She stood up, and shook loose her hair. It was long and auburn and it fell around her shoulders gorgeously, and Peter remembered the sweet lady he had married eight years ago, when he was a bright young writer working hard on his first novel. He smiled. "You look nice," he said.

Kathy seemed startled. "You *are* feeling morose," she said. "Are you sure you don't have a fever?"

"No fever. Just a memory, and a lot of regrets."

"Ah," she said. She walked back toward their bedroom, and snapped the towel at him in passing. "C'mon, captain. Your team is going to be waiting, and all this heavy philosophy has given me quite an appetite."

The food was fine, but the dinner was awful.

They ate thick slabs of rare prime rib, with big baked potatoes and lots of fresh vegetables. The wine looked expensive and tasted wonderful. Afterwards, they had their choice of three desserts, plus fresh-ground coffee and several delicious liqueurs. Yet the meal was strained and unpleasant, Peter thought. Steve Delmario was in pretty bad shape even before he came to the table, and while he was there he drank wine as if it were water, getting louder and fuzzier in the process. E.C. Stuart was coldly quiet, his fury barely held in check behind an icy, aloof demeanor. And Bunnish thwarted every one of Peter's attempts to move conversation to safe neutral ground.

His genial expansiveness was a poor mask for gloating, and he insisted on opening old wounds from their college years. Every time Peter recounted an anecdote that was amusing or harmless, Bunnish smiled and countered with one that stank of hurt and rejection.

Finally, over coffee, E.C. could stand no more of it. "Pus," he said loudly, interrupting Bunnish. It was about the third word he'd permitted himself the entire meal. "Pus and more pus. Bunnish, what's the point? You've brought us here: You've got us trapped here, with you. Why? So you can prove that we treated you shabbily back in college? Is that the idea? If so, fine. You've made your point. You were treated shabbily. I am ashamed, I am guilty. Mea culpa, mea culpa, mea maxima culpa. Now let's end it. It's over."

"Over?" said Bunnish, smiling. "Perhaps it is. But you've changed E.C. Back when I was the butt of your jokes, you'd recount them for weeks. *Over* wasn't so final then, was it? And what about my game with Vesselere in the nationals? When that was over, did we forget it? Oh, no, we did not. That game was played in December, you'll recall. I heard about it until I graduated in May. At every meeting. That game was *never* over for me. Delmario liked to show me a different checkmate every time I saw him. Our dear captain refrained from playing me in any league matches for the rest of the year. And you, E.C., you liked to greet me with, 'Say, Bunny, lost any big ones lately?' You even reprinted that game in the club newsletter, and mailed it in to *Chess Life*. No doubt all this seems like ancient history to you. I have this trick memory, though. I can't forget things quite so easily. I remember it all. I remember the way Vesselere sat there, with his hands folded on his stomach, never moving, staring at me out of those itty bitty eyes of his. I remember the way he moved his pieces, very carefully, very daintily, lifting each one between thumb and forefinger. I remember wandering into the halls between moves, to get a drink of water, and seeing Norten over by the wall charts, talking to Mavora from the A team. You know what he was saying? He was gesturing with his hands, all worked up, and he was telling him, *He's going to blow it, damn it, he's going to blow it!* Isn't that right, Peter? And Les looked over at me as I passed, and said, *Lose this one and your ass is grass, Bunny!* He was another endearing soul. I remember all the people who kept coming to look at my game. I remember Norten standing in the corner with Hal Winslow, the two mighty captains, talking heatedly. Winslow was all rumpled and needed a shave and he had his clipboard, and he was trying to figure out who'd finish where if we won, or tied, or lost. I remember how it felt when I tipped over my king, too. I remember the way Delmario started kicking the wall, the way E.C. shrugged and glanced up at the ceiling, and the way Peter came over and just said *Bunnish!* and shook his head. You see? My trick memory is as tricky as ever, and I haven't forgotten a thing. And especially I haven't forgotten that game. I can recite all the moves to you right now, if you'd like."

"Shit," said Steve Delmario. "Only one important move to recite, Bunny. Knight takes pawn, that's the move you ought to recite. The sac, the winning sac, the one you didn't play. I forget what kind of feeble thing you did instead."

Bunnish smiled. "My move was king to knight one," he said. "To protect my rook pawn. I'd castled long, and Vesselere was threatening to snatch it."

"Pawn, shmawn," said Delmario. "You had him busted. The sac would have gutted that whale like nobody's goddamned business. What a laugh that would have been. The bunny rabbit beating the whale. Old Hal Winslow would have been so shocked he would have dropped his clipboard. But you blew it, guarding some diddlysquat little pawn. You blew it."

"So you told me," said Bunnish. "And told me, and told me."

"Look," Peter said, "I don't see the sense in rehashing all of this. Steve is drunk, Bruce. You can see that. He doesn't know what he's saying."

"He knows exactly what he's saying, Norten," Bunnish replied. He smiled thinly and removed his glasses. Peter was startled by his eyes. The hatred there was almost tangible, and there was something else as well, something old and bitter and somehow *trapped*. The eyes passed lightly over Kathy, who was sitting quietly amidst all the old hostility, and touched Steve Delmario, Peter Norten, and E.C. Stuart each in turn, with vast loathing and vast amusement.

"Enough," Peter said, almost pleadingly.

"NO!" said Delmario. The drink had made him belligerent. "It's not enough, it'll never be enough, goddamn it. Get out a set, Bunny! I dare you! We'll analyze it right now, go over the whole thing again, I'll show you how you pissed it all away." He pulled himself to his feet.

"I have a better idea," said Bunnish. "Sit down, Delmario."

Delmario blinked uncertainly, and then fell back into his chair.

"Good," said Bunnish. "We'll get to my idea in a moment, but first I'm going to tell you all a story. As Archie Bunker once said, revenge is the best way to get even. But it isn't revenge unless the victim knows. So I'm going to tell you. I'm going to tell you exactly how I've ruined your lives."

"Oh, come off it!" E.C. said.

"You never did like stories, E.C.," Bunnish said. "Know why? Because when someone tells a story, they become the center of attention. And you always needed to be the center of attention, wherever you were. Now you're not the center of anything, though. How does it feel to be insignificant?"

E.C. gave a disgusted shake of his head and poured himself more coffee. "Go on, Bunnish," he said. "Tell your story. You have a captive audience."

"I do, don't I?" Bunnish smiled. "All right. It all begins with that game. Me and Vesselere. I did *not* blow that game. It was never won."

Delmario made a rude noise.

"I know," Bunnish continued, unperturbed, "now, but I did not know then. I thought that you were right. I'd thrown it all away, I thought. It ate at me. For years and years, more years than you would believe. Every night I went to sleep replaying that game in my head. That game blighted my entire life. It became an obsession. I wanted only one thing—another chance. I wanted to go back, somehow, to choose another line, to make different moves, to come out a winner. I'd picked the wrong variation, that was all. I knew that if I had another chance, I'd do better. For more than fifty years, I worked toward that end, and that end alone."

Peter swallowed a mouthful of cold coffee hastily and said, "What? Fifty years? You mean five, don't you?"

"Fifty," Bunnish repeated.

"You are insane," said E.C.

"No," said Bunnish. "I am a genius. Have you ever heard of time travel, any of you?"

"It doesn't exist," said Peter. "The paradoxes . . ."

Bunnish waved him quiet. "You're right and you're wrong, Norten. It exists, but only in a sort of limited fashion. Yet that is enough. I won't bore you with mathematics none of you can understand. Analogy is easier. Time is said to be the fourth dimension, but it differs from the other three in one conspicuous way—our consciousness moves along it. From past to present only, alas. Time itself does not flow, no more than, say, width can flow. Our minds flicker from one instant of time to the next. This analogy was my starting point. I reasoned that if consciousness can move in one direction, it can move in the other direction as well. It took me fifty years to work out the details, however, and make what I call a *flashback* possible.

"That was in my first life, gentlemen, a life of failure and ridicule and poverty. I tended my obsession and did what I had to so as to keep myself fed. And I hated you, each of you, for every moment of those fifty years. My bitterness was inflamed as I watched each of you succeed, while I struggled and failed. I met Norten once, twenty years after college, at an autographing party. You were so patronizing. It was then that I determined to ruin you, all of you.

"And I did. What is there to say? I perfected my device at the age of seventy-one. There is no way to move matter through time, but *mind*, mind is a different issue. My device would send my mind back to any point in my own lifetime that I chose, superimpose my consciousness with all of its memories on the consciousness of my earlier self. I could take nothing with me, of course." Bunnish smiled and tapped his temple significantly. "But I still had my photographic memory. It was more than enough. I memorized things I would need to know in my new life, and I flashed back to my youth. I was given another chance, a chance to make some different moves in the game of life. I did."

Steve Delmario blinked. "Your body," he said blurrily. "What happened to your body, huh?"

"An interesting question. The kick of the flashback kills the would-be time-traveller. The body, that is. The timeline itself goes on, however. At least my equations indicate that it should. I've never been around to witness it. Meanwhile, changes in the past create a new, variant timeline."

"Oh, alternate tracks," Delmario said. He nodded. "Yeah."

Kathy laughed. "I can't believe I'm sitting here listening to all this," she said. "And that *he*"—she pointed to Delmario—"is taking it seriously."

E.C. Stuart had been looking idly at the ceiling, with a disdainful, faintly tolerant smile on his face. Now he straightened. "I agree," he said to Kathy. "I am not so gullible as you were, Bruce," he told Bunnish, "and if you are trying to get some laughs by having us swallow this crock of shit, it isn't going to work."

Bunnish turned to Peter. "Captain, what's your vote?"

"Well," said Peter carefully, "all this is a little hard to credit, Bruce. You spoke of the game becoming an obsession with you, and I think that's true. I think you ought to be talking to a professional about this, not to us."

"A professional what?" Bunnish said.

Peter fidgeted uncomfortably. "You know. A shrink or a counselor."

Bunnish chuckled. "Failure hasn't made you any less patronizing," he said. "You were just as bad in the bookstore, in that line where you turned out to be a successful novelist."

Peter sighed. "Bruce, can't you see how pathetic these delusions of yours are? I mean, you've obviously been quite a success, and none of us have done as well, but even that wasn't enough for you, so you've constructed all these elaborate fantasies about how *you* have been the one behind our various failures. Vicarious, imaginary revenge."

"Neither vicarious nor imaginary, Norten," Bunnish snapped. "I can tell you exactly how I did it."

"Let him tell his stories, Peter," E.C. said. "Then maybe he'll let us out of this funny farm."

"Why thank you, E.C.," Bunnish said. He looked around the table with smug satisfaction, like a man about to live out a dream he has cherished for a long, long time. Finally he fastened on Steve Delmario. "I'll start with you," he said, "because in fact, I *did* start with you. You were easy to destroy, Delmario, because you were

always so limited. In the original timeline, you were as
wealthy as I am in this one. While I spent my life per-
fecting my flashback device, you made fast fortunes in
the wide world out there. Electronic games at first, later
more basic stuff, home computers, that sort of thing. You
were born for that, and you were the best in the business,
inspired and ingenious.

"When I flashed back, I simply took your place. Before
using my device, I studied all your early little games,
your cleverest ideas, the basic patents that came later
and made you so rich. And I memorized all of them,
along with the dates on which you'd come up with each
and every one. Back in the past, armed with all this fore-
knowledge, it was child's play to beat you to the punch.
Again and again. In those early years, Delmario, didn't
it ever strike you as strange the way I anticipated every
one of your small brainstorms? I'm living *your* life,
Delmario."

Delmario's hand had begun to tremble as he listened.
His face looked dead. "God damn you," he said. "God
damn you."

"Don't let him get to you, Steve," E.C. put in. "He's
just making this up to see us squirm. It's all too absurd
for words."

"But it's *true*," Delmario wailed, looking from E.C. to
Bunnish and then, helplessly, at Peter. Behind the thick
lenses his eyes seemed wild. "Peter, what he said—all
my ideas—he was always ahead of me, he, he, I *told* you,
he—"

"Yes," Peter said firmly, "and you told Bruce too, when
we were talking earlier. Now he's just using your fears
against you."

Delmario opened his mouth, but no words came out.

"Have another drink," Bunnish suggested.

Delmario stared at Bunnish as if he were about to leap
up and strangle him. Peter tensed himself to intervene.

But then, instead, Delmario reached out for a half-empty wine bottle, and filled his glass sloppily.

"This is contemptible, Bruce," E.C. said.

Bunnish turned to face him. "Delmario's ruin was easy and dramatic," he said. "You were more difficult, Stuart. He had nothing to live for but his work, you see, and when I took that away from him, he just collapsed. I only had to anticipate him a half-dozen times before all of his belief in himself was gone, and he did the rest himself. But you, E.C., you had more resources."

"Go on with the fairy tale, Bunnish," E.C. said in a put-upon tone.

"Delmario's ideas had made me rich," Bunnish said. "I used the money against you. Your fall was less satisfying and less resounding than Delmario's. He went from the heights to the pits. You were only a moderate success to begin with, and I had to settle for turning you into a moderate failure. But I managed. I pulled strings behind the scenes to lose you a number of large accounts. When you were with Foote, Cone I made sure another agency hired away a copywriter named Allerd, just before he came up with a campaign that would have rebounded to your credit. And remember when you left that position to take a better-paying slot at a brand new agency? Remember how quickly that agency folded, leaving you without an income? That was me. I've given your career twenty or thirty little shoves like that. Haven't you ever wondered at how infallibly wrong most of your professional moves have been, Stuart? At your bad luck?"

"No," said E.C. "I'm doing well enough, thank you."

Bunnish smiled. "I played one other little joke on you, too. You can thank me for that case of herpes you picked up last year. The lady who gave it to you was well paid. I had to search for her for a good number of years until I found the right combination—an out-of-work actress who was young and gorgeous and precisely your type, yet sufficiently desperate to do just about anything, and gifted with an incurable venereal disease as well. How did you like her, Stuart? It's your fault, you know. I just put her in your path, you did the rest yourself. And I thought it was so fitting, after my blind date and all."

E.C.'s expression did not change. "If you think this is going to break me down or make me believe you, you're way off base. All this proves is that you've had me investigated, and managed to dig up some dirt on my life."

"Oh," said Bunnish. "Always so skeptical, Stuart. Scared that if you believe, you'll wind up looking foolish. Tsk." He turned toward Peter. "And you, Norten. You. Our fearless leader. You were the most difficult of all."

Peter met Bunnish's eyes and said nothing.

"I read your novel, you know," Bunnish said casually.

"I've never published a novel."

"Oh, but you have! In the original timeline, that is. Quite a success too. The critics loved it, and it even appeared briefly on the bottom of the *Times* bestseller list."

Peter was not amused. "This is so obvious and pathetic," he said.

"It was called *Beasts in a Cage*, I believe," Bunnish said.

Peter had been sitting and listening with contempt, humoring a sick, sad man. Now, suddenly, he sat upright as if slapped.

He heard Kathy suck in her breath. "My God," she said.

E.C. seemed puzzled. "Peter? What is it? You look . . ."

"No one knows about that book," Peter said. "How the hell did you find out? My old agent, you must have gotten the title from him. Yes. That's it, isn't it?"

"No," said Bunnish, smiling complacently.

"You're lying!"

"Peter, what is it?" said E.C. "Why are you so upset?"

Peter looked at him. "My book," he said. *"I . . . Beasts in a Cage* was . . ."

"There was such a book?"

"Yes," Peter said. He swallowed nervously, feeling confused and angry. "Yes, there was. I . . . after college. My first novel." He gave a nervous laugh. "I thought it would be the first. I had . . . had a lot of hopes. It was ambitious. A serious book, but I thought it had commercial possibilities as well. The circus. It was about the circus, you know how I was always fascinated by the circus. A metaphor for life, I thought, a kind of life, but very colorful too, and dying, a dying institution. I thought I could write the great circus novel. After college, I travelled with Ringling Brothers' Blue Show for a year, doing research. I was a butcher, I . . . that's what they call the vendors in the stands, you see. A year of research, and I took two years to write the novel. The central character was a boy who worked with the big cats. I finally finished it and sent it off to my agent, and less than three weeks after I'd gotten it into the mail, I, I . . ." He couldn't finish.

But E.C. understood. He frowned. "That circus bestseller? What was the title?"

"*Blue Show*," Peter said, the words bitter in his mouth. "By Donald Hastings Sullivan, some old hack who'd written fifty gothics and a dozen formula westerns, all under pen names. Such a book, from such a writer. No one could believe it. E.C., *I* couldn't believe it. It was *my* book, under a different title. Oh, it wasn't word-for-word. *Beasts in a Cage* was a lot better written. But the story, the background, the incidents, even a few of the character names . . . it was frightening. My agent never marketed my book. He said it was too much like *Blue Show* to be publishable, that no one would touch it. And even if I did get it published, he warned me, I would be labelled derivative at best, and a plagiarist at worst. It looked like a ripoff, he said. Three years of my life, and he called it a ripoff. We had words. He fired me, and I couldn't get another agent to take me on. I never wrote another book. The first one had taken too much out of me." Peter turned to Bunnish. "I destroyed my manuscript, burned every copy. No one knew about that book except my agent, me, and Kathy. How did you find out?"

"I told you," said Bunnish. "I read it."

"You damned liar!" Peter said. He scooped up a glass in a white rage, and flung it down the table at Bunnish's smiling face, wanting to obliterate that complacent grin, to see it dissolve into blood and ruin. But Bunnish ducked and the glass shattered against a wall.

"Easy, Peter," E.C. said. Delmario was blinking in owlish stupidity, lost in an alcoholic haze. Kathy was gripping the edge of the table. Her knuckles had gone white.

"Methinks our captain doth protest too much," Bunnish said, his dimples showing. "You know I'm telling the truth, Norten. I read your novel. I can recite the whole plot to prove it." He shrugged. "In fact, I did recite the whole plot. To Donald Hastings Sullivan, who wrote *Blue Show* while in my employ. I would have done it myself, but I had no aptitude for writing. Sully was glad for the chance. He got a handsome flat fee and we split the royalties, which were considerable."

"You son of a bitch," Peter said, but he said it without force. He felt his rage ebbing away, leaving behind it only a terrible sickly feeling, the certainty of defeat. He felt cheated and helpless and, all of a sudden, he realized that he believed Bunnish, believed every word of his preposterous story. "It's true, isn't it?" he said. "It is really true. You did it to me. You. You stole my words, my dreams, all of it."

Bunnish said nothing.

"And the rest of it," Peter said, "the other failures, those were all you too, weren't they? After *Blue Show*, when I went into journalism . . . that big story that evaporated on me, all my sources suddenly denying everything or vanishing, so it looked like I'd made it all up. The assignments that evaporated, all those lawsuits, plagiarism, invasion of privacy, libel, every time I turned around I was being sued. Two years, and they just about ran me out of the profession. But it wasn't bad luck, was it? It was you. You stole my *life.*"

"You ought to be complimented, Norten. I had to break you twice. The first time I managed to kill your literary career with *Blue Show,* but then while my back was turned you managed to become a terribly popular journalist. Prize-winning, well known, all of it, and by then it was too late to do anything. I had to flash back once more to get you, do everything all over."

"I ought to kill you, Bunnish," Peter heard himself say.

E.C. shook his head. "Peter," he said, in the tone of a man explaining something to a high-grade moron, "this is all an elaborate hoax. Don't take Bunny seriously."

Peter stared at his old teammate. "No, E.C. It's true. It's all true. Stop worrying about being the butt of a joke, and think about it. It makes sense. It explains everything that has happened to us."

E.C. Stuart made a disgusted noise, frowned, and fingered the end of his mustache.

"Listen to your captain, Stuart," Bunnish said.

Peter turned back to him. "Why? That's what I want to know. *Why?* Because we played jokes on you? Kidded you? Maybe we were rotten, I don't know, it didn't seem to be so terrible at the time. You brought a lot of it on yourself. But whatever we might have done to you, we never deserved this. We were your teammates, your friends."

Bunnish's smile curdled, and the dimples disappeared. "You were *never* my friends."

Steve Delmario nodded vigorously at that. "You're no friend of mine, Funny Bunny, I tell you that. Know what you are? A *wimp.* You were always a goddamn wimp, that's why nobody ever liked you, you were just a damn wimp loser with a crewcut. Hell, you think you were the only one ever got kidded? What about me, the ol' last man on earth, huh, what about that? What about the jokes E.C. played on Pete, on Les, on all the others?" He took a drink. "Bringing us here like this, that's another damn wimp thing to do. You're the same Bunny you always were. Wasn't enough to *do* something, you had to brag about it, let everybody know. And if somethin' went wrong, was never your fault, was it? You only lost 'cause the room was too noisy, or the lighting was bad, whatever." Delmario stood up. "You make me sick. Well, you screwed up all our lives maybe, and now you told us about it. Good for you. You had your damn wimp fun. Now let us out of here."

"I second that motion," said E.C.

"Why, I wouldn't think of it," Bunnish replied. "Not just yet. We haven't played any chess yet. A few games for old times' sake."

Delmario blinked, and moved slightly as he stood holding the back of his chair. "The *game*," he said, suddenly reminded of his challenge to Bunnish of a few minutes ago. "We were goin' to play over the game."

Bunnish folded his hands neatly in front of him on the table. "We can do better than that," he said. "I am a very fair man, you see. None of you ever gave me a chance, but I'll give one to you, to each of you. I've stolen your lives. Wasn't that what you said, Norten? Well, *friends,* I'll give you a shot at winning those lives back. We'll play a little chess. We'll replay the game, from the critical position. I'll take Vesselere's side and you can have mine. The three of you can consult, if you like, or I'll play you one by one. I don't care. All you have to do is beat me. Win the game you say I should have won, and I'll let you go, and give you anything you like. Money, property, a job, whatever."

"Go t' hell, wimp," Delmario said. "I'm not interested in your damn money."

Bunnish picked up his glasses from the table and donned them, smiling widely. "Or," he said, "if you prefer, you can win a chance to use my flashback device. You can go back then, anticipate me, do it all over, live the lives you were destined to live before I dealt myself in. Just think of it. It's the best opportunity you'll ever have, any of you, and I'm making it so *easy*. All you have to do is win a won game."

"Winning a won game is one of the hardest things in chess," Peter said sullenly. But even as he said it, his mind was racing, excitement stirring deep in his gut. It was a chance, he thought, a chance to reshape the ruins of his life, to make it come out right. To obliterate the wrong turnings, to taste the wine of success instead of the wormwood of failure, to avoid the mockery that his marriage to Kathy had become. Dead hopes rose like ghosts to dance again in the graveyard of his dreams. He had to take the shot, he knew. He *had* to.

Steve Delmario was there before him. "I can win that goddamned game," he boomed drunkenly. "I could win it with my eyes shut. You're on, Bunny. Get out a set, damn you!"

Bunnish laughed and stood up, putting his big hands flat on the tabletop and using them to push himself to his feet. "Oh no, Delmario. You're not going to have the excuse of being drunk when you lose. I'm going to crush you when you are cold stone sober. Tomorrow. I'll play you tomorrow."

Delmario blinked furiously. "Tomorrow," he echoed.

Later, when they were alone in their room, Kathy turned on him. "Peter," she said, "let's get out of here. Tonight. Now."

Peter was sitting before the fire. He had found a small chess set in the top drawer of his bedside table, and had set up the critical position from Vesselere-Bunnish to study it. He scowled at the distraction and said, "Get out? How the hell do you propose we do that, with our car locked up in that garage?"

"There's got to be a phone here somewhere. We could search, find it, call for help. Or just walk."

"It's December, and we're in the mountains miles from anywhere. We try to walk out of here and we could freeze to death. No." He turned his attention back to the chessboard and tried to concentrate.

"*Peter*," she said angrily.

He looked up again. "What?" he snapped. "Can't you see I'm busy?"

"We have to do *something*. This whole scene is insane. Bunnish needs to be locked up."

"He was telling the truth," Peter said.

Kathy's expression softened, and for an instant there was something like sorrow on her face. "I know," she said softly.

"You know," Peter mimicked savagely. "You know, do you? Well, do you know how it *feels*? That bastard is going to pay. He's responsible for every rotten thing that has happened to me. For all I know, he's probably responsible for you."

Kathy's lips moved only slightly, and her eyes moved not at all, but suddenly the sorrow and sympathy were gone from her face, and instead Peter saw familiar pity, well-honed contempt. "He's just going to crush you again," she said coldly. "He wants you to lust after this chance, because he intends to deny it to you. He's going to beat you, Peter. How are you going to like that? How are you going to live with it, afterwards?"

Peter looked down at the chess pieces. "That's what he intends, yeah. But he's a moron. This is a *won* position. It's only a matter of finding the winning line, the right variation. And we've got three shots at it. Steve goes first. If he loses, E.C. and I will be able to learn from his mistakes. I won't lose. I've lost everything else, maybe, but not this. This time I'm going to be a winner. You'll see."

"I'll see, all right," Kathy said. "You pitiful bastard."

Peter ignored her, and moved a piece. Knight takes pawn.

Kathy remained in the suite the next morning. "Go play your damn games if you like," she told Peter. "I'm going to soak in the hot tub, and read. I want no part of this."

"Suit yourself," Peter said. He slammed the door behind him, and thought once again what a bitch he'd married.

Downstairs, in the huge living room, Bunnish was setting up the board. The set he'd chosen was not ornate and expensive like the one in the corner, with its pieces glued into place. Sets like that looked good for decorative purposes, but were useless in serious play. Instead Bunnish had shifted a plain wooden table to the center of the room, and fetched out a standard tournament set: a vinyl board in green and white that he unrolled carefully, a well-worn set of Drueke pieces of standard Staunton design, cast in black and white plastic with lead weights in the bases, beneath the felt, to give them a nice heft. He placed each piece into position from memory, without once looking at the game frozen on the expensive inlaid board across the room. Then he began to set a double-faced chess clock. "Can't play without the clock, you know," he said, smiling. "I'll set it exactly the same as it stood that day in Evanston."

When everything was finished, Bunnish surveyed the board with satisfaction and seated himself behind Vesselere's Black pieces. "Ready?" he asked.

Steve Delmario sat down opposite him, looking pale and terribly hung-over. He was holding a big tumbler full of orange juice, and behind his thick glasses his eyes moved nervously. "Yeah," he said. "Go on."

Bunnish pushed the button that started Delmario's clock.

Very quickly, Delmario reached out, played knight

takes pawn—the pieces clicked together softly as he made the capture—and used the pawn he'd taken to punch the clock, stopping his own timer and starting Bunnish's.

"The sac," said Bunnish. "What a surprise." He took the knight.

Delmario played bishop takes pawn, saccing another piece. Bunnish was forced to capture with his king. He seemed unperturbed. He was smiling faintly, his dimples faint creases in his big cheeks, his eyes clear and sharp and cheerful behind his tinted eyeglasses.

Steve Delmario was leaning forward over the board, his dark eyes sweeping back and forth over the position, back and forth, over and over again as if double checking that everything was really where he thought it was. He crossed and uncrossed his legs. Peter, standing just behind him, could almost feel the tension beating off Delmario in waves, twisting him. Even E.C. Stuart, seated a few feet distant in a big comfortable armchair, was staring at the game intently. The clock ticked softly. Delmario lifted his hand to move his queen, but hesitated with his fingers poised above it. His hand trembled.

"What's the matter, Steve?" Bunnish asked. He steepled his hands just beneath his chin, and smiled when Delmario looked up at him. "You hesitate. Don't you know? He who hesitates is lost. Uncertain, all of a sudden? Surely that can't be. You were always so certain before. How many mates did you show me? How many?"

Delmario blinked, frowned. "I'm going to show you one more, Bunny," he said furiously. His fingers closed on his queen, shifted it across the board. "Check."

"Ah," said Bunnish. Peter studied the position. The double sac had cleared away the pawns in front of the Black king, and the queen check permitted no retreat. Bunnish marched his king up a square, toward the center of the board, toward the waiting White army. Surely he was lost now. His own defenders were all over on the queenside, and the enemy was all around him. But Bunnish did not seem worried.

Delmario's clock was ticking as he examined the position. He sipped his juice, shifted restlessly in his seat. Bunnish yawned, and grinned tauntingly. "You were the winner that day, Delmario. Beat a Master. The only winner. Can't you find the win now? Where are all those mates, eh?"

"There's so many I don't know which one to go with, Bunny," Steve said. "Now shut up, damn you. I'm trying to think."

"Oh," said Bunnish. "Pardon."

Delmario consumed ten minutes on his clock before he reached out and moved his remaining knight. "Check."

Bunnish advanced his king again.

Delmario licked his lips, slid his queen forward a square. "Check."

Bunnish's king went sideways, toward the safety of the queenside.

Delmario flicked a pawn forward. "Check."

Bunnish had to take. He removed the offending pawn with his king, smiling complacently.

With the file open, Delmario could bring his rooks into play. He shifted one over. "Check."

Bunnish's harried king moved again.

Now Delmario moved the rook forward, sliding it right up the file to confront the enemy king face to face. "Check!" he said loudly.

Peter sucked in his breath sharply, without meaning to. The rook was hanging! Bunnish could just snatch it off. He stared at the position over Delmario's shoulder. Bunnish could take the rook with his king, all right, but then the other rook came over, the king had to go back, then if the queen shifted just one square . . . yes . . . too many mate threats in that variation. Black had lots of resources, but they all ended in disaster. But if Bunnish took with his knight instead of his king, he left that square unguarded . . . hmmm . . . queen check, king up, bishop comes in . . . no, mate was even quicker that way.

Delmario drained his orange juice and set the empty tumbler down with self-satisfied firmness.

Bunnish moved his king diagonally forward. The only possible move, Peter thought. Delmario leaned forward. Behind him, Peter leaned forward too. The White pieces were swarming around Black's isolated king now, but how to tighten the mating net? Steve had three different checks, Peter thought. No, four, he could do that too. He watched and analyzed in silence. The rook check was no good, the king just retreated, and further checks simply drove him to safety. The bishop? No, Bunnish could trade off, take with his rook—he was two pieces up, after all. Several subvariations branched off from the two queen checks. Peter was still trying to figure out where they led, when Delmario reached out suddenly, grabbed a pawn from in front of his king, and moved it up two squares. He slammed it down solidly, and slapped the clock. Then he sat back and crossed his arms. "Your move, Bunny," he said.

Peter studied the board. Delmario's last move didn't give check, but the pawn advance cut off an important escape square. Now that threatened rook check was no longer innocuous. Instead of being chased back to safety, the Black king got mated in three. Of course, Bunnish had a tempo now, it was his move, he could bring up a defender. His queen now, could . . . no, then queen check, king back, rook check, and the Black queen fell . . . bishop maybe . . . no, check there and mate in one, unstoppable. The longer Peter looked at the position, the fewer defensive resources he saw for Black. Bunnish could delay the loss, but he couldn't stop it. He was smashed!

Bunnish did not look smashed. Very calmly he picked

up a knight and moved it to queen's knight six. "Check," he said quietly.

Delmario stared. Peter stared. E.C. Stuart got up out of his chair and drifted closer, his finger brushing back his mustache as he considered the game. The check was only a time-waster, Peter thought. Delmario could capture the knight with either of two pawns, or he could simply move his king. Except . . . Peter scowled . . . if White took with the bishop pawn, queen came up with check, king moved to the second, queen takes rook pawn with check, king . . . no, that was no good. White got mated by force. The other way seemed to bring on the mate even faster, after the queen checked from the eighth rank.

Delmario moved his king up.

Bunnish slid a bishop out along a diagonal. "Check."

There was only one move. Steve moved his king forward again. He was being harassed, but his mating net was still intact, once the checks had run their course.

Bunnish flicked his knight backward, with another check.

Delmario was blinking and twisting his legs beneath the table. Peter saw that if he brought his king back, Bunnish had a forced series of checks leading to mate . . . but the Black knight hung now, to both rook and queen, and . . . Delmario captured it with the rook.

Bunnish grabbed White's advanced pawn with his queen, removing the cornerstone of the mating net. Now Delmario could play queen takes queen, but then he lost his queen to a fork, and after the trade-offs that followed he'd be hopelessly busted. Instead he retreated his king.

Bunnish made a tsking noise and captured the White knight with his queen, again daring Delmario to take it. With knight and pawn both gone, Delmario's mating threats had all dissipated, and if White snatched that Black queen, there was a check, a pin, take, take, take, and . . . Peter gritted his teeth together . . . and White would suddenly be in the endgame down a piece, hope-lessly lost. No. There had to be something better. The position still had a lot of play in it. Peter stared, and analyzed.

Steve Delmario stared too, while his clock ticked. The clock was one of those fancy jobs, with a move counter. It showed that he had to make seven more moves to reach time control. He had just under fifteen minutes remaining. Some time pressure, but nothing serious.

Except that Delmario sat and sat, eyes flicking back and forth across the board, blinking. He took off his thick glasses and cleaned them methodically on his shirttail. When he slid them back on, the position had not changed. He stared at the Black king fixedly, as if he were willing it to fall. Finally he started to get up. "I need a drink," he said.

"I'll get it," Peter snapped. "Sit down. You've only got eight minutes left."

"Yeah," Delmario said. He sat down again. Peter went to the bar and made him a screwdriver. Steve drained half of it in a gulp, never taking his eyes from the chessboard.

Peter happened to glance at E.C. Stuart. E.C. shook his head and cast his eyes up toward the ceiling. Not a word was spoken, but Peter heard the message: *forget it.*

Steve Delmario sat there, growing more and more agitated. With three minutes remaining on his clock, he reached out his hand, thought better of it, and pulled back. He shifted in his seat, gathered his legs up under him, leaned closer to the board, his nose a bare couple inches above the chessmen. His clock ticked.

He was still staring at the board when Bunnish smiled and said, "Your flag is down, Delmario."

Delmario looked up, blinking. His mouth hung open. "Time," he said urgently. "I just need time to find the win, got to be here someplace, got to, all those checks . . ."

Bunnish rose. "You're out of time, Delmario. Doesn't matter anyway. You're dead lost."

"NO! No I'm not, damn you, there's a win . . ."

Peter put a hand on Steve's shoulder. "Steve, take it easy," he said. "I'm sorry. Bruce is right. You're busted here."

"No," Delmario insisted. "I know there's a winning combo, I just got to . . . got to . . . only . . ." His right hand, out over the board, began to shake, and he knocked over his own king.

Bunnish showed his dimples. "Listen to your captain, winner-boy," he said. Then he looked away from Delmario, to where E.C. stood scowling. "You're next, Stuart. Tomorrow. Same time, same place."

"And if I don't care to play?" E.C. said disdainfully.

Bunnish shrugged. "Suit yourself," he said. "I'll be here, and the game will be here. I'll start your clock on time. You can lose over the board or lose by forfeit. You lose either way."

"And me?" Peter said.

"Why, captain," said Bunnish. "I'm saving *you* for last."

Steve Delmario was a wreck. He refused to leave the chessboard except to mix himself fresh drinks. For the rest of the morning and most of the afternoon he remained glued to his seat, drinking like a fish and flicking the chess pieces around like a man possessed, playing and replaying the game. Delmario wolfed down a couple sandwiches that Peter made up for him around lunchtime, but there was no talking to him, no calming him. Peter tried. In an hour or so, Delmario would be passed out from the booze he was downing in such alarming quantities.

Finally he and E.C. left Delmario alone, and went upstairs to his suite. Peter knocked on the door. "You decent, Kathy? E.C. is with me."

She opened the door. She had on jeans and a t-shirt. "Decent as I ever get," she said. "Come on in. How did the great game come out?"

Delmario lost," Peter said. "It was a close thing, though. I thought we had him for a moment."

Kathy snorted.

"So what now?" E.C. said.

"You going to play tomorrow?"

E.C. shrugged. "Might as well. I've got nothing to lose."

"Good," Peter said. "You can beat him. Steve almost won, and we both know the shape he's in. We've got to analyze, figure out where he went wrong."

E.C. fingered his mustache. He looked cool and thoughtful. "That pawn move," he suggested. "The one that didn't give check. It left White open for that counterattack."

"It also set up the mating net," Peter said. He looked over his shoulder, saw Kathy standing with her arms crossed. "Could you get the chessboard from the bedroom?" he asked her. When she left, Peter turned back to E.C. "I think Steve was already lost by the time he made that pawn move. That was his only good shot—lots of threats there. Everything else just petered out after a few checks. He went wrong before that, I think."

"All those checks," E.C. said. "One too many, maybe?"

"Exactly," said Peter. "Instead of driving him into a checkmate, Steve drove him into safety. You've got to vary somewhere in there."

"Agreed."

Kathy arrived with the chess set and placed it on the low table between them. As Peter swiftly set up the critical position, she folded her legs beneath her and sat on the floor. But she grew bored very quickly when they began to analyze, and it wasn't long before she got to her feet again with a disgusted noise. "Both of you are crazy," she said. "I'm going to get something to eat."

"Bring us back something, will you?" Peter asked.
"And a couple of beers?" But he hardly noticed it when
she placed the tray beside them.

They stayed at it well into the night. Kathy was the
only one who went down to dine with Bunnish. When
she returned, she said, "That man is *disgusting*," so
emphatically that it actually distracted Peter from the
game. But only for an instant.

"Here, try this," E.C. said, moving a knight, and Peter
looked back quickly.

"I see you decided to play, Stuart," Bunnish said the
next morning.

E.C., looking trim and fresh, his sandy hair carefully
combed and brushed, a steaming mug of black coffee in
hand, nodded briskly. "You're as sharp as ever, Brucie."

Bunnish chuckled.

"One point, however," E.C. said, holding up a finger.
"I still don't believe your cock-and-bull story about time-
travel. We'll play this out, alright, but we'll play for
money, not for one of your flashbacks. Understood?"

"You jokers are such suspicious types," Bunnish said.
He sighed. "Anything you say, of course. You want
money. Fine."

"One million dollars."

Bunnish smiled broadly. "Small change," he said. "But
I agree. Beat me, and you'll leave here with one million.
You'll take a check, I hope?"

"A certified check." E.C. turned to Peter. "You're my
witness," he said, and Peter nodded. The three of them
were alone this morning. Kathy was firm in her disinterest, and Delmario was in his room sleeping off his binge.

"Ready?" Bunnish asked.

"Go on."

Bunnish started the clock. E.C. reached out and played
the sacrifice. Knight takes pawn. His motions were crisp
and economical. Bunnish captured, and E.C. played the

bishop sac without a second's hesitation. Bunnish captured again, pushed the clock.

E.C. Stuart brushed back his mustache, reached down, and moved a pawn. No check.

"Ah," Bunnish said. "An improvement. You have something up your sleeve, don't you? Of course you do. E.C. Stuart always has something up his sleeve. The hilarious, unpredictable E.C. Stuart. Such a joker. So imaginative."

"Play chess, Brucie," snapped E.C.

"Of course." Peter drifted closer to the board while Bunnish studied the position. They had gone over and over the game last night, and had finally decided that the queen check that Delmario had played following the double sac was unsound. There were several other checks in the position, all tempting, but after hours of analysis he and E.C. had discarded those as well. Each of them offered plenty of traps and checkmates should Black err, but each of them seemed to fail against correct play, and they had to assume Bunnish would play correctly.

E.C.'s pawn move was a more promising line. Subtler. Sounder. It opened lines for White's pieces, and interposed another barrier between Black's king and the safety of the queenside. Suddenly White had threats everywhere. Bunnish had serious troubles to chew on now.

He did not chew on them nearly as long as Peter would have expected. After studying the position for a bare couple minutes, he picked up his queen and snatched off White's queen rook pawn, which was undefended. Bunnish cupped the pawn in his hand, yawned, and slouched back in his chair, looking lazy and unperturbed.

E.C. Stuart permitted himself a brief scowl as he looked over the position. Peter felt uneasy as well. That move ought to have disturbed Bunnish more than it had, he thought. White had so many threats ... last night they had analyzed the possibilities exhaustively, playing and replaying every variation and subvariation until they were sure that they had found the win. Peter had gone to sleep feeling almost jubilant. Bunnish had a dozen feasible defenses to their pawn thrust. They'd had no way of knowing which one he would choose, so they had satisfied themselves that each and every one ultimately ended in failure.

Only now Bunnish had fooled them. He hadn't played *any* of the likely defenses. He had just ignored E.C.'s mating threats, and gone pawnsnatching as blithely as the rankest patzer. Had they missed something? While E.C. considered the best reply, Peter drew up a chair to the side of the board so he could analyze in comfort.

There was nothing, he thought, nothing. Bunnish had a check next move, if he wanted it, by pushing his queen to the eighth rank. But it was meaningless. E.C. hadn't weakened his queenside the way Steve had yesterday, in his haste to find a mate. If Bunnish checked, all Stuart had to do was move his king up to queen two. Then the Black queen would be under attack by a rook, and forced to retreat or grab another worthless pawn. Meanwhile, Bunnish would be getting checkmated in the middle of the board. The more Peter went over the variations, the more convinced he became that there was no way Bunnish could possibly work up the kind of counterattack he had used to smash Steve Delmario.

E.C., after a long and cautious appraisal of the board, seemed to reach the same conclusion. He reached out coolly and moved his knight, hemming in Bunnish's lonely king once and for all. Now he threatened a queen check that would lead to mate in one. Bunnish could capture the dominating knight, but then E.C. just recaptured with a rook, and checkmate followed soon threafter, no matter how Bunnish might wriggle on the hook.

Bunnish smiled across the board at his opponent, and

lazily shoved his queen forward a square to the last rank. "Check," he said.

E.C. brushed back his moustache, shrugged, and played his king up. He punched the clock with a flourish. "You're lost," he said flatly.

Peter was inclined to agree. That last check had accomplished nothing; in fact, it seemed to have worsened Black's plight. The mate threats were still there, as unstoppable as ever, and now Black's queen was under attack as well. He could pull it back, of course, but not in time to help with the defense. Bunnish ought to be frantic and miserable.

Instead his smile was so broad that his fat cheeks were threatening to crack in two. "Lost?" he said. "Ah, Stuart, this time the joke is on you!" He giggled like a teen-age girl, and brought his queen down the rank to grab off White's rook. "Check!"

Peter Norten had not played a game of tournament chess in a long, long time, but he still remembered the way it had felt when an opponent suddenly made an unexpected move that changed the whole complexion of a game: the brief initial confusion, the *what is that?* feeling, followed by panic when you realized the strength of the unanticipated move, and then the awful swelling gloom that built and built as you followed through one losing variation after another in your head. There was no worse moment in the game of chess.

That was how Peter felt now.

They had missed it totally. Bunnish was giving up his queen for a rook, normally an unthinkable sacrifice, but not in this position. E.C. *had* to take the offered queen. But if he captured with his king, Peter saw with sudden awful clarity, Black had a combination that won the farm, which meant he had to use the other rook, pulling it off its crucial defense of the central knight . . . and then . . . oh, *shit*!

E.C. tried to find another alternative for more than

fifteen minutes, but there was no alternative to be found. He played rook takes queen. Bunnish quickly seized his own rook and captured the knight that had moved so menacingly into position only two moves before. With ruthless precision, Bunnish then forced the trade-off of one piece after another, simplifying every danger off the board. All of a sudden they were in the endgame. E.C. had a queen and five pawns; Bunnish had a rook, two bishops, a knight, and four pawns, and—ironically—his once-imperiled king now occupied a powerful position in the center of the board.

Play went on for hours, as E.C. gamely gave check after check with his rogue queen, fighting to pick up a loose piece or perhaps draw by repetition. But Bunnish was too skilled for such desperation tactics. It was only a matter of technique.

Finally E.C. tipped over his king.

"I thought we looked at every possible defense," Peter said numbly.

"Why, captain," said Bunnish cheerfully. "Every attempt to defend loses. The defending pieces block off escape routes or get in the way. Why should I help mate myself? I'd rather let you try to do that."

"I *will* do that," Peter promised angrily. "Tomorrow."

Bunnish rubbed his hands together. "I can scarcely wait!"

That night the post-mortem was held in E.C.'s suite; Kathy—who had greeted their glum news with an "I told you so" and a contemptuous smile—had insisted that she didn't want them staying up half the night over a chessboard in *her* presence. She told Peter he was behaving like a child, and they had angry words before he stormed out.

Steve Delmario was going over the morning's loss with E.C. when Peter joined them. Delmario's eyes looked awfully bloodshot, but otherwise he appeared sober, if haggard. He was drinking coffee. "How does it look?" Peter asked when he pulled up a seat.

"Bad," E.C. said.

Delmario nodded. "Hell, worse'n bad, it's starting to look like that damn sac is unsound after all. I can't believe it, I just can't, it all looks so promising, got to be something there. *Got* to. But I'm damned if I can find it."

E.C. added, "The surprise he pulled today is a threat in a number of variations. Don't forget, we gave up two pieces to get to this position. Unfortunately, that means that Brucie can easily afford to give some of that material back to get out of the fix. He still comes out ahead, and wins the endgame. We've found a few improvements on my play this morning—"

"That knight doesn't have to drop," interjected Delmario.

" . . . but nothing convincing," E.C. concluded.

"You ever think," Delmario said, "that maybe the Funny Bunny was *right*? That maybe the sac don't work, maybe the game was never won at all?" His voice had a note of glum disbelief in it.

"There's one thing wrong with that," Peter said.

"Oh?"

"Ten years ago, after Bunnish had blown the game and the match, Robinson Vesselere *admitted* that he had been lost."

E.C. looked thoughtful. "That's true. I'd forgotten that."

"Vesselere was almost a Senior Master. He had to know what he was talking about. The win is there. I mean to find it."

Delmario clapped his hands together and whooped gleefully. "Hell yes, Pete, you're right! Let's go!"

"At last the prodigal spouse returns," Kathy said pointedly when Peter came in. "Do you have any idea what time it is?"

She was seated in a chair by the fireplace, though the fire had burned down to ashes and embers. She wore a dark robe, and the end of the cigarette she was smoking was a bright point in the darkness. Peter had come in smiling, but now he frowned. Kathy had once been a heavy smoker, but she'd given it up years ago. Now she only lit a cigarette when she was very upset. When she lit up, it usually meant they were headed for a vicious row.

"It's late," Peter said. "I don't know how late. What does it matter?" He'd spent most of the night with E.C. and Steve, but it had been worth it. They'd found what they had been looking for. Peter had returned tired but elated, expecting to find his wife asleep. He was in no mood for grief. "Never mind about the time," he said to her, trying to placate. "We've *got* it, Kath."

She crushed out her cigarette methodically. "Got what? Some new move you think is going to defeat our psychopathic host? Don't you understand that I don't give a damn about this stupid game of yours? Don't you listen to a thing I say? I've been waiting up half the night, Peter. It's almost three in the morning. I want to talk."

"Yeah?" Peter snapped. Her tone had gotten his back up. "Did you ever think that maybe I didn't want to listen? Well, think it. I have a big game tomorrow. I need my sleep. I can't afford to stay up till dawn screaming at you. Understand? Why the hell are you so hot to talk anyway? What could you possibly have to say that I haven't heard before, huh?"

Kathy laughed nastily. "I could tell you a few things about your old friend Bunnish that you haven't heard before."

"I doubt it."

"Do you? Well, did you know that he's been trying to get me into bed for the past two days?"

She said it tauntingly, throwing it at him. Peter felt as if he had been struck. *"What?"*

"Sit down," she snapped, "and listen."

Numbly, he did as she bid him. "Did you?" he asked, staring at her silhouette in the darkness, the vaguely ominous shape that was his wife.

"Did I? Sleep with him, you mean? Jesus, Peter, how can you ask that? Do you loathe me that much? I'd sooner sleep with a roach. That's what he reminds me of anyway." She gave a rueful chuckle. "He isn't exactly a sophisticated seducer, either. He actually offered me money."

"Why are you telling me this?"

"To knock some goddamned sense into you! Can't you see that Bunnish is trying to destroy you, all of you, any way he can? He didn't want me. He just wanted to get at you. And you, you and your moron teammates, are playing right into his hands. You're becoming as obsessed with that idiot chess game as *he* is." She leaned forward. Dimly, Peter could make out the lines of her face. "Peter," she said almost imploringly, "don't play him. He's going to beat you, love, just like he beat the others."

"I don't think so, *love*," Peter said from between clenched teeth. The endearment became an epithet as he hurled it back at her. "Why the hell are you always so ready to predict defeat for me, huh? Can't you ever be supportive, not even for a goddamned minute? If you won't help, why don't you just bug off? I've had all I can stand of you, damn it. Always belittling me, mocking. You've never believed in me. I don't know why the hell you married me, if all you wanted to do was make my life a hell. *Just leave me alone!"*

For a long moment after Peter's outburst there was silence. Sitting there in the darkened room, he could almost feel her rage building—any instant now he expected to hear her start screaming. Then he would scream back, and she would get up and break something, and he would grab her, and then the knives would come out in earnest. He closed his eyes, trembling, feeling close to tears. He didn't want this, he thought. He really didn't.

But Kathy fooled him. When she spoke, her voice was surprisingly gentle. "Oh, Peter," she said. "I never meant to hurt you. Please. I love you."

He was stunned. "Love me?" he said wonderingly.

"Please listen. If there is anything at all left between us, please just listen to me for a few minutes. Please."

"All right," he said.

"Peter, I *did* believe in you once. Surely you must remember how good things were in the beginning? I was supportive then, wasn't I? The first few years, when you were writing your novel? I worked, I kept food on the table, I gave you the time to write."

"Oh, yes," he said, anger creeping back into his tone. Kathy had thrown that at him before, had reminded him forcefully of how she'd supported them for two years while he wrote a book that turned out to be so much waste paper. "Spare me your reproaches, huh? It wasn't my fault I couldn't sell the book. You heard what Bunnish said."

"I wasn't reproaching you, damn it!" she snapped. "Why are you always so ready to read criticism into every word I say?" She shook her head, and got her voice back under control. "Please, Peter, don't make this harder than it is. We have so many years of pain to overcome, so many wounds to bind up. Just hear me out.

"I was trying to say that I did believe in you. Even after the book, after you burned it . . . even then. You made it hard, though. I didn't think you were a failure, but *you* did, and it changed you, Peter. You let it get to you. You gave up writing, instead of just gritting your teeth and doing another book."

"I wasn't tough enough, I know," he said. "The loser. The weakling."

"*Shut up!*" she said in exasperation. "I didn't say that, *you* did. Then you went into journalism. I still believed. But everything kept going wrong. You got fired, you got sued, you became a disgrace. Our friends started drifting away. And all the time you insisted that none of it was your fault. You lost all the rest of your self-confidence. You didn't dream any more. You whined, bitterly and incessantly, about your bad luck."

"You never helped."

"Maybe not," Kathy admitted. "I tried to, at the start, but it just got worse and worse and I couldn't deal with it. You weren't the dreamer I'd married. It was hard to remember how I'd admired you, how I'd respected you. Peter, you loathed yourself so much that there was no way to keep the loathing from rubbing off on me."

"So?" Peter said. "What's the point, Kathy?"

"I never left you, Peter," she said. "I could have, you know. I wanted to. I stayed, through all of it, all the failures and all the self-pity. Doesn't that say anything to you?"

"It says you're a masochist," he snapped. "Or maybe a sadist."

That was too much for her. She started to reply, and her voice broke, and she began to weep. Peter sat where he was and listened to her cry. Finally the tears ran out, and she said, quietly, "Damn you. Damn you. I hate you."

"I thought you loved me. Make up your mind."

"You ass. You insensitive creep. Don't you understand, Peter?"

"Understand *what*?" he said impatiently. "You said listen, so I've been listening, and all you've been doing is rehashing all the same old stuff, recounting all my inadequacies. I heard it all before."

"Peter, can't you see that this week has changed *everything*? If you'd only stop hating, stop loathing me and yourself, maybe you could see it. We have a chance again, Peter. If we try. Please."

"I don't see that anything has changed. I'm going to play a big chess game tomorrow, and you know how much it means to me and my self-respect, and you don't care. You don't care if I win or lose. You keep telling me I'm *going* to lose. You're *helping* me to lose by making me argue when I should be sleeping. What the hell has changed? You're the same damn bitch you've been for years."

"I will tell you what has changed," she said. "Peter, up until a few days ago, both of us thought you were a failure. But you aren't! *It hasn't been your fault.* None of it. Not bad luck, like you kept saying, and not personal inadequacy either, like you really thought. Bunnish has done it all. Can't you see what a difference that makes? You've never had a chance, Peter, but you have one now. There's no reason you shouldn't believe in yourself. We *know* you can do great things! Bunnish admitted it. We can leave here, you and I, and start all over again. You could write another book, write plays, do anything you want. You have the talent. You've never lacked it. We can dream again, believe again, love each other again. Don't you see? Bunnish had to gloat to complete his revenge, but by gloating he's *freed* you!"

Peter sat very still in the dark room, his hand clenching and unclenching on the arm of the chair as Kathy's words sunk in. He had been so wrapped up in the chess game, so obsessed with Bunnish's obsession, that he had never seen it, never considered it. *It wasn't me,* he thought wonderingly. *All those years, it was never me.* "It's true," he said in a small voice.

"Peter?" she said, concerned.

He heard the concern, heard more than that, heard love in her voice. So many people, he thought, make such grand promises, promise better or worse, promise rich or poorer, and bail out as soon as things turn the least bit sour in a relationship. But she had stayed, through all of it, the failures, the disgrace, the cruel words and the poisonous thoughts, the weekly fights, the poverty. She had stayed.

"Kathy," he said. The next words were very hard. "I love you, too." He started to get up and move toward her, and began to cry.

They arrived late the next morning. They showered together, and Peter dressed with unusual care. For some reason, he felt it was important to look his best. It was a new beginning, after all. Kathy came with him. They entered the living room holding hands. Bunnish was already behind the board, and Peter's clock was ticking. The others were there too. E.C. was seated patiently in a chair. Delmario was pacing. "Hurry up," he said when Peter came down the stairs. "You've lost five minutes already."

Peter smiled. "Easy, Steve," he said. He went over and took his seat behind the White pieces. Kathy stood behind him. She looked gorgeous this morning, Peter thought.

"It's your move, captain," Bunnish said, with an unpleasant smile.

"I know," Peter said. He made no effort to move, scarcely even looked at the board. "Bruce, why do you hate me? I've been thinking about that, and I'd like to know the answer. I can understand about Steve and E.C. Steve had the presumption to win when you lost, and he rubbed your nose in that defeat afterwards. E.C. made you the butt of his jokes. But why me? What did I ever do to you?"

Bunnish looked briefly confused. Then his face grew hard. "You. You were the worst of them all."

Peter was startled. "I never . . ."

"The big captain," Bunnish said sarcastically. "That day ten years ago, you never even *tried*. You took a quick grandmaster draw with your old friend Hal Winslow. You could have tried for a win, played on, but you didn't. Oh, no. You never cared how much more pressure you put on the rest of us. And when we lost, you didn't take any of the blame, not a bit of it, even though you gave up half a point. It was all *my* fault. And that wasn't all of it, either. Why was *I* on first board, Norten? All of us on the B team had approximately the same rating. How did I get the honor of being board one?"

Peter thought for a minute, trying to recall the strategies that had motivated him ten years before. Finally he nodded. "You always lost the big games, Bruce. It made sense to put you up on board one, where you'd face the other teams' big guns, the ones who'd probably beat whoever we played there. That way the lower boards would be manned by more reliable players, the ones we could count on in the clutch."

"In other words," Bunnish said, "I was a write-off. You expected me to lose, while you won matches on the lower boards."

"Yes," Peter admitted. "I'm sorry."

"Sorry," mocked Bunnish. "You *made* me lose, expected me to lose, and then tormented me for losing, and now you're sorry. You didn't play chess that day. You never played chess. You were playing a bigger game, a game that lasted for years, between you and Winslow of U.C. And the team members were your pieces and your pawns. Me, I was a sac. A gambit. That was all. And it didn't work anyway. Winslow beat you. You *lost.*"

"You're right," Peter admitted. "I lost. I think I understand now. Why you did all the things you've done."

"You're going to lose again now," Bunnish said. "*Move,* before your clock runs out." He nodded down at the checkered wasteland that lay between them, at the complex jumble of Black and White pieces.

Peter glanced at the board with disinterest. "We analyzed until three in the morning last night, the three of us. I had a new variation all set. A single sacrifice, instead of the double sac. I play knight takes pawn, but I hold back from the bishop sac, swing my queen over instead. That was the idea. It looked pretty good. But it's unsound, isn't it?"

Bunnish stared at him. "Play it, and we'll find out!"

"No," said Peter. "I don't want to play."

"*Pete!*" Steve Delmario said in consternation. "You got to, what are you saying, beat this damn bastard."

Peter looked at him. "It's no good, Steve."

There was a silence. Finally Bunnish said, "You're a coward, Norten. A coward and a failure and a weakling. Play the game out."

"I'm not interested in the game, Bruce. Just tell me. The variation is unsound."

Bunnish made a disgusted noise. "Yes, yes," he snapped. "It's unsound. There's a countersac, I give up a rook to break up your mating threats, but I win a piece back a few moves later."

"All the variations are unsound, aren't they?" Peter said.

Bunnish smiled thinly.

"White doesn't have a won game at all," Peter said. "We were wrong, all those years. You never blew the win. You never *had* a win. Just a position that looked good superficially, but led nowhere."

"Wisdom, at last," Bunnish said. "I've had computers print out every possible variation. They take forever, but I've had lifetimes. When I flashed back—you have no idea how many times I have flashed back, trying one new idea after another—that is always my target point, that day in Evanston, the game with Vesselere. I've tried every move there is to be tried in that position, every wild idea. It makes no difference. Vesselere always beats me. All the variations are unsound."

"But," Delmario protested, looking bewildered, "Vesselere *said* he was lost. He *said* so!"

Bunnish looked at him with contempt. "I had made him sweat a lot in a game he should have won easily. He was just getting back. He was a vindictive man, and he knew that by saying that he'd make the loss that much more painful." He smirked. "I've taken care of *him* too, you know."

E.C. Stuart rose up from his chair and straightened his vest. "If we're done now, Brucie, maybe you would be so kind as to let us out of Bunnishland?"

"*You* can go," Bunnish said. "And that drunk, too. But not Peter." He showed his dimples. "Why, Peter has almost won, in a sense. So I'm going to be generous. You know what I'm going to do for you, captain? I'm going to let you use my flashback device."

"No thank you," Peter said.

Bunnish stared, befuddled. "What do you mean, no? Don't you understand what I'm giving you? You can wipe out all your failures, try again, make some different moves. Be a success in another timeline."

"I know. Of course, that would leave Kathy with a dead body in *this* timeline, wouldn't it? And you with the satisfaction of driving me to something that uncannily resembles suicide. No. I'll take my chances with the future instead of the past. With Kathy."

Bunnish let his mouth droop open. "What do you care about her? She hates you anyway. She'll be better off with you dead. She'll get the insurance money and you'll get somebody better, somebody who cares about you."

"But I do care about him," Kathy said. She put a hand on Peter's shoulder. He reached up and touched it, and smiled.

"Then you're a fool too," Bunnish cried. "He's nothing, he'll *never* be anything. I'll see to that."

Peter stood up. "I don't think so, somehow. I don't think you can hurt us anymore. Any of us." He looked at the others. "What do you think, guys?"

E.C. cocked his head thoughtfully, and ran a finger

along the underside of his mustache. "You know," he said, "I think you're right."

Delmario just seemed baffled, until all of a sudden the light broke across his face, and he grinned. "You can't steal ideas I haven't come up with yet, can you?" he said to Bunnish. "Not in this timeline, anyhow." He made a loud whooping sound and stepped up to the chessboard. Reaching down, he stopped the clock. "Checkmate," he said. "Checkmate, checkmate, *checkmate!*"

Less than two weeks later, Kathy knocked softly on the door of the study. "Wait a sec!" Peter shouted. He typed out another sentence, then flicked off the typewriter and swiveled in his chair. "C'mon in."

She opened the door and smiled at him. "I made some tuna salad, if you want to take a break for lunch. How's the book coming?"

"Good," Peter said. "I should finish the second chapter today, if I keep at it." She was holding a newspaper, he noticed. "What's that?"

"I thought you ought to see this," she replied, handing it over.

She'd folded it open to the obits. Peter took it and read. Millionaire electronics genius Bruce Bunnish had been found dead in his Colorado home, hooked up to a strange device that had seemingly electrocuted him. Peter sighed.

"He's going to try again, isn't he?" Kathy said.

Peter put down the newspaper. "The poor bastard. He can't see it."

"See what?"

Peter took her hand and squeezed it. "All the variations are unsound," he said. It made him sad. But after lunch, he soon forgot about it, and went back to work.

CLOSING TIME

The world ended on a slow Tuesday night.

The rain had been coming down heavily since mid-afternoon, and trade was lousy. Hank was washing some beer steins and listening to Barney Dale relate his marital woes. He had heard all of Barney's marital woes before, but there was nothing else to do. The Happy Hour crowd had departed early tonight, and Barney was the only customer in the joint.

"Nothing I do pleases her," Barney was mumbling into his draft. He was a short, balding, elderly fellow whose wife had been browbeating him for forty years now. Hank had been earwitness to at least five of those years. "I'll really catch it tonight," Barney said, "Out drinking beer, she hates that, and she's *bigger* than me. She—"

That was when the door swung open and Milton stalked in, wet and angry. He stood in the open door, rain pattering on the asphalt of the parking lot behind him, while his eyes swept back and forth across the dim, empty barroom. "Where is he?" he said loudly. "I'm going to kill the mothafuckah, I swear I am."

Hank sighed. It was going to be another one of those nights. "First close the door, Milt," he called out. "The rain's coming in."

"Oh," said Milton. Underneath his temper, he was actually kind of a sweetheart, though you'd never know it to look at him. He stood six foot seven, with fists the size of cinder blocks, and twice as hard. "Sorry," he said, a bit abashed. He closed the door carefully and came striding over to the bar, working on his glower with every step. He was drenched, and his shoes squished when he walked, but his anger was so palpable you almost expected the moisture to come boiling off as steam.

"The usual, Milt?" Hank asked. He flicked water off a stein, wiped it desultorily with his towel, and stood it next to the others.

"Yeah," said Milton. He yanked out a barstool and sat down next to Barney, who was blinking at him in mildly inebriated astonishment. "And you tell me where that jiveass turkey has got himself to," he added.

"Who is it has you so worked up?" Hank asked, as he pulled out the creme de menthe and set to work on the grasshopper.

"Sleazy Pete," Milton growled. "I'm going to wring his skinny lil' neck for him. Where the hell is he? He hangs around here Tuesdays, don't he? I know he does. You tell that bastid he ain't gonna duck me, no way."

Hank spun a coaster onto the bar and placed the grass-hopper on top of it. Milton wrapped one huge meaty hand around it, and glared over at Barney Dale as if daring him to make a comment. Barney suddenly discovered something of enormous interest in the bottom of his stein.

"You're too early," Hank said. "Pete will be in a little over four hours from now."

Milton sipped his grasshopper and grunted.

Barney raised his stein and smiled tentatively. Hank took it and drew him another. As he set it down, Barney said, "Now how do you know just when he's going to be in, Hank? You one of them ESP fellows my missus is always reading me about from the *Enquirer*?"

Hank smiled. "ESP don't come into it. Pete's a regular. I know my regulars. I know where they live, and what they do for a buck, and how many kids they got, and what kinds of cars they drive. And I sure as hell know when they come in. Pete usually comes in early, except for Tuesdays during the summers. He always goes to a movie or a ballgame on Tuesdays. He'll be in a couple hours before closing time." Hank picked up another stein and dipped it into the dishwater.

"I'll wait," Milton said. "When that sumbitch comes in, I'll bust his goddamn head, you wait and see."

"Sure thing," Hank agreed. He didn't like trouble in his place, but he wasn't too worried. He knew his regulars. Milton couldn't hold his grasshoppers, and he was a maudlin, amiable drunk. By the time Sleazy Pete wandered in, Milt would be a pussycat. "Why are you so corked off at Pete?" Hank asked conversationally. Anything was better than Barney's marital woes. "I thought you two were buddies."

"*Buddies!*" Milton roared. "I'll kill the mothafuckah. He gypped me. Here, take a look at this." He pulled something out of his pocket and tossed it onto the bar.

Barney Dale sipped his beer and stared at the thing curiously, not bold enough to reach for it. Hank set down the stein he was washing, came over, and picked it up. It was a round amulet, on a heavy metal chain. He held it up to the light, and it twisted slowly. "Gold?" he asked.

"Hell, no," Milton said. "Brass. Even Pete ain't stupid enough to sell it if it was gold."

The amulet had a nice heft to it. Hank examined it more closely. All around the outside rim were little carvings of animals, all kinds of animals. In the center was a milky white stone of some sort. Thin lines ran in from the animals to the stone, like spokes on a wheel. "Interesting," Hank said. "What's the crystal in the middle?"

"Glass," said Milton. "Milkglass. Sleazy Pete said it was moonstone, whatever the hell that is, but it ain't."

Hank put the amulet back on the bar. "Can I look at it?" Barney asked, timidly. Milton stared at him and nodded.

"Pete sold it to you?" Hank said. Sleazy Pete ran a little, used bookstore and bric-a-brac shop a few blocks away, and was always coming in with one piece of junk or another and trying to sell it to some drunk. This wouldn't be the first time it had gotten him in trouble.

"Damn right," Milton said. "Lying lil' weasel. Got fifty bucks out of me for that ugly thing. I mean to get it back if I got to take it out of his hide."

"Why'd you buy it? Think it was gold?"

Milton frowned, finished his grasshopper, and signalled for another. "Hell, no," he said. "Do I look stupid or something? Knew it weren't no gold. Only I was drunk, and Pete said the damn thing was magic. You know. A fucking magic amulet."

"Ah," said Hank. "So you bought it because you thought it was magic, and it wasn't."

Milton looked pained. He stared morosely at the bar, shredding his coaster in his big hands. Hank gave him another with his grasshopper. "That ain't it, exactly," Milton said finally, with a touch of reluctance. "It's magic all right, but not like Pete said it'd be."

Hank looked up from his dishwater. "What?" he said. Barney Dale was staring too, looking from the amulet to

Milton and then down again, blinking his watery blue eyes as if he couldn't believe what he was hearing.

"You heard me," Milton said, frowning again. "The damn thing works. Only . . ." He paused, a bit perplexed. "Maybe I ought to start at the beginning."

"That's generally a good place to start," Hank said. He was thinking that maybe it would be an interesting night after all, at least for a Tuesday.

"It was a couple weeks back," Milton said. "Right in here, this very damn place. I had a bit to drink, you know, and Sleazy Pete comes over and shows me that thing and gives me this pitch about its powers. It was supposed to be, like, a thing for *changing.*"

"Changing?" Hank said.

Milton waved his hand irritably. "Shiftin' shape, that's what that bastid Pete called it. You know, werewolf stuff, like in them old movies. Only this thing don't change you into no wolf, Pete says, which was fine with me, 'cause I didn't see no sense in running around ripping out anybody's throat, you know? He says it'll change me into a bird. Says he used it himself, during the full moon, which is the only time it works, and he changed into this big hawk, flew around all night. Only Pete has got this thing about heights, you know, so he didn't want the change. Only it ain't something you got any choice about, he says. If you own the goddamned amulet, when that ol' moon comes pokin' up, you change.

"Well, hell, *I* ain't got no thing about heights, and I always wanted to fly, you know, only I never had the goddamn money. Sounded like it'd be a lot of fun. So we dickered over the price for a bit, and finally I bought the damn thing and took it home and waited for the next full moon."

Barney had the amulet in his hand. "Last night was the first night of the full moon," he said, peering cautiously over at Milton.

"Damn right it was," Milton said.

"And you didn't change?" Hank asked.

"Shit, I *changed* all right, but not into a goddamn hawk. I'm gonna kill me that lying sumbitch, I tell you. He really sold me a bill of goods. Worst fuckin' night of my life."

There was a brief silence. Neither one of them wanted to press him. Finally Barney Dale cleared his throat and said, "If you don't mind me asking, er, exactly what kind of change did you experience?"

Milton took a long sip from his grasshopper, then turned slowly and deliberately on his stool to face Barney. Beneath his thick, bushy eyebrows, his eyes were squinty and mean. "What's your name again, little man?"

Barney swallowed. "Er, Barney. Barney Dale."

Milton smiled. "Listen up good, Mister Barney Dale. I'm gonna answer your question, you hear. But you better not laugh. I'm telling you out front. You laugh and I'm gonna twist your little head clean off and drop kick it about fifty yards down the goddamned street. You got that?"

"Er," said Barney. "Yes. Sure. I wouldn't dream of laughing."

"Real good," said Milton. "Well, the thing of it is, I turned into a rabbit."

Barney didn't laugh, Hank had to give him that. He was too scared to laugh. Hank didn't laugh either, but he found himself fighting to suppress a grin. "A rabbit?" he said.

"A rabbit. You know, a goddamn Easter bunny. Hippidy hop, hippidy hop. One of *them.*"

"Oh," said Barney. He peered down at the amulet again, and adjusted his glasses.

"A rabbit ain't no hawk," Milton said.

"That's true," Hank agreed.

"It was a goddamned nightmare, I tell you, and that mothafuckah is going to pay for every goddamned minute of hell I went through. City ain't no place for a rabbit."

"Not even a wererabbit," Hank said, smiling.

"No, sir. Nearly got run down by cars, and this one cat cornered me in this alley, and I was lucky to get out with my skin, and later on there was this dog chased me for miles, I swear. And the kids, the stinkin' little brats, they were the worst. Some of 'em threw stones and some wanted to catch me and make me a pet. All goddamned night it was just hop, hop, hop, one fucking thing after another." He shuddered. "My legs are sore as hell, too. I swear, when Pete comes in, I'm going to take this goddamn amulet of his and shove it up where the sun don't shine."

Barney Dale was turning the amulet round and round in his hands. "There's no rabbit on here," he said.

"What?" Milton snapped.

Barney put the disc on the bar between them. "Look," he said, "there's no rabbit. I thought perhaps these pictures here along the rim gave some indication of how it worked. You see? If there was a hawk, and then a rabbit, well, that would make sense, wouldn't it? Then we could see what followed, and no doubt the next bearer of the amulet would turn into that, whatever it might be. Only there's no rabbit, see? Here's a bird"—he pointed—"and there's a wolf, and some kind of big cat, and all kinds of other predators, but there's no rabbit. I think these are just decorative."

Milton grunted. "Decorative. So what? Hell, I bet Pete turned into a rabbit too, them pictures don't mean nothing. He knew what he was gettin' rid of, you bet he did. I'm going to kill him."

Barney glanced at his watch. "Er," he said, "pardon me, but you will run into a little problem there."

Milton looked over, incredulous. "You think I'm going to have a *problem* beating the hell out of a lil' nothing like Sleazy Pete?"

"I'm afraid you are," said Barney. "Hank said that Pete won't be in until a few hours before closing." He looked

at his watch again. "And, if I have the correct time,
moonrise will be along in about forty minutes or so. Long
before closing time. You'll be a rabbit when Pete arrives,
if what you've said is true."

Milton winced as if struck. "Oh, shit," he said. He
looked around wildly. "Hank," he squealed, "you've gotta
help me. Keep me here till dawn. Don't let no kids get
me."

Hank shrugged. He was enjoying this immensely.
"Anything for a regular," he said. "I got some lettuce in
the fridge, too. And we can probably win a few bar bets
with you, if anybody ever comes in."

Barney hefted the amulet in his hand. "I've got a better idea," he said. "I'll buy this from you."

Milton stared. "You'll *what*?"

"I'll buy it," Barney repeated, amiably. "Fifty dollars,
you said? Here." He pulled out his wallet, extracted two
twenties and a ten, and laid them on the bar. "Go on,
pick it up, and then the amulet will be off your hands.
You won't change, and when your friend comes in, you
can beat him to a bloody pulp." He hefted the amulet
again. It looked like a tiny golden wheel in his hand, with
a cloudy white dented hubcap. "What do you say?"

Milton looked at Barney for a long moment, then gave
a whoop of laughter and snatched up the money.
"Brother, you're on!" he said. "Hell, I don't know what
your game is, but I don't figure on spending no more
time as no rabbit if I can help it. Hell, I'll even buy you
a beer."

Barney slid the amulet into his pocket and stood up.
"Thank you, but I'll have to decline, I'm afraid. I have
to get home. My wife will kill me." He smiled slyly and
started for the door.

"Barney," Hank called out, "wait a sec." He was
unbearably curious. "What are you figuring?"

Barney smiled broadly. "It's a nice piece of brasswork,

you know. I bet it's worth a lot more than fifty dollars, even if it isn't magic."

"But what if it is?" Hank asked. "Aren't you worried about changing?"

Barney shrugged. "Not especially. I'm going to give it to my wife, you see. She'll make a *wonderful* rabbit." He chuckled. "Good evening, gentlemen. I'll see you tomorrow."

They listened to him drive off. "Poor woman's got quite a surprise coming," said Milton. He handed Hank one of Barney's twenties. "Set me up with another."

"You still waiting for Pete?"

"Sure am," Milton said. "I figure I'll kill him anyway, just on account of last night. That's fair, ain't it?"

Hank smiled and shrugged. Three grasshoppers all ready. By the time Sleazy Pete made his appearance, Milton would be all sweetness and light.

A little over a half hour later, though, Milton looked up from his drink and said, "Hey, listen up! The rain stopped."

Hank listened. "I believe you're right," he said. Then, still listening, he got a cold feeling all of a sudden as he heard the sound of a car pulling up outside. It was a very distinctive sound, the putt-putt-putt of an old car whose muffler has long ago ceased muffling. It came to a halt with a screech of worn brakes and a dull cough. Hank knew it instantly: Sleazy Pete's clunker. "So much for ESP," he said.

Milton looked at him curiously, but he didn't have time to inquire, for just then the door opened and Pete came sauntering in, all skin and bones and tattered denim and long blonde hair. "Hey, guys," he called out cheerfully. "What's happening? Game got rained out tonight. Hi, Hank. Hi, Milt."

Milton turned on his stool. "You," he said. "You are going to die." He got up and roared and started across the barroom, waving a fist the size of a wrecking ball.

Sleazy Pete gave one long look before he broke and spun and raced for the door and the parking lot. Milton followed, bellowing with rage.

Hank sighed and reached under the bar for his Louisville slugger. What a business, he thought. He followed them outside, prepared to subdue Milton by force if he threatened any real bodily harm to Pete.

Pete was sprinting for his car, but Milton was bigger and faster, and he caught him just as he was opening the door, yanked him back and spun him around, seized his shirtfront and lifted him bodily into the air. Sleazy Pete screamed and kicked. "I'm going to kill you, you mothafuckah," Milton said, and he slammed Pete down across the hood of his car, hard.

"Now, Milton," Hank said. "Cut it out. You know I can't allow this."

"Think it's fun to turn me into a rabbit, huh?" Milton said. "Maybe I'll just turn you into chopmeat and we'll see how much fun that is, huh?"

"Milton," Hank said, a little more forcefully. "Stop. I mean it now."

"Let me alone!" Pete yelled. "You're crazy! I don't know nothing about no rabbit!"

Milton smiled and balled up a huge fist.

"*Milton!*" Hank shouted, and he brought his baseball bat down hard on the fender of Pete's car. There was a satisfying loud thunk.

Milton, startled, looked over at Hank.

"Let him go," Hank said. He hefted the bat.

Milton frowned and released his hold on Sleazy Pete. "Oh, hell," he said. "I wasn't gonna hurt him, just muss him up a little."

"He's mussed enough," Hank observed drily. Sleazy Pete had earned his name. His denims were ragged and patched and dirty, his hair was a wild scraggle, and even his car was a twenty-year-old rambling wreck, partly faded red and mostly primer grey. Pete had never gotten around to finishing the paint job.

Pete sat up on the hood of his car, panting. "Jesus," he said. "You're one crazy fucker. What the hell's wrong?"

"He says the magic amulet you sold him turned him into a rabbit," Hank said, before Milton could reply. "He didn't like it."

"Damn right I didn't," said Milton.

"A *rabbit*? That can't be right. A werehawk, that's what it was for. I used it myself. It turned you into a bird, it had to."

"I know birds, I know rabbits. It turned me into a goddamned bunny rabbit, you mothafuckah!"

Sleazy Pete scratched at his beard and looked perplexed. "That's interesting," he said. "I guess it works different on everyone who owns it. Maybe that pattern of animals on the rim has something to do . . ."

"Hell, no," Milton said. "We looked at that. Just decorative. Ain't no rabbits on there."

Pete looked even more puzzled. "Then I don't get it . . . I . . . wait, wait a sec, maybe it's like a mystic key to your true nature, you know. I'm a sort of freewheeling dude, so I turned into a hawk, and you . . ." He saw where that was heading and stopped abruptly.

Milton made an ominous growling noise and grabbed him again. "You telling me I'm a *rabbit*?" he roared. "Damn it, you *are* going to die!"

Hank swore under his breath and slammed the bat down on the fender again. "Cut it *out*!" he said.

They stopped. Milton grunted and let go. Pete shook his head. "Look at whatcha done to my *car*!" he wailed. The second blow had left a big dent in the fender. "Jesus, Hank."

"Sorry," the barman said. "I'll stand you to one on the house. No one is going to notice one more dent on this thing anyhow. It's an old piece of junk and you know it."

"It's a *classic*," Pete insisted. He ran his hand over the

fender, frowning. Then he climbed off the hood and stood up. "Three free rounds, I insist. A real classic."

"One," said Hank. "I saved your life, and the car's a deathtrap. What the hell is it, anyhow?"

"You don't know your classic automobiles," Pete said, affronted. "This is a Falcon, one of the first. Ford. Wonderful little car."

Hank had stopped listening all of a sudden. He looked around. The parking lot was dark, the asphalt still slick with the recent rain, but he could make out his own van down by the corner of the building. There was only one other car in the lot. He pointed to it with his bat. "That's yours, isn't it?" he said to Milton.

"Yeah," Milton said, frowning suspiciously.

"VW?"

"Yeah," said Milton. "Brand new. A Rabbit. It gets real good . . ." He stopped, and awareness dawned in his eyes.

Hank laughed.

Pete looked from one car to another. "Oh, Jesus," he said, cradling his head in his hands. "Where the hell is that thing now? We got to keep it safe. There are all kind of . . . cougars, bobcats, hell, they could *kill* somebody. . . ."

"What does he drive, Hank?" Milton demanded. "You know him, right? What kind of car has he got?"

Hank shook his head ruefully. "Poor Barney. We're safe enough. He's got a VW too. Only his is older."

Milton nodded. "Oh, shit. A Beetle."

"Poor Barney," Hank repeated.

"What a night he's going to have," said Milton.

Hank sighed and turned to go back into his establishment. But he stopped when he heard Sleazy Pete say, "Hey, look."

"The moon," Milton said, with a glance. Off where Pete was pointing, the sky was beginning to lighten. "The goddamn full moon. Guess it's started for the poor bastid. Hope his wife don't step on him."

That was when Hank went cold all over. He dropped the bat. It clattered on the pavement and rolled. Then he pulled out his key and turned and locked the door to his bar.

"Hey," said Milton, "it ain't closing time."

"Oh, yes it is," Hank replied. He pointed to where the sky was growing brighter and brighter. "That isn't the moon. It's too overcast to see the moon, and anyhow that's the wrong direction." But by then none of them could mistake the glow for moonlight. It was swelling visibly, eating up half the sky, and its heart burned like the noonday sun, too bright to look upon.

"Oh, shit," Milton said, shielding his eyes and staggering back against the wall.

"He bought it for his wife," Hank said sadly.

Pete asked the last question. "What does she . . ." he began, but the flesh had melted off his bones before he could finish, and he ended with a terrible shrill scream.

Hank had only seen it once, the night that Barney's wife had come to drag him home. Barney had been so plastered that she'd needed help getting him to the car, so Hank had obliged, and he remembered, he remembered. He had a good memory for things like that.

"A Nova," he said, as the world turned incandescent.

UNDER SIEGE

On the high ramparts of Vargon, Colonel Bengt Anttonen stood alone and watched phantasms race across the
ice.

The world was snow and wind and bitter, burning cold.
The winter sea had frozen hard around Helsinki, and in
its icy grip it held the six island citadels of the great
fortress called Sveaborg. The wind was a knife drawn
from a sheath of ice. It cut through Anttonen's uniform,
chafed at his cheeks, brought tears to his eyes and froze
them as they trickled down his face. The wind howled
around the towering gray granite walls, forced its way
through doors and cracks and gun emplacements, insinu-
ated itself everywhere. Out upon the frozen sea, it
snapped and shrieked at the Russian artillery, and sent

puffs of snow from the drifts running and swirling over the ice like strange white beasts, ghostly animals all a-sparkle, wearing first one shape and then another, changing constantly as they ran.

They were creatures as malleable as Anttonen's thoughts. He wondered what form they would take next and where they were running to so swiftly, these misty children of snow and wind. Perhaps they could be taught to attack the Russians. He smiled, savoring the fancy of the snow beasts unleashed upon the enemy. It was a strange, wild thought. Colonel Bengt Anttonen had never been an imaginative man before, but of late his mind had often been taken by such whimsies.

Anttonen turned his face into the wind again, welcoming the chill, the numbing cold. He wanted it to cool his fury, to cut into the heart of him and freeze the passions that seethed there. He wanted to be numb. The cold had turned even the turbulent sea into still and silent ice; now let it conquer the turbulence within Bengt Anttonen. He opened his mouth, exhaled a long plume of breath that rose from his reddened cheeks like steam, inhaled a draught of frigid air that went down like liquid oxygen.

But panic came in the wake of that thought. Again, it was happening again. What was liquid oxygen? Cold, he knew somehow; colder than the ice, colder than this wind. Liquid oxygen was bitter and white, and it steamed and flowed. He knew it, knew it as certainly as he knew his own name. But *how*?

Anttonen turned from the ramparts. He walked with long swift strides, his hand touching the hilt of his sword as if it could provide some protection against the demons that had invaded his mind. The other officers were right; he was going mad, surely. He had proved it this afternoon at the staff meeting.

The meeting had gone very badly; as they all had of late. As always, Anttonen had raised his voice against the others, hopelessly, stupidly. He was right, he *knew* that. Yet he knew also that he could not convince them, and that each word further undermined his status, further damaged his career.

Jägerhorn had brought it on once again. Colonel F. A. Jägerhorn was everything that Anttonen was not; dark and handsome, polished and politic, an aristocrat with an aristocrat's control. Jägerhorn had important connections, Jägerhorn had influential relatives, Jägerhorn had a charmed career. And, most importantly, Jägerhorn had the confidence of Vice-Admiral Carl Olof Cronstedt, commandant of Sveaborg.

At the meeting, Jägerhorn had had a sheaf of reports.

"The reports are wrong," Anttonen had insisted. "The Russians do not outnumber us. And they have barely forty guns, sir. Sveaborg mounts ten times that number."

Cronstedt seemed shocked by Anttonen's tone, his certainty, his insistence. Jägerhorn simply smiled. "Might I ask how you come by this intelligence, Colonel Anttonen?" he asked.

That was the question Bengt Anttonen could never answer. "I know," he said stubbornly.

Jägerhorn rattled the papers in his hand. "My own intelligence comes from Lieutenant Klick, who is in Helsinki and has direct access to reliable reports of enemy plans, movements, and numbers." He looked to Vice-Admiral Cronstedt. "I submit, sir, that this information is a good deal more reliable than Colonel Anttonen's mysterious certainties. According to Klick, the Russians outnumber us already, and General Suchtelen will soon be receiving sufficient reinforcements to enable him to launch a major assault. Furthermore, they have a formidable amount of artillery on hand. Certainly more than the forty pieces that Colonel Anttonen would have us believe the extent of their armament."

Cronstedt was nodding, agreeing. Even then Anttonen could not be silent. "Sir," he insisted, "Klick's reports must be discounted. The man cannot be trusted. Either he is in the pay of the enemy or they are deluding him."

Cronstedt frowned. "That is a grave charge, Colonel."

"Klick is a fool and a damned Anjala traitor!"

Jägerhorn bristled at that, and Cronstedt and a number of junior officers looked plainly aghast. "Colonel," the commandant said, "it is well known that Colonel Jägerhorn has relatives in the Anjala League. Your comments are offensive. Our situation here is perilous enough without my officers fighting among themselves over petty political differences. You will offer an apology at once."

Given no choice, Anttonen had tendered an awkward apology. Jägerhorn accepted with a patronizing nod.

Cronstedt went back to the papers. "Very persuasive," he said, "and very alarming. It is as I have feared. We have come to a hard place." Plainly his mind was made up. It was futile to argue further. It was at times like this that Bengt Anttonen most wondered what madness had possessed him. He would go to staff meetings determined to be circumspect and politic, and no sooner would he be seated than a strange arrogance would seize him. He argued long past the point of wisdom; he denied obvious facts, confirmed in written reports from reliable sources; he spoke out of turn and made enemies on every side.

"No, sir," he said, "I beg of you, disregard Klick's intelligence. Sveaborg is vital to the spring counteroffensive. We have nothing to fear if we can hold out until the ice melts. Once the sea lanes are open, Sweden will send help."

Vice-Admiral Cronstedt's face was drawn and weary, an old man's face. "How many times must we go over this? I grow tired of your argumentative attitude, and I am quite aware of Sveaborg's importance to the spring offensive. The facts are plain. Our defenses are flawed, and the ice makes our walls accessible from all sides. Sweden's armies are being routed—"

"We know that only from the newspapers the Russians allow us, sir," Anttonen blurted. "French and Russian papers. Such news is unreliable."

Cronstedt's patience was exhausted. "Quiet!" he said, slapping the table with an open palm. "I have had enough of your intransigence, Colonel Anttonen. I respect your patriotic fervor, but not your judgement. In the future, when I require your opinion, I shall ask for it. Is that clear?"

"Yes, sir," Anttonen had said.

Jägerhorn smiled. "If I may proceed?"

The rebuke had been as smarting as the cold winter wind. It was no wonder Anttonen had felt driven to the cold solitude of the battlements afterwards.

By the time he returned to his quarters, Bengt Anttonen's mood was bleak and confused. Darkness was falling, he knew. Over the frozen sea, over Sveaborg, over Sweden and Finland. And over America, he thought. Yet the afterthought left him sick and dizzy. He sat heavily on his cot, cradling his head in his hands. America, America, what madness was that, what possible difference could the struggle between Sweden and Russia make to that infant nation so far away?

Rising, he lit a lamp, as if light would drive the troubling thoughts away, and splashed some stale water on his face from the basin atop the modest dresser. Behind the basin was the mirror he used for shaving; slightly warped and dulled by corrosion, but serviceable. As he dried his big, bony hands, he found himself staring at his own face, the features at once so familiar and so oddly, frighteningly strange. He had unruly graying hair, dark gray eyes, a narrow straight nose, slightly sunken cheeks, a square chin. He was too thin, almost gaunt. It was a stubborn, common, plain face. The face he had worn all his life. Long ago, Bengt Anttonen had grown resigned to the way he looked. Until recently, he scarcely gave his appearance any thought. Yet now he stared at himself, unblinking, and felt a disturbing fascination welling up inside him, a sense of satisfaction, a pleasure in the cast of his image that was alien and troubling.

Such vanity was sick, unmanly, another sign of madness. Anttonen wrenched his gaze from the mirror. He lay himself down with a will.

For long moments he could not sleep. Fancies and visions danced against his closed eyelids, sights as fantastic as the phantom animals fashioned by the wind: flags he did not recognize, walls of polished metal, great storms of fire, men and women as hideous as demons asleep in beds of burning liquid. And then, suddenly, the thoughts were gone, peeled off like a layer of burned skin. Bengt Anttonen sighed uneasily, and turned in his sleep . . .

. . . before the awareness is always the pain, and the pain comes first, the only reality in a still quiet empty world beyond sensation. For a second, an hour I do not know where I am and I am afraid. And then the knowledge comes to me; returning, I am returning, in the return is always pain, I do not want to return, but I must. I want the sweet clean purity of ice and snow, the bracing touch of the winter wind, the healthy lines of Bengt's face. But it fades, fades though I scream and clutch for it, crying, wailing. It fades, fades, and then is gone.

I sense motion, a stirring all around me as the immersion fluid ebbs away. My face is exposed first. I suck in air through my wide nostrils, spit the tubes out of my bleeding mouth. When the fluid falls below by ears, I hear a gurgling, a greedy sucking sound. The vampire machines feed on the juices of my womb, the black blood of my second life. The cold touch of air on my skin pains me. I try not to scream, manage to hold the noise down to a whimper.

Above, the top of my tank is coated by a thin ebony film that has clung to the polished metal. I can see my reflection. I'm a stirring sight, nostril hairs a-quiver on my noseless face, my right cheek bulging with a swollen greenish tumor. Such a handsome devil. I smile, showing a triple row of rotten teeth, fresh new incisors pushing up among them like sharpened stakes in a field of yellow toadstools. I wait for release. The tank is too damned small, a coffin. I am buried alive, and the fear is a palpable weight upon me. They do not like me. What if they just leave me in here to suffocate and die? "Out!" I whisper, but no one hears.

Finally the lid lifts and the orderlies are there. Rafael and Slim. Big strapping fellows, blurred white collossi with flags sewn above the pockets of their uniforms. I cannot focus on their faces. My eyes are not so good at the best of times, and especially bad just after a return. I know the dark one is Rafe, though, and it is he who reaches down and unhooks the i.v. tubes and the telemetry, while Slim gives me my injection. Ahhh. Good. The hurt fades. I force my hands to grasp the sides of the tank. The metal feels strange; the motion is clumsy, deliberate, my body slow to respond. "What took you so long?" I ask.

"Emergency," says Slim. "Rollins." He is a testy, laconic sort, and he doesn't like me. To learn more, I would have to ask question after question. I don't have the strength. I concentrate instead on pulling myself to a sitting position. The room is awash with a bright blue-white fluorescent light. My eyes water after so long in darkness. Maybe the orderlies think I'm crying with joy to be back. They're big but not too bright. The air has an astringent, sanitized smell and the hard coolness of air conditioning. Rafe lifts me up from the coffin, the fifth silvery casket in a row of six, each hooked up to the computer banks that loom around us. The other coffins are all empty now. I am the last vampire to rise this night, I think. Then I remember. Four of them are gone, have been gone for a long time. There is only Rollins and myself, and something has happened to Rollins.

They set me in my chair and Slim moves behind me, rolls me past the empty caskets and up the ramps to debriefing. "Rollins," I ask him.

"We lost him."

I didn't like Rollins. He was even uglier than me, a wizened little homunculus with a swollen, oversized cranium and a distorted torso without arms or legs. He had real big eyes, lidless, so he could never close them. Even asleep, he looked like he was staring at you. And he had no sense of humor. No goddamned sense of humor at all. When you're a geek, you got to have a sense of humor. But whatever his faults, Rollins was the only one left, besides me. Gone now. I feel no grief, only a numbness.

The debriefing room is cluttered but somehow impersonal. They wait for me on the other side of the table. The orderlies roll me up opposite them and depart. The table is a long formica barrier between me and my superiors, maybe a *cordon sanitaire*. They cannot let me get too close, after all, I might be contagious. They are normals. I am ... what am I? When they conscripted me, I was classified as a HM₃. Human Mutation, third category. Or a hum-three, in the vernacular. The hum-ones are the non-viables, stillborns and infant deaths and living veggies. We got millions of 'em. The hum-twos are viable but useless, all the guys with extra toes and webbed hands and funny eyes. Got thousands of them. But us hum-threes are a fucking *elite*, so they tell us. That's when they draft us. Down here, inside the Graham Project bunker, we get new names. Old Charlie Graham himself used to call us his "timeriders" before he croaked, but that's too romantic for Major Salazar. Salazar prefers the official government term: G.C., for Graham Chrononaut. The orderlies and grunts turned G.C. into "geek," of course, and we turned it right back on 'em, me and Nan and Creeper, when they were still with us. *They* had a terrific sense of humor, now. The killer geeks, we called ourselves. Six little killer geeks riding the time-stream biting the heads off vast chickens of probability. Heigh-ho.

And then there was one.

Salazar is pushing papers around on the table. He looks sick. Under his dark complexion I can see an unhealthy greenish tinge, and the blood vessels in his nose have burst beneath the skin. None of us are in good shape down here, but Salazar looks worse than most. He's been gaining weight, and it looks bad on him. His uniforms are all too tight now, and there won't be any fresh ones. They've closed down the commissaries and the mills, and in a few years we'll all be wearing rags. I've told Salazar he ought to diet, but no one will listen to a geek, except when the subject is chickens. "Well," Salazar says to me, his voice snapping. A hell of a way to start a debriefing. Three years ago, when it began, he was full of starch and vinegar, very correct and military, but even the Maje has no time left for decorum now.

"What happened to Rollins?" I ask.

Doctor Veronica Jacobi is seated next to Salazar. She used to be chief headshrinker down here, but since Graham Crackers went and expired she's been heading up the whole scientific side of the show. "Death trauma," she says, professionally. "Most likely, his host was killed in action."

I nod. Old story. Sometimes the chickens bite back. "He accomplish anything?"

"Not that we've noticed," Salazar says glumly.

The answer I expected. Rollins had gotten rapport with some ignorant grunt of a footsoldier in the army of Charles XII. I had this droll mental picture of him marching the guy up to his loon of a teenaged king and trying to tell the boy to stay away from Poltava. Charles probably hanged him on the spot—though, come to think of it, it had to be something quicker, or else Rollins would have had time to disengage.

"Your report," prompts Salazar.

"Right, Maje," I say lazily. He hates to be called Maje, though not so much as he hated Sally, which was what Creeper used to call him. Us killer geeks are an insolent lot. "It's no good," I tell them. "Cronstedt is going to meet with General Suchtelen and negotiate for surrender. Nothing Bengt says sways him one damned bit. I been pushing too hard. Bengt thinks he's going crazy. I'm afraid he may crack."

"All timeriders take that risk," Jacobi says. "The longer you stay in rapport, the stronger your influence grows on the host, and the more likely it becomes that your presence will be felt. Few hosts can deal with that perception." Ronnie has a nice voice, and she's always polite to me. Well-scrubbed and tall and calm and even friendly, and above all ineffably polite. I wonder if she'd be as polite if she knew that she'd figured prominently in my masturbation fantasies ever since we'd been down here? They only put five women into the Cracker Box, with thirty-two men and six geeks, and she's by far the most pleasant to contemplate.

Creeper liked to contemplate her, too. He even bugged her bedroom, to watch her in action. She never knew. Creeper had a talent for that stuff, and he'd rig up these tiny little audio-video units on his workbench and plant them everywhere. He said that if he couldn't live life, at least he was going to watch it. Once night he invited me into his room, when Ronnie was entertaining big, red-haired Captain Halliburton, the head of the base security, and her fella in those early days. I watched, yeah; got to confess that I watched. But afterward I got angry. Told Creeper he had no right to spy on Ronnie, or on any of them. "They make us spy on our hosts," he said, "right inside their fucking *heads*, you geek.

Turnabout is fair play." I told him it was different, but I got so mad I couldn't explain why.

It was the only fight Creeper and me ever had. In the long run, it didn't mean much. He went on watching, without me. They never caught the little sneak, but it didn't matter, one day he went timeriding and didn't come back. Big strong Captain Halliburton died too, caught too many rads on those security sweeps, I guess. As far as I know, Creeper's hookup is still in place; from time to time I've thought about going in and taking a peek, to see if Ronnie has herself a new lover. But I haven't. I really don't want to know. Leave me with my fantasies and my wetdreams; they're a lot better anyway.

Salazar's fat fingers drum upon the table. "Give us a full report on your activities," he says curtly.

I sigh and give them what they want, everything in boring detail. When I'm done, I say, "Jägerhorn is the key to the problem. He's got Cronstedt's ear. Anttonen don't."

Salazar is frowning. "If only you could establish rapport with Jägerhorn," he grumbles. What a futile whiner. He knows that's impossible.

"You takes what you gets," I tell him. "If you're going to wish impossible wishes, why stop at Jägerhorn? Why not Cronstedt? Hell, why not the goddamned *Czar*?"

"He's right, Major," Veronica says. "We ought to be grateful that we've got a link with Anttonen. At least he's a colonel. That's better than we did in any of the other target periods."

Salazar is still unhappy. He's a military historian by trade. He thought this would be easy when they transferred him out from West Point, or what was left of it. "Anttonen is peripheral," he declares. "We must reach the key figures. Your chrononauts are giving me footnotes, bystanders, the wrong men in the wrong place at the wrong time. It is impossible."

"You knew the job was dangerous when you took it,"

I say. A killer geek quoting Superchicken; I'd get thrown out of the union if they knew. "We don't get to pick and choose."

The Maje scowls at me. I yawn. "I'm tired of this," I say. "I want something to eat. Some ice cream. I want some rocky road ice cream. Seems funny, don't it? All that goddamned ice, and I come back wanting ice cream." There is no ice cream, of course. There hasn't been any ice cream for half a generation, anywhere in the godforsaken mess they call a world. But Nan used to tell me about it. Nan was the oldest geek, the only one born before the big crash, and she had lots of stories about the way things used to be. I liked it best when she talked about ice cream. It was smooth and cold and sweet, she said. It melted on your tongue, and filled your mouth with liquid, delicious cold. Sometimes she would recite the flavors for us, as solemnly as Chaplain Todd reading his Bible: vanilla and strawberry and chocolate, fudge swirl and praline, rum raisin and heavenly hash, banana and orange sherbet and mint chocolate chip, pistachio and butterscotch and coffee and cinnamon and butter pecan. Creeper used to make up flavors to poke fun at her, but there was no getting to Nan. She just added his inventions to her list, and spoke fondly thereafter of anchovy almond and liver chip and radiation ripple, until I couldn't tell the real flavors from the made-up ones any more, and didn't really care.

Nan was the first we lost. Did they have ice cream in St. Petersburg back in 1917? I hope they did. I hope she got a bowl or two before she died.

Major Salazar is still talking, I realize. He has been talking for some time. " . . . our last chance now," he is saying. He begins to babble about Sveaborg, about the importance of what we are doing here, about the urgent need to *change* something somehow, to prevent the Soviet Union from ever coming into existence, and thus forestall the war that has laid the world to waste. I've heard it all before, I know it all by heart. The Maje has terminal verbal diarrhea, and I'm not so dumb as I look.

It was all Graham Cracker's idea, the last chance to win the war or maybe just save ourselves from the plagues and bombs and the poisoned winds. But the Maje was the historian, so he got to pick all the targets, when the computers had done their probability analysis. He had six geeks and he got six tries. "Nexus points," he called 'em. Critical points in history. Of course, some were better than others. Rollins got the Great Northern War, Nan got the Revolution, Creeper got to go all the way back to Ivan the Terrible, and I got Sveaborg. Impregnable, invincible Sveaborg. Gibraltar of the North.

"There is no reason for Sveaborg to surrender," the Maje is saying. It is his own ice cream litany. History and tactics give him the sort of comfort that butter brickle gave to Nan. "The garrison is seven thousand strong, vastly outnumbering the besieging Russians. The artillery inside the fortress is much superior. There is plenty of ammunition, plenty of food. If Sveaborg only holds out until the sea lanes are open, Sweden will launch its counteroffensive and the siege will be broken easily. The entire course of the war may change! You must make Cronstedt listen to reason."

"If I could just lug back a history text and let him read what they say about him, I'm sure he'd jump through flaming hoops," I say. I've had enough of this. "I'm tired," I announce. "I want some food." Suddenly, for no apparent reason, I feel like crying. "I want something to eat, damn it, I don't want to talk anymore, you hear, I want *something to eat.*"

Salazar glares, but Veronica hears the stress in my voice, and she is up and moving around the table. "Easy enough to arrange," she says to me, and to the Maje, "We've accomplished all we can for now. Let me get him some food." Salazar grunts, but he dares not object. Veronica wheels me away, toward the commissary.

Over stale coffee and a plate of mystery meat and overcooked vegetables, she consoles me. She's not half bad at it; a pro, after all. Maybe, in the old days, she wouldn't have been considered especially striking—I've seen the old magazines, after all, even down here we have our old *Playboys*, our old video tapes, our old novels, our old record albums, our old funny books, nothing *new* of course, nothing recent, but lots and lots of the old junk. I ought to know, I practically mainline the stuff, when I'm not flailing around inside Bengt's cranium, I'm planted in front of my tube, running some old TV show or a movie, maybe reading a paperback at the same time, trying to imagine what it would be like to live back then, before they screwed up everything. So I know all about the old standards, and maybe it's true that Ronnie ain't up to, say, Bo or Marilyn or Brigitte or Garbo. Still, she's nicer to look at than anybody else down in this damned septic tank. And the rest of us don't quite measure up either. Creeper wasn't no Groucho, no matter how hard he tried; me, I look just like Jimmy Cagney, but the big green tumor and all the extra yellow teeth and the want of a nose spoil the effect, just a little.

I push my fork away with the meal half-eaten. "It has no taste. Back then, food had *taste*."

Veronica laughs. "You're lucky. You get to taste it. For the rest of us, this is all there is."

"Lucky? Ha-ha. I know the difference, Ronnie. You don't. Can you miss something you never had?" I'm sick of talking about it, though; I'm sick of it all. "You want to play chess?"

She smiles and gets up in search of our set. An hour later, she's won the first game and we're starting the second. There are about a dozen chess players down here in the Cracker Box; now that Graham and Creeper are gone, I can beat all of them except Ronnie. The funny thing is, back in 1808 I could probably be world champion. Chess has come a long way in the last two hundred years, and I've memorized openings that those old guys never even dreamed of.

"There's more to the game than book openings," Veronica says, and I realize I've been talking aloud.

"I'd still win," I insist. "Hell, those guys have been dead for centuries, how much fight can they put up?"

She smiles, and moves a knight. "Check," she says.

I realize that I've lost again. "Some day I've got to learn to play this game," I say. "Some world champion."

Veronica begins to put the pieces back in the box. "This Sveaborg business is a kind of chess game too," she says conversationally, "a chess game across time, us and the Swedes against the Russians and the Finnish nationalists. What move do you think we should make against Cronstedt?"

"Why did I know that the conversation was going to come back to that?" I say. "Damned if I know. I suppose the Maje has an idea."

She nods. Her face is serious now. Pale soft face, framed by dark hair. "A desperate idea. These are desperate times."

What would it be like if I did suceed, I wonder? If I changed something? What would happen to Veronica and the Maje and Rafe and Slim and all the rest of them? What would happen to *me*, lying there in my coffin full of darkness? There are theories, of course, but no one really knows. "I'm a desperate man, ma'am," I say to her, "ready for any desperate measures. Being subtle sure hasn't done diddlysquat. Let's hear it. What do I gotta get Bengt to do now? Invent the machine gun? Defect to the Russkis? Expose his privates on the battlements? What?"

She tells me.

I'm dubious. "Maybe it'll work," I say. "More likely, it'll get Bengt slung into the deepest goddamned dungeon that place has. They'll really think he's nuts. Jägerhorn might just shoot him outright."

"No," she says. "In his own way, Jägerhorn is an idealist. A man of principle. I agree, it is a chancy move. But you don't win chess games without taking chances. Will you do it?"

She has such a nice smile; I think she likes me. I shrug. "Might as well," I say. "Can't dance."

". . . shall be allowed to dispatch two couriers to the King, the one by the northern, the other by the southern road. They shall be furnished with passports and safeguards, and every possible facility shall be given them for accomplishing their journey. Done at the island of Lonan, 6 April, 1808."

The droning voice of the officer reading the agreement stopped suddenly, and the staff meeting was deathly quiet. A few of the Swedish officers stirred uneasily in their seats, but no one spoke.

Vice-Admiral Cronstedt rose slowly. "This is the agreement," he said. "In view of our perilous position, it is better than we could have hoped for. We have used a third of our powder already, our defenses are exposed to attack from all sides because of the ice, we are outnumbered and forced to support a large number of fugitives who rapidly consume our provisions. General Suchtelen might have demanded our immediate surrender. By the grace of God, he did not. Instead we have been allowed to retain three of Sveaborg's six islands, and will regain two of the others, should five Swedish ships-of-the-line arrive to aid us before the third of May. If Sweden fails us, we must surrender. Yet the fleet shall be restored to Sweden at the conclusion of the war, and this immediate truce will prevent any further loss of life."

Cronstedt sat down. At his side, Colonel Jägerhorn came crisply to his feet. "In the event the Swedish ships do not arrive on time, we must make plans for an orderly surrender of the garrison." He launched into a discussion of the details.

Bengt Anttonen sat quietly. He had expected the news, had somehow known it was coming, but it was no less dismaying for all that. Cronstedt and Jägerhorn had negotiated a disaster. It was foolish. It was craven. It was hopelessly doomed. Immediate surrender of Wester-Svartö, Langörn, and Oster-Lilla-Svartö, the rest of the garrison to come later, capitulation deferred for a meaningless month. History would revile them. School children would curse their names. And he was helpless.

When the meeting at last ended, the others rose to depart. Anttonen rose with them, determined to be silent, to leave the room quietly for once, to let them sell Sveaborg for thirty pieces of silver if they would. But as he tried to turn, the compulsion seized him, and he went instead to where Cronstedt and Jägerhorn lingered. They both watched him approach. In their eyes, Anttonen thought he could see a weary resignation.

"You must not do this," he said heavily.

"It is done," Cronstedt replied. "The subject is not open for further discussion, Colonel. You have been warned. Go about your duties." He climbed to his feet, turned to go.

"The Russians are cheating you," Anttonen blurted.

Cronstedt stopped and looked at him.

"Admiral, please, you must listen to me. This provision, this agreement that we will retain the fortress if five ships-of-the-line reach us by the third of May, it is a fraud. The ice will not have melted by the third of May. No ship will be able to reach us. The armistice agreement provides that the ships must have entered Sveaborg's harbor by noon on the third of May. General Suchtelen will use the time afforded by the truce to move his guns and gain control of the sea approaches. Any ship attempting to reach Sveaborg will come under heavy attack. And there is more. The messengers you are sending to the King, sir, they—"

Cronstedt's face was ice and granite. He held up a

hand. "I have heard enough. Colonel Jägerhorn, arrest this madman." He gathered up his papers, refusing to look Anttonen in the face, and strode angrily from the room.

"Colonel Anttonen, you are under arrest," Jägerhorn said, with surprising gentleness in his voice. "Don't resist, I warn you, that will only make it worse."

Anttonen turned to face the other colonel. His heart was sick. "You will not listen. None of you will listen. Do you know what you are doing?"

"I think I do," Jägerhorn said.

Anttonen reached out and grabbed him by the front of his uniform. "You do *not*. You think I don't know what you are, Jägerhorn? You're a nationalist, damn you. This is the great age of nationalism. You and your Anjala League, your damned Finnlander noblemen, you're all Finnish nationalists. You resent Sweden's domination. The Czar has promised you that Finland will be an autonomous state under his protection, so you have thrown off your loyalty to the Swedish crown."

Colonel F.A. Jägerhorn blinked. A strange expression flickered across his face before he regained his composure. "You cannot know that," he said. "No one knows the terms—I—"

Anttonen shook him bodily. "History is going to laugh at you, Jägerhorn. Sweden will lose this war, because of you, because of Sveaborg's surrender, and you'll get your wish, Finland will become an autonomous state under the Czar. But it will be no freer than it is now, under Sweden. You'll swap your King like a second-hand chair at a flea market, for the butchers of the Great Wrath, and gain nothing by the transaction."

"Like a . . . a market for fleas? What is that?"

Anttonen scowled. "A flea market, a flea . . . I don't know," he said. He released Jägerhorn, turned away. "Dear God, I do know. It is a place where . . . where things are sold and traded. A fair. It has nothing to do with fleas, but it is full of strange machines, strange smells." He ran his fingers through his hair, fighting not to scream. "Jägerhorn, my head is full of demons. Dear God, I must confess. Voices, I hear voices day and night, even as the French girl, Joan, the warrior maid. I know things that will come to pass." He looked into Jägerhorn's eyes, saw the fear there, and held his hands up, entreating now. "It is no choice of mine, you must believe that. I pray for silence, for release, but the whispering continues, and these strange fits seize me. They are not of my doing, yet they must be sent for a reason, they must be true, or why would God torture me so? Have mercy, Jägerhorn. Have mercy on me, and listen!"

Colonel Jägerhorn looked past Anttonen, his eyes searching for help, but the two of them were quite alone. "Yes," he said. "Voices, like the French girl. I did not understand."

Anttonen shook his head. "You hear, but you will not believe. You are a patriot, you dream you will be a hero. You will be no hero. The common folk of Finland do not share your dreams. They remember the Great Wrath. They know the Russians only as ancient enemies, and they hate. They will hate you as well. And Cronstedt, ah, poor Admiral Cronstedt. He will be reviled by every Finn, every Swede, for generations to come. He will live out his life in this new Grand Duchy of Finland, on a Russian stipend, and he will die a broken man on April 7, 1820, twelve years and one day after he met with Suchtelen on Lonan and gave Sveaborg to Russia. Later, years later, a man named Runeberg will write a series of poems about this war. Do you know what he will say of Cronstedt?"

"No," Jägerhorn said. He smiled uneasily. "Have your voices told you?"

"They have taught me the words by heart," said Bengt Anttonen. He recited:

> *Call him the arm we trusted in,*
> *that shrank in time of stress,*
> *call him Affliction, Scorn, and Sin,*
> *and Death and Bitterness,*
> *but mention not his former name,*
> *lest they should blush who bear the same.*

"That is the glory you and Cronstedt are winning here, Jägerhorn," Anttonen said bitterly. "That is your place in history. Do you like it?"

Colonel Jägerhorn had been carefully edging around Anttonen; there was a clear path between him and the door. But now he hesitated. "You are speaking madness," he said. "And yet—and yet—how could you have known of the Czar's promises? You would almost have me believe you. Voices? Like the French girl? The voice of God, you say?"

Anttonen sighed. "God? I do not know. Voices, Jägerhorn, that is all I hear. Perhaps I am mad."

Jägerhorn grimaced. "They will revile us, you say? They will call us traitors and denounce us in poems?"

Anttonen said nothing. The madness had ebbed; he was filled with a helpless despair.

"No," Jägerhorn insisted. "It is too late. The agreement is signed. We have staked our honor on it. And Vice-Admiral Cronstedt, he is so uncertain. His family is here, and he fears for them. Suchtelen has played him masterfully and we have done our part. It cannot be undone. I do not believe this madness of yours, yet even if I believed, there is no hope for it, nothing to be done. The ships will not come in time. Sveaborn must yield, and the war must end with Sweden's defeat. How could it be otherwise? The Czar is allied with Bonaparte himself, he cannot be resisted!"

"The alliance will not last," Anttonen said, with a rueful smile. "The French will march on Moscow and it will destroy them as it destroyed Charles XII. The winter will be their Poltava. All of this will come too late for Finland, too late for Sveaborg."

"It is too late even now," Jägerhorn said. "Nothing can be changed."

For the first time, Bengt Anttonen felt the tiniest glimmer of hope. "It is not too late."

"What course do you urge upon us, then? Cronstedt has made his decision. Should we mutiny?"

"There will be a mutiny in Sveaborg, whether we take part or not. It will fail."

"What then?"

Bengt Anttenon lifted his head, stared Jägerhorn in the eyes. "The agreement stipulates that we may send two couriers to the King, to inform him of the terms, so the Swedish ships may be dispatched on time."

"Yes. Cronstedt will choose our couriers tonight, and they will leave tomorrow, with papers and safe passage furnished by Suchtelen."

"You have Cronstedt's ear. See that I am chosen as one of the couriers."

"You?" Jägerhorn looked doubtful. "What good will that serve?" He frowned. "Perhaps this voice you hear is the voice of your own fear. Perhaps you have been under siege too long, and it has broken you, and now you hope to run free."

"I can prove my voices speak true," Anttonen said.

"How?" snapped Jägerhorn.

"I will meet you tomorrow at dawn at Ehrensvärd's tomb, and I will tell you the names of the couriers that Cronstedt has chosen. If I am right, you will convince him to send me in the place of one of those chosen. He will agree, gladly. He is anxious to be rid of me."

Colonel Jägerhorn rubbed his jaw, considering. "No one could know the choices but Cronstedt. It is a fair test." He put out his hand. "Done."

They shook. Jägerhorn turned to go. But at the doorway he turned back. "Colonel Anttonen," he said, "I have forgotten my duty. You are in my custody. Go to your own quarters and remain there, until the dawn."

"Gladly," said Anttonen. "At dawn, you will see that I am right."

"Perhaps," said Jägerhorn, "but for all our sakes, I shall hope very much that you are wrong."

... and the machines suck away the liquid night that enfolds me, and I'm screaming, screaming so loudly that Slim draws back, a wary look on his face. I give him a broad geekish smile, rows on rows of yellow rotten teeth. "Get me out of here, turkey," I shout. The pain is a web around me, but this time it doesn't seem as bad, this time I can almost stand it, this time the pain is *for* something.

They give me my shot, and lift me into my chair, but this time I'm eager for the debriefing. I grab the wheels and give myself a push, breaking free of Rafe, rolling down the corridors like I used to do in the old days, when Creeper was around to race me. There's a bit of a problem with one ramp, and they catch me there, the strong silent guys in their ice cream suits (that's what Nan called 'em, anyhow), but I scream at them to leave me alone. They do. Surprises the hell out of me.

The Maje is a little startled when I come rolling into the room all by my lonesome. He starts to get up. "Are you ..."

"Sit down, Sally," I say. "It's good news. Bengt psyched out Jägerhorn good. I thought the kid was gonna wet his pants, believe me. I think we got it socked. I'm meeting Jägerhorn tomorrow at dawn to clinch the sale." I'm grinning, listening to myself. Tomorrow, hey, I'm talking about 1808, but tomorrow is how it feels. "Now here's the sixty-four thousand dollar question. I need to know the names of the two guys that Cronstedt is going to try and send to the Swedish king. Proof, y'know? Jägerhorn says he'll get me sent if I can convince him. So you look up those names for me, Maje, and once I say the magic words, the duck will come down and give us Sveaborg."

"This is very obscure information," Salazar complains. "The couriers were detained for weeks, and did not even arrive in Stockholm until the day of the surrender. Their names may be lost to history." What a whiner, I'm thinking; the man is never satisfied.

Ronnie speaks up for me, though. "Major Salazar, those names had better not be lost to history, or to us. You were our military historian. It was your job to research each of the target periods *thoroughly*." The way she's talking to him, you'd never guess he was the boss. "The Graham Project has every priority. You have our computer files, our dossiers on the personnel of Sveaborg, and you have access to the war college at New West Point. Maybe you can even get through to someone in what remains of Sweden. I don't care how you do it, but it must be done. The entire project could rest on this piece of information. The entire world. Our past and our future. I shouldn't need to tell you that." She turns to me. I applaud. She smiles. "You've done well," she says. "Would you give us the details?"

"Sure," I say. "It was a piece of cake. With ice cream on top. What'd they used to call that?"

"A la mode."

"Sveaborg a la mode," I say, and I serve it up to them. I talk and talk. When I finally finish, even the Maje looks grudgingly pleased. Pretty damn good for a geek, I think. "OK," I say when I'm done with the report. "What's next? Bengt gets the courier job, right? And I get the message through somehow. Avoid Suchtelen, don't get detained, the Swedes send in the cavalry."

"Cavalry?" Sally looks confused.

"It's a figure of speech," I say, with unusual patience.

The Maje nods. "No," he says. "The couriers—it's true that General Suchtelen lied, and held them up as an extra form of insurance. The ice might have melted, after all. The ships might have come through in time. But it was an unnecessary precaution. That year, the ice around Helsinki did not melt until well after the deadline date." He gives me a solemn stare. He has never looked sicker, and the greenish tinge of his skin undermines the effect he's trying to achieve. "We must make a bold stroke. You will be sent out as a courier, under the terms of the truce. You and the other courier will be brought before General Suchtelen to receive your safe conducts through Russian lines. That is the point at which you will strike. The affair is settled, and war in those days was an honorable affair. No one will expect treachery."

"Treachery?" I say. I don't like the sound of what I'm hearing.

For a second, the Maje's smile looks almost genuine; he's finally lit on something that pleases him. "Kill Suchtelen," he says.

"Kill Suchtelen?" I repeat.

"Use Anttonen. Fill him with rage. Have him draw his weapon. Kill Suchtelen."

I see. A new move in our crosstime chess game. The geek gambit.

"They'll kill Bengt," I say.

"You can disengage," Salazar says.

"Maybe they'll kill him fast," I point out. "Right there, on the spot, y'know."

"You take that risk. Other men have given their lives for our nation. This is war." The Maje frowns. "Your success may doom us all. When you change the past, the present as it now exists may simply cease to exist, and us with it. But our nation will live, and millions we have lost will be restored to us. Healthier, happier versions of ourselves will enjoy the rich lives that were denied us. You yourself will be born whole, without sickness or deformity."

"Or talent," I say. "In which case I won't be able to go back to do this, in which case the past stays unchanged."

"The paradox does not apply. You have been briefed on this. The past and the present and future are not co-temporanious. And it will be Anttonen who effects the change, not yourself. He is of that time." The Maje is impatient. His thick, dark fingers drum on the table top. "Are you a coward?"

"Fuck you and the horse you rode in on," I tell him. "You don't get it. I could give a shit about me. I'm better off dead. But they'll kill *Bengt.*"

He frowns."What of it?"

Veronica has been listening intently. Now she leans across the table and touches my hand, gently. "I understand. You identify with him, don't you?"

"He's a good man," I say. Do I sound defensive? Very well, then; I *am* defensive. "I feel bad enough that I'm driving him around the bend, I don't want to get him killed. I'm a freak, a geek, I've lived my whole life under siege and I'm going to die here, but Bengt has people who love him, a life ahead of him. Once he gets out of Sveaborg, there's a whole world out there."

"He has been dead for almost two centuries," Salazar says.

"I was inside his head this afternoon," I snap.

"He will be a casualty of war," the Maje says. "In war, soldiers die. It is a fact of life, then as now."

Something else is bothering me. "Yeah, maybe, he's a soldier, I'll buy that. He knew the job was dangerous when he took it. But he cares about *honor,* Sally. A little thing we've forgotten. To die in battle sure, but you want me to make him a goddamned *assassin,* have him violate a flag of truce. He's an honorable man. They'll revile him."

"The ends justify the means," says Salazar bluntly. "Kill Suchtelen, kill him under the flag of truce, yes. It will kill the truce as well. Suchtelen's second-in-command is far less wily, more prone to outbursts of temper, more eager for a spectacular victory. You will

tell him that Cronstedt *ordered* you to cut down Suchtelen. He will shatter the truce, will launch a furious
attack against the fortress, an attack that Sveaborg,
inpregnable as it is, will easily repulse. Russian casualties
will be heavy, and Swedish determination will be fired
by what they will see as Russian treachery. Jägerhorn,
with proof before him that the Russian promises are
meaningless, will change sides. Cronstedt, the hero of
Ruotsinsalmi, will become the hero of Sveaborg as well.
The fortress will hold. With the spring the Swedish fleet
will land an army at Sveaborg, behind Russian lines,
while a second Swedish army sweeps down from the
north. The entire course of the war will change. When
Napoleon marches on Moscow, a Swedish army will
already hold St. Petersburg. The Czar will be caught in
Moscow, deposed, executed. Napoleon will install a pup-
pet government, and when his retreat comes, it will be
north, to link up with his Swedish allies at St. Petersburg.
The new Russian regime will not survive Bonaparte's fall,
but the Czarist restoration will be as short-lived as the
French restoration, and Russia will evolve toward a lib-
eral parliamentary democracy. The Soviet Union will
never come into being to war against the United States."
He emphasizes his final words by pounding his fist on
the conference table.

"Sez you," I say mildly.

Salazar gets red in the face. "That is the computer
projection," he insists. He looks away from me, though.
Just a quick little averting of the eyes, but I catch it.
Funny. He can't look me in the eyes.

Veronica squeezes my hand. "The projection may be
off," she admits. "A little or a lot. But it is all we have.
And this is our last chance. I understand your concern
for Anttonen, really I do. It's only natural. You've been
part of him for months now, living his life, sharing his
thoughts and feelings. Your reservations do you credit.
But now millions of lives are in the balance, against the

life of this one man. This one, dead man. It's your decision. The most important decision in all of human history, perhaps, and it rests with you alone." She smiles. "Think about it carefully, at least."

When she puts it like that, and holds my little hand all the while, I'm powerless to resist. Ah, Bengt. I look away from them, sigh. "Break out the booze tonight," I say wearily to Salazar, "the last of that old pre-war stuff you been saving."

The Maje looks startled, discomfited; the jerk thought his little cache of prewar Glenlivet and Irish Mist and Remy Martin was a well-kept secret. And so it was until Creeper planted one of his little bugs, heigh-ho. "I do not think drunken revelry is in order," Sally says. Defending his treasure. He's homely and mean-spirited, but nobody ever said he wasn't selfish.

"Shut up and come across," I say. Tonight I ain't gonna be denied. I'm giving up Bengt, the Maje can give up some booze. "I want to get shitfaced," I tell them. "It's time to drink to the goddamned dead and toast the living, past and present. It's in the rules, damn you. The geek always gets a bottle before he goes out to meet the chickens."

Within the central courtyard of the Vargon citadel, Bengt Anttonen waited in the predawn chill. Behind him stood Ehrensvärd's tomb, the final resting place of the man who had built Sveaborg, and now slept securely within the bosom of his creation, his bones safe behind her guns and her thick granite walls, guarded by all her daunting might. He had built her impregnable, and impregnable she stood, so none would come to disturb his rest. But now they wanted to give her away.

The wind was blowing. It came howling down out of a black empty sky, stirred the barren branches of the trees that stood in the empty courtyard, and cut through Anttonen's warmest coat. Or perhaps it was another sort of chill that lay upon him; the chill of fear. Dawn was almost at hand. Above, the stars were fading. And his head was empty, echoing, mocking. Light would soon break over the horizon, and with the light would come Colonel Jägerhorn, hard-faced, imperious, demanding, and Anttonen would have nothing to say to him.

He heard footsteps. Jägerhorn's boots rang on the stones. Anttonen turned to face him, watching him climb the few small steps up to Ehrensvard's memorial. They stood a foot apart, conspirators huddled against the cold and darkness. Jägerhorn gave him a curt, short nod. "I have met with Cronstedt."

Anttonen opened his mouth. His breath steamed in the frigid air. And just as he was about to succumb to the emptiness, about to admit that his voices had failed him, something whispered deep inside him. He spoke two names.

There was such a long silence that Anttonen once again began to fear. Was it madness after all, and not the voice of God? Had he been wrong? But then Jägerhorn looked down, frowning, and clapped his gloved hands together in a gesture that spoke of finality. "God help us all," he said, "but I believe you."

"I will be the courier?"

"I have already broached the subject with Vice-Admiral Cronstedt," Jägerhorn said. "I have reminded him of your years of service, your excellent record. You are a good soldier and a man of honor, damaged only by your own patriotism and the pressure of the siege. You are that sort of warrior who cannot bear inaction, who must always be doing something. You deserve more than arrest and disgrace, I have argued. As a courier, you will redeem yourself, I have told him I have no doubt of it. And by removing you from Sveaborg, we will remove also a source of tension and dissent around which mutiny might grow. The Vice-Admiral is well aware that a good many of the men are most unwilling to honor our pact with Suchtelen. He is convinced." Jägerhorn smiled wanly. "I am nothing if not convincing, Anttonen. I can marshall an argument as Bonaparte marshalls his armies. So this victory is ours. You are named courier."

"Good," said Anttonen. Why did he feel so sick at heart? He should have been full of jubilation.

"What will you do?" Jägerhorn asked. "For what purpose do we conspire?"

"I will not burden you with that knowledge," Anttonen replied. It was knowledge he lacked himself. He must be the courier, he had known that since yesterday, but the why of it still eluded him, and the future was cold as the stone of Ehrensvard's tomb, as misty as Jägerhorn's breath. He was full of a strange foreboding, a sense of approaching doom.

"Very well," said Jägerhorn. "I pray that I have acted wisely in this." He removed his glove, offered his hand. "I will count on you, on your wisdom and your honor."

"My honor," Bengt repeated. Slowly, too slowly, he took off his own glove to shake the hand of the dead man standing there before him. Dead man? He was no dead man; he was live, warm flesh. But it was frigid there under those bare trees, and when Anttonen clasped Jägerhorn's hand, the other's skin felt cold to the touch.

"We have had our differences," said Jägerhorn, "but we are both Finns, after all, and patriots, and men of honor, and now too we are friends."

"Friends," Anttonen repeated. And in his head, louder than it had ever been before, so clear and strong it seemed almost as if someone had spoken behind him, came a whisper, sad somehow, and bitter. *C'mon, Chicken Little,* it said, *shake hands with your pal, the geek.*

Gather ye Four Roses while ye may, for time is still a-flying, and this same geek what smiles today tomorrow may be dying. Heigh-ho, drunk again, second night inna row, chugging all the Maje's good booze, but what does it matter, he won't be needing it. After this next little timeride, he won't even exist, or that's what they tell me. In fact, he'll never have existed, which is a real weird thought. Old Major Sally Salazar, his big thick fingers, his greenish tinge, the endearing way he had of whining and bitching, he sure seemed real this afternoon at that last debriefing, but now it turns out there never was any such person. Never was a Creeper, never a Rafe or a Slim, Nan never ever told us about ice cream and reeled off the names of all those flavors, butter pecan and rum raisin are one with Ninevah and Tyre, heigh-ho. Never happened, nope, and I slug down another shot, drinking alone, in my room, in my cubicle, the savior at this last liquid supper, where the hell are all my fucking apostles? Ah, drinking, drinking, but not with me.

They ain't s'posed to know, nobody's s'posed to know but me and the Maje and Ronnie, but the word's out, yes it is, and out there in the corridors it's turned into a big wild party, boozing and singing and fighting, a little bit of screwing for those lucky enough to have a partner, of which number I am not one, alas. I want to go out and join in, hoist a few with the boys, but no, the Maje says no, too dangerous, one of the motley horde might decide that even this kind of has-been life is better than a never-was non-life, and therefore off the geek, ruining everybody's plans for a good time. So here I sit on geek row, in my little room boozing alone, surrounded by five other little rooms, and down at the end of the corridor is a most surly guard, pissed off that he isn't out there getting a last taste, who's got to keep me in and the rest of them out.

I was sort of hoping Ronnie might come by, you know, to share a final drink and beat me in one last game of chess and maybe even play a little kissey-face, which is a ridiculous fantasy on the face of it, but somehow I don't wanna die a virgin, even though I'm not really going to die, since once the trick is done, I won't ever have lived at all. It's goddamned noble of me if you ask me and you got to cause there ain't nobody else around to ask. Another drink now but the bottle's almost empty; I'll have to ring the Maje and ask for another. Why won't Ronnie come by? I'll never be seeing her again, after tomorrow, tomorrow-tomorrow and two-hundred-years-ago-tomorrow. I could refuse to go, stay here and keep the happy lil' family alive, but I don't think she'd like that. She's a lot more sure than me. I asked her this afternoon if Sally's projections could tell us about the side effects. I mean, we're changing this war, and we're keeping Sveaborg and (we hope) losing the Czar and (we hope) losing the Soviet Union and (we sure as hell hope) maybe losing the big war and all, the bombs and the rads and the plagues and all that good stuff, even radiation ripple ice cream which was the Creeper's favorite flavor, but what if we lose other stuff? I mean, with Russia so changed and all, are we going to lose Alaska? Are we gonna lose vodka? Are we going to lose George Orwell? Are we going to lose Karl Marx? We tried to lose Karl Marx, actually, one of the other geeks, Blind Jeffey, he went back to take care of Karlie, but it didn't work out. Maybe vision was too damn much for him. So we got to keep Karl, although come to think of it, who cares about Karl Marx, are we gonna lose Groucho? No Groucho, no Groucho ever, I don't like that concept, last night I shot a geek in my pyjamas and how he got in my pyjamas I'll never know, but maybe, who the hell knows how us geeks get anyplace, all these damn dominoes falling every which way, knocking over other dominoes, dominoes was never my game, I'm a chess player, world chess champion in temporal exile, that's me, dominoes is a dumb damn game. What if it don't work, I asked Ronnie, what if we take out Russia, and, well, Hitler wins World War II so we wind up swapping missiles and germs and bio-toxins with Nazi Germany? Or England? Or fucking Austria-Hungary, maybe, who can say? The superpower

Austria-Hungary, what a thought, last night I shot a Hapsburg in my pyjamas, the geeks put him there, heigh-ho.

Ronnie didn't make me no promises, kiddies. Best she could do was shrug and tell me this story about a horse. This guy was going to get his head cut off by some old-timey king, y'see, so he pipes up and tells the king that if he's given a year, he'll teach the king's horse to talk. The king likes this idea, for some reason, maybe he's a Mister Ed fan, I dunno, but he gives the guy a year. And afterwards, the guy's friends say, hey, what is this, you can't get no horse to talk. So the guy says, well, I got a year now, that's a long time, all kinds of things could happen. Maybe the king will die. Maybe I'll die. Maybe the horse will die. Or maybe the horse will talk.

I'm too damn drunk, I am I am, and my head's full of geeks and talking horses and falling dominoes and unrequited love, and all of a sudden I got to see her. I set down the bottle, oh so carefully, even though it's empty, don't want no broken glass on geek row, and I wheel myself out into the corridor, going slow, I'm not too coordinated right now. The guard is at the end of the hall, looking wistful. I know him a little bit. Security guy, big black fellow, name of Dex. "Hey, Dex," I say as I come wheeling up, "screw this shit, let's us go party, I want to see lil' Ronnie." He just looks at me, shakes his head. "C'mon," I say. I bat my baby-blues at him. Does he let me by? Does the Pope shit in the woods? Hell no, old Dex says, "I got my orders, you stay right here." All of a sudden I'm mad as hell, this ain't fair, I want to see Ronnie. I gather up all my strength and try to wheel right by him. No cigar; Dex turns, blocks my way, grabs the wheelchair and pushes. I go backwards fast, spin around when a wheel jams, flip over and out of the chair. It hurts. Goddamn it hurts. If I had a nose, I woulda bloodied it, I bet. "You stay where you are, you fucking freak," Dex tells me. I start to cry, damn him anyhow, and he watches me as I get my chair upright and pull myself into it. I sit there staring at him. He stands there staring at me. "Please," I say finally. He shakes his head. "Go get her then," I say. "Tell her I want to see her." Dex grins. "She's busy," he tells me. "Her and Major Salazar. She don't want to see you."

I stare at him some more. A real withering, intimidating stare. He doesn't wither or look intimidated. It can't be, can it? Her and the Maje? Her and old Sally Greenface? No way, he's not her type, she's got better taste than that, I know she has. Say it ain't so, Joe. I turn around, start back to my cubicle. Dex looks away. Heigh-ho, fooled him.

Creeper's room is the one beyond mine, the last one at the end of the hall. Everything's just like he left it. I turn on the set, play with the damn switches, trying to figure out how it works. My mind isn't at its sharpest right at this particular minute, it takes me a while, but finally I get it, and I jump from scene to scene down in the Cracker Box, savoring all these little vignettes of life in these United States as served up by Creeper's clever ghost. Each scene has its own individual charm. There's a gang bang going on in the commissary, right on top of one of the tables where Ronnie and I used to play chess. Two huge security men are fighting up in the airlock area; they've been at it a long time, their faces are so bloody I can't tell who the hell they are, but they keep at it, staggering at each other blindly, swinging huge awkward fists, grunting, while a few others stand around and egg them on. Slim and Rafe are sharing a joint, leaning up against my coffin. Slim thinks they ought to rip out all the wires, fuck up everything so I can't go timeriding. Rafe thinks it'd be easier to just bash my head in. Somehow I don't think he loves me no more. Maybe I'll cross him off my Christmas list. Fortunately for the geek, both of them are too stoned and screwed up to do anything at all. I watch a half-dozen other scenes, and finally, a little reluctantly, I go to Ronnie's room, where I watch her screwing Major Salazar.

Heigh-ho, as Creeper would say, what'd you expect, really?

I could not love thee, dear, so much, loved I not honor more. She walks in beauty like the night. But she's not so pretty, not really, back in 1808 there were lovelier women, and Bengt's just the man to land 'em too, although Jägerhorn probably does even better. My Veronica's just the queen bee of a corrupt poisoned hive, that's all. They're done now. They're talking. Or rather the Maje is talking, bless his soul, he's into his ice cream litany, he's just been making love to Ronnie and now he's lying there in bed talking about Sveaborg, damn him. " . . . only a thirty per cent chance that the massacre will take place," he's saying, "the fortress is very strong, formidably strong, but the Russians have the numbers, and if they do bring up sufficient reinforcements, Cronstedt's fears may prove to be substantial. But even that will work out. The assassination, well, the rules will be suspended, they'll slaughter everyone inside, but Sveaborg will become a sort of Swedish Alamo, and the branching paths ought to come together again. Good probability. The end results will be the same." Ronnie isn't listening to him, though; there's a look on her face I've never seen, drunken, hungry, scared, and now she's moving lower on him and doing something I've only seen in my fantasies, and now I don't want to watch anymore, no, oh no, no, oh no.

General Suchtelen had established his command post on the outskirts of Helsinki, another clever ploy. When Sveaborg turned its cannon on him, every third shot told upon the city the fortress was supposed to protect, until Cronstedt finally ordered the firing stopped. Suchtelen took advantage of that concession as he had all the rest. His apartments were large and comfortable; from his windows, across the white expanse of ice and snow, the gray form of Sveaborg loomed large. Colonel Bengt Anttenon stared at it morosely as he waited in the ante-room with Cronstedt's other courier and the Russians who had escorted them to Suchtelen. Finally the inner doors opened and the dark Russian captain emerged. "The general will see you now," he said.

General Suchtelen sat behind a wide wooden desk. An aide stood by his right arm. A guard was posted at the door, and the captain entered with the Swedish couriers. On the broad, bare expanse of the desk was an inkwell, a blotter, and two signed safe conducts, the passes that would take them through the Russian lines to Stockholm and the Swedish king, one by the southern and the other by the northern route. Suchtelen said something, in Russian; the aide provided a translation. Horses had been provided, and fresh mounts would be available for them along the way, orders had been given. Anttonen listened to the discussion with a curiously empty feeling and a vague sense of disorientation. Suchtelen was going to let them go. Why did that surprise him? Those were the terms of the agreement, after all, those were the conditions of the truce. As the translator droned on, Anttonen felt increasingly lost and listless. He had conspired to get himself here, the voices had told him to, and now here he was, and he did not know why, nor did he know what he was to do.

They handed him one of the safe conducts, placed it in his outstretched hand. Perhaps it was the touch of the paper; perhaps it was something else. A sudden red rage filled him, an anger so fierce and blind and all-consuming that for an instant the world seemed to flicker and vanish and he was somewhere else, seeing naked bodies twining in a room whose walls were made of pale green blocks. And then he was back, the rage still hot within him, but cooling now, cooling quickly. They were staring at him, all of them. With a sudden start, Anttonen realized that

he had let the safe conduct fall to the floor, that his hand
had gone to the hilt of his sword instead, and the blade
was now half-drawn, the metal shining dully in the sunlight that streamed through Suchtelen's window. Had
they acted more quickly, they might have stopped him,
but he had caught them all by surprise. Suchtelen began
to rise from his chair, moving as if in slow motion. Slow
motion, Bengt wondered briefly, what was that? But he
knew, he knew. The sword was all the way out now. He
heard the captain shout something behind him, the aide
began to go for his pistol, but Quick Draw McGraw he
wasn't, Bengt had the drop on them all, heigh-ho. He
grinned, spun the sword in his hand, and offered it, hilt
first, to General Suchtelen.

"My sword, sir, and Colonel Jägerhorn's compliments,"
Bengt Anttonen heard himself say with something
approaching awe. "The fortress is in your grasp. Colonel
Jägerhorn suggests that you hold up our passage for a
month. I concur. Detain us here, and you are certain of
victory. Let us go, and who knows what chance misfor-
tune might occur to bring the Swedish fleet? It is a long
time until the third of May. In such a time, the king
might die, or the horse might die, or you or I might die.
Or the horse might talk."

The translator put away his pistol and began to trans-
late; the other courier began to protest, ineffectually.
Bengt Anttonen found himself possessed of an eloquence
that even his good friend Jägerhorn might envy. He
spoke on and on. He had one moment of strange weakness, when his stomach churned and his head swam, but
somehow he knew it was nothing to be alarmed at, it
was just the pills taking effect, it was just a monster dying
far away in a metal coffin full of night, and then there
were none, heigh-ho, one siege was ending and another
would go on and on, and what did it matter to Bengt,
the world was a big, crisp, cold, jeweled oyster. He
thought this was the beginning of a beautiful friendship,

and what the hell, maybe he'd save their asses after all, if he happened to feel like it, but he'd do it his way.

After a time, General Suchtelen, nodding, reached out and accepted the proferred sword.

Colonel Bengt Anttonen reached Stockholm on the third of May, in the Year of Our Lord Eighteen-Hundred-and-Eight, with a message for Gustavus IV Adolphus, King of Sweden. On the same date, Sveaborg, impregnable Sveaborg, Gibraltar of the North, surrendered to the inferior Russian forces.

At the conclusion of hostilities, Colonel Anttonen resigned his commission in the Swedish army and became an emigré, first to England, and later to America. He took up residence in New York City, where he married, fathered nine children, and became a well-known and influential journalist, widely respected for his canny ability to sense coming trends. When events proved him wrong, as happened infrequently, Anttonen was always surprised. He was a founder of the Republican Party, and his writings were instrumental in the election of John Charles Fremont to the Presidency in 1856.

In 1857, a year before his death, Anttonen played Paul Morphy in a New York chess tournament, and lost a celebrated game. Afterward, his only comment was, "I could have beat him at dominoes," a phrase that Morphy's biographers are fond of quoting.

THE GLASS FLOWER

Once, when I was just a girl in the first flush of my true youth, a young boy gave me a glass flower as a token of his love.

He was a rare and precious boy, though I confess that I have long forgotten his name. So too was the flower he gave me. On the steel and plastic worlds where I have spent my lives, the ancient glassblower's art is lost and forgotten, but the unknown artisan who had fashioned my flower remembered it well. My flower has a long and delicate stem, curved and graceful, all of fine thin glass, and from that frail support the bloom explodes, as large as my fist, impossibly exact. Every detail is there, caught, frozen in crystal for eternity; petals large and small crowding each other, bursting from the center of the blossom in a slow transparent riot, surrounded by a crown of six wide drooping leaves, each with its tracery of veins intact, each unique. It was as if an alchemist had been wandering through a garden one day, and in a moment of idle play had transmuted an especially large and beautiful flower into glass.

All that it lacks is life.

I kept that flower with me for near two hundred years, long after I had left the boy who gave it to me and the world where he had done the giving. Through all the varied chapters of my lives, the glass flower was always close at hand. It amused me to keep it in a vase of polished wood, and set it near a window. Sometimes the leaves and petals would catch the sun and flash brilliantly for an incandescent instant; at other times they would filter and fracture the light, scattering blurred rainbows on my floor. Often towards dusk, when the world was dimmer, the flower would seem to fade entirely from view, and I might sit staring at an empty vase. Yet, when the morning came, the flower would be back again. It never failed me.

The glass flower was terribly fragile, but no harm ever came to it. I cared for it well; better, perhaps, than I have ever cared for anything, or anyone. It out-lasted a dozen lovers, more than a dozen professions, and more worlds and friends than I can name. It was with me in my youth on Ash and Erikan and Shamdizar, and later on Rogue's Hope and Vagabond, and still later when I had grown old on Dam Tullian and Lilith and Gulliver. And when I finally left human space entirely, put all my lives and all the worlds of men behind me, and grew young again, the glass flower was still at my side.

And, at very long last, in my castle built on stilts, in my house of pain and rebirth where the game of mind is played, amid the swamps and stinks of Croan'dhenni, far from all humanity save those few lost souls who seek us out—it was there too, my glass flower.

On the day Kleronomas arrived.

"Joachim Kleronomas," I said.

"Yes."

There are cyborgs and then there are cyborgs. So many worlds, so many different cultures, so many sets of values and levels of technologies. Some cyberjacks are half organic, some more, some less; some sport only a single metal hand, the rest of their cyberhalves cleverly concealed beneath the flesh. Some cyborgs wear synthaflesh that is indistinguishable from human skin, though that is no great feat, given the variety of skin to be seen among the thousand worlds. Some hide the metal and flaunt the flesh; with others the reverse is true.

The man who called himself Kleronomas had no flesh to hide or flaunt. A cyborg he called himself, and a cyborg he was in the legends that had grown up around his name, but as he stood before me, he seemed more a robot, insufficiently organic to pass even as android.

He was naked, if a thing of metal and plastic can be naked. His chest was jet; some shining black alloy or smooth plastic, I could not tell. His arms and legs were transparent plasteel. Beneath that false skin, I could see the dark metal of his duralloy bones, the power-bars and flexors that were muscles and tendons, the micromotors and sensing computers, the intricate pattern of lights racing up and down his superconductive neurosystem. His fingers were steel. On his right hand, long silver claws sprang rakishly from his knuckles when he made a fist.

He was looking at me. His eyes were crystalline lenses set in metal sockets, moving back and forth in some green translucent gel. They had no visible pupils; behind each implacable crimson iris burned a dim light that gave his stare an ominous red glow. "Am I that fascinating?" he asked me. His voice was surprisingly natural; deep and resonant, with no metallic echoes to corrode the humanity of his inflections.

"Kleronomas," I said. "Your name is fascinating, certainly. A very long time ago, there was another man of that name, a cyborg, a legend. You know that, of course. He of the Kleronomas Survey. The founder of the Academy of Human Knowledge on Avalon. Your ancestor? Perhaps metal runs in your family."

"No," said the cyborg. "Myself. I am Joachim Kleronomas."

I smiled for him. "And I'm Jesus Christ. Would you care to meet my Apostles?"

"You doubt me, Wisdom?"

"Kleronomas died on Avalon a thousand years ago."

"No," he said. "He stands before you now."

"Cyborg," I said, "this is Croan'dhenni. You would not have come here unless you sought rebirth, unless you sought to win new life in the game of mind. So be warned. In the game of mind, your lies will be stripped away from you. Your flesh and your metal and your illusions, we will take them all, and in the end there will be only you, more naked and alone than you can ever imagine. So do not waste my time. It is the most precious thing I have, time. It is the most precious thing any of us have. Who are you, cyborg?"

"Kleronomas," he said. Was there a mocking note in his voice? I could not tell. His face was not built for smiling. "Do you have a name?" he asked me.

"Several," I said.

"Which do you use?"

"My players call me Wisdom."

"That is a title, not a name," he said.

I smiled. "You are travelled, then. Like the real Kleronomas. Good. My birth name was Cyrain. I suppose, of all my names, I am most used to that one. I wore it for the first fifty years of my life, until I came to Dam Tullian and studied to be a Wisdom and took a new name with the title."

"Cyrain," he repeated. "That alone?"

"Yes."

"On what world were you born, then?"

"Ash."

"Cyrain of Ash," he said. "How old are you?"

"In standard years?"

"Of course."

I shrugged. "Close to two hundred. I've lost count."

"You look like a child, like a girl close to puberty, no more."

"I am older than my body," I said.

"As am I," he said. "The curse of the cyborg, Wisdom, is that parts can be replaced."

"Then you're immortal?" I challenged him.

"In one crude sense, yes."

"Interesting," I said. "Contradictory. You come here to me, to Croan'dhenni and its Artifact, to the game of mind. Why? This is a place where the dying come, cyborg, in hopes of winning life. We don't get many immortals."

"I seek a different prize," the cyborg said.

"Yes?" I prompted.

"Death," he told me. "Life. Death. Life."

"Two different things," I said. "Opposites. Enemies."

"No," said the cyborg. "They are the same."

Six hundred standard years ago, a creature known in legend as The White landed among the Croan'dhenni in the first starship they had ever seen. If the descriptions in Croan'dhic folklore can be trusted, then The White was of no race I have ever encountered, nor heard of, though I am widely travelled. This does not surprise me. The manrealm and its thousand worlds (perhaps there are twice that number, perhaps less, but who can keep count?), the scattered empires of Fyndii and Damoosh and g'vhern and N'or Talush, and all the other sentients who are known to us or rumored of, all this together, all those lands and stars and lives colored by passion and blood and history, sprawling proudly across the light-years, across the black gulfs that only the *volcryn* ever truly know, all of this, all of our little universe . . . it is only an island of light surrounded by a vastly greater area of greyness and myth that fades ultimately into the black of ignorance. And *this* only in one small galaxy, whose uttermost reaches we shall never know, should we endure a billion years. Ultimately, the sheer size of things will defeat us, however we may strive or scream; that truth I am sure of.

But I do not defeat easily. That is my pride, my last and only pride; it is not much to face the darkness with, but it is something. When the end comes, I will meet it raging.

The White was like me in that. It was a frog from a pond beyond ours, a place lost in the grey where our little lights have not yet shone on the dark waters. Whatever sort of creature it might have been, whatever burdens of history and evolution it carried in its genes, it was nonetheless my kin. Both of us were angry mayflies, moving restlessly from star to star because we, alone among our fellows, knew how short our day. Both of us found a destiny of sorts in these swamps of Croan'dhenni.

The White came utterly alone to this place, set down its little starship (I have seen the remains: a toy, that ship, a trinket, but with lines that are utterly alien to me, and deliciously chilling), and, exploring, found something.

Something older than itself, and stranger.

The Artifact.

Whatever strange instruments it had, whatever secret alien knowledge it possessed, whatever instinct bid it enter; all lost now, and none of it matters. The White knew, knew something the native sentients had never guessed, knew the purpose of the Artifact, knew how it might be activated. For the first time in—a thousand years? A million? For the first time in a long while, the game of mind was played. And The White changed, emerged from the Artifact as something else, as the first. The first mindlord. The first master of life and death. The first painlord. The first lifelord. The titles are born, worn, discarded, forgotten, and none of them matter.

Whatever I am, The White was the first.

Had the cyborg asked to meet my Apostles, I would not have disappointed him. I gathered them when he left me. "The new player," I told them, "calls himself Kleronomas. I want to know who he is, what he is, and what he hopes to gain. Find out for me."

I could feel their greed and fear. The Apostles are a useful tool, but loyalty is not for them. I have gathered to me twelve Judas Iscariots, each of them hungry for that kiss.

"I'll have a full scan worked up," suggested Doctor Lyman, pale weak eyes considering me, flatterer's smile trembling.

"Will he consent to an interface?" asked Deish Green-9, my own cyberjack. His right hand, sunburned red-black flesh, was balled into a fist; his left was a silver ball that cracked open to exude a nest of writhing metallic tendrils. Beneath his heavy beetling brow, where he should have had eyes, a seamless strip of mirrorglass was set into his skull. He had chromed his teeth. His smile was very bright.

"We'll find out," I said.

Sebastian Cayle floated in his tank, a twisted embryo with a massive monstrous head, flippers moving vaguely, huge blind eyes regarding me through turgid greenish fluids as bubbles rose all around his pale naked flesh. *He is a Liar* came the whisper in my head. *I will find the truth for you, Wisdom.*

"Good," I told him.

Tr'k'nn'r, my Fyndii mindmute, sang to me in a high shrill voice at the edge of human hearing. He loomed above them all like a stickman in a child's crude drawing, a stickman three meters tall, excessively jointed, bending in all the wrong places at all the wrong angles, assembled of old bones turned gray as ash by some ancient fire. But the crystalline eyes beneath his brow ridge were fervid as he sang, and fragrant black fluids ran from the bottom of his lipless vertical mouth. His song was of pain and screaming and nerves set afire, of secrets revealed, of truth dragged steaming and raw from all its hidden crevasses.

"No," I said to him. "He is a cyborg. If he feels pain it is only because he wills it. He would shut down his receptors and turn you off, loneling, and your song would turn to silence."

The neurowhore Shayalla Loethen smiled with resignation. "Then there's nothing for me to work on either, Wisdom?"

"I'm not sure," I admitted. "He has no obvious genitalia, but if there's anything organic left inside him, his pleasure centers might be intact. He claims to have been male. The instincts might still be viable. Find out."

She nodded. Her body was soft and white as snow, and sometimes as cold, when she wanted cold, and sometimes white hot, when that was her desire. Those lips that curled upwards now with anticipation were crimson and alive. The garments that swirled around her changed shape and color even as I watched, and sparks began to play along her fingertips, arcing across her long, painted nails.

"Drugs?" asked Braje, biomed, gengineer, poisoner. She sat thinking, chewing some tranq of her own devising, her swollen body as damp and soft as the swamps outside. "Truetell? Agonine? Esperon?"

"I doubt it," I said.

"Disease," she offered. "Manthrax or gangrene. The slow plague, and we've got the cure?" She giggled.

"No," I said curtly.

And the rest, and on and on. They all had their suggestions, their ways of finding out things I wanted to know, of making themselves useful to me, of earning my gratitude. Such are my Apostles. I listened to them, let myself be carried along by the babble of voices, weighed, considered, handed out orders, and finally I sent them all away, all but one.

Khar Dorian will be the one to kiss me when that day finally comes. I do not have to be a Wisdom to know that truth.

The rest of them want something of me. When they get it, they will be gone. Khar got his desire long ago, and still he comes back and back and back, to my world and my bed. It is not love of me that brings him back, nor the beauty of the young body I wear, nor anything as simple as the riches he earns. He has grander things in mind.

"He rode with you," I said. "All the way from Lilith. Who is he?"

"A player," Dorian said, grinning at me crookedly, taunting me. He is breathtakingly beautiful. Lean and hard and well fit, with the arrogance and rough-hewn masculine sexuality of a thirty-year-old, flush with health and power and hormones. His hair is blond and long and unkempt. His jaw is clean and strong, his nose straight and unbroken, his eyes a hale, vibrant blue. But there is something old living behind those eyes, something old and cynical and sinister.

"Dorian," I warned him, "don't try games with me. He is more than just a player. Who is he?"

Khar Dorian got up, stretched lazily, yawned, grinned. "Who he says he is," my slaver told me. "Kleronomas."

* * *

Morality is a closely knit garment that binds tightly when it binds at all, but the vastnesses that lie between the stars are prone to unravelling it, to plucking it apart into so many loose threads, each brightly colored, but forming no discernible pattern. The fashionable Vagabonder is a rustic spectacular on Cathaday, the Ymirian swelters on Vess, the Vessman freezes on Ymir, and the shifting lights the Fellanei wear instead of cloth provoke rape, riot, and murder on half a dozen worlds. So it is with morals. Good is no more constant than the cut of a lapel; the decision to take a sentient life weighs no more heavily than the decision to bare one's breasts, or hide them.

There are worlds on which I am a monster. I stopped caring a long time ago. I came to Croan'dhenni with my own fashion sense, and no concern for the aesthetic judgments of others.

Khar Dorian calls himself a slaver, and points out to me that we do, indeed, deal in human flesh. He can call himself what he likes. I am no slaver; the charge offends me. A slaver sells his clients into bondage and servitude, deprives them of freedom, mobility, and time, all precious commodities. I do no such thing. I am only a thief. Khar and his underlings bring them to me from the swollen cities of Lilith, from the harsh mountains and cold wastes of Dam Tullian, from the rotting tenements along the canals of Vess, from spaceport bars on Fellanora and Cymeranth and Shrike, from wherever he can find them, he takes them and brings them to me, and I steal from them and set them free.

A lot of them refuse to go.

They cluster outside my castle walls in the city they have built, toss gifts to me as I pass, call out my name, beg favors of me. I have left them freedom, mobility, and time, and they squander it all in futility, hoping to win back the one thing I have stolen.

I steal their bodies, but they lose their souls themselves.

And perhaps I am unduly harsh to call myself a thief.
These victims Khar brings me are unwilling players in
the game of mind, but no less players for all that. Others
pay so very dearly and risk so very much for the same
privilege. Some we call players and some we call prizes,
but when the pain comes and the game of mind begins,
we are all the same, all naked and alone without riches
or health or status, armed with only the strength that lies
within us. Win or lose, live or die, it is up to us and us
alone.

I give them a chance. A few have even won. Very few,
true, but how many thieves give their victims any chance
at all?

The Steel Angels, whose worlds lie far from Croan'-
dhenni on the other side of human space, teach their
children that strength is the only virtue and weakness the
only sin, and preach that the truth of their faith is written
large on the universe itself. It is a difficult point to argue.
By their creed, I have every moral right to the bodies I
take, because I am stronger and therefore better and
more holy than those born to that flesh.

The little girl born in my present body was not a Steel
Angel, unfortunately.

"And baby makes three," I said, "even if baby is made
of metal and plastic and names himself a legend."

"Eh?" Rannar looked at me blankly. He is not as
widely traveled as me, and the reference, something I
have dredged up from my forgotten youth on some world
he's never walked, escapes him entirely. His long, sour
face wore a look of patient bafflement.

"We have three players now," I told him carefully.
"We can play the game of mind."

That much Rannar understood. "Ah yes, of course. I'll
see to it at once, Wisdom."

Craimur Delhune was the first. An ancient thing,
almost as old as me, though he had done all of his living

in the same small body. No wonder it was worn out. He was hairless and shrivelled, a wheezing half-blind travesty, his flesh full of alloplas and metal implants that labored day and night just to keep him alive. It was not something they could do much longer, but Craimur Delhune had not had enough living yet, and so he had come to Croan'dhenni to pay for the flesh and begin all over again. He had been waiting nearly half a standard year.

Rieseen Jay was a stranger case. She was under fifty and in decent health, though her flesh bore its own scars. Rieseen was jaded. She had sampled every pleasure Lilith offered, and Lilith offers a good many pleasures. She had tasted every food, flowed with every drug, sexed with males, females, aliens, and animals, risked her life skiing the glaciers, baiting pit-dragons, fighting in the soar-wars for the delectation of holofans everywhere. She thought a new body would be just the thing to add spice to life. Maybe a male body, she thought, or an alien's offcolor flesh. We get a few like her.

And Joachim Kleronomas made three.

In the game of mind, there are seats for seven. Three players, three prizes, and me.

Rannar offered me a thick portfolio, full of photographs and reports on the prizes newly arrived on Khar Dorian's ships, on the *Bright Phoenix* and the *Second Chance* and the *New Deal* and the *Fleshpot* (Khar has always had a certain black sense of humor). The majordomo hovered at my elbow, solicitous and helpful, as I turned the pages and made my selections. "She's delicious," he said once, at a picture of a slim Vessgirl with frightened yellow eyes that hinted at a hybrid gene-mix. "Very strong and healthy, that one," he said later, as I considered a hugely muscled youth with green eyes and waist-long braided black hair. I ignored him. I always ignore him.

"Him," I said, taking out the file of a boy as slender

as a stiletto, his ruddy skin covered with tattoos. Khar had purchased him from the authorities on Shrike, where he'd been convicted of killing another sixteen year old. On most worlds Khar Dorian, the infamous free trader, smuggler, raider, and slaver, had a name synonomous with evil; parents threatened their children with him. On Shrike he was a solid citizen who did the community great service by buying up the garbage in the prisons.

"Her," I said, setting aside a second photograph, of a pudgy young woman of about thirty standard whose wide green eyes betrayed a certain vacancy. From Cymeranth, her file said. Khar had dropped one of his raiders into a coldsleep facility for the mentally damaged and helped himself to some young, healthy, attractive bodies. This one was soft and fat, but that would change once an active mind wore the flesh again. The original owner had sucked up too much dreamdust.

"And it," I said. The third file was that of a g'vhern hatchling, a grim looking individual with fierce magenta eye-crests and huge, leathery batwings that glistened with iridescent oils. It was for Rieseen Jay, who thought she might like to try a nonhuman body. If she could win it.

"Very good, Wisdom," said Rannar approvingly. He was always approving. When he had come to Croan'-dhenni, his body was grotesque; he'd been caught in bed with the daughter of his employer, a V'lador knight of the blood, and the punishment was extensive ritual mutilation. He did not have the price of a game. But I'd had two players waiting for almost a year, one of whom was dying of manthrax, so when Rannar offered me ten years of faithful service to make up the difference, I accepted.

Sometimes I had my regrets. I could feel his eyes on my body, could sense his mind stripping away the soft armor of my clothes to fasten, leechlike, on my small, budding breasts. The girl he'd been found with was not much younger than the flesh I now wore.

* * *

My castle is built of obsidian.

North of here, far north, in the smoky polar wastelands where eternal fires burn against a purple sky, the black volcanic glass lies upon the ground like common stone. It took thousands of Croan'dhic miners nine standard years to find enough for my purposes and drag it all back to the swamps, over all those barren kilometers. It took hundreds of artisans another six years to cut and polish it and fit it all together into the dark shimmering mosaic that is my home. I judged the effort worthwhile.

My castle stands on four great jagged pillars high up above the smells and damp of the Croan'dhic swampland, ablaze with colored lights whose ghosts glimmer within the black glass. My castle gleams; a thing of beauty, austere and forbidding, supreme and apart from the shantytown that has grown up around it, where the losers and discards and dispossessed huddle hopelessly in floating reed-huts, festering treehouses, and hovels on half-rotted wooden stilts. The obsidian appeals to my aesthetic sense, and I find its symbolism appropriate to this house of pain and rebirth. Life is born in the heat of sexual passion as obsidian is born in volcanic fire. The clean truth of light can sometimes flow through its blackness, beauty seen dimly through darkness, and like life, it is terribly fragile, with edges that can be dangerously sharp.

Inside my castle are rooms on rooms, some panelled over with fragrant native woods and covered with furs and thick carpets, some left bare and black, ceremonial chambers where dark reflections move through glass walls and footsteps click brittle against glass floors. In the center, at the very apex, rises an onion-shaped obsidian tower, braced by steel. Within the dome, a single chamber.

I ordered the castle built, replacing an older and much shabbier structure, and to that single tower chamber, I caused the Artifact to be moved.

It is there that the game of mind is played.

My own suite is at the base of the tower. The reasons for that were symbolic as well. None achieve rebirth without first passing through me.

I was breaking fast in bed, on butterfruit and raw fish and strong black coffee, with Khar Dorian stretched out languid and insolent beside me, when my scholar Apostle, Alta-k-Nahr, came to me with her report.

She stood at the foot of my bed, her back twisted like a great question mark by her disease, her long features permanently set in a grimace of distaste, her skin shot through with swollen veins like great blue worms, and she told me of her researches on the historical Kleronomas in a voice unnecessarily soft.

"His full name was Joachim Charle Kleronomas," she said, "and he was native to New Alexandria, a first generation colony less than seventy light years from Old Earth. Records of his birthdate, childhood, and adolescence are fragmentary and contradictory. The most popular legends indicate his mother was a high-ranking officer on a warship of the 13th Human Fleet, under Stephen Cobalt Northstar, and that Kleronomas met her only twice. He was gestated in a hireling host-mother and reared by his father, a minor scholar at a library on New Alexandria. My opinion is that this tale of his origin explains, a bit too neatly, how Kleronomas came to combine both the scholastic and martial traditions; therefore I question its reliability.

"More certain is the fact that he joined the military at a very early age, in those last days of the Thousand Years War. He served initially as systems tech on a screamer-class raider with the 17th Human Fleet, distinguished himself in deepspace actions off El Dorado and Arturius and in the raids on Hrag Druun, after which he was promoted to cadet and given command training. By the time the 17th was shifted from its original base on Fenris to a minor sector capital called Avalon, Kleronomas had earned further distinction, and was the third-in-command of the dropship *Hannibal*. But in the raids on Hruun-Fourteen, the *Hannibal* took heavy damage from Hrangan defenders, and was finally abandoned. The screamer in which Kleronomas escaped was disabled by enemy fire and crashed planetside, killing everyone aboard. He was the sole survivor. Another screamer picked up what was left of him, but he was so near dead and horribly maimed that they shoved him into cryostorage at once. He was taken back to Avalon, but resources were few and demands many, and they had no time to bother reviving him. They kept him under for years.

"Meanwhile, the Collapse was in progress. It had been in progress all of his lifetime, actually, but communications across the width of the old Federal Empire were so slow that no one knew it. But a single decade saw the revolt on Thor, the total disintegration of the 15th Human Fleet, and Old Earth's attempt to remove Stephen Cobalt Northstar from command of the 13th, which led inevitably to the secession of Newholme and most of the other first generation colonies, to Northstar's obliteration of Wellington, to civil war, breakaway colonies, lost worlds, the fourth great expansion, the hellfleet legend, and ultimately the sealing of Old Earth and the effective cessation of commercial starflight for a generation. Longer than that, far far longer, on some more remote worlds, many of which devolved to near-savagery or developed odd variant cultures.

"Out on the front, Avalon had its own first-hand experience of the Collapse when Rajeen Tober, commanding the 17th Fleet, refused to submit to the civil authorities and took his ships deep into the Tempter's Veil to found his own personal empire safe from both Hrangan and human retaliation. The departure of the 17th left Avalon essentially defenseless. The only warships still in the sector were the ancient hulks of the 5th Human Fleet, which had last seen combat nearly seven centuries earlier, when Avalon was a very distant strikebase against the Hrangans. About a dozen capital-class ships and thirty-odd smaller craft of the 5th remained in orbit around Avalon, most needing extensive repairs, all functionally obsolete. But they were the only defenders left to a frightened world, so Avalon determined to refit and restore them. To crew these museum pieces, Avalon turned to its cryonic wards, and began to thaw every combat veteran on hand, including Joachim Kleronomas. The damage he had sustained was extensive, but Avalon needed every last body. Kleronomas returned more machine than man. A cyborg."

I leaned forward to interrupt Alta's recitation. "Are there any pictures of him as he was then?" I asked her.

"Yes. Both before and after. Kleronomas was a big man, with blue-black skin, a heavy outthrust jaw, gray eyes, long pure white hair. After the operation, the jaw and the bottom half of his face were gone entirely, replaced with seamless metal. No mouth, no nose. He took nourishment intravenously. One eye was lost, replaced by a crystal sensor with IR/UV range. His right arm and the entire right half of his chest was cybered, steel plate, duralloy mesh, plastic. A third of his inner organs were synthetic. And they gave him a jack, of course, and built in a small computer. From the beginning, Kleronomas disdained cosmetics; he looked exactly like what he was."

I smiled. "But what he was, that was still a good deal more fleshy than our new guest?"

"True," said my scholar. "The rest of the history is more well known. There weren't many officers among the revived. Kleronomas was given his own command, a small courier-class ship. He served for a decade, pursuing the scholarly studies in history and anthropology that were his private passion, and rising higher and higher in the ranks while Avalon waited for ships that never came and built more and more ships of its own. There were no trades, no raids; the interregnum had come.

"Finally, a bolder civil leadership decided to risk a few of its ships and find out how the rest of human civilization had fared. Six of the ancient 5th Fleet dreadnaughts were refitted as science survey craft and sent out. Kleronomas was given command of one of them. Of those survey ships, two were lost on their missions, and three others returned within two years carrying minimal information on a handful of the closest systems, prompting the Avalonians to reinitiate starflight on a very limited local basis. Kleronomas was thought lost.

"He was not lost. When the small, limited goals of the original survey were completed, he decided to continue rather than return to Avalon. He became obsessed with the next star, and the next after that, and the next after that. He took his ship on and on. There were mutinies, desertions, dangers to be faced and fought, and Kleronomas dealt with them all. As a cyborg, he was immensely long-lived. The legends say he became ever more metallic as the voyage went on, and on Eris discovered the matrix crystal and expanded his intellectual abilities by orders of magnitude through the addition of the first crystal-matrix computer. That particular story fits his character; he was obsessed not only with the acquisition of knowledge, but with its retention. Altered so, he would never forget.

"When he finally returned to Avalon, more than a hundred standard years had passed. Of the men and women who had left Avalon with him, Kleronomas alone survived; his ship was manned by the descendants of its original crew, plus those recruits he had gathered on the worlds he visited. But he had surveyed four hundred and forty-nine planets, and more asteroids, comets, and satellites than anyone would have dreamed possible. The information he brought back became the foundation upon which the Academy of Human Knowledge was built, and the crystal samples, incorporated into existing systems, became the medium in which that knowledge was stored, eventually evolving into the academy's vast Artificial Intelligences and the fabled crystal towers of Avalon. The resumption of large-scale starflight soon thereafter was the real end of the interregnum. Kleronomas himself served as the first academy administrator until his death, which supposedly came on Avalon in ai-42, that is, forty-two standard years after the day of his return."

I laughed. "Excellent," I told Alta-k-Nahr. "He's a fraud, then. Dead at least seven hundred years." I looked at Khar Dorian, whose long fine hair was spread across the pillow as he nibbled on a heel of mead bread. "You are slipping, Khar. He fooled you."

Khar swallowed, grinned. "Whatever you say, Wisdom," he said, in a tone that told me he was anything but contrite. "Shall I kill him for you?"

"No," I said. "He is a player. In the game of mind, there are no imposters. Let him play. Let him play."

Days later, when the game had been scheduled, I called the cyborg to me. I saw him in my office, a large room with deep scarlet carpeting, where my glass flower sits by the great window that overlooks my battlements and the swamp town below.

His face was without expression. Of course, of course. "You summoned me, Cyrain of Ash."

"The game is set," I told him. "Four days from today."

"I am pleased," he said.

"Would you like to see the prizes?" I offered him the files; the boy, the girl, the hatchling.

He glanced at them briefly, without interest.

"I am told," I said to him, "that you have spent a lot of time wandering these past days. Inside my castle, and outside in the town and the swamps."

"True," he said. "I do not sleep. Knowledge is my

diversion, my addiction. I was curious to learn what sort of place this was."

Smiling, I said, "And what sort of place is it, cyborg?"

He could not smile, nor frown. His tone was even, polite. "A vile place," he said. "A place of despair and degradation."

"A place of eternal, undying hope," I said.

"A place of sickness, of the body and the soul."

"A place where the sick grow well," I countered.

"And where the well grow sick," the cyborg said. "A place of death."

"A place of life," I said. "Isn't that why you came? For life?"

"And death," he said. "I have told you, they are the same."

I leaned forward. "And I have told you, they are very different. You make harsh judgments, cyborg. Rigidity is to be expected in a machine, but this fine, precious moral sensitivity is not."

"Only my body is machine," he said.

I picked up his file. "That is not my understanding," I said. "Where is your morality in regard to lying? Especially so transparent a lie?" I opened the file flat on my desk. "I've had a few interesting reports from my Apostles. You've been extraordinarily cooperative."

"If you wish to play the game of mind, you cannot offend the painlord," he said.

I smiled. "I'm not as easily offended as you might think." I searched through the reports. "Doctor Lyman did a full scan on you. He finds you an ingenious construct. And made entirely of plastic and metal. There is nothing organic left inside you, cyborg. Or should I call you robot? Can computers play the game of mind, I wonder? We will certainly find out. You have three of them, I see. A small one in what should be your brain case that attends to motor functions, sensory input and internal monitoring, a much larger library unit occupying most of your lower torso, and a crystal matrix in your chest." I looked up. "Your heart, cyborg?"

"My mind," he said. "Ask your Doctor Lyman, and he will tell of other cases like mine. What is a human mind? Memories. Memories are data. Character, personality, individual volition. Those are programming. It is possible to imprint the whole of a human mind upon a crystal matrix computer."

"And trap the soul in the crystal?" I said. "Do you believe in souls?"

"Do you?" he asked.

"I must. I am mistress of the game of mind. It would seem to be required of me." I turned to the other reports my Apostles had assembled on this construct who called himself Kleronomas. "Deish Green-9 interfaced with you. He says you have a system of incredible sophistication, that the speed of your circuitry greatly exceeds human thought, that your library contains far more accessible information than any single organic brain could retain even were it able to make full use of its capacity, and that the mind and memories locked within that crystal matrix are that of one Joachim Kleronomas. He swears to that."

The cyborg said nothing. Perhaps he might have smiled then, had he the capacity.

"On the other hand," I said, "my scholar Alta-k-Nahr assures me that Kleronomas is dead seven hundred years. Who am I to believe?"

"Whomever you choose," he said indifferently.

"I might hold you here and send to Avalon for confirmation," I said. I grinned. "A thirty-year voyage in, thirty more years back out. Say a year to research the question. Can you wait sixty-one years to play, cyborg?"

"As long as necessary," he said.

"Shayalla says you are thoroughly asexual."

"That capacity was lost from the day they remade me," he said. "My interest in the subject lingered for some centuries afterwards, but finally that too faded. If I choose, I have access to a full range of erotic memories of the days when I wore organic flesh. They remain as fresh as the day they were entered into my computer. Once locked in crystal, memories cannot fade, as with a human brain. They are there, waiting to be tapped. But for centuries now, I have had no inclination to recall them."

I was intrigued. "You cannot forget," I said.

"I can erase," he said. "I can choose not to remember."

"If you are among the winners in our little game of mind, you will regain your sexuality."

"I am aware of that. It will be an interesting experience. Perhaps then I will choose to tap those ancient memories."

"Yes," I said, delighted. "You'll begin to use them, and at precisely the same instant you will begin to forget them. There is a loss there, cyborg, as sharp as your gain."

"Gain or loss. Living and dying. I have told you, Cyrain, they cannot be separated."

"I don't accept that," I said. It was at issue with all I believe, all I am; his repetition of the lie annoyed me. "Braje says you cannot be affected by drugs or disease. Obvious. You could be dismantled, though. Several of my Apostles have offered to dispose of you, at my command. My aliens are especially bloodthirsty, it seems."

"I have no blood," he said. Sardonic? Or was it all the power of suggestion?

"Your lubricants might suffice," I said dryly. "Tr'k'nn'r would test your capacity for pain. AanTerg Moonscorer, my g'vhern aerialist, has offered to drop you from a great height."

"That would be an unconscionable crime by nest standards."

"Yes and no," I said. "A nestborn g'vhern would be

aghast at the suggestion that flight be thus perverted. My Apostle, on the other hand, would be more aghast at the suggestion of birth control. Flapping those oily leather wings you'll find the mind of a half-sane cripple from New Rome. This is Croan'dhenni. We are not as we seem."

"So it appears."

"Jonas has offered to destroy you too, in a less dramatic but equally effective fashion. He's my largest Apostle. Deformed by runaway glands. The patron saint of advanced automatic weaponry, and my chief of security."

"Obviously you have declined these offers," the cyborg said.

I leaned back. "Obviously," I said, "though I always reserve the right to change my mind."

"I am a player," he said. "I have paid Khar Dorian, have bribed the Croan'dhic port-guards, have paid your major-domo and yourself. Inwards, on Lilith and Cymeranth and Shrike and other worlds where they speak of this black palace and its half-mythical mistress, they say that your players are treated with fairness."

"Wrong," I said. "I am never fair, cyborg. Sometimes I am just. When the whim takes me."

"Do you threaten all your players as you have threatened me?" he asked.

"No," I admitted. "I'm making a special exception in your case."

"Why?" he asked.

"Because you're dangerous," I said, smiling. We had come to the heart of it at last. I shuffled through all my Apostolic bulls, and extracted the last of them, the most important. "At least one of my Apostles you have never met, but he knows you, cyborg, knows you better than you would dream."

The cyborg said nothing.

"My pet telepath," I said. "Sebastian Cayle. He's blind and twisted and I keep him in a big jar, but he has his uses. He can probe through walls. He has stroked the crystals of your mind, friend, and tripped the binary synapses of your id. His report is a bit cryptic, but admirably terse." I slid it across the desk for the cyborg to read.

A haunted labyrinth of thought. The steel ghost. The truth within the lie, life in death and death in life. He will take everything from you if he can. Kill him now.

"You are ignoring his advice," the cyborg said.

"I am," I told him.

"Why?"

"Because you're a mystery, one I plan to solve when we play the game of mind. Because you're a challenge, and it has been a long time since I was challenged. Because you dare to judge me and dream of destroying me, and it has been ages since anyone found the courage to do either of those things."

Obsidian makes a dark, distorted mirror, but one that suits me. We take our reflections for granted all our lives, until the hour comes when our eyes search for the familiar features and find instead the image of a stranger. You cannot know the meaning of horror or of fascination until you take that first long gaze from a stranger's eyes, and raise an unfamiliar hand to touch the other's cheek, and feel those fingers, light and cool and afraid, brush against your skin.

I was already a stranger when I came to Croan'dhenni more than a century ago. I knew my face, as well I should, having worn it nearly ninety years. It was the face of a woman who was both hard and strong, with deep lines around her gray eyes from squinting into alien suns, a wide mouth not without its generosity, a nose once broken that had not healed straight, short brown hair in perpetual disarray. A comfortable face, and one that I had a certain affection for. But I lost it somewhere, perhaps during my years on Gulliver, lost it when I was too busy to notice. By the time I reached Lilith, the first stranger had begun to haunt my mirrors. She was an old woman, old and wrinkled. Her eyes were grey and rheumy and starting to dim, her hair white and thin, with patches of pinkish scalp showing through; the edge of her mouth trembled, there were broken capillaries in her nose, and beneath her chin lay several folds of soft gray flesh like the wattles of a hen. Her skin was soft and loose, where mine had always been taut and flush with health, and there was another thing, a thing you could not see in the mirror—a smell of sickness that enveloped her like the cheap perfume of an aged courtesan, a pheromone for death.

I did not know her, this old sick thing, nor did I cherish her company. They say that age and sickness come slowly on worlds like Avalon and Newholme and Prometheus; legends claim death no longer comes at all on Old Earth behind its shining walls. But Avalon and Newholme and Prometheus were far away, and Old Earth is sealed and lost to us, and I was alone on Lilith with a stranger in my mirror. And so I took myself beyond the manrealm, past the furthest reach of human arms, to the wet dimness of Croan'dhenni, where whispers said a new life could be found. I wanted to look into a mirror once more, and find the old friend that I had lost.

Instead I found more strangers.

The first was the painlord itself; mindlord, lifelord, master of life and death. Before my coming, it had ruled here forty-odd standard years. It was Croand'hic, a native, a great bulbous thing with swollen eyes and mottled blue-green skin, a grotesque parody of a toad with slender, double-jointed arms and three long verticle maws like wet black wounds in its fragrant flesh. When I looked upon it, I could taste its weakness; it was vastly fat, a sea of spreading blubber with an odor like rotten eggs, where the Croand'hic guards and servants were well-muscled and hard. But to topple the mindlord, you must become the mindlord. When we played the game of mind I took its life, and woke in that vile body.

It is no easy thing for a human mind to wear an alien skin; for a day and a night I was lost inside that hideous flesh, sorting through sights and sounds and smells that made no more sense than the images in nightmare, screaming, clawing for control and sanity. I survived. A triumph of spirit over flesh. When I was ready, another game of mind was called, and this time I emerged with the body of my choice.

She was a human. Thirty-nine years of age by her reckoning, healthy, plain of face but strong of body, a professional gambler who had come to Croan'dhenni for the ultimate game. She had long red-brown hair and eyes whose blue-green color reminded me of the seas of Gulliver. She had some strength, but not enough. In those distant days, before the coming of Khar Dorian and his slavers' fleet, few humans found their way to Croan'dhenni. My choice was limited. I took her.

That night I looked into the mirror again. It was still a stranger's face, hair too long, eyes of the wrong hue, a nose as straight as the blade of a knife, a careful guarded mouth that had done too little smiling.

Years afterward, when that body began to cough blood from some infernal pestilence out of the Croan'dhic swamps, I built a room of obsidian mirrors to meet each new stranger. Years pass more swiftly than I care to think while that room remains sealed and inviolate, but always, finally, the day comes when I know I will be visiting it once more, and then my servants climb the stairs and polish the black mirrors to a fine dark sheen, and when the game of mind is done I ascend alone and strip off my clothing and stand and turn in solitude, slow dancing with the images of others.

High, sharp cheekbones and dark eyes sunk in deep

hollows beneath her brow. A face shaped like a heart, surrounded by a nimbus of wild black hair, large pale breasts tipped with brown.

Taut lean muscles moving beneath oiled red-brown skin, long fingernails sharp as claws, a narrow pointed chin, brown hair like wire bristles cut in a thin high stripe across her scalp and halfway down her back, the hot scent of rut heavy between her thighs. My thighs? On a thousand worlds, humanity changes in a thousand different ways.

Massive boney head looking down at the world from near three meters height, beard and hair blending into one leonine mane as bright as beaten gold, strength written large in every bone and sinew, the broad flat chest with its useless red nipples, the strangeness of the long, soft penis between my legs. Too much strangeness for me; the penis stayed soft all the months I wore that body, and that year my mirrored room was opened twice.

A face very like the one that I remember. But how well do I remember? A century was gone to dust, and I kept no likenesses of the faces I had worn. From my first youth long ago, only the glass flower remained. But she had short brown hair, a smile, gray-green eyes. Her neck was too long, her breasts too small, perhaps. But she was close, close, until she grew old, and the day came when I glimpsed another stranger walking beside me inside the castle walls.

And now the haunted child. In the mirrors she looks like a daughter of dreams, the daughter I might have birthed had I been far lovelier than I ever was. Khar brought her to me, a gift he said, a most beautiful gift, to repay me in kind after I had found him gray and impotent, hoarse of voice and scarred of face, and made him young and handsome.

She is perhaps eleven years old, perhaps twelve. Her body is gaunt and awkward, but the beauty is there, locked inside, just beginning to blossom. Her breasts are budding now, and her blood first came less than half a year ago. Her hair is silver-gold, long and straight, a glittering cascade that falls nearly to her heels. Her eyes are large in her small face, and they are the deepest, purest violet. Her face is something sculpted. She was bred to be thus, no doubt of that; genetic tailoring has made the Shrikan trade-lords and the wealthy of Lilith and Fellanora a breathtakingly beautiful folk.

When Khar brought her to me, she was shy of seven, her mind already gone, a whimpering animal thing screaming in a dark locked room within her skull. Khar says she was that way when he bought her, the dispossessed daughter of a Fellanei robber baron toppled and executed for political crimes, his family and friends and retainers slain with him or turned into mindless sexual playthings for his victorious enemies. That is what Khar says. Most of the time I even believe him.

She is younger and prettier than I can ever remember being, even in my lost first youth on Ash, where a nameless boy gave me a glass flower. I hope to wear this sweet flesh for as many years as I wore the body I was born to. If I dwell here long enough, perhaps the day will come when I can look into a dark mirror and see my own face again.

One by one they ascended unto me; through Wisdom to rebirth, or so they hoped.

High above the swamps, locked within my tower, I prepared for them in the changing chamber, hard by my unimpressive throne. The Artifact is not prepossessing; a rudely shaped bowl of some soft alien alloy, charcoal gray in color and faintly warm to the touch, with six niches spaced evenly around the rim. They are seats; cramped, hard, uncomfortable seats, designed for obviously nonhuman physiognomies, but seats nonetheless. From the floor of the bowl rises a slender column that blossoms into another seat, the awkward cup that enthrones . . .

choose the title you like best. Painlord, mindlord, lifelord, giver and taker, operator, trigger, master. All of them are me. And others before me, the chain rattling back to The White and perhaps earlier, to the makers, the unknowns who fashioned this machine in the dimness of distant eons.

If the chamber has its drama, that is my doing. The walls and ceiling are curved, and fashioned laboriously of a thousand individual pieces of polished obsidian. Some shards are cut very thin, so the gray light of the Croan'-dhic sun can force its way through. Some shards are so thick as to be almost opaque. The room is one color, but a thousand shades, and for those who have the wit to see it, it forms a great mosaic of life and death, dreams and nightmares, pain and ecstacy, excess and emptiness, everything and nothing, blending one into the other, around and around unending, a circle, a cycle, the worm that eats its own tail forever, each piece individual and fragile and razor-edged and each part of a greater picture that is vast and black and brittle.

I stripped and handed my clothing to Rannar, who folded each garment neatly. The cup is topless and egg-shaped. I climbed inside and folded my legs beneath me in a lotus, the best possible compromise between the lines of the Artifact and the human physique. The interior walls of the machine began to bleed; glistening red-black fluid beading on the gray metal of the egg, each globule swelling fatter and heavier until it burst. Streams trickled down the smooth, curved walls, and the moisture began to collect at the bottom. My bare skin burned where the fluid touched me. The flow came faster and heavier, the fire creeping up my body, until I was half immersed.

"Send them in," I told Rannar. How many times have I said those words? I have lost count.

The prizes were led in first. Khar Dorian came with the tattooed boy. "There," Khar said offhandedly, gesturing to a seat while smiling lasciviously for me, and the hard youth, this killer, this wild bloody tough, shrank away from his escort and took the place assigned to him. Braje, my biomed, brought the woman. They too are of a kind, pallid, overweight, soft. Braje giggled as she fastened the manacles about her complaisant charge. The hatchling fought, its lean muscles writhing, its great wings beating together in a dramatic but ultimately ineffectual thunderclap as huge, glowering Jonas and his men forced it down into its niche. As they manacled it into place, Khar Dorian grinned and the g'vhern made a high, thin whistling sound that hurt the ears.

Craimur Delhune had to be carried in by his aides and hirelings. "There," I told them, pointing, and they propped him awkwardly into one of the niches. His shrunken, wizened face stared at me, half-blind eyes darting around the chamber like small, feral beasts, his mouth sucking greedily, as if his rebirth was done and he sought a mother's breast. He was blind to the mosaic; for him, it was only a dark room with black glass walls.

Rieseen Jay swaggered in, bored by my chamber before she even entered it. She saw the mosaic but gave it only a cursory glance, as something beneath her notice, too tiresome to study. Instead she made a slow circuit of the niches, inspecting each of the prizes like a butcher examining the meat. She lingered longest in front of the hatchling, seeming to delight in its struggles, its obvious fear, the way it hissed and whistled at her and glared from those fierce, bright eyes. She reached out to touch a wing, and leapt back, laughing, when the hatchling bit at her. Finally she took herself to a seat, where she sprawled languidly, waiting for the game to begin.

Finally Kleronomas.

He saw the mosaic at once, stopped, stared up at it, his crystalline eyes scanning slowly around the room, halting here and there again to study some fine detail. He paused so long that Rieseen Jay grew impatient, and snapped at him to take a seat. The cyborg studied her, metal face unreadable. "Quiet," I said.

He finished his study of the dome, taking his own time, and only then seated himself in the final empty niche. The way he took his place was as if all the seats had been vacant and this was his choice, selected by him alone.

"Clear the room," I commanded. Rannar bowed and gestured them out, Jonas and Braje and the others. Khar Dorian went last, and made a gesture at me as he took his leave. Meaning what? Good luck? Perhaps. I heard Rannar seal the door.

"Well?" demanded Rieseen Jay.

I gave her a look that silenced her. "You are all seated in the Siege Perilous," I said. I always began with those words. No one ever understood. This time . . . Kleronomas, perhaps. I watched the mask that was his face. Within the crystal of his eyes, I saw a slight shifting motion, and tried to find a meaning in it. "There are no rules in the game of mind. But I have rules, for when it is over, when you are back in my domain.

"Those of you who are here unwillingly, if you are strong enough to hold the flesh you wear, it is yours forever. I give it to you freely. No prize plays more than once. Hold fast to your birthflesh and when it is done, Khar Dorian will take you back to the world he found you on and set you loose with a thousand standards and your freedom.

"Those players who find rebirth this day, who rise in strange flesh when this game is ended, remember that what you have won or lost is your own doing, and spare me your regrets and recriminations. If you are dissatisfied with the outcome of this gaming, you may of course play again. If you have the price.

"One last warning. For all of you. This is going to hurt. This is going to hurt more than anything you ever imagined."

So saying, I began the game of mind.

Once more.

What can you say about pain?

Words can trace only the shadow of the thing itself. The reality of hard, sharp physical pain is like nothing else, and it is beyond language. The world is too much with us, day and night, but when we hurt, when we really hurt, the world melts and fades and becomes a ghost, a dim memory, a silly unimportant thing. Whatever ideals, dreams, loves, fears, and thoughts we might have had become ultimately unimportant. We are alone with our pain, it is the only force in the cosmos, the only thing of substance, the only thing that matters, and if the pain is bad enough and lasts long enough, if it is the sort of agony that goes on and on, then all the things that are our humanity melt before it and the proud sophisticated computer that is the human brain becomes capable of but a single thought:

Make it stop, make it STOP!

And if the pain does eventually stop, afterwards, with the passage of time, even the mind that has experienced it becomes unable to comprehend it, unable to remember how bad it truly was, unable to describe it so as to even approach the terrible truth of what it felt like when it was happening.

In the game of mind, the agony of the painfield is like no other pain, like nothing I have ever experienced.

The painfield does no harm to the body, leaves no marks, no scars, no injuries, no signs to mark its passing. It touches the mind directly with an agony beyond my power to express. How long does it last? A question for relativists. It lasts but the smallest part of a microsecond, and it lasts forever.

The Wisdoms of Dam Tullian are masters of a hundred different disciplines of mind and body, and they teach their acolytes a technique for isolating pain, dissociating from it, pushing it away and thus transcending it. I had been a Wisdom for half my life when I first played the game of mind. I used all I had been taught, all the tricks and truths I had mastered and learned to rely on. They were utterly useless. This was a pain that did not touch the body, a pain that did not race along the nerve paths, a pain that filled the mind so completely and so shatteringly that not even the smallest part of you was free to think or plan or meditate. The pain was you, and you were the pain. There was nothing to dissociate from, no cool sanctum of thought where you might retreat.

The painfield was infinite and eternal, and from that ceaseless and unthinkable agony there was only one sure surcease. It was the old one, the true one, the same balm that has been succor to billions of men and women, and even the smallest of the beasts of the field, since the beginning of time. Pain's dark lord. My enemy, my lover. Again, yet again, wanting only an end to suffering, I rushed to his black embrace.

Death took me, and the pain ended.

On a vast, echoey plain in a place beyond life, I waited for the others.

Dim shadows taking form from the mists. Four, five, yes. Have we lost some of them? It would not surprise me. In three games out of four, a player finds his truth in death and seeks no further. This time? No. I see the sixth shape striding out of the writhing fog, we are all here, I look around myself once more, count three, four, five, six, seven, and me, me, eight.

Eight?

That's wrong, that's very wrong. I am dizzy, disoriented. Nearby someone is screaming. A little girl, sweet-faced, innocent, dressed in pastels and pretty gems. She does not know how she got here, she does not understand, her eyes are lost and childish and far too trusting, and the pain has woken her from a dreamdust languor to a strange land full of fear.

I raise a small, strong hand, gaze at the thick brown fingers, the patch of callous by my thumb, the blunt wide nails trimmed to the quick. I make a fist, a familiar gesture, and in my hand a mirror takes shape from the iron of my will and the quicksilver of my desire. Within its glittering depths I see a face. It is the face of a woman who is both hard and strong, with deep lines around her grey eyes from squinting into alien suns, a wide mouth not without its generosity, a nose once broken that has not healed straight, short brown hair in perpetual disarray. A comfortable face. It gives me comfort now.

The mirror dissolves into smoke. The land, the sky, everything is shifting and uncertain. The sweet little girl is still screaming for her daddy. Some of the others are staring at me, lost. There is a young man, plain of face, his black hair swept back straight and feathered with color in a style that has not been the fashion on Gulliver for a century. His body looks soft, but in his eyes I see a hard edge that reminds me of Khar Dorian. Rieseen Jay seems stunned, wary, frightened, but still she is recognizably Rieseen Jay; whatever else might be said of her, she has a strong sense of who she is. Perhaps that will even be enough. The g'vhern looms near her, far larger here than it seemed before, its body glistening with oil as it spreads demonic wings and begins to whip the fog into long gray ribbons. In the game of mind, it wears no manacles; Rieseen Jay looks long, and cowers away from it. So too does another player, a wisty grey shape covered by a blaze of tattoos, his face a pale blur with neither purpose nor definition. The little girl screams on and on. I turn away from them, leave them to their own devices, and face the final player.

A big man, his skin the color of polished ebony with a dark blue undertone where his long muscles flex as he stretches. He is naked. His jaw is square and heavy, jutting sharply forward. Long hair surrounds his face and falls past his shoulders, hair as white and crisp as fresh bedsheets, as white as the untouched snow of a world that men have never walked. As I watch him, his thick, dark penis stirs against his leg, swells, grows erect. He smiles at me. "Wisdom," he says.

Suddenly I'm naked too.

I frown, and now I wear an ornate suit of armor, overlapping plates of gilded duralloy, filigreed with forbidding runes, and beneath my arm is a matching antique helmet, festooned with a plume of bright feathers. "Joachim Kleronomas," I say. His penis grows and thickens until it is an absurd fat staff that presses hard against the flatness of his stomach. I cover it, and him, in a uniform from a history text, all black and silver, with the bluegreen globe of Old Earth sewn on his right sleeve and twin silver galaxies swirling on his collar.

"No," he says, amused, "I never reached that rank," and the galaxies are gone, replaced by a circle of six silver stars. "And for most of my time, Wisdom, my allegiance was to Avalon, not Earth." His uniform is less martial, more functional, a simple grey-green jumpsuit with a black fabric belt and a pocket heavy with pens. Only the silver circle of stars remains. "There," he says.

"Wrong," I tell him. "Wrong still." And when I am done talking, only the uniform remains. Inside the cloth the flesh is gone, replaced by silver-metal mockery, a shining empty thing with a toaster for a head. But only for an instant. Then the man is back, frowning, unhappy. "Cruel," he says to me. The hardness of his penis strains at the fabric of his crotch.

Behind him, the eighth man, the ghost who ought not be here, the misplaced phantom, makes a soft whispery sound, a sound like the rustling of dry dead leaves in a cold autumn wind.

He is a thin, shadowy thing, this intruder. I must look at him very hard to see him at all. He is much smaller than Kleronomas, and he gives the impression of being old and frail, though his flesh is so wispy, so insubstantial, that it is hard to be sure. He is a vision suggested by the random drift of the fog, perhaps, an echo dressed in faded white, but his eyes glow and shimmer and they are trapped and afraid. He reaches out to me. The flesh of his hand is translucent, pulled tightly over grey ancient bones.

I back away, uncertain. In the game of mind, the lightest touch can have a terrible reality.

Behind me I hear more screaming, the terrible wild sound of someone in an ecstacy of fear. I turn.

It has begun in earnest now. The players are seeking their prey. Craimur Delhune, young and vital and far more muscular than he was a moment ago, stands with a flaming sword in one hand, swinging it easily at the tattooed boy. The boy is on his knees, shrieking, trying to cover himself with upraised arms, but Delhune's bright blade passes through the grey shadowflesh unimpeded, and slices at the shining tattoos. He removes them from the boy surgically, swing by swing, and they drift upwards in the misty air, shining images of life cut free of the grey skin on which they were imprisoned. Delhune snatches them as they float by and swallows them whole. Smoke drifts from his nostrils and his open mouth. The boy screams and cringes. Soon there will be nothing left but shadow.

The hatchling has taken to the air. It circles above us, keening at us in its high, thin voice as its wings thunder.

Rieseen Jay has had second thoughts, it seems. She stands above the whimpering little girl, who grows less little with each passing moment. Jay is changing her. She is older now, fatter, her eyes just as frightened but far more vacant. Wherever she turns her head, mirrors appear and sing taunts at her with fat wet lips. Her flesh swells and swells, tearing free of her poor, frayed clothing; thin lines of spittle run down her chin, She wipes at it, crying, but it only flows faster, and now it turns pink with blood. She is enormous, gross, revolting. "That's you," the mirrors say. "Don't look away. Look at yourself. You're not a little girl. Look, look, look. Aren't you pretty? Aren't you sweet? Look at you, look at you." Rieseen Jay folds her arms, smiles with satisfaction.

Kleronomas looks at me with cold judgment on his face. A band of black cloth wraps itself about my eyes. I blink, vanish it, glare at him. "I'm not blind," I say. "I see them. It is not my fight."

The fat woman is as large as a truck, as pale and soft as a maggot. She is naked and immense and with each blink of Jay's eye she grows more monstrous. Huge white breasts burst forth from her face, hands, thighs, and the brown meaty nipples open gaping mouths and began to sing. A thick green penis appears above her vagina, curls down, enters her. Cancers blossom on her skin like a field of dark flowers. And everywhere are the mirrors, blinking in and out, reflecting and distorting and enlarging, relentlessly showing her everything she is, documenting every grotesque fancy that Jay inflicts upon her. The fat woman is hardly human. From a mouth the size of my head, gumless and bleeding, she issues forth a sound like the wailing of the damned. Her flesh begins to smoke and tremble.

The cyborg points. All the mirrors explode.

The mist is full of daggers, shards of slivered glass flying everywhere. One comes at me and I make it gone. But the others, the others . . . they curve like smart missiles, become an aerial flotilla, attack. Rieseen Jay is pierced in a thousand places, and the blood drips from her eyes, her breasts, her open mouth. The monster is a little girl again, crying.

"A moralist," I say to Kleronomas.

He ignores me, turns to look at Craimur Delhune and the shadow boy. Tattooes flame to new life upon the youth's skin, and in his hand a sword appears and takes fire. Delhune takes a step back, unnerved. The boy touches his flesh, mouths some silent oath, rises warily.

"An altruist," I say. "Giving succor to the weak."

Kleronomas turns. "I hold no brief with slaughter."

I laugh at him. "Maybe you're just saving them for yourself, cyborg. If not, you had better grow wings fast, before your prize flies away."

His face is cold. "My prize is in front of me," he says.

"Somehow I knew that," I reply, donning my plumed helmet. My armor is alive with golden highlights, my sword is a spear of light.

My armor is as black as the pit, and the designs worked upon it, black on black, are of spiders and snakes and human skulls and faces a-writhe with pain. My long straight silver sword turns to obsidian, and twists into a grotesquerie of barbs and hooks and cruel spikes. He has a sense of drama, this damned cyborg. "No," I say. "I will not be cast as evil." I am gold and silver once more, shining, and my plumes are red and blue. "Wear the suit yourself if you like it so much."

It stands before me, black and hideous, the helmet open on a grinning skull. Kleronomas sends it away. "I need no props," he says. His grey-and-white ghost flitters at his side, plucking at him. Who is that? I wonder yet again.

"Fine," I say. "Then we'll dispense with the symbols."

My armor is gone.

I hold out my bare, open hand. "Touch me," I say. "Touch me, cyborg."

As his hand reaches out to mine, metal creeps up his long dark fingers.

In the game of mind, even more than in life, image and metaphor are everything.

The place beyond time, the endless fog-shrouded plain, the cold sky and the uncertain earth beneath us, even that is illusion. It is mine, all of it, a setting—

however unearthly, however surreal—against which the players may act out their tawdry dramas of dominance and submission, conquest and despair, death and rebirth, rape and mind-rape. Without my shaping, my vision and the visions of all the other painlords through the eons, they would have no ground below, no sky above, no place to set their feet, no feet to set. The reality offers not even the scant comfort of the barren landscape I give them. The reality is chaos, unendurable, outside of space and time, bereft of matter or energy, without measurement and therefore frighteningly infinite and suffocatingly claustrophobic, terribly eternal and achingly brief. In that reality the players are trapped; seven minds locked into a telepathic gestalt, into a congress so intimate it cannot be borne by most. And therefore they shrink away, and the very first things we create, in a place where we are gods (or devils, or both), are the bodies we have left behind. Within these walls of flesh we take our refuge and try to order chaos.

The blood has the taste of salt; but there is no blood, only illusion. The cup holds a black and bitter drink; but there is no cup, only an image. The wounds are open and raw, dripping anguish; but there are no wounds, no body to be wounded, only metaphor, symbol, conjuring. Nothing is real, and everything can hurt, can kill, can evoke a lasting madness.

To survive, the players must be resilient, disciplined, stable, and ruthless; they must possess a ready imagination, an extensive vocabulary of symbols, a certain amount of psychological insight. They must find the weakness in their opponent, and hide their own phobias thoroughly. The rules are simple. Believe in everything; believe in nothing. Hold tight to yourself and your sanity.

Even when they kill you, it has no meaning, unless you believe that you have died.

Upon this plain of illusion where these all-too-mutable bodies whirl and feint in a trite pavane that I have seen a thousand times before, plucking swords and mirrors and monsters from the air to throw at one another like jugglers gone mad, the most frightening thing of all is a simple touch.

The symbolism is direct, the meaning clear. Flesh upon flesh. Stripped of metaphor, stripped of protection, stripped of masks. Mind upon mind. When we touch, the walls are down.

Even time is illusory in the game of mind; it runs as fast, or as slow, as we desire.

I am Cyrain, I tell myself, born of Ash, far-traveled, a Wisdom of Dam Tullian, master of the game of mind, mistress of the obsidian castle, ruler of Croan'dhenni, mindlord, painlord, lifelord, whole and immortal and invulnerable. Enter me.

His fingers are cool and hard.

I have played the game of mind before, have clasped hands with others who thought themselves strong. In their minds, in their souls, in them, I have seen things. In dark grey tunnels I have traced the graffiti of their ancient scars. The quicksand of their insecurities has clutched at my boots. I have smelled the rank odor of their fears, great swollen beasts who dwell in a palpable living darkness. I have burned my fingers on the hot flesh of lusts who will not speak a name. I have ripped the cloaks from their still, quiet secrets. And then I have taken it all, been them, lived their lives, drunk the cold draught of their knowledge, rummaged through their memories. I have been born a dozen times, have suckled at a dozen teats, have lost a dozen virginities, male and female.

Kleronomas was different.

I stood in a great cavern, alive with lights. The walls and floor and ceiling were translucent crystal, and all around me spires and cones and twisted ribbons rose bright and red and hard, cold to the touch yet alive, the soulsparks moving through them everywhere. A crystalline fairy city in a cave. I touched the nearest outcropping, and the memory flooded into me, the knowledge as clear and sharp and certain as the day it had been etched there. I turned and looked around with new eyes, now discerning rigid order where initially I had perceived only chaotic beauty. It was clean. It took my breath away. I looked everywhere for the vulnerability, the door of gangrenous flesh, the pool of blood, the place of weeping, the shuffling unclean thing that must live deep inside him, and I found nothing, nothing, nothing, only perfection, only the clean sharp crystal, so very red, glowing from within, growing, changing, yet eternal. I touched it once again, wrapping my hand about an outcropping that rose in front of me like a stalagmite. The knowledge was mine. I began to walk, touching, touching, drinking everywhere. Glass flowers bloomed on every side, fantastic scarlet blooms, fragile and beautiful. I took one and sniffed at it, but it had no scent. The perfection was daunting. Where was his weakness? Where was the hidden flaw in this diamond that would enable me to crack it with a single sharp blow?

Here within him there was no decay.

Here there was no place for death.

Here nothing lived.

It felt like home.

And then in front of me the ghost took form, grey and gaunt and unsteady. His bare feet sent up thin tendrils of smoke as they trod lightly on the gleaming crystals underneath, and I caught the scent of burning meat. And I smiled. The spectre haunted the crystal maze, but every touch meant pain and destruction. "Come here," I said. He looked at me. I could see the lights on the far side of the cavern through the haze of his uncertain flesh. He moved to me and I opened my arms to him, entered him, possessed him.

*   *   *

I seated myself upon a balcony in the highest tower of my castle, and drank from a small cup of fragrant black coffee laced with brandy. The swamps were gone; instead I gazed upon mountains, hard and cold and clean. They rose blue-white all around me, and from the highest peak flew a plume of snow crystals caught in a steady endless wind. The wind cut through me, but I scarcely felt it. I was alone and at peace, and the coffee tasted good, and death was far away.

He walked out upon the balcony, and seated himself upon one of the parapets. His pose was casual, insolent, confident. "I know you," he said. It was the ultimate threat.

I was not afraid. "I know you," I said. "Shall I conjure up your ghost?"

"He will be here soon enough. He is never far from me."

"No," I said. I sipped my coffee, and let him wait. "I am stronger than you," I told him finally. "I can win the game, cyborg. You were wrong to challenge me."

He said nothing.

I set down my cup, drained and empty, passed my hand across it, smiled as my glass flower grew and spread its colorless transparent petals. A broken rainbow crawled across the table.

He frowned. Color crept into my flower. It softened and drooped, the rainbow was banished. "The other was not real," he said. "A glass flower is not alive."

I held up his rose, pointed at the broken stem. "This flower is dying," I said. In my hands, it became glass once again. "A glass flower lasts forever."

He transmuted the glass back to living tissue. He was stubborn, I will say that for him. "Even dying, it lives."

"Look at its imperfections," I said. I pointed them out, one by one. "Here an insect has gnawed upon it. Here a petal has grown malformed, here, these dark splotches, those are blight, here the wind has bent it. And look what I can do." I took the largest, prettiest petal between thumb and forefinger, ripped it off, fed it to the wind. "Beauty is no protection. Life is terribly vulnerable. And ultimately, all of it ends like this." In my hand, the flower turned brown and shrivelled and began to rot. Worms festered upon it briefly, and foul black fluids ran from it, and then it was dust. I crumpled it, blew it away, and from behind his ear I plucked another flower. Glass.

"Glass is hard," he said, "and cold."

"Warmth is a byproduct of decay, the stepchild of entropy." I told him.

Perhaps he would have replied, but we were no longer alone. Over the crennellated edge of the parapets the ghost came crawling, pulling himself up with frail grey-white hands that left bloody stains upon the purity of my stone. He stared at us wordlessly, a half-transparent whispering in white. Kleronomas averted his eyes.

"Who is he?" I ask.

The cyborg could not answer.

"Do you even remember his name?" I asked him. He replied with silence, and I laughed at them both. "Cyborg, you judged me, found my morality suspect, my actions tainted, but whatever I might be, I am nothing to you. I steal their bodies. You've taken his mind. Haven't you? *Haven't you?*"

"I never meant to," he said.

"Joachim Kleronomas died on Avalon seven hundred years ago, just as they say he did. Steel and plastic he might wear, but inside he was still rotting flesh, even at the end, and with all flesh there comes a time when the cells die. A thin flat line on a machine, glowing in the darkness, and an empty metal shell. The end of a legend. What did they do then? Scoop out the brain and bury it beneath some oversized monument? No doubt." The coffee was strong and sweet; here it never grew lukewarm, because my will did not permit it. "But they did not bury the machine, did they? That expensive, sophisticated cybernetic organism, the library computer with its wealth of knowledge, the crystal matrix with all its frozen memories. All that was too valuable to discard. The good scientists of Avalon kept it in an interface with the Academy's main system, correct? How many centuries passed before one of them decided to don that cyborg body again, and keep his own death at bay?"

"Less than one," the cyborg said. "Less than fifty standard years."

"He should have erased you," I said. "But why? His brain would be riding the machine, after all. Why deny himself access to all that marvelous knowledge, why destroy those crystallized memories? Why, when he could savor them instead? How much better to have a whole second lifetime at his disposal, to be able to access wisdom he had never earned, recollect places he had never been and people he had never met." I shrugged, and looked at the ghost. "Poor stupid thing. If you'd ever played the game of mind, you might have understood."

What can the mind be made of, if not memories? Who are we, after all? Only who we think we are, no more, no less.

Etch your memories on diamond, or on a block of rancid meat, those are the choices. Bit by bit the flesh must die, and give way to steel and metal. Only the diamond memories survive to drive the body. In the end no flesh remains, and the echoes of lost memories are ghostly scratchings on the crystal.

"He forgot who he was," the cyborg said. "I forgot who I was, rather. I began to think . . . he began to think he was me." He looked up at me, his eyes locked on mine. They were red crystal, those eyes, and behind them I could see a glow. His skin was taking on a hard, polished sheen, silvering as I watched. And this time he was doing it himself. "You have your own weaknesses," he said, pointing.

Where it curls about the handle of my coffee cup, my

hand has grown black, and spotted with corruption. I could smell the decay. Flesh began to flake off, and beneath I saw the bloody bone, bleaching to grim whiteness. Death crept up my bare arm, inexorably. I suppose it was meant to fill me with horror. It only filled me with disgust.

"No," I said. My arm was whole and healthy. "No," I repeated, and now I was metal, silver-bright and undying, eyes like opals, glass flowers twined through platinum hair. I could see my reflection gleaming upon the polished jet of his chest; I was beautiful. Perhaps he could see himself as well, mirrored in my chrome, for just then he turned his head away.

He seemed so strong, but on Croan'dhenni, in my castle of obsidian, in this house of pain and rebirth where the game of mind is played, things are not always as they seem.

"Cyborg," I said to him, "you are lost."

"The other players," he began.

"No." I pointed. "He will stand between you and any victim you might choose. Your ghost. Your guilt. He will not allow it. You will not allow it."

The cyborg could not look at me. "Yes," in a voice tainted by metal and corroded by despair.

"You will live forever," I said.

"No. I will go on forever. It is different, Wisdom. I can tell you the precise temperature reading of any environment, but I cannot feel heat or cold. I can see into the infrared and the ultraviolet, can magnify my sensors to count every pore on your skin, but I am blind to what I think must be your beauty. I desire life, real life, with the seed of death growing inexorably within it, and therefore giving it meaning."

"Good," I said, satisfied.

He finally looked at me. Trapped in that shining metal face were two pale, lost, human eyes. "Good?"

"I make my own meaning, cyborg, and life is the

enemy of death, not its mother. Congratulations. You've won. And so have I." I rose and reached across the table, plunged my hand through the cold black chest, and ripped the crystal heart from his breast. I held it up and it shone, brighter and brighter, its scarlet rays dancing brilliantly upon the cold dark mountains of my mind.

I opened my eyes.

No, incorrect; I activated my sensors once again, and the scene in the chamber of change came into focus with a clarity and sharpness I had never experienced. My obsidian mosaic, black against black, was now a hundred different shades, each distinct from the others, the pattern crisp and clear. I was seated in a niche along the rim; in the center cup, the child-woman stirred and blinked large violet eyes. The door opened and they came to her, Rannar soliticious, Khar Dorian aloof, trying to conceal his curiosity, Braje giggling as she gave her shots.

"No," I announced to them. My voice was too deep, too male. I adjusted it. "No, here," I said, sounding more like myself.

Their stares were like the cracking of whips.

In the game of mind, there are winners and there are losers.

The cyborg's interference had its effects, perhaps. Or perhaps not, perhaps before the game was over, the pattern would have been the same. Craimur Delhune is dead; they gave his corpse to the swamps last evening. But the vacancy is gone from the eyes of the pudgy young dreamduster, and she is dieting and exercising even now, and when Khar Dorian leaves, he will take her back to Delhune's estates on Gulliver.

Rieseen Jay complains that she was cheated. I believe she will linger here, outside, in the city of the damned. No doubt that will cure her boredom. The g'hvern struggles to speak, and has painted elaborate symbols on its wings. The tattooed boy leapt from the castle battlements a few hours after his return, and impaled himself upon the jagged obsidian spikes far below, flapping his arms until the last instant. Wings and fierce eyes do not equate with strength.

A new mindlord has begun to reign. She has commanded them to start on a new castle, a structure shaped from living woods, its foundations rooted deep in the swamps, its exterior covered with vines and flowers and other living things. "You will get insects," I have warned her, "parasites and stinging flies, miner-worms in the wood, blight in your foundation, rot in your walls. You will have to sleep with netting over your bed. You will have to kill, constantly, day and night. Your wooden castle will swim in a miasma of little deaths, and in a few years the ghosts of a million insects will swarm your halls by night."

"Nonetheless," she says, "my home will be warm and alive, where yours was cold and brittle."

We all have our symbols, I suppose.

And our fears.

"Erase him," she has warned me. "Blank the crystal, or in time he will consume you, and you will become another ghost in the machine."

"Erase him?" I might have laughed, if the mechanism permitted laughter. I can see right through her. Her soul is scrawled upon that soft, fragile face. I can count her pores and note each flicker of doubt in the pupils of those violet eyes. "Erase *me*, you mean. The crystal is home to us both, child. Besides, I do not fear him. You miss the point. Kleronomas was crystal, the ghost organic meat, the outcome inevitable. My case is different. I am as crystalline as he is, and just as eternal."

"Wisdom—" she began.

"Wrong," I said.

"Cyrain, if you prefer—"

"Wrong again. Call me Kleronomas." I have been many things through my long and varied lives, but I have never been a legend. It has a certain cachet.

The little girl looked at me. "I am Kleronomas," she said in a high sweet voice, her eyes baffled.

"Yes," I said, "and no. Today we are both Kleronomas. We have lived the same lives, done the same things, stored the same memories. But from this day on, we walk different paths. I am steel and crystal, and you are childflesh. You wanted life, you said. Embrace it, it's yours, and all that goes with it. Your body is young and healthy, just beginning to blossom, your years will be long and full. Today you think you are still Kleronomas. And tomorrow?

"Tomorrow you will learn about lust again, and open your little thighs to Khar Dorian, and shudder and cry out as he rides you to orgasm. Tomorrow you will bear children in blood and pain, and watch them grow and age and bear children of their own, and die. Tomorrow you will ride through the swamps and the dispossessed will toss you gifts, and curse you, and praise you, and pray to you. Tomorrow new players will arrive, begging for bodies, for rebirth, for another chance, and tomorrow Khar's ships will land with a new load of prizes, and all your moral certainties will be tested, and tested again, and twisted to new shapes. Tomorrow Khar and Jonas or Sebastien Cayle will decide that they have waited long enough, and you'll taste the honeyed treason of their kiss, and perhaps you'll win, or perhaps you'll lose. There's no certainty to it. But there's one sure thing I can promise. On the day after tomorrow, long years from now though they will not seem long once passed, death will begin to grow inside you. The seed is already planted. Perhaps it will be some disease blooming in one of those small sweet breasts Rannar would so dearly love to suckle, perhaps a fine thin wire pulled tight across your throat as you sleep, perhaps a sudden solar flare that will burn this planet clean. It will come, though, and sooner than you think."

"I accept it," she said. She smiled as she spoke; I think she really meant it. "All of it, every part. Life and death. I have been without it for a long time, Wis—Kleronomas."

"Already you're forgetting things," I observed. "Every day you will lose more. Today we both remember. We remember the crystal caverns of Eris, the first ship we ever served on, the lines of our father's face. We remember what Tomas Chung said when we decided not to turn back to Avalon, and the other words he said as he lay dying. We remember the last woman we ever made love to, the shape and smell of her, the taste of her breasts, the noises she made when we pleasured her. She's been dead and gone eight hundred years, but she lives in our memories. But she's dying in yours, isn't she? Today you are Kleronomas. Yet I am him as well, and I am Cyrain of Ash, and a small part of me is still our ghost, poor sad man. But when tomorrow comes, I'll hold tight to all I am, and you, you'll be the mindlord, or perhaps just a sex-slave in some perfumed brothel on Cymeranth, or a scholar on Avalon, but in any case a different person than you are now."

She understood; she accepted. "So you'll play the game of mind forever," she said, "and I will never die."

"You will die," I pointed out. "Most certainly. Kleronomas is immortal."

"And Cyrain of Ash."

"Her too. Yes."

"What will you do?" she asked me.

I went to the window. The glass flower was there, in its simple wooden vase, its petals refracting the light. I looked up at the source of that light, the brilliant sun of Croan'dhenni burning in the clear midday sky. I could look straight into it now, could focus on the sunspots and the flaming towers of its prominences. I made a small conscious adjustment to the crystal lenses of my eyes, and the empty sky was full of stars, more stars than I had ever seen before, more stars than I could possibly have imagined.

"Do?" I said, still gazing up at those secret starfields, visible to me alone. They brought to mind my obsidian mosaic. "There are worlds I've never been to," I told my sister-twin, father, daughter, enemy, mirror-image, whatever she was. "There are things I don't yet know, stars that even now I cannot see. What will I do? Everything. To begin with, everything."

As I spoke, a fat striped insect flew through the open window on six gossamer wings that trilled the air too fast for human sight, though I could count every languid beat if I so chose. It landed briefly on my glass flower, found neither scent nor pollen, and slipped back outside. I watched it go, growing smaller and smaller, dwindling in the distance, until at last I had telescoped my vision to the maximum, and the small dying bug was lost among the swamps and stars.

PORTRAITS OF HIS CHILDREN

Richard Cantling found the package leaning up against his front door, one evening in late October when he was setting out for his walk. It annoyed him. He had told his postman repeatedly to ring the bell when delivering anything too big to fit through the mail slot, yet the man persisted in abandoning the packages on the porch, where any passerby could simply walk off with them. Although, to be fair, Cantling's house was rather isolated, sitting on the river bluffs at the end of a cul de sac, and the trees effectively screened it off from the street. Still, there was always the possibility of damage from rain or wind or snow.

Cantling's displeasure lasted only an instant. Wrapped in heavy brown paper and carefully sealed with tape, the

package had a shape that told all. Obviously a painting.
And the hand that had block-printed his address in heavy
green marker was unmistakeably Michelle's. Another
self-portrait then. She must be feeling repentant.

He was more surprised than he cared to admit, even
to himself. He had always been a stubborn man. He
could hold grudges for years, even decades, and he had
the greatest difficulty admitting any wrong. And Michelle,
being his only child, seemed to take after him in all of
that. He hadn't expected this kind of gesture from her.
It was . . . well, sweet.

He set aside his walking stick to lug the package inside,
where he could unwrap it out of the damp and the blus-
tery October wind. It was about three feet tall, and unexpectedly heavy. He carried it awkwardly, shutting the
door with his foot and struggling down the long foyer
toward his den. The brown drapes were tightly closed; the
room was dark, and heavy with the smell of dust. Cantling
had to set down the package to fumble for the light.

He hadn't used his den much since that night, two
months ago, when Michelle had gone storming out. Her
self-portrait was still sitting up above the wide slate mantle. Below, the fireplace badly wanted cleaning, and on
the built-in bookshelves his novels, all bound in handsome dark leather, stood dusty and disarrayed. Cantling
looked at the old painting and felt a brief wash of anger
return to him, followed by depression. It had been such
a nasty thing for her to do. The portrait had been quite
good, really. Much more to his taste than the tortured
abstractions that Michelle liked to paint for her own pleasure, or the trite paperback covers she did to make her
living. She had done it when she was twenty, as a birthday gift for him. He'd always been fond of it. It captured
her as no photograph had ever done, not just the lines
of her face, the high angular cheekbones and blue eyes
and tangled ash-blond hair, but the personality inside.
She looked so young and fresh and confident, and her

smile reminded him so much of Helen, and the way she had smiled on their wedding day. He'd told Michelle more than once how much he'd like that smile.

And so, of course, it had been the smile that she'd started on. She used an antique dagger from his collection, chopped out the mouth with four jagged slashes. She'd gouged out the wide blue eyes next, as if intent on blinding the portrait, and when he came bursting in after her, she'd been slicing the canvas into ribbons with long angry crooked cuts. Cantling couldn't forget that moment. So ugly. And to do something like that to her own work, he couldn't imagine it. He had tried to picture himself mutilating one of his books, tried to comprehend what might drive one to such an act, and he had failed utterly. It was unthinkable, beyond even imagination.

The mutilated portrait still hung in its place. He'd been too stubborn to take it down, and yet he could not bear to look at it. So he had taken to avoiding his den. It wasn't hard. The old house was a huge, rambling place, with more rooms than he could possibly need or want, living alone as he did. It had been built a century ago, when Perrot had been a thriving river town, and they said that a succession of steamer captains had lived there. Certainly the steamboat gothic architecture and all the gingerbread called up visions of the glory days of the river, and he had a fine view of the Mississippi from the third-story windows and the widow's walk. After the incident, Cantling had moved his desk and his typewriter to one of the unused bedrooms and settled in there, determined to let the den remain as Michelle had left it until she came back with an apology.

He had not expected that apology quite so soon, however, nor in quite this form. A tearful phone call, yes— but not another portrait. Still, this was nicer somehow, more personal. And it was a gesture, the first step toward a reconciliation. Richard Cantling knew too well that he was incapable of taking that step himself, no matter how lonely he might become. He had left all his New York friends behind when he moved out to this Iowa river town, and had formed no local friendships to replace them. That was nothing new. He had never been an outgoing sort. He had a certain shyness that kept him apart, even from those few friends he did make. Even from his family, really. Helen had often accused him of caring more for his characters than for real people, an accusation that Michelle had picked up on by the time she was in her teens. Helen was gone too. They'd divorced ten years ago, and she'd been dead for five. Michelle, infuriating as she could be, was really all he had left. He had missed her, missed even the arguments.

He thought about Michelle as he tore open the plain brown paper. He would call her, of course. He would call her and tell her how good the new portrait was, how much he liked it. He would tell her that he'd missed her, invite her to come out for Thanksgiving. Yes, that would be the way to handle it. No mention of their argument, he didn't want to start it all up again, and neither he nor Michelle was the kind to back down gracefully. A family trait, that stubborn willful pride, as ingrained as the high cheekbones and squarish jaw. The Cantling heritage.

It was an antique frame, he saw. Wooden, elaborately carved, very heavy, just the sort of thing he liked. It would mesh with his Victorian decor much better than the thin brass frame on the old portrait. Cantling pulled the wrapping paper away, eager to see what his daughter had done. She was nearly thirty now—or was she past thirty already? He never could keep track of her age, or even her birthdays. Anyway, she was a much better painter than she'd been at twenty. The new portrait ought to be striking. He ripped away the last of the wrappings and turned it around.

His first reaction was that it was a fine, fine piece of work, maybe the best thing that Michelle Cantling had ever done.

Then, belatedly, the admiration washed away, and was replaced by anger. It wasn't her. It wasn't Michelle. Which meant it wasn't a replacement for the portrait she had so willfully vandalized. It was . . . something else.

Someone else.

It was a face he had never before laid eyes on. But it was a face he recognized as readily as if he had looked on it a thousand times. Oh yes.

The man in the portrait was young. Twenty, maybe even younger, though his curly brown hair was already well-streaked with gray. It was unruly hair, disarrayed as if the man had just come from sleep, falling forward into his eyes. Those eyes were a bright green, lazy eyes somehow, shining with some secret amusement. He had high Cantling cheekbones, but the jawline was all wrong for a relative. Beneath a wide, flat nose, he wore a sardonic smile; his whole posture was somehow insolent. The portrait showed him dressed in faded dungarees and a ravelled WMCA Good Guy sweatshirt, with a half-eaten raw onion in one hand. The background was a brick wall covered with graffiti.

Cantling had created him.

Edward Donohue. Dunnahoo, that's what they'd called him, his friends and peers. The other characters in Richard Cantling's first novel, *Hangin' Out*. Dunnahoo had been the protagonist. A wise guy, a smart mouth, too damn bright for his own good. Looking down at the portrait, Cantling felt as if he'd known him for half his life. As indeed he had, in a way. Known him and, yes, cherished him, in the peculiar way a writer can cherish one of his characters.

Michelle had captured him true. Cantling stared at the painting and it all came back to him, all the events he had bled over so long ago, all the people he had fashioned and described with such loving care. He remembered Jocko, and the Squid, and Nancy, and Ricci's Pizzeria where so much of the book's action had taken place (he could see it vividly in his mind's eye), and the business with Arthur and the motorcycle, and the climactic pizza fight. And Dunnahoo. Dunnahoo especially. Smarting off, fooling around, hanging out, coming of age. "Fuck 'em if they can't take a joke," he said. A dozen times or so. It was the book's closing line.

For a moment, Richard Cantling felt a vast, strange affection well up inside him, as if he had just been reunited with an old, lost friend.

And then, almost as an afterthought, he remembered all the ugly words that he and Michelle had flung at each other that night, and suddenly it made sense. Cantling's face went hard. "Bitch," he said aloud. He turned away in fury, helpless without a target for his anger. "Bitch," he said again, as he slammed the door of the den behind him.

"Bitch," he had called her.

She turned around with the knife in her hand. Her eyes were raw and red from crying. She had the smile in her hand. She balled it up and threw it at him. "Here, you bastard, you like the damned smile so much, here it is."

It bounced off his cheek. His face was reddening. "You're just like your mother," he said. "She was always breaking things too."

"You gave her good reason, didn't you?"

Cantling ignored that. "What the hell is wrong with you? What the hell do you think you're going to accomplish with this stupid melodramatic gesture? That's all it is, you know. Bad melodrama. Who the hell do you think you are, some character in a Tennessee Williams play? Come off it, Michelle. If I wrote a scene like this in one of my books, they'd laugh at me."

"This isn't one of your goddamned books!" she screamed. "This is real life. *My* life. I'm a real person, you son of

a bitch, not a character in some damned book." She whirled, raised the knife, slashed and slashed again.

Cantling folded his arms against his chest as he stood watching. "I hope you're enjoying this pointless exercise."

"I'm enjoying the hell out of it," Michelle yelled back.

"Good. I'd hate to think it was for nothing. This is all very revealing, you know. That's your own face you're working on. I didn't think you had that much self-hate in you."

"If I do, we know who put it there, don't we?" She was finished. She turned back to him, and threw down the knife. She had begun to cry again, and her breath was coming hard. "I'm leaving. Bastard. I hope you're ever so fucking happy here, really I do."

"I haven't done anything to deserve this," Cantling said awkwardly. It was not much of an apology, not much of a bridge back to understanding, but it was the best he could do. Apologies had never come easily to Richard Cantling.

"You deserve a thousand times worse," Michelle had screamed back at him. She was such a pretty girl, and she looked so ugly. All that nonsense about anger making people beautiful was a dreadful cliche, and wrong as well; Cantling was glad he'd never used it. "You're supposed to be my father," Michelle said. "You're supposed to love me. You're supposed to be my father, and you *raped me*, you bastard."

Cantling was a light sleeper. He woke in the middle of the night, and sat up in bed shivering, with the feeling that something was wrong.

The bedroom seemed dark and quiet. What was it? A noise? He was very sensitive to noise. Cantling slid out from under the covers and donned his slippers. The fire he'd enjoyed before retiring for the night had burned down to embers, and the room was chilly. He felt for his tartan robe, hanging from the foot of the big antique four-poster, slipped into it, cinched the belt, and moved quietly to the bedroom door. The door creaked a little at times, so he opened it very slowly, very cautiously. He listened.

Someone was downstairs. He could hear them moving around.

Fear coiled in the pit of his stomach. He had no gun up here, nothing like that. He didn't believe in that. Besides, he was supposed to be safe. This wasn't New York. He was supposed to be safe here in quaint old Perrot, Iowa. And now he had a prowler in his house, something he had never faced in all of his years in Manhattan. What the hell was he supposed to do?

The police, he thought. He'd lock the door and call the police. He moved back to the bedside, and reached for the phone.

It rang.

Richard Cantling stared at the telephone. He had two lines; a business number hooked up to his recording machine, and an unlisted personal number that he gave only to very close friends. Both lights were lit. It was his private number ringing. He hesitated, then scooped up the receiver. "Hello."

"The man himself," the voice said. "Don't get weird on me, dad. You were going to call the cops, right? Stupid. It's only me. Come down and talk."

Cantling's throat felt raw and constricted. He had never heard that voice before, but he knew it, he knew it. "Who is this?" he demanded.

"Silly question," the caller replied. "You know who it is."

He did. But he said, "Who?"

"Not who. Dunnahoo." Cantling had written that line. "You're not real."

"There were a couple of reviewers who said that too. I seem to remember how it pissed you off, back then."

"You're not *real*," Cantling insisted.

"I'm cut to the goddamned quick," Dunnahoo said. "If I'm not real, it's your fault. So quit getting on my case about it, OK? Just get your ass in gear and hustle it downstairs so we can hang out together." He hung up.

The lights went out on the telephone. Richard Cantling sat down on the edge of his bed, stunned. What was he supposed to make of this? A dream? It was no dream. What could he do?

He went downstairs.

Dunnahoo had built a fire in the living room fireplace, and was settled into Cantling's big leather recliner, drinking Pabst Blue Ribbon from a bottle. He smiled lazily when Cantling appeared under the entry arch. "The man," he said. "Well, don't you look half-dead. Want a beer?"

"Who the hell are you?" Cantling demanded.

"Hey, we been round that block already. Don't bore me. Grab a beer and park your ass by the fire."

"An actor," Cantling said. "You're some kind of goddamned actor. Michelle put you up to this, right?"

Dunnahoo grinned. "An actor? Well, that's fuckin' unlikely, ain't it? Tell me, would you stick something that weird in one of your novels? No way, Jose. You'd never do it yourself and if somebody else did it, in one of them workshops or a book you were reviewing, you'd rip his fuckin' liver out."

Richard Cantling moved slowly into the room, staring at the young man sprawled in his recliner. It was no actor. It was Dunnahoo, the kid from his book, the face from the portrait. Cantling settled into a high, overstuffed armchair, still staring. "This makes no sense," he said. "This is like something out of Dickens."

Dunnahoo laughed. "This ain't no fucking Christmas Carol, old man, and I sure ain't no ghost of Christmas past."

Cantling frowned; whoever he was, that line was out of character. "That's wrong," he snapped. "Dunnahoo didn't read Dickens. Batman and Robin, yes, but not Dickens."

"I saw the movie, dad," Dunnahoo said. He raised the beer bottle to his lips and had a swallow.

"Why do you keep calling me dad?" Cantling said. "That's wrong too. Anachronistic. Dunnahoo was a street kid, not a beatnik."

"You're telling me? Like I don't know or something?" He laughed. "Shit man, what the hell else should I call you?" He ran his fingers through his hair, pushing it back out of his eyes. "After all, I'm still your fuckin' first-born."

She wanted to name it Edward, if it turned out to be a boy. "Don't be ridiculous, Helen," he told her.

"I thought you liked the name Edward," she said.

He didn't know what she was doing in his office anyway. He was working, or trying to work. He'd told her never to come into his office when he was at the typewriter. When they were first married, Helen was very good about that, but there had been no dealing with her since she'd gotten pregnant. "I do like the name Edward," he told her, trying hard to keep his voice calm. He hated being interrupted. "I like the name Edward a lot. I love the goddamned name Edward. That's why I'm using it for my protagonist. Edward, that's his name. Edward Donohue. So we can't use it for the baby because I've already used it. How many times do I have to explain that?"

"But you never *call* him Edward in the book," Helen protested.

Cantling frowned. "Have you been reading the book again? Damn it, Helen, I *told* you I don't want you messing around with the manuscript until it's done."

She refused to be distracted. "You never call him Edward," she repeated.

"No," he said. "That's right. I never call him Edward.

I call him Dunnahoo, because he's a street kid, and because that's his street name, and he doesn't like to be called Edward. Only it's still his name, you see. Edward is his name. He doesn't like it, but it's his fucking *name,* and at the end he tells someone that his name is Edward, and that's real damned important. So we can't name the kid Edward, because *he's* named Edward, and I'm tired of this discussion. If it's a boy, we can name it Lawrence, after my grandfather."

"But I don't *want* to name him Lawrence," she whined. "It's so old-fashioned, and then people will call him Larry, and I hate the name Larry. Why can't you call the character in your book Lawrence?"

"Because his name is Edward."

"This is our baby I'm carrying," she said. She put a hand on her swollen stomach, as if Cantling needed a visual reminder.

He was tired of arguing. He was tired of discussing. He was tired of being interrupted. He leaned back in his chair. "How long have you been carrying the baby?"

Helen look baffled. "You know. Seven months now. And a week."

Cantling leaned forward and slapped the stack of manuscript pages piled up beside his typewriter. "Well, I've been carrying *this* baby for three damned years now. This is the fourth fucking draft, and the last one. He was named Edward on the first draft, and on the second draft, and on the third draft, and he's damn well going to be named Edward when the goddamned novel comes out. He'd been named Edward for *years* before that night of fond memory when you decided to surprise me by throwing away your diaphragm, and thereby got yourself knocked up."

"It's not fair," she complained. "He's only a character. This is our baby."

"Fair? You want fair? OK. I'll make it fair. Our first-born son will get named Edward. How's that for fair?"

Helen's face softened. She smiled shyly.

He held up a hand before she had a chance to say anything. "Of course, I figure I'm only about a month away from finishing this damn thing, if you ever stop interrupting me. You've got a little further to go. But that's as fair as I can make it. You pop before I type THE END and you got the name. Otherwise, my baby here"—he slapped the manuscript again—"is first-born."

"You can't," she started.

Cantling resumed his typing.

"My first-born," Richard Cantling said.

"In the flesh," Dunnahoo said. He raised his beer bottle in salute, and said, "To fathers and sons, hey!" He drained it with one long swallow and flipped the bottle across the room end over end. It smashed in the fireplace.

"This is a dream," Cantling said.

Dunnahoo gave him a raspberry. "Look, old man, face it, I'm here." He jumped to his feet. "The prodigal returns," he said, bowing. "So where the fuck is the fatted calf and all that shit? Least you coulda done was order a pizza."

"I'll play the game," Cantling said. "What do you want from me?"

Dunnahoo grinned. "Want? Who, me? Who the fuck knows? I never knew what I wanted, you know that. Nobody in the whole fucking book knew what they wanted."

"That was the point," Cantling said.

"Oh, I get it," Dunnahoo said. "I'm not dumb. Old Dicky Cantling's boy is anything but dumb, right?" He wandered off toward the kitchen. "There's more beer in the fridge. Want one?"

"Why not?" Cantling asked. "It's not every day my oldest son comes to visit. Dos Equis with a slice of lime, please."

"Drinking fancy Spic beer now, huh? Shit. What ever happened to Piels? You could suck up Piels with the best of them, once upon a time." He vanished through the kitchen door. When he returned he was carrying two bottles of Dos Equis, holding them by the necks with his fingers jammed down into the open mouths. In his other hand he had a raw onion. The bottles clanked together as he carried them. He gave one to Cantling. "Here. I'll suck up a little culture myself."

"You forgot the lime," Cantling said.

"Get your own fuckin' lime," Dunnahoo said. "Whatcha gonna do, cut off my allowance?" He grinned, tossed the onion lightly into the air, caught it, and took a big bite. "Onions," he said. "I owe you for that one, dad. Bad enough I have to eat raw onions, I mean, shit, but you fixed it so I don't even *like* the fucking things. You even said so in the damned book."

"Of course," Cantling said. "The onion had a dual function. On one level, you did it just to prove how tough you were. It was something none of the others hanging out at Ricci's could manage. It gave you a certain status. But on a deeper level, when you bit into an onion you were making a symbolic statement about your appetite for life, your hunger for it all, the bitter and the sharp parts as well the sweet."

Dunnahoo took another bite of onion. "Horseshit," he said. "I ought to make you eat a fucking onion, see how you like it."

Cantling sipped at his beer. "I was young. It was my first book. It seemed like a nice touch at the time."

"Eat it raw," Dunnahoo said. He finished the onion.

Richard Cantling decided this cozy domestic scene had gone on long enough. "You know, Dunnahoo or whoever you are," he said in a conversational tone, "you're not what I expected."

"What did you expect, old man?"

Cantling shrugged. "I made you with my mind instead

of my sperm, so you've got more of me in you than any child of my flesh could ever have. You're me."

"Hey," said Dunnahoo, "not fucking guilty. I wouldn't be you on a bet."

"You have no choice. Your story was built from my own adolescence. First novels are like that. Ricci's was really Pompeii Pizza in Newark. Your friends were my friends. And you were me."

"That so?" Dunnahoo replied, grinning.

Richard Cantling nodded.

Dunnahoo laughed. "You should be so fuckin' lucky, dad."

"What does that mean?" Cantling snapped.

"You live in a dream world, old man, you know that? Maybe you like to pretend you were like me, but there ain't no way it's true. I was the big man at Ricci's. At Pompeii, you were the four-eyes hanging out back by the pinball machine. You had me balling my fuckin' brains out at sixteen. You never even got bare tit till you were past twenty, off in that college of yours. It took you weeks to come up with the wisecracks you had me tossing off every fuckin' time I turned around. All those wild crazy things I did in that book, some of them happened to Dutch and some of them happened to Joey and some of them never happened at all, but none of them happened to you, old man, so don't make me laugh."

Cantling flushed a little. "I was writing fiction. Yes, I was a bit of a misfit in my youth, but . . ."

"A nerd," Dunnahoo said. "Don't fancy it up."

"I was not a nerd," Cantling said, stung. *"Hangin' Out* told the truth. It made sense to use a protagonist who was more central to the action than I'd been in real life. Art draws on life but it has to shape it, rearrange it, give it structure, it can't simply replicate it. That's what I did."

"Nah. What *you* did was to suck off Dutch and Joey and the rest. You helped yourself to their lives, man, and took credit for it all yourself. You even got this weird fuckin' idea that I was based on you, and you been thinking that so long you believe it. You're a leech, dad. You're a goddamned thief."

Richard Cantling was furious. "Get out of here!" he said.

Dunnahoo stood up, stretched. "I'm fuckin' wounded. Throwing your baby boy out into the cold Ioway night, old man? What's wrong? You liked me well enough when I was in your damn book, when you could control every thing I did and said, right? Don't like it so well now that I'm real, though. That's your problem. You never did like real life half as well as you liked books."

"I like life just fine, thank you," Cantling snapped.

Dunnahoo smiled. Standing there, he suddenly looked washed out, insubstantial. "Yeah?" he said. His voice seemed weaker than it had been.

"Yeah!" Cantling replied.

Now Dunnahoo was fading visibly. All the color had drained from his body, and he looked almost transparent. "Prove it," he said. "Go into your kitchen, old man, and take a great big bite out of your fuckin' raw onion of life." He tossed back his hair, and laughed, and laughed, and laughed, until he was quite gone.

Richard Cantling stood staring at the place where he had been for a long time. Finally, very tired, he climbed upstairs to bed.

He made himself a big breakfast the next morning; orange juice and fresh-brewed coffee, English muffins with lots of butter and blackberry preserves, a cheese omelette, six strips of thick-sliced bacon. The cooking and the eating were supposed to distract him. It didn't work. He thought of Dunnahoo all the while. A dream, yes, some crazy sort of dream. He had no ready explanation for the broken glass in the fireplace or the empty beer bottles in his living room, but finally he found one. He had experienced some sort of insane drunken somnabulist episode, Cantling decided. It was the stress of the on-going quarrel with Michelle, of course, triggered by the portrait she'd sent him. Perhaps he ought to see someone about it, a doctor or a psychologist or someone.

After breakfast, Cantling went straight to his den, determined to confront the problem directly and resolve it. Michelle's mutilated portrait still hung above the fireplace. A festering wound, he thought; it had infected him, and the time had come to get rid of it. Cantling built a fire. When it was going good, he took down the ruined painting, dismantled the metal frame—he was a thrifty man, after all—and burned the torn, disfigured canvas. The oily smoke made him feel clean again.

Next there was the portrait of Dunnahoo to deal with. Cantling turned to consider it. A good piece of work, really. She had captured the character. He could burn it, but that would be playing Michelle's own destructive game. Art should never be destroyed. He had made his mark in the world by creation, not destruction, and he was too old to change. The portrait of Dunnahoo had been intended as a cruel taunt, but Cantling decided to throw it back in his daughter's teeth, to make a splendid celebration of it. He would hang it, and hang it prominently. He knew just the place for it.

Up at the top of the stairs was a long landing; an ornate wooden bannister overlooked the first floor foyer and entry hall. The landing was fifteen feet long, and the back wall was entirely blank. It would make a splendid portrait gallery, Cantling decided. The painting would be visible to anyone entering the house, and you would pass right by it on the way to any of the second floor rooms. He found a hammer and some nails and hung Dunnahoo in a place of honor. When Michelle came back to make peace, she would see him there, and no doubt leap to the conclusion that Cantling had totally missed the point of her gift. He'd have to remember to thank her effusively for it.

Richard Cantling was feeling much better. Last night's conversation was receding into a bad memory. He put it firmly out of his mind and spent the rest of the day writing letters to his agent and publisher. In the late afternoon, pleasantly weary, he enjoyed a cup of coffee and some butter streusel he'd hidden away in the refrigerator. Then he went out on his daily walk, and spent a good ninety miniutes hiking along the river bluffs with a fresh, cold wind in his face.

When he returned, a large square package was waiting on his porch.

He leaned it up against an armchair, and settled into his recliner to study it. It made him uneasy. It had an effect, no doubt of it. He could feel an erection stirring against his leg, pressing uncomfortably against his trousers.

The portrait was . . . well, frankly erotic.

She was in bed, a big old antique four-poster, much like his own. She was naked. She was half-turned in the painting, looking back over her right shoulder; you saw the smooth line of her backbone, the curve of her right breast. It was a large, shapely, and very pretty breast; the aureole was a pale pink and very large, and her nipple was erect. She was clutching a rumpled sheet up to her chin, but it did little to conceal her. Her hair was red-gold, her eyes green, her smile playful. Her smooth young skin had a flush to it, as if she had just risen from a bout of lovemaking. She had a peace symbol tattooed high on the right cheek of her ass. She was obviously very young. Richard Cantling knew just how young: she was eighteen, a child-woman, caught in that precious time between innocence and experience when sex is just a wonderfully exciting new toy. Oh yes, he knew a lot about her. He knew her well.

Cissy.

He hung her portrait next to Dunnahoo.

*   *   *

Dead Flowers was Cantling's title for the book. His editor changed it to *Black Roses;* more evocative, he said, more romantic, more upbeat. Cantling fought the change on artistic grounds, and lost. Afterwards, when the novel made the bestseller lists, he managed to work up the grace to admit that he'd been wrong. He sent Brian a bottle of his favorite wine.

It was his fourth novel, and his last chance. *Hangin' Out* had gotten excellent reviews and had sold decently, but his next two books had been panned by the critics and ignored by the readers. He had to do something different, and he did. *Black Roses* turned out to be highly controversial. Some reviewers loved it, some loathed it. But it sold and sold and sold, and the paperback sale and the film option (they never made the movie) relieved him of financial worries for the first time in his life. They were finally able to afford a down payment on a house, transfer Michelle to a private school and get her those braces; the rest of the money Cantling invested as shrewdly as he was able. He was proud of *Black Roses* and pleased by its success. It made his reputation.

Helen hated the book with a passion.

On the day the novel finally fell off the last of the lists, she couldn't quite conceal her satisfaction. "I knew it wouldn't last forever," she said.

Cantling slapped down the newspaper angrily. "It lasted long enough. What the hell's wrong with you? You didn't like it before, when we were barely scraping by. The kid needs braces, the kid needs a better school, the kid shouldn't have to eat goddamn peanut butter and jelly sandwiches every day. Well, that's all behind us. And you're more pissed off than ever. Give me a little credit. Did you like being married to a failure?"

"I don't like being married to a pornographer," Helen snapped at him.

"Fuck you," Cantling said.

She gave him a nasty smile. "When? You haven't touched me in weeks. You'd rather be fucking your Cissy."

Cantling stared at her. "Are you crazy, or what? She's a character in a book I wrote. That's all."

"Oh go to hell," Helen said furiously. "You treat me like I'm a goddamned idiot. You think I can't read? You think I don't know? I read your shitty book. I'm not stupid. The wife, Marsha, dull ignorant boring Marsha, cud-chewing mousy Marsha, that cow, that nag, that royal pain-in-the-ass, that's me. You think I can't tell? I can tell, and so can my friends. They're all very sorry for me. You love me as much as Richardson loved Marsha. Cissy's just a character, right, like hell, like bloody hell." She was crying now. "You're in love with her, damn you. She's your own little wetdream. If she walked in the door right now you'd dump me as fast as Richardson dumped good old Marsha. Deny it. Go on, deny it, I dare you!"

Cantling regarded his wife incredulously. "I don't believe you. You're jealous of a character in my book. You're jealous of someone who doesn't exist."

"She exists in your head, and that's the only place that matters with you. Of course you want to fuck her. Of course your damned book was a big seller. You think it was because of your writing? It was on account of the sex, on account of *her*!"

"Sex is an important part of life," Cantling said defensively. "It's a perfectly legitimate subject for art. You want me to pull down a curtain every time my characters go to bed, is that it? Coming to terms with sexuality, that's what *Black Roses* is all about. Of course it had to be written explicitly. If you weren't such a damned prude you'd realize that."

"I'm not a prude!" Helen screamed at him. "Don't you dare call me one, either." She picked up one of the breakfast plates and threw it at him. Cantling ducked; the plate shattered on the wall behind him. "Just because

I don't like your goddamned filthy book doesn't make me a prude."

"The novel has nothing to do with it," Cantling said. He folded his arms against his chest but kept his voice calm. "You're a prude because of the things you do in bed. Or should I say the things you won't do?" He smiled.

Helen's face was red; beet red, Cantling thought, and rejected it, too old, too trite. "Oh, yes, but she'll do them, won't she?" Her voice was pure acid. "Cissy, your cute little Cissy. She'll get a sexy little tattoo on her ass if you ask her to, right? She'll do it outdoors, she'll do it in all kinds of strange places, with people all around. She'll wear kinky underwear, she thinks it's fun. She'll let you come in her mouth whenever you like. She's always ready and she doesn't have any stretch marks and she has eighteen-year-old tits, and she'll *always* have eighteen-year-old tits, won't she? How the hell do I compete with that, huh? How? How? *HOW?*"

Richard Cantling's own anger was a cold, controlled, sarcastic thing. He stood up in the face of her fury and smiled sweetly. "Read the book," he said. "Take notes."

He woke suddenly, in darkness, to the light touch of skin against his foot.

Cissy was perched on top of the footboard, a red satin sheet wrapped around her, a long slim leg exploring under his blankets. She was playing footsie with him, and smiling mischievously. "Hi, daddy," she said.

Cantling had been afraid of this. It had been in his mind all evening. Sleep had not come easily. He pulled his foot away and struggled to a sitting position.

Cissy pouted. "Don't you want to play?" she asked.

"I," he said, "I don't believe this. This can't be real."

"It can still be fun," she said.

"What the hell is Michelle doing to me? How can this be happening?"

She shrugged. The sheet slipped a little; one perfect red-tipped eighteen-year-old breast peeked out.

"You still have eighteen-year-old tits," Cantling said numbly. "You'll always have eighteen-year-old tits."

Cissy laughed. "Sure. You can borrow them, if you like, daddy. I'll bet you can think of something interesting to do with them."

"Stop calling me daddy," Cantling said.

"Oh, but you *are* my daddy," Cissy said in her little-girl voice.

"Stop that!" Cantling said.

"Why? You want to, daddy, you want to play with your little girl, don't you?" She winked. "Vice is nice but incest is best. The families that play together stay together." She looked around. "I like four-posters. You want to tie me up, daddy? I'd like that."

"No," Cantling said. He pushed back the covers, got out of bed, found his slippers and robe. His erection throbbed against his leg. He had to get away, he had to put some distance between him and Cissy, otherwise . . . he didn't want to think about otherwise. He busied himself making a fire.

"I like that," Cissy said when he got it going. "Fires are so romantic."

Cantling turned around to face her again. "Why you?" he asked, trying to stay calm. "Richardson was the protagonist of *Black Roses*, not you. And why skip to my fourth book? Why not somebody from *Family Tree* or *Rain*?"

"Those gobblers?" Cissy said. "Nobody real there. You didn't really want Richardson, did you? I'm a lot more fun." She stood up and let go of the satin sheet. It puddled about her ankles, the flames reflected off its shiny folds. Her body was soft and sweet and young. She kicked free of the sheet and padded toward him.

"Cut it out, Cissy," Cantling barked.

"I won't bite," Cissy said. She giggled. "Unless you

want me to. Maybe I should tie *you* up, huh?" She put her arms around him, gave him a hug, turned up her face for a kiss.

"Let go of me," he said, weakly. Her arms felt good. She felt good as she pressed up against him. It had been a long time since Richard Cantling had held a woman in his arms; he didn't like to think about how long. And he had never had a woman like Cissy, never, never. But he was frightened. "I can't do this," he said. "I can't. I don't want to."

Cissy reached through the folds of his robe, shoved her hand inside his briefs, squeezed him gently. "Liar," she said. "You want me. You've always wanted me. I'll bet you used to stop and jack off when you were writing the sex scenes."

"No," Cantling said. "Never."

"Never?" She pouted. Her hand moved up and down. "Well, I bet you wanted to. I bet you got hard, anyway. I bet you got hard every time you described me."

"I," he said. The denial would not come. "Cissy, please."

"Please," she murmured. Her hand was busy. "Yes, please." She tugged at his briefs and they fluttered to the floor. "Please," she said. She untied his robe and helped him out of it. "Please." Her hand moved along his side, played with his nipples; she stepped closer, and her breasts pressed lightly against his chest. "Please," she said, and she looked up at him. Her tongue moved between her lips.

Richard Cantling groaned and took her in his trembling arms.

She was like no woman he had ever had. Her touch was fire and satin, electric, and her secret places were sweet as honey.

In the morning she was gone.

Cantling woke late, too exhausted to make himself

breakfast. Instead he dressed and walked into town, to a small cafe in a quaint hundred-year-old brick building at the foot of the bluffs. He tried to sort things out over coffee and blueberry pancakes.

None of it made any sense. It could not be happening, but it was; denial accomplished nothing. Cantling forked down a mouthful of homemade blueberry pancake, but the only taste in his mouth was fear. He was afraid for his sanity. He was afraid because he did not understand, did not want to understand. And there was another, deeper, more basic fear.

He was afraid of what would come next. Richard Cantling had published nine novels.

He thought of Michelle. He could phone her, beg her to call it off before he went mad. She was his daughter, his flesh and blood, surely she would listen to him. She loved him. Of course she did. And he loved her too, no matter what she might think. Cantling knew his faults. He had examined himself countless times, under various guises, in the pages of his books. He was impossibly stubborn, willful, opinionated. He could be rigid and unbending. He could be cold. Still, he thought of himself as a decent man. Michelle . . . she had inherited some of his perversity, she was furious at him, hate was so very close to love, but surely she did not mean to do him serious harm.

Yes, he could phone Michelle, ask her to stop. Would she? If he begged her forgiveness, perhaps. That day, that terrible day, she'd told him that she would never forgive him, never, but she couldn't have meant that. She was his only child. The only child of his flesh, at any rate.

Cantling pushed away his empty plate and sat back. His mouth was set in a hard rigid line. Beg for mercy? He did not like that. What had he done, after all? Why couldn't they understand? Helen had never understood and Michelle was as blind as her mother. A writer must

live for his work. What had he done that was so terrible?
What had he done that required forgiveness? Michelle
ought to be the one phoning him.

The hell with it, Cantling thought. He refused to be
cowed. He was right; she was wrong. Let Michelle call
him if she wanted a rapprochement. She was not going
to terrify him into submission. What was he so afraid of,
anyway? Let her send her portraits, all the portraits she
wanted to paint. He'd hang them up on his walls, display
the paintings proudly (they were really a homage to his
work, after all), and if the damned things came alive at
night and prowled through his house, so be it. He'd enjoy
their visits. Cantling smiled. He'd certainly enjoyed Cissy,
no doubt of that. Part of him hoped she'd come back.
And even Dunnahoo, well, he was an insolent kid, but
there was no real harm in him, he just liked to mouth
off.

Why, now that he stopped to consider it, Cantling
found that the possibilities had a certain intoxicating
charm. He was uniquely privileged. Scott Fitzgerald
never attended one of Gatsby's fabulous parties, Conan
Doyle could never really sit down with Holmes and Wat-
son, Nabokov never actually tumbled Lolita. What would
they have said to the idea?

The more he considered things, the more cheerful he
became. Michelle was trying to rebuke him, to frighten
him, but she was really giving him a delicious experience.
He could play chess with Sergei Tederenko, the cynical
emigre hustler from *En Passant*. He could argue politics
with Frank Corwin, the union organizer from his Depression novel, *Times Are Hard*. He might flirt with beautiful
Beth McKenzie, go dancing with crazy old Miss Aggie,
seduce the Danzinger twins and fulfill the one sexual
fantasy that Cissy had left untouched, yes, certainly, what
the hell had he been afraid of? These were his own
creations, his characters, his friends and family.

Of course, there was the new book to consider. Can-

tling frowned. That was a disturbing thought. But Michelle
was his daughter, she loved him, surely she wouldn't go
that far. No, of course not. He put the idea firmly aside
and picked up his check.

He expected it. He was almost looking forward to it.
And when he returned from his evening constitutional,
his cheeks red from the wind, his heart beating just a
little faster in anticipation, it was there waiting for him,
the familiar rectangle wrapped in plain brown paper.
Richard Cantling carried it inside carefully. He made
himself a cup of coffee before he unwrapped it, deliberately prolonging the suspense to savor the moment,
delighting in the thought of how deftly he'd turned
Michelle's cruel little plan on its head.

He drank his coffee, poured a refill, drank that. The
package stood a few feet away. Cantling played a little
game with himself, trying to guess whose portrait might
be within. Cissy had said something about none of the
characters from *Family Tree* or *Rain* being real enough.
Cantling mentally reviewed his life's work, trying to
decide which characters seemed most real. It was a
pleasant speculation, but he could reach no firm con-
clusions. Finally he shoved his coffee cup aside and
moved to undo the wrappings. And there it was.

Barry Leighton.

Again, the painting itself was superb. Leighton was
seated in a newspaper city room, his elbow resting on
the gray metal case of an old manual typewriter. He wore
a rumpled brown suit and his white shirt was open at
the collar and plastered to his body by perspiration. His
nose had been broken more than once, and was spread
all across his wide, homely, somehow comfortable face.
His eyes were sleepy. Leighton was overweight and jowly
and rapidly losing his hair. He'd given up smoking but
not cigarettes; an unlit Camel dangled from one corner
of his mouth. "As long as you don't light the damned

things, you're safe," he'd said more than once in Cantling's novel *Byeline*.

The book hadn't done very well. It was a depressing book, all about the last week of a grand old newspaper that had fallen on bad times. It was more than that, though. Cantling was interested in people, not newspapers; he had used the failing paper as a metaphor for failing lives. His editor had wanted to work in some kind of strong, sensational subplot, have Leighton and the others on the trail of some huge story that offered the promise of redemption, but Cantling had rejected that idea. He wanted to tell a story about small people being ground down inexorably by time and age, about the inevitability of loneliness and defeat. He produced a novel as gray and brittle as newsprint. He was very proud of it.

No one read it.

Cantling lifted the portrait and carried it upstairs, to hang beside those of Dunnahoo and Cissy. Tonight should be interesting, he thought. Barry Leighton was no kid, like the others; he was a man of Cantling's own years. Very intelligent, mature. There was a bitterness in Leighton, Cantling knew very well; a disappointment that life had, after all, yielded so little, that all his bylines and big stories were forgotten the day after they ran. But the reporter kept his sense of humor through all of it, kept off the demons with nothing but a mordant wit and an unlit Camel. Cantling admired him, would enjoy talking to him. Tonight, he decided, he wouldn't bother going to bed. He'd make a big pot of strong black coffee, lay in some Seagram's 7, and wait.

It was past midnight and Cantling was rereading the leatherbound copy of *Byeline* when he heard ice cubes clinking together in the kitchen. "Help yourself, Barry," he called out.

Leighton came through the swinging door, tumbler in hand. "I did," he said. He looked at Cantling through heavily lidded eyes, and gave a little snort. "You look old enough to be my father," he said. "I didn't think anybody could look *that* old."

Cantling closed the book and set it aside. "Sit down," he said. "As I recall, your feet hurt."

"My feet always hurt," Leighton said. He settled himself into an armchair and swallowed a mouthful of whiskey. "Ah," he said, "that's better."

Cantling tapped the novel with a fingertip. "My eighth book," he said. "Michelle skipped right over three novels. A pity. I would have liked to meet some of those people."

"Maybe she wants to get to the point," Leighton suggested.

"And what is the point?"

Leighton shrugged. "Damned if I know. I'm only a newspaperman. Five Ws and an H. You're the novelist. You tell me the point."

"My ninth novel," Cantling suggested. "The new one."

"The last one?" said Leighton.

"Of course not. Only the most recent. I'm working on something new right now."

Leighton smiled. "That's not what my sources tell me."

"Oh? What do your sources say?"

"That you're an old man waiting to die," Leighton said. "And that you're going to die alone."

"I'm fifty-two," Cantling said crisply. "Hardly old."

"When your birthday cake has got more candles than you can blow out, you're old," said Leighton dryly. "Helen was younger than you, and she died five years ago. It's in the mind, Cantling. I've seen young octogenarians and old adolescents. And you, you had liver spots on your brain before you had hair on your balls."

"That's unfair," Cantling protested.

Leighton drank his Seagram's. "Fair?" he said. "You're too old to believe in fair, Cantling. Young people live life. Old people sit and watch it. You were born old. You're a watcher, not a liver." He frowned. "Not a liver, jeez, what a figure of speech. Better a liver than a gall bladder, I guess. You were never a gall bladder either. You've been full of piss for years, but you don't have any gall at all. Maybe you're a kidney."

"You're reaching, Barry," Cantling said. "I'm a writer. I've always been a writer. That's my life. Writers observe life, they report on life. It's in the job description. You ought to know."

"I do know," Leighton said. "I'm a reporter, remember? I've spent a lot of long gray years writing up other peoples' stories. I've got no story of my own. You know that, Cantling. Look what you did to me in *Byeline*. The *Courier* croaks and I decide to write my memoirs and what happens?"

Cantling remembered. "You blocked. You rewrote your old stories, twenty-year-old stories, thirty-year-old stories. You had that incredible memory. You could recall all the people you'd ever reported on, the dates, the details, the quotes. You could recite the first story you'd had bylined word for word, but you couldn't remember the name of the first girl you'd been to bed with, couldn't remember your ex-wife's phone number, you couldn't . . . you couldn't . . ." His voice failed.

"I couldn't remember my daughter's birthday," Leighton said. "Where do you get those crazy ideas, Cantling?"

Cantling was silent.

"From life, maybe?" Leighton said gently. "I was a good reporter. That was about all you could say about me. You, well, maybe you're a good novelist. That's for the critics to judge, and I'm just a sweaty newspaperman whose feet hurt. But even if you are a good novelist, even if you're one of the great ones, you were a lousy husband, and a miserable father."

"No," Cantling said. It was a weak protest.

Leighton swirled his tumbler; the ice cubes clinked and clattered. "When did Helen leave you?" he asked.

"I don't ... ten years ago, something like that. I was in the middle of the final draft of *En Passant*."

"When was the divorce final?"

"Oh, a year later. We tried reconciliation, but it didn't take. Michelle was in school, I remember. I was writing *Times Are Hard*."

"You remember her third grade play?"

"Was that the one I missed?"

"The one you missed? You sound like Nixon saying, 'Was that the time I lied?' That was the one Michelle had the lead in, Cantling."

"I couldn't help that," Cantling said. "I wanted to come. They were giving me an award. You don't skip the National Literary League dinner. You can't."

"Of course not," said Leighton. "When was it that Helen died?"

"I was writing *Byeline*," Cantling said.

"Interesting system of dating you've got there. You ought to put out a calendar." He swallowed some whiskey.

"All right," Cantling said. "I'm not going to deny that my work is important to me. Maybe too important, I don't know. Yes, the writing has been the biggest part of my life. But I'm a decent man, Leighton, and I've always done my best. It hasn't all been like you're implying. Helen and I had good years. We loved each other once. And Michelle ... I loved Michelle. When she was a little girl, I used to write stories just for her. Funny animals, space pirates, silly poems. I'd write them up in my spare time and read them to her at bedtime. They were something I did just for Michelle, for love."

"Yeah," Leighton said cynically. "You never even thought about getting them published."

Cantling grimaced. "That ... you're implying ... that's a distortion. Michelle loved the stories so much, I thought maybe other kids might like them too. It was just an idea. I never did anything about it."

"Never?"

Cantling hesitated. "Look, Bert was my friend as well as my agent. He had a little girl of his own. I showed him the stories once. Once!"

"I can't be pregnant," Leighton said. "I only let him fuck me once. Once!"

"He didn't even like them," Cantling said.

"Pity," replied Leighton.

"You're laying this on me with a trowel, and I'm not guilty. No, I wasn't father of the year, but I wasn't an ogre either. I changed her diaper plenty of times. Before *Black Roses*, Helen had to work, and I took care of the baby every day, from nine to five."

"You hated it when she cried and you had to leave your typewriter."

"Yes," Cantling said. "Yes, I hated being interrupted, I've always hated being interrupted, I don't care if it was Helen or Michelle or my mother or my roommate in college, when I'm writing I don't like to be interrupted. Is that a fucking capital crime? Does that make me inhuman? When she cried, I went to her. I didn't like it, I hated it, I resented it, but I *went to her*."

"When you heard her," said Leighton. "When you weren't in bed with Cissy, dancing with Miss Aggie, beating up scabs with Frank Corwin, when your head wasn't full of their voices, yeah, sometimes you heard, and when you heard you went. Congratulations, Cantling."

"I taught her to read," Cantling said. "I read her *Treasure Island* and *Wind in the Willows* and *The Hobbit* and *Tom Sawyer*, all kinds of things."

"All books you wanted to reread anyway," said Leighton. "Helen did the real teaching, with Dick and Jane."

"*I hate Dick and Jane!*" Cantling shouted.

"So?"

"You don't know what you're talking about," Richard Cantling said. "You weren't there. Michelle was there. She loved me, she still loves me. Whenever she got hurt, scraped her knee or got her nose bloodied, whatever it was, it was me she'd run to, never Helen. She'd come crying to me and I'd hug her and dry her tears and I'd tell her ... I used to tell her ..." But he couldn't go on. He was close to tears himself; he could feel them hiding the corners of his eyes.

"I know what you used to tell her," said Barry Leighton in a sad, gentle voice.

"She remembered it," Cantling said. "She remembered it all those years. Helen got custody, they moved away, I didn't see her much, but Michelle always remembered, and when she was all grown up, after Helen was gone and Michelle was on her own, there was this time she got hurt, and I ... I ..."

"Yes," said Leighton. "I know."

The police were the ones that phoned him. Detective Joyce Brennan, that was her name, he would never forget that name. "Mister Cantling?" she said.

"Yes?"

"Mister Richard Cantling?"

"Yes," he said. "Richard Cantling the writer." He had gotten strange calls before. "What can I do for you?"

She identified herself. "You'll have to come down to the hospital," she said to him. "It's your daughter, Mister Cantling. I'm afraid she's been assaulted."

He hated evasion, hated euphemism. Cantling's characters never passed away, they died; they never broke wind, they farted. And Richard Cantling's daughter ... "Assaulted?" he said. "Do you mean she's been assaulted or do you mean she's been raped?"

There was a silence on the other end of the line. "Raped," she said at last. "She's been raped, Mister Cantling."

"I'll be right down," he said.

She had in fact been raped repeatedly and brutally. Michelle had been as stubborn as Helen, as stubborn as

Cantling himself. She wouldn't take his money, wouldn't take his advice, wouldn't take the help he offered her through his contacts in publishing. She was going to make it on her own. She waitressed in a coffee house in the Village, and lived in a large, drafty, and run-down warehouse loft down by the docks. It was a terrible neighborhood, a dangerous neighborhood, and Cantling had told her so a hundred times, but Michelle would not listen. She would not even let him pay to install good locks and a security system. It had been very bad. The man had broken in before dawn on a Friday morning. Michelle was alone. He had ripped the phone from the wall and held her prisoner there through Monday night. Finally one of the busboys from the coffee house had gotten worried and come by, and the rapist had left by the fire escape.

When they let him see her, her face was a huge purple bruise. She had burn marks all over her, where the man had used his cigarette, and three of her ribs were broken. She was far beyond hysteria. She screamed when they tried to touch her; doctors, nurses, it didn't matter, she screamed as soon as they got near. But she let Cantling sit on the edge of the bed, and take her in his arms, and hold her. She cried for hours, cried until there were no more tears in her. Once she called him "Daddy," in a choked sob. It was the only word she spoke; she seemed to have lost the capacity for speech. Finally they tranquilized her to get her to sleep.

Michelle was in the hospital for two weeks, in a deep state of shock. Her hysteria waned day by day, and she finally became docile, so they were able to fluff her pillows and lead her to the bathroom. But she still would not, or could not, speak. The psychologist told Cantling that she might never speak again. "I don't accept that," he said. He arranged Michelle's discharge. Simultaneously he decided to get them both out of this filthy hellhole of a city. She had always loved big old spooky houses, he remembered, and she used to love the water, the sea, the river, the lake. Cantling consulted realtors, considered a big place on the coast of Maine, and finally settled on an old steamboat gothic mansion high on the bluffs of Perrot, Iowa. He supervised every detail of the move.

Little by little, recovery began.

She was like a small child again, curious, restless, full of sudden energy. She did not talk, but she explored everything, went everywhere. In spring she spent hours up on the widow's walk, watching the big towboats go by on the Mississippi far below. Every evening they would walk together on the bluffs, and she would hold his hand. One day she turned and kissed him suddenly, impulsively, on his cheek. "I love you, daddy," she said, and she ran away from him, and as Cantling watched her run, he saw a lovely, wounded woman in her mid-twenties, and saw too the gangling, coltish tomboy she had been.

The dam was broken after that day. Michelle began to talk again. Short, childlike sentences at first, full of childish fears and childish naivete. But she matured rapidly, and in no time at all she was talking politics with him, talking books, talking art. They had many a fine conversation on their evening walks. She never talked about the rape, though; never once, not so much as a word.

In six months she was cooking, writing letters to friends back in New York, helping with the household chores, doing lovely things in the garden. In eight months she had started to paint again. That was very good for her; now she seemed to blossom daily, to grow more and more radiant. Richard Cantling didn't really understand the abstractions his daughter liked to paint, he preferred representational art, and best of all he loved the self-portrait she had done for him when she was still an art major in college. But he could feel the pain in these new canvasses of hers, he could sense that she was engaged in an exorcism of sorts, trying to squeeze the pus from some wound deep inside, and he approved. His writing has been a balm for his own wounds more than once. He envied her now, in a way. Richard Cantling had not written a word for more than three years. The crashing commercial failure of *Byeline*, his best novel, had left him blocked and impotent. He'd thought perhaps the change of scene might restore him as well as Michelle, but that had been a vain hope. At least one of them was busy.

Finally, late one night after Cantling had gone to bed, his door opened and Michelle came quietly into his bedroom and sat on the edge of his bed. She was barefoot, dressed in a flannel nightgown covered with tiny pink flowers. "Daddy," she said, in a slurred voice.

Cantling had woken when the door opened. He sat up and smiled for her. "Hi," he said. "You've been drinking."

Michelle nodded. "I'm going back," she said. "Needed some courage, so's I could tell you."

"Going back?" Cantling said. "You don't mean to New York? You can't be serious!"

"I got to," she said. "Don't be mad. I'm better now."

"Stay here. Stay with me. New York is uninhabitable, Michelle."

"I don't want to go back. It scares me. But I got to. My friends are there. My work is there. My life is back there, daddy. My friend Jimmy, you remember Jimmy, he's art director for this little paperback house, he can get me some cover assignments, he says. He wrote. I won't have to wait tables any more."

"I don't believe I'm hearing this," Richard Cantling said. "How can you go back to that damned city after what happened to you there?"

"That's why I have to go back," Michelle insisted. "That guy, what he did . . . what he did to me . . ." Her voice caught in her throat. She drew in her breath, got hold of herself. "If I don't go back, it's like he ran me out of town, took my whole life away from me, my friends, my art, everything. I can't let him get away with that, can't let him scare me off. I got to go back and take up what's mine, prove that I'm not afraid."

Richard Cantling looked at his daughter helplessly. He reached out, gently touched her long, soft hair. She had finally said something that made sense in his terms. He would do the same thing, he knew. "I understand," he said. "It's going to be lonely here without you, but I understand, I do."

"I'm scared," Michelle said. "I bought plane tickets. For tomorrow."

"So soon?"

"I want to do it quickly, before I lose my nerve," she said. "I don't think I've ever been this scared. Not even . . . not even when it was happening. Funny, huh?"

"No," said Cantling. "It makes sense."

"Daddy, hold me," Michelle said. She pressed herself into his arms. He hugged her and felt her body tremble.

"You're shaking," he said.

She wouldn't let go of him. "You remember, when I was real little, I used to have those nightmares, and I'd come bawling into your bedroom in the middle of the night and crawl into bed between you and mommy."

Cantling smiled. "I remember," he said.

"I want to stay here tonight," Michelle said, hugging him even more tightly. "Tomorrow I'll be back there, alone. I don't want to be alone tonight. Can I, daddy?"

Cantling disengaged gently, looked her in the eyes. "Are you sure?"

She nodded; a tiny, quick, shy nod. A child's nod.

He threw back the covers and she crept in next to him. "Don't go away," she said. "Don't even go to the bathroom, okay? Just stay right here with me."

"I'm here," he said. He put his arms around her, and Michelle curled up under the covers with her head on his shoulder. They lay together that way for a long time. He could feel her heart beating inside her chest. It was a soothing sound; soon Cantling began to drift back to sleep.

"Daddy?" she whispered against his chest.

He opened his eyes. "Michelle?"

"Daddy, I have to get rid of it. It's inside me and it's poison. I don't want to take it back with me. I have to get rid of it."

Cantling stroked her hair, long slow steady motions, saying nothing.

"When I was little, you remember, whenever I fell down or got in a fight, I'd come running to you, all teary, and show you my booboo. That's what I used to call it when I got hurt, remember, I'd say I had a booboo."

"I remember," Cantling said.

"And you, you'd always hug me and you'd say, 'Show me where it hurts,' and I would and you'd kiss it and make it better, you remember that? Show me where it hurts?"

Cantling nodded. "Yes," he said softly.

Michelle was crying quietly. He could feel the wetness soaking through the top of his pajamas. "I can't take it back with me, daddy. I want to show you where it hurts. Please. Please."

He kissed the top of her head. "Go on."

She started at the beginning, in a halting whisper.

When dawn light broke through the bedroom windows, she was still talking. They never slept. She cried a lot, screamed once or twice, shivered frequently despite the weight of the blankets; Richard Cantling never let go of her, not once, not for a single moment. She showed him where it hurt.

Barry Leighton sighed. "It was a far, far better thing you did than you had ever done," he said. "Now if you'd only gone off to that far, far better rest right then and there, that very moment, everything would have been fine." He shook his head. "You never did know when to write Thirty, Cantling."

"Why?" Cantling demanded. "You're a good man, Leighton, tell me. Why is this happening. Why?"

The reporter shrugged. He was beginning to fade now. "That was the W that always gave me the most trouble," he said wearily. "Pick the story, and let me loose, and I could tell you the who and the what and the when and the where and even the how. But the *why* . . . ah, Cantling, you're the novelist, the whys are your province, not mine. The only Y that I ever really got on speaking terms with was the one goes with MCA."

Like the Cheshire cat, his smile lingered long after the rest of him was gone. Richard Cantling sat staring at the empty chair, at the abandoned tumbler, watching the whiskey-soaked ice cubes melt slowly.

He did not remember falling asleep. He spent the night in the chair, and woke stiff and achey and cold. His dreams had been dark and shapeless and full of fear. He had slept well into the afternoon; half the day was gone. He made himself a tasteless breakfast in a kind of fog. He seemed distant from his own body, and every motion was slow and clumsy. When the coffee was ready, he poured a cup, picked it up, dropped it. The mug broke into a dozen pieces. Cantling stared down at it stupidly, watching rivulets of hot brown liquid run between the tiles. He did not have the energy to clean it up. He got a fresh mug, poured more coffee, managed to get down a few swallows.

The bacon was too salty; the eggs were runny, disgusting. Cantling pushed the meal away half-eaten, and drank more of the black, bitter coffee. He felt hung-over, but he knew that booze was not the problem.

Today, he thought. It will end today, one way or the other. She will not go back. *Byeline* was his eighth novel, the next to the last. Today the final portrait would arrive. A character from his ninth novel, his last novel. And then it would be over.

Or maybe just beginning.

How much did Michelle hate him? How badly had he wronged her? Cantling's hand shook; coffee slopped over the top of the mug, burning his fingers. He winced, cried out. Pain was so inarticulate. Burning. He thought of smouldering cigarettes, their tips like small red eyes. His stomach heaved. Cantling lurched to his feet, rushed to the bathroom. He got there just in time, gave his breakfast to the bowl. Afterwards he was too weak to move. He lay slumped against the cold white porcelain, his head swimming. He imagined somebody coming up behind him, taking him by the hair, forcing his face down into the water, flushing, flushing, laughing all the while, saying dirty, dirty, I'll get you clean, you're so dirty, flushing, flushing so the toilet ran and ran, holding his face down so the water and the vomit filled his mouth, his nostrils, until he could hardly breathe, until the world was almost black, until it was almost over, and then up again, laughing while he sucked in air, and then pushing him down again, flushing again, and again and again and again. But it was only his imagination. There was no one there. No one. Cantling was alone in the bathroom.

He forced himself to stand. In the mirror his face was gray and ancient, his hair filthy and unkempt. Behind him, leering over his shoulder, was another face. A man's face, pale and drawn, with black hair parted in the middle and slicked back. Behind a pair of small round glasses were eyes the color of dirty ice, eyes that moved constantly, frenetically, wild animals caught in a trap. They would chew off their own limbs to be free, those eyes. Cantling blinked and the face was gone. He turned on the cold tap, plunged his cupped hands under the stream, splashed water on his face. He could feel the stubble of his beard. He needed to shave. But there wasn't time, it wasn't important, he had to . . . he had to. . .

He had to do something. Get out of there. Get away, get to someplace safe, somewhere his children couldn't find him.

But there was nowhere safe, he knew.

He had to reach Michelle, talk to her, explain, plead. She loved him. She *would* forgive him, she had to. She would call it off, she would tell him what to do.

Frantic, Cantling rushed back to the living room, snatched up the phone. He couldn't remember Michelle's number. He searched around, found his address book, flipped through it wildly. There, there; he punched in the numbers.

The phone rang four times. Then someone picked it up.

"Michelle—" he started.

"Hi," she said. "This is Michelle Cantling, but I'm not in right now. If you'll leave your name and number when you hear the tone, I'll get back to you, unless you're selling something."

The beep sounded. "Michelle, are you there?" Cantling said. "I know you hide behind the machine sometimes, when you don't want to talk. It's me. Please pick up. Please."

Nothing.

"Call me back, then," he said. He wanted to get it all in; his words tumbled over each other in their haste to get out. "I, you, you can't do it, please, let me explain, I never meant, I never meant, please . . ." There was the beep again, and then a dial tone. Cantling stared at the phone, hung up slowly. She would call him back. She had to, she was his daughter, they loved each other, she had to give him the chance to explain.

Of course, he had tried to explain before.

His doorbell was the old-fashioned kind, a brass key

that projected out of the door. You had to turn it by hand, and when you did it produced a loud, impatient metallic rasp. Someone was turning it furiously, turning it and turning it and turning it. Cantling rushed to the door, utterly baffled. He had never made friends easily, and it was even harder now that he had become so set in his ways. He had no real friends in Perrot, a few acquaintances perhaps, but no one who would come calling so unexpectedly, and twist the bell with such energetic determination.

He undid his chain and flung the door open, wrenching the bell key out of Michelle's fingers.

She was dressed in a belted raincoat, a knitted ski cap, a matching scarf. The scarf and a few loose strands of hair were caught in the wind, moving restlessly. She was wearing high, fashionable boots and carrying a big leather shoulder bag. She looked good. It had been almost a year since Cantling had seen her, on his last Christmas visit to New York. It had been two years since she'd moved back east.

"Michelle," Cantling said. "I didn't ... this is quite a surprise. All the way from New York and you didn't even tell me you were coming?"

"No," she snapped. There was something wrong with her voice, her eyes. "I didn't want to give you any warning, you bastard. You didn't give me any warning."

"You're upset," Cantling said. "Come in, let's talk."

"I'll come in all right." She pushed past him, kicked the door shut behind her with so much force that the buzzer sounded again. Out of the wind, her face got ever harder. "You want to know why I came? I am going to tell you what I think of you. Then I'm going to turn around and leave, I'm going to walk right out of this house and out of your fucking life, just like mom did. She was the smart one, not me. I was dumb enough to think you loved me, crazy enough to think you cared."

"Michelle, don't," Cantling said. "You don't understand. I do love you. You're my little girl, you—"

"Don't you *dare!*" she screamed at him. She reached into her shoulder bag. "You call this *love*, you rotten bastard!" She pulled it out and flung it at him.

Cantling was not as quick as he'd been. He tried to duck, but it caught him on the side of his neck, and it hurt. Michelle had thrown it hard, and it was a big, thick, heavy hardcover, not some flimsy paperback. The pages fluttered as it tumbled to the carpet; Cantling stared down at his own photograph on the back of the dustwrapper. "You're just like your mother," he said, rubbing his neck where the book had hit. "She always threw things too. Only you aim better." He smiled weakly.

"I'm not interested in your jokes," Michelle said. "I'll never forgive you. Never. Never ever. All I want to know is how you can do this to me, that's all. You tell me. You tell me now."

"I," Cantling said. He held his hands out helplessly. "Look, I . . . you're upset now, why don't we have some coffee or something, and talk about it when you calm down a little. I don't want a big fight."

"I don't give a fuck what you want," Michelle screamed. "I want to talk about it right now!" She kicked the fallen book.

Richard Cantling felt his own anger building. It wasn't right for her to yell at him like that, he didn't deserve this attack, he hadn't done anything. He tried not to say anything for fear of saying the wrong thing and escalating the situation. He knelt and picked up his book. Without thinking, he brushed it off, turned it over almost tenderly. The title glared up at him; stark, twisted red letters against a black background, the distorted face of a pretty young woman, mouth open in a scream. *Show Me Where It Hurts.*

"I was afraid you'd take it the wrong way," Cantling said.

"The *wrong way*!" Michelle said. A look of incredulity passed across her face. "Did you think I'd *like* it?"

"I, I wasn't sure," said Cantling. "I hoped . . . I mean, I was uncertain of your reaction, and so I thought it would be better not to mention what I was working on, until, well . . ."

"Until the fucking thing was in the bookstore windows," Michelle finished for him.

Cantling flipped past the title page. "Look," he said, holding it out, "I dedicated it to you." He showed her:

To Michelle, who knew the pain.

Michelle swung at it, knocked it out of Cantling's hands. "You bastard," she said. "You think that makes it better? You think your stinking dedication excuses what you did? Nothing excuses it. I'll never forgive you."

Cantling edged back a step, retreating in the face of her fury. "I didn't do anything," he said stubbornly. "I wrote a book. A novel. Is that a crime?"

"You're my *father*," she shrieked. "You knew . . . you knew, you bastard, you knew I couldn't bear to talk about it, to talk about what happened. Not to my lovers or my friends or even my therapist. I can't, I just *can't*, I can't even think about it, you knew. I told you, I told only you, because you were my daddy and I trusted you and I had to get it out, and I told you, it was private, it was just between us, you knew, but what did you do? You wrote it all up in a goddamned book and *published* it for millions of people to read! Damn you, damn you. Were you planning to do that all along, you sonofabitch? Were you? That night in bed, were you memorizing every word?"

"I," said Cantling. "No, I didn't memorize anything, I just, well, I just remembered it. You're taking it all wrong, Michelle. The book's not about what happened to you. Yes, it's inspired by that, that was the starting point, but it's fiction, I changed things, it's just a novel."

"Oh yeah, daddy, you changed things all right. Instead

of Michelle Cantling it's all about Nicole Mitchell, and she's a fashion designer instead of an artist, and she's also kind of stupid, isn't she? Was that a change or is that what you think, that I was stupid to live there, stupid to let him in like that? It's all fiction, yeah. It's just a coincidence that it's about this girl that gets held prisoner and raped and tortured and terrorized and raped some more, and that you've got a daughter who was held prisoner and raped and tortured and terrorized and raped some more, right, just a fucking coincidence!"

"You don't understand," Cantling said helplessly.

"No, *you* don't understand. You don't understand what it's like. This is your biggest book in years, right? Number one bestseller, you've never been number one before, haven't even been on the lists since *Times Are Hard,* or was it *Black Roses*? And why not, why not number one, this isn't no boring story about a has-been newspaper, this is *rape,* hey, what could be hotter? Lots of sex and violence, torture and fucking and terror, and doncha know, *it really happened,* yeah." Her mouth twisted and trembled. "It was the worst thing that ever happened to me. It was all the nightmares that have ever been. I still wake up screaming sometimes, but I was getting better, it was behind me. And now it's there in every bookstore window, and all my friends know, everybody knows, strangers come up to me at parties and tell me how sorry they are." She choked back a sob; she was halfway between anger and tears. "And I pick up your book, your fucking no good book, and there it is again, in black and white, all written down. You're such a fucking *good* writer, daddy, you make it all so real. A book you can't put down. Well, I put it down but it didn't help, it's all there, now it will always be there, won't it? Every day somebody in the world will pick up your book and read it and I'll get raped again. That's what you did. You finished the job for him, daddy. You violated me, took me without my consent, just like he did. You raped me. You're my own father and you raped me!"

"You're not being fair," Cantling said. "I never meant to hurt you. The book ... Nicole is strong and smart. It's the man who's the monster. He uses all those different names because fear has a thousand names, but only one face, you see. He's not just a man, he's the darkness made flesh, the mindless violence that waits out there for all of us, the gods that play with us like flies, he's a symbol of all—"

"He's the man who raped me! He's not a symbol!"

She screamed it so loudly that Richard Cantling had to retreat in the face of her fury. "No," he said. "He's just a character. He's ... Michelle, I know it hurts, but what you went through, it's something people should know about, should think about, it's a part of life. Telling about life, making sense of it, that's the job of literature, that's my job. Someone had to tell your story. I tried to make it true, tried to do my—"

His daughter's face, red and wet with tears, seemed almost feral for a moment, unrecognizable, inhuman. Then a curious calm passed across her features. "You got one thing right," she said. "Nicole didn't have a father. When I was a little kid I'd come to you crying and my daddy would say show me where it hurts, and it was a private thing, a special thing, but in the book Nicole doesn't have a father, he says it, you gave it to him, he says show me where it hurts, he says it all the time. You're so ironic. You're so clever. The way he said it, it made him so real, more real than when he *was* real. And when you wrote it, you were right. That's what the monster says. Show me where it hurts. That's the monster's line. Nicole doesn't have a father, he's dead, yes, that was right too. I don't have a father. No I don't."

"Don't you talk to me like that," Richard Cantling said. It was terror inside him; it was shame. But it came out anger. "I won't have that, no matter what you've been through. I'm your father."

"No," Michelle said, grinning crazy now, backing away from him. "No, I don't have a father, and you don't have any children, no, unless it's in your books. Those are your children, your only children. Your books, your damned fucking books, those are your children, those are your children, those are your children." Then she turned and ran past him, down the foyer. She stopped at the door to his den. Cantling was afraid of what she might do. He ran after her.

When he reached the den, Michelle had already found the knife and set to work.

Richard Cantling sat by his silent phone and watched his grandfather clock tick off the hours toward darkness.

He tried Michelle's number at three o'clock, at four, at five. The machine, always the machine, speaking in a mockery of her voice. His messages grew more desperate. It was growing dim outside. His light was fading.

Cantling heard no steps on his porch, no knock on his door, no rasping summons from his old brass bell. It was an afternoon as silent as the grave. But by the time evening had fallen, he knew it was out there. A big square package, wrapped in brown paper, addressed in a hand he had known well. Inside a portrait.

He had not understood, not really, and so she was teaching him.

The clock ticked. The darkness grew thicker. The sense of a waiting presence beyond his door seemed to fill the house. His fear had been growing for hours. He sat in the armchair with his legs pulled up under him, his mouth hanging open, thinking, remembering. Heard cruel laughter. Saw the dim red tips of cigarettes in the shadows, moving, circling. Imagined their small hot kisses on his skin. Tasted urine, blood, tears. Knew violence, knew violation, of every sort there was. His hands, his voice, his face, his face, his face. The character with a dozen names, but fear had only a single face. The youngest of his children. His baby. His monstrous baby.

He had been blocked for so long, Cantling thought. If only he could make her understand. It was a kind of impotence, not writing. He had been a writer, but that was over. He had been a husband, but his wife was dead. He had been a father, but she got better, went back to New York. She left him alone, but that last night, wrapped in his arms, she told him the story, she showed him where it hurt, she gave him all that pain. What was he to do with it?

Afterwards he could not forget. He thought of it constantly. He began to reshape it in his head, began to grope for the words, the scenes, the symbols that would make sense of it. It was hideous, but it was life, raw strong life, the grist for Cantling's mill, the very thing he needed. She had showed him where it hurt; he could show them all. He did resist, he did try. He began a short story, an essay, finished some reviews. But it returned. It was with him every night. It would not be denied.

He wrote it.

"Guilty," Cantling said in the darkened room. And when he spoke the word, a kind of acceptance seemed to settle over him, banishing the terror. He was guilty. He had done it. He would accept the punishment, then. It was only right.

Richard Cantling stood and went to his door.

The package was there.

He lugged it inside, still wrapped, carried it up the stairs. He would hang him beside the others, beside Dunnahoo and Cissy and Barry Leighton, all in a row, yes. He went for his hammer, measured carefully, drove the nail. Only then did he unwrap the portrait, and look at the face within.

It captured her as no other artist had ever done, not just the lines of her face, the high angular cheekbones and blue eyes and tangled ash-blond hair, but the personality inside. She looked so young and fresh and confident, and he could see the strength there, the courage, the stubbornness. But best of all he liked her smile. It was a lovely smile, a smile that illuminated her whole face. The smile seemed to remind him of someone he had known once. He couldn't remember who.

Richard Cantling felt a strange, brief sense of relief, followed by an even greater sense of loss, a loss so terrible and final and total that he knew it was beyond the power of the words he worshipped.

Then the feeling was gone.

Cantling stepped back, folded his arms, studied the four portraits. Such excellent work; looking at the paintings, he could almost feel their presence in his house.

Dunnahoo, his first-born, the boy he wished he'd been.

Cissy, his true love.

Barry Leighton, his wise and tired alter-ego.

Nicole, the daughter he'd never had.

His people. His characters. His children.

A week later, another, much smaller, package arrived. Inside the carton were copies of four of his novels, a bill, and a polite note from the artist inquiring if there would be any more commissions.

Richard Cantling said no, and paid the bill by check.

POUL ANDERSON

Poul Anderson is one of the most honored authors of our time. He has won seven Hugo Awards, three Nebula Awards, and the Gandalf Award for Achievement in Fantasy, among others. His most popular series include the Polesotechnic League/Terran Empire tales and the Time Patrol series. Here are fine books by Poul Anderson available through Baen Books:

THE GAME OF EMPIRE

A *new* novel in Anderson's Polesotechnic League/Terran Empire series! Diana Crowfeather, daughter of Dominic Flandry, proves well capable of following in his adventurous footsteps.

FIRE TIME

Once every thousand years the Deathstar orbits close enough to burn the surface of the planet Ishtar. This is known as the Fire Time, and it is then that the barbarians flee the scorched lands, bringing havoc to the civilized South.

AFTER DOOMSDAY

Earth has been destroyed, and the handful of surviving humans must discover which of three alien races is guilty before it's too late.

THE BROKEN SWORD

It is a time when Christos is new to the land, and the Elder Gods and the Elven Folk still hold sway. In 11th-century Scandinavia Christianity is beginning to replace the old religion, but the Old Gods still have power, and men are still oppressed by the folk of the Faerie. "Pure gold!"—Anthony Boucher.

THE DEVIL'S GAME

Seven people gather on a remote island, each competing for a share in a tax-free fortune. The "contest" is ostensibly sponsored by an eccentric billionaire—but the rich man is in league with an alien masquerading as a demon . . . or is it the other way around?

THE ENEMY STARS

Includes for the first time the sequel to "The Enemy Stars"; "The Ways of Love." Fast-paced adventure science fiction from a master.

SEVEN CONQUESTS

Seven brilliant tales examine the many ways human beings—most dangerous and violent of all species—react under the stress of conflict and high technology.

STRANGERS FROM EARTH

Classic Anderson: A stranded alien spends his life masquerading as a human, hoping to contact his own world. He succeeds, but the result is a bigger problem than before . . . What if our reality is a fiction? Nothing more than a book written by a very powerful Author? Two philosophers stumble on the truth and try to puzzle out the Ending . . .

PRAISE FOR
LOIS MCMASTER BUJOLD

What the critics say:

The Warrior's Apprentice: "Now here's a fun romp through the spaceways—not so much a space opera as space ballet.... it has all the 'right stuff.' A lot of thought and thoughtfulness stand behind the all-too-human characters. Enjoy this one, and look forward to the next."   —Dean Lambe, *SF Reviews*

"The pace is breathless, the characterization thoughtful and emotionally powerful, and the author's narrative technique and command of language compelling. Highly recommended."   —*Booklist*

Brothers in Arms: "... she gives it a geniune depth of character, while reveling in the wild turnings of her tale. ... Bujold is as audacious as her favorite hero, and as brilliantly (if sneakily) successful."   —*Locus*

"Miles Vorkosigan is such a great character that I'll read anything Lois wants to write about him. ... a book to re-read on cold rainy days." —Robert Coulson, *Comics Buyer's Guide*

Borders of Infinity: "Bujold's series hero Miles Vorkosigan may be a lord by birth and an admiral by rank, but a bone disease that has left him hobbled and in frequent pain has sensitized him to the suffering of outcasts in his very hierarchical era.... Playing off Miles's reserve and cleverness, Bujold draws outrageous and outlandish foils to color her high-minded adventures."   —*Publishers Weekly*

Falling Free: "In *Falling Free* Lois McMaster Bujold has written her fourth straight superb novel. ... How to break down a talent like Bujold's into analyzable components? Best not to try. Best to say 'Read, or you will be missing something extraordinary.'" —Roland Green, *Chicago Sun-Times*

The Vor Game: "The chronicles of Miles Vorkosigan are far too witty to be literary junk food, but they rouse the kind of craving that makes popcorn magically vanish during a double feature."   —Faren Miller, *Locus*

MORE PRAISE FOR
LOIS MCMASTER BUJOLD

What the readers say:

"My copy of *Shards of Honor* is falling apart I've reread it so often.... I'll read whatever you write. You've certainly proved yourself a grand storyteller."
—Liesl Kolbe, Colorado Springs, CO

"I experience the stories of Miles Vorkosigan as almost viscerally uplifting.... But certainly, even the weightiest theme would have less impact than a cinder on snow were it not for a rousing good story, and good storytelling with it. This is the second thing I want to thank you for.... I suppose if you boiled down all I've said to its simplest expression, it would be that I immensely enjoy and admire your work. I submit that, as literature, your work raises the overall level of the science fiction genre, and spiritually, your work cannot avoid positively influencing all who read it."
—Glen Stonebraker, Gaithersburg, MD

" 'The Mountains of Mourning' [in *Borders of Infinity*] was one of the best-crafted, and simply best, works I'd ever read. When I finished it, I immediately turned back to the beginning and read it again, and I can't remember the last time I did that."   —Betsy Bizot, Lisle, IL

"I can only hope that you will continue to write, so that I can continue to read (and of course buy) your books, for they make me laugh and cry and think ... rare indeed."   —Steven Knott, Major, USAF

What do you say?

Send me these books!

Shards of Honor • 72087-2 • $4.99 ____
The Warrior's Apprentice • 72066-X • $4.50 ____
Ethan of Athos • 65604-X • $4.99 ____
Falling Free • 65398-9 • $4.99 ____
Brothers in Arms • 69799-4 • $3.95 ____
Borders of Infinity • 69841-9 • $4.99 ____
The Vor Game • 72014-7 • $4.99 ____
Barrayar • 72083-X • $4.99 ____

Lois McMaster Bujold:
Only from Baen Books

If these books are not available at your local bookstore, just check your choices above, fill out this coupon and send a check or money order for the cover price to Baen Books, Dept. BA, P.O. Box 1403, Riverdale, NY 10471.

NAME: _____

ADDRESS: _____

_____

I have enclosed a check or money order in the amount of $ _____.